WARRIOR ROGUE

NANCY J. COHEN

OGP
ORANGE
GROVE
PRESS

Chapter One

"If he doesn't show up in the next ten minutes, I'll kill him." Jennifer Dyhr paced back and forth on the Tokyo film set for a video game commercial. Their lead actor, Keith Monroe, was more than an hour overdue. What could have happened to him?

"I called his hotel room." Sandi tapped her pen on the clipboard cradled in her arm. Dressed in a prim suit, she looked more like a schoolteacher than a fashion designer's assistant. "He didn't answer, so I left a message. Ditto for his cell."

"The jerk. You'd think he would be more reliable." Jen tucked a stray hair behind her ear. Her twist was coming undone, same as her composure.

"It's the producer's problem, not yours."

"Oh, yeah? Who else could we get to look the part of a vengeful Norse god?" She waved a hand. "If you recall, I'm the one who recommended Keith for the role. I wouldn't have won this project without him."

"Don't be so hard on yourself. Like, your costumes have nothing to do with Keith's no show."

Sandi's calm tone failed to reassure her. "The producer might not see it that way. He'll lump us Americans together and blame me for Keith's behavior."

"Oh, come on, Jen. He's lucky to have you. You're the best in the field."

"True." Jen squared her shoulders. Inspired by visions from the past, she'd made her mark on the fashion industry and garnered numerous awards for her designs based on Viking influence. She'd become as much a celebrity as the stars who wore her garments.

Nonetheless, Jen had yet to introduce her line overseas. If she wanted her company to expand, she needed gigs like this one to show she could compete in the global marketplace.

"I hope Keith wasn't in an accident." Her heart raced at the thought. "Maybe we should call the hospitals."

"You can suggest that to Mr. Nakamura." Sandi bobbed her head in a warning nod.

Jen braced herself as the director hurried over. A lanky man with black hair, Mr. Nakamura wore a perpetual scowl and his tense posture like a seasoned samurai.

"Keith Monroe is passed out drunk in his hotel room," the translator interpreted after a rapid-fire dialogue by the director. A boyish-faced youth, Akeno had confided to Jen his wish to work on the film crew someday.

"You're kidding," Jen blurted before remembering her place. "I mean, I'm so sorry. Please accept my apologies for Keith's irresponsible behavior."

She bowed her head in deference, expecting a tongue-lashing in response. Her Japanese associates would need someone to take the blame. Jen only hoped this snag wouldn't damage the reputation she'd worked so hard to build.

"The producer has already called the casting office for a replacement," Akeno said after another spate of dialogue from his employer, whose irate tone matched his angry eyes.

"We need a guy with the right build," she reminded them. "Blond hair and blue eyes would be a bonus."

While they waited for the stand-in actor to arrive, Jen inspected the stitching on her costumes.

"Jen, this woman's seam is splitting." Sandi indicated one of the extras portraying a villager.

Jen cursed under her breath. "Did she sit down? I told her not to bend. This shift barely fits around her hips."

She grabbed a needle and thread from her kit as the director herded everyone to take their places on set. The storyline involved a barbarian ravaging a peaceful village until a Norse god appeared to battle him.

It amazed her how the sound stage looked like a real Viking town with thatched roof houses spewing smoke from holes in the roofs, vendors lining a busy market street, and wood planked walkways leading toward a fake pier rimmed with barrels of wine.

The village street bustled with action as actors walked through their paces and chatted amongst themselves. She could almost smell the sheep dung and wood smoke.

Uh-oh. Her visions often started with a sensory impression. Quickly, Jen wrapped up her repair and stashed away her kit. Reality receded as a white haze swept into her mind.

When her eyes focused again, she was strolling down the village street in the distant past.

Her gown swished against her leather boots as she beamed a friendly smile to the blacksmith. Across the road, the fur peddler waved. She nodded him a greeting, her nose wrinkling at the smell of fish emanating from the wharf. Shivering, she drew the edges of her shawl closer together, as a stiff breeze blew off the sea.

Shrieks of surprise made her vision evaporate. A man charged into view from around the corner onto the studio set.

A naked man.

Jen stared at him, aghast. What kind of joke was this?

Lacerations marred his body, and heavens above, what a magnificent body the man had. Her glance dropped from his massive shoulders to his muscled chest and then down to his very masculine package. The glory of him stole her breath.

"Where am I? What's happened?" His wild-eyed look and combative stance froze the actors on set.

His American accent startled Jen. *Brilliant, just brilliant.* Who else but their stand-in for Keith Monroe would show up with such melodrama? She should have recognized him at once from his wheat blond hair and blue eyes, but she'd been too focused on his, ah, other parts.

She fought an urge to fan herself, the heat from the spotlights raising her temperature. Or maybe that wasn't what caused her to feel so hot all over.

The man's gaze slammed into hers, and time stood still. The distance between them shrunk, blotting out their surroundings, until only the two of them stood facing each other on a plain where mist swirled at their feet. Their heartbeats pounded a sensual rhythm in harmony.

In her mind's eye, she shed her clothes as a hunger she'd never known swept through her. A hunger for him.

Shaking her head, she reoriented herself. Much as she'd like to admire his physique all day long, they had to get moving. Time was money as far as the producer was concerned. This guy needed to be clothed, fast.

"Sandi, get me Keith's costume and tell the makeup artist we need her." Jen's voice came out as a high-pitched squeak. She cleared her throat. "Our new stand-in has done a great job on those fake wounds, so he shouldn't need more than a touch-up."

Mr. Nakamura hustled over with the translator in tow. He jabbed his finger at the new guy. "You there, what is your name?"

The actor stiffened but didn't respond. He glanced at the other crew members who had stopped to watch. A look of confusion spread over his face. His jaw tightened, a day's growth of bristle adding authenticity to his role.

"What's your name?" Jen spoke in a loud tone like people did to foreigners who could hear perfectly well but didn't understand.

"I am Paz Hadar." His dimples deepened as he regarded her. "Who are you?"

His slow, lazy perusal generated warmth throughout her body. Those devilish eyes roamed from her hair, to her rayon maxi dress, to her low-heeled sandals. A gleam of appreciation entered his expression, making her heart beat faster.

"I'm Jennifer Dyhr, the costume designer." Jen pronounced her last name like deer. "You are inappropriately dressed, Mr. Hadar. Or undressed, I should say."

Mr. Nakamura's lips compressed. "Tell him he has ten minutes to get ready. I am not amused by his dramatic entrance. He is only a substitute for our star."

"*Hai*, Mr. Nakamura-san."

Jen gave him a deferential bow. After he walked away, she signaled to Paz. The man sauntered over as though strolling about naked was a normal occurrence. Had he meant to disrupt the set and attract everyone's attention?

No matter. She had to make him look like a vengeful Norse god. Standing before her, the man towered over her five-foot eight frame by at least six inches.

Moisture glistened on his skin. His hair hung in damp clumps, as if he'd just come from a swim. He must have been near the studio to rush over, disrobe, and apply his makeup.

However, he'd forgotten to remove his watch. Having been so focused on his other *attributes*, she hadn't noticed the fancy dial before. Further up his forearm was a broad gash. When she touched the edge, he winced as though it hurt for real. Unable to help herself, she let her fingers slide up his arm, outlining his firm bicep. He drew in a sharp breath but didn't move.

Her glance roamed to his chest, where a tangle of golden hair tempted her to feel its texture. His scent entered her nostrils, a strange mixture of sea air and salt.

Her temples pounded. Oh, no. Afraid she'd segue into another vision, she grabbed the trousers Sandi brought over and thrust them at him.

When he just stood there, she clucked her tongue. "What's the matter with you? Put these on. And take your watch off. It doesn't belong in this scene."

He plucked the pants from her fingers and pulled them on while she averted her gaze. When he muttered under his breath, she dared to look again. Poor fellow fumbled with the drawstring ties at his waist as though he didn't know what to do with them. Good God, what planet did he come from?

She grabbed the ends, pulled tight, and tied a bow, all the while conscious of his proximity and powerful musculature.

Standing so close, she had a terrible urge to feast her eyes on him. He was quite the man, and it had been a while since she'd split with her last boyfriend.

Resolutely looking into his crystalline eyes, she moistened her lips. Her throat had gone dry when she touched his skin. "I hope you've been briefed on your role."

His brow furrowed. "Of course. I know what to do."

His deep voice resonated through her like warm honey, turning her bones fluid and making her belly flip-flop.

Best to finish this as fast as possible.

She offered him a linen shirt next followed by a brick red tunic. When she'd studied what Vikings had worn, she had been pleased to learn they dyed their fabrics in bold shades. Wealthy people wore clothing trimmed in silk with gold or silver threads. These styles became the inspiration for her unique designs.

Paz donned the garments and stuffed his watch into a pants pocket. After he secured a leather belt around his waist, she gave him a cloak to fasten at his shoulder with a faux gold brooch. The cobalt color brought out the ocean blue of his eyes. He glanced at her, and she blushed to be caught staring.

She stepped away as he tugged on his boots. The makeup artist bustled over to bring some order to his unruly hair and to dab cover-up on the dark shadows under his eyes. Odd that he hadn't fixed that problem when he'd applied his fake lacerations. And was that scratch on his cheekbone starting to smear?

The director called for everyone to take their places. Jen retreated with Sandi to a spot off to the side where they could observe. Ready for any wardrobe disasters, she prayed they'd get this done in as few takes as possible.

Mr. Nakamura issued instructions, but the new guy wasn't listening. He tensed as the pace picked up. Jen swallowed. Did he understand what his role required?

"Action," the director yelled in the equivalent Japanese.

Lars Anderson, the Scandinavian actor hired to play the bad guy, charged onto the set wearing what accounted for full battle armor in those days: a chain mail tunic and conical helmet complete with metal eye and nose guards. He looked ferocious with his full beard, blazing eyes, and feral grin. Swinging a long-handled battle-axe, he gave a chilling war whoop.

Fake blood sprayed as he attacked the villagers. Carnage resulted. Or rather, what would appear to be carnage on screen. While the other actors screamed in mock fright, the man called Paz reached behind his back. A startled look crossed his face as though he expected to find a weapon there.

Chaos broke around him. Jen hoped he knew his moves. He was supposed to use his magical power to stop the villain dead in his tracks.

That didn't appear to be his intention. Instead, Paz launched himself at Lars as though the hounds of hell were on his heels.

Pow, thunk, thud.

His fists and feet aimed practiced blows at his opponent.

Lars didn't even have time to feign a defense. He raised his arms, but Paz's punches hit home with unswerving accuracy.

Along with the cast and crew, Jen watched in fascinated horror. Were the cameras getting this? The director observed in stunned silence as his cameramen kept filming.

Paz smashed the hapless actor on the jaw. With a howl of pain mingled with surprise, Lars wheeled around. Jen's heart leapt into her throat when Paz lunged for a stick on the ground.

Her eyes widened. Was that a yardstick? Someone must have left it there by mistake. What did Paz want with it?

Stop, she wanted to say but her mouth wouldn't form the word. *Wrong prop. And you're playing a Norse god. You don't need a weapon.*

Paz twirled the yardstick like a staff before striking Lars at mid-thigh. The stick snapped, but Paz kept his motion flowing, following through with a kick to the same spot. Lars cried out, his legs crumpling. He went down, flat on his back.

Immediately, Paz planted a foot on Lars's chest and pointed the broken yardstick at his throat. His arms tensed.

In another instant, he'd put a lethal vent into the guy's trachea. What was the matter with him?

"Don't move," Jen hollered, recovering her voice.

Paz hesitated, stick poised in the air.

"You're hurting him. Haven't you filmed a fight scene before?"

"Fight scene?" Paz's brow creased, as he regarded her with puzzlement.

Meanwhile, crew members rushed forward to break the men apart. One man put out an arm to hold Paz back, while another helped Lars to his feet.

"Where's the first aid station? Ow, my leg." Lars cast Paz a scathing glance. "What's wrong with you, mate? You cudda killed me."

Blood oozed from a cut on his bottom lip. He yanked the helmet off his head and swiped his mouth. "I'm bleeding, you idiot. If I have any marks on my face, my career is ruined. Ruined! You'll hear from my lawyer." With a growl, he limped backstage and out of sight.

Jen scuttled over. Could this day get any worse?

She gripped Paz's arm. "Didn't you study fight scene choreography when you took acting classes? You could have seriously injured Mr. Anderson."

Across the room, the director spouted a torrent of words at the crew. Jen was sure he must be chewing them out. It wasn't their fault, for heaven's sake.

"What do you mean?" Paz shook her off. "He was butchering those villagers. I couldn't stand by and let that beast murder people."

She stared into his confused blue eyes. "Paz, they were acting. You know, pretending," she explained when he shook his head in bewilderment. "This set, all that blood, it's fake."

"I don't understand. People were screaming, fleeing in panic." He lifted his chin. "It is my duty as a Drift Lord to protect them."

"You're playing a Norse god. You were supposed to use magic to defeat your enemy and not pick up a stick on the ground. A yardstick, no less! Didn't you get a script?"

"Your words have no meaning for me." He rubbed a hand over his weary face. His fingers came back stained with crimson. "Is this fake, too? My head pounds as though hit by a hammer."

"Good Lord, you're really bleeding." Jen examined the gash on the side of his head. "These wounds are real. No wonder you're so out of it. What happened to you?"

"I remember an impact, and then… nothing."

Her mind somersaulted on what she knew about the guy. He showed up here naked and confused, and everyone assumed he'd prepared for his role. Had the poor fellow been in such a rush to take the job that he'd had an accident along the way? A concussion would explain his strange behavior.

She crooked her finger, signaling Sandi who'd been consulting with the makeup artist.

"Yuki says she didn't touch the cuts on this man's face because he had done such a good job of applying paint." Sandi squinted at him. "That stuff is smearing, but she's afraid to come any closer to fix it."

"That's because his wounds are real." Jen turned to Paz. "This is my assistant, Sandi. We're both concerned about you. Tell us what happened on the way here. You must have been in an accident."

"Accident… yes. No. The images are—how do you say it? My mind is unclear."

Mr. Nakamura broke off from his conversation and strode in their direction. From his taut posture and pinched face, Jen expected a reprimand.

"Security said no one drove through the studio entrance." Poor Akeno looked as though he had swallowed a lemon pit as he translated the director's words. "How did this man get here?"

"I think he may have been in an accident." Jen glanced at Paz. His lips were clamped together, his complexion pale. *Don't pass out*, she pleaded silently. *We need to take you to a doctor.* "He could have left his car behind, walked the rest of the way, and stumbled through the gate. A head injury would account for his confusion."

Sandi's eyebrows lifted. "I've known a lot of desperate actors in my time, but this? If he really got whacked on the head, he belongs in the hospital."

"You're right. I'll take him."

For some reason, she felt drawn to the newcomer. Maybe it was the lost look in his eyes, or perhaps his unstable state of health. Being ill in a foreign country could be terrifying, and he could use her support.

Sandi drew her aside. "Are you nuts? You don't know anything about this guy. Like, he could get violent again."

"I'll be all right. He seems to respond to me, so I can get him through the hospital hoopla. In the meantime, check on Keith and see if he's on his way yet. I'm counting on you for damage control."

The translator gestured to her. "Miss Dyhr, the director wants this actor's contact information."

Did he plan to press charges against the poor guy, too? She shouldn't be surprised. Mr. Nakamura would need to save face in the producer's view. Forget their opinion of her—it must be blown to hell by this incident.

Jen had been completely unaware Norse mythology interested video gamers until Sandi pointed out a couple of games titled *Viking Warrior: Bridge to Asgard* and *Valkyrie Knights*. This revelation had opened a whole realm of possibility for her. She'd designed wardrobes for feature films and magazine shoots galore, but never an ad for a video game company.

She'd been so excited when her hairstylist brought the Japanese producer into her Manhattan showroom, and he'd called afterward to offer a job. It gave her the perfect opportunity to extend her brand.

"Mr. Nakamura, this man needs medical attention." She

thrust her chin forward, determined to salvage her reputation by assuming responsibility. "With your permission, I'll take him to the hospital. If Keith still isn't here by the time I return, I promise to call the casting office myself for a replacement. I'm so sorry for the delay."

After giving him another respectful bow, she turned to Sandi. "I'll order my driver to bring the car around. Try to appease the big wigs while I'm gone. We have to find some way to salvage this situation."

Jen led Paz backstage to change into some borrowed street clothes. Then she herded the newcomer out the exit and into the busy midday traffic.

Chapter Two

Paz came to his senses in the back seat of a ground vehicle beside a beautiful woman. What had she called herself? Jennifer, although the short blonde addressed her as Jen. He remembered that much from the nightmarish barbarian attack.

When he'd regained consciousness earlier, he had no idea where he had landed. The first people he'd seen had been the costumed characters, making him think he had been cast back in time to the Viking era. Jen had been an anomaly. He'd focused on her at once, ignoring the others around them. Then came the attack on the villagers. He'd reacted automatically as per his training.

Once he realized it was a film set, he deduced that he must have spatial shifted from his point of origin in Orlando, Florida. That meant he'd traversed a spontaneous rift in the space-time continuum. Things would only get worse unless he accomplished his mission, and until then, he had to survive.

Jen sat alongside him. She wore her raven hair secured in a twist, highlighting the delicate angles of her face. Her long dress stuck to the cushion, pulling on her bodice and giving him a tantalizing view of her cleavage.

By Odin's grace, he didn't need this distraction now. He had to find out what happened to his team.

At his last recollection, they'd stormed an enemy facility housing a jamming device that blocked their sensor readings. Their objective had been to destroy the antenna and its power source. Paz had no idea if his friends had succeeded. A beefy

Trollek soldier had shoved him into a pit filled with a chopping, whirling mechanism.

He'd hit his head and bounced off a wall, tumbling to the bottom where the sea rushed in a torrential current. Yanked underwater and tossed about like a particle of sand, he'd lost his clothing and his consciousness.

Paz didn't remember much else until he awoke backstage at the film studio. Hearing voices, he'd stumbled in their direction and rounded a corner onto the village set. His face heated when he remembered his natural state and people's stares.

"Where should I take you?" Jen asked in a soft tone.

"That depends. Where are we?" He glanced out the window. Neon signs advertised a sword museum, an arts center, and a department store. He could read the English well enough with his implanted universal translator.

"I thought the doctor did a neurological exam on you. He said you were clear to go." Jen's eyes widened in alarm.

A healer at their medical center had cleaned and treated his wounds. He'd been fortunate none of his injuries were more serious than a crack on the head and minor lacerations, meaning he could resume his mission.

"I know we're in Tokyo. I meant to ask where we are headed?"

Relief flitted across her face. "Let me see if Keith made it to the set first before we make any decisions."

Jen pulled out a rectangular object from her handbag. Paz recognized it as the crude communication device called a cellular phone. He smiled inwardly. As communications officer for the Drift Lords, he could upgrade that to a Class IV Portable Intel Platform, or PIP, with the proper added components.

Jen punched numbers on her touchpad. "Hello, Sandi?" She held the phone to her ear. "Yes, it's me. What's going on?"

Her forehead scrunched as she listened. "You're kidding. The producer loved the take? I don't believe it." A pause. "Hmm, good question. I'll get back to you on that one."

While she spoke, Paz stared at the jumble of tall buildings that went by in a blur as their driver shot through an intersection, barely missing a bicyclist.

Jen hung up and stuffed the phone back in her handbag. Her narrowed gaze swung toward him.

"Okay, who are you?"

"I told you. My name is Paz Hadar."

"That's not what I meant. Keith still isn't there, and Sandi says the actor sent by the casting office arrived shortly after we left the studio. If you're not the man they sent, who the hell are you?"

He liked the way her dark brown eyes blazed when she was angry. How would they change when she got aroused?

Get that idea out of your head. She's not your type.

Just look at her expensive diamond earrings and manicured nails, at her fashionable clothing and confident posture. She oozed wealth and sophistication.

He steered clear of women like Jennifer Dyhr for the same reason he'd left home.

"I am a Drift Lord on a mission." He didn't see any reason to lie.

"A Drift Lord? What's that?"

"If I tell you, I'll have to kill you." He grinned at the moue of displeasure on her face.

"Please don't joke with me. I'm trying to help you."

"Very well. I am a warrior sent to banish the horde back to where they belong." He watched for her reaction and was gratified when she stared at him as though he'd sprouted wings.

"The horde? Okay, fella. Maybe you are some kind of agent on a mission, and you ran afoul of the bad guys. You know what? I'll drop you off at the nearest consulate. They can help you get home or complete your job. Whatever."

"You are correct. It was the bad guys, as you call them, who did this to me."

He sank back in his seat and closed his eyes, memories

flooding him. Along with them rode a sense of pain. His team had been captured by the enemy. One of their own had betrayed them. Paz had no way of knowing the final outcome of the battle because he'd been pushed into the pit, presumably left for dead.

"May I borrow your communication device? I wish to call my colleagues to let them know I'm all right." And to find out if any of them survived.

"You mean my cell phone?" Jen fished it from her purse and handed it to him. "Maybe you should ask them to arrange for your return home."

"Indeed, I shall." But when he dialed their emergency number, no one answered. Even if his mates were on board the *Protector* rather than planet-side, they should receive the transmission. The fact that even Zohar, their captain and crown prince of the Star Empire, did not respond made Paz's jaw tighten.

In silence, he handed Jen back her phone. It was up to him now to complete their assignment. Failure would mean the destruction not only of this world but thousands of others.

His duty was clear. He would send the Trolleks back where they belonged, or he'd die trying.

****

Jen ordered the driver to head for the American Embassy. She'd drop Paz off there where hopefully he could reconnect with his friends. He'd gone quiet, staring out the window, his profile frozen in consternation. Aware of his hulking presence beside her, she inched away on the seat. His magnetism tended to draw her closer, but they'd only just met and caution prevailed.

He looked a wreck, his jaw unshaven, and his hair askew. Maybe he *had* been attacked. A mugging would account for his confusion and injuries. In that case, the man was lucky he hadn't been hurt worse. But shouldn't he have recovered his senses by now? All this talk of Drift Lords and secret missions made her wonder about his sanity.

He seemed to be a decent guy otherwise. Growing up in Palm Beach had taught her to discern between men who were sincere in their admiration and men who wanted something from her. She yearned to find a guy who had enough cash and clout that he wouldn't need hers. A prominent businessman might fit the bill, but she had yet to meet a magnate who lit her fire. Her dream of marrying a partner with whom to share her successes and start a family seemed to grow ever distant.

She sneaked a glance sideways at her companion. He'd be fabulous in the role of a vengeful Norse god if he really knew how to act. Actually, with his powerful physique, he'd make a striking model for her upcoming Spring line. Maybe he'd consider a change in careers? He didn't have to be sane. Just looking like a hunk would work well enough.

"Tell me, are you an actor at all, or do you have another job?"

He gave her an oblique glance. "When I am not employed in my current position, I work in telecom."

Jen gripped her seat as their driver jammed on the brakes. A trio of motorcyclists zoomed past a yellow light. Outside, solemn-faced workers scurried down the street while tourists craned their necks to regard the billboards. A popular department store loomed ahead.

The car jerked forward after the traffic signal changed.

"How would you like to do something different?" Jen smiled encouragingly. "You'd make a great model for my designs. I could teach you what you need to know if you come to Manhattan. You'd make a lot more money than you do repairing telephone equipment."

She assumed that's what he did, based on his vague reply that he worked in telecom. That's like a garbage man saying he worked in sanitation.

Paz's gaze seared into her. Did he believe her offer to be sincere, or did he think she was proposing he become her next boy toy? A restless feeling washed over her at the notion. Hot and cold impulses raced up her spine as the image of him naked popped into her mind. His scent drifted into her nostrils, reminiscent of a sunny day at the beach. She crossed her legs and then uncrossed them.

Her cell phone's strident ring shattered the moment. Jen retrieved her unit, wondering what was wrong with her. The man was a total stranger, for heaven's sake. She should never have gotten involved with him. Sandi was probably calling to see what was taking her so long in returning.

"Hey, hon, it's Dad."

Jen's stomach lurched. Getting a call from her father during business hours on a Wednesday sent up a red flag.

"What's the matter? Is everything all right?"

"No, it's not," he replied in a terse tone. "The Board of Trustees has called an emergency meeting to vote on the merger. You need to be here to convince them to hold out. I need more time to talk to Yeager Capital Investments."

Jen cursed under her breath. She'd inherited her aunt's shares in the family business empire, and with it came a Board position. Her cousin Clifford, Aunt Alba's son, had contested the will but hadn't won. Now he'd changed tactics to try for a hostile takeover instead.

"Can't you stall until I'm home? I have a flight booked for Friday. We're almost finished filming."

"Cliff has come up with a new challenge, Jen. It concerns you personally. I've hired a business jet. It'll be waiting for you on the tarmac."

Jen sighed. She supposed Sandi could pack her things and send them along later. Meanwhile, her assistant could handle the rest of the details with Mr. Nakamura. "Okay. I'm in the car now. I'll go straight to the airport."

"I knew I could count on you, pumpkin. Let me know your ETA. I'll send a car to pick you up when you arrive."

"That's not necessary. I'll get a cab when I reach Palm Beach. Bye, Dad."

Severing the connection, she pursed her lips. The family

business served more as an anchor around her neck than an asset. The management skills she'd learned from her father, though, had helped when she formed her own design company.

Sitting beside her on the backseat, Paz patted her hand. "I couldn't help overhearing, and I'm sorry if you received troubling news."

"I have to go home. It's a family business matter." Jen's voice hardened.

"Don't you have any siblings who can step in?"

"Nope, it's just me and my parents."

"Is it true you will be flying to Florida?" "Yes, my father chartered a private jet."

They'd probably have to make a few refueling stops along the way. Guess she wouldn't be headed back to Manhattan just yet. Hopefully she could conclude the business at home before Fashion Week, because she still had a ton of work to do in preparation for their show even though her staff was fully capable.

Awareness crept into her that Paz's hand still covered hers. His large palm conveyed reassurance and warmth and sent tingles of pleasure along her nerves. "I'm heading straight for the airport." She slipped her hand away. "We need to drop you off first. I'll give you the address of my showroom in New York. If you're really interested in modeling, meet me there."

When he didn't respond, Jen gave him a sharp glance. His gaze fixed on her left wrist where she wore the watch Mom had given her on her sixteenth birthday. Silence stretched between them, until he raised his eyes to meet hers.

"I accept your offer of employment." His grin dispelled the gloom she'd felt only moments before.

"I'll accompany you on your aircraft."

"Pardon me, but who invited you?"

Maybe she'd been too hasty in offering him a job. She knew nothing about him except that he'd lied about being Keith's stand-in. Then again, he hadn't actually claimed to be the actor's replacement. They'd all just assumed he was the guy.

He lifted an eyebrow. "You need me, whether you know it or not. Tell me, have you ever felt a compulsion to learn about the past? Your past?"

Her breath hitched. "What do you mean?" He couldn't know about her visions. No one knew. Well, Aunt Alba had known when she was alive, but Jen had told nobody else. They'd think she was nuts.

Paz surveyed her with a devilish gleam in his eye. "I'll bet you've always been strangely drawn to the Viking age."

Her stomach somersaulted. Oh, God. He did know. "You... how do you know this?"

He grinned, his dimples deepening. "Now that I've seen your timepiece, I know a lot about you. Take me along on your journey, and I'll explain."

"My timepiece?" She felt like a parrot.

"Are you aware that symbol etched on its face is a rune?"

She ground her teeth together. The man might be loony, but he knew things no one else did. Hadn't Aunt Alba said the inscription looked like runic lettering?

She'd just warn the pilot to keep the door securely locked to the flight deck while en route to the States.

"What about your passport? You'll need one to get through Customs." Huh. Maybe that would stump him.

"I'll worry about it once we arrive."

"That's a bit blasé. You have no ID, no money, and nobody to bail you out. How do you expect to get around, even if Immigration does let you into the States, which is unlikely?"

His shoulder lifted in a shrug. "I'll improvise. Don't be concerned. It won't reflect on you."

It had better not. I already have the fallout to deal with from your snafu on set. Sandi wants to know who you are, if not the actor's stand-in sent by the agency.

Sensing that he wouldn't take no for an answer, Jen issued new orders to the driver, who then crossed lanes and made a turn.

Paz fell silent, his gaze directed at the passing scenery. His forehead creased as though troubles plagued him.

"Are you having second thoughts?" She tapped his arm. "I can still drop you off along the way. Maybe there's someplace else you need to be?"

His somber gaze swung toward her. "No, I'm just thinking it's been a while since I—"

"Since you what?" *Shaved? You got that right buddy. You could use a few personal grooming tools.*

"Never mind. But it might be a good idea for us to pinch the deal." He edged closer.

"Don't you mean cinch the deal?" *Why did he act like such a foreigner? Maybe he wasn't from the U.S. but merely had an American accent.*

He leaned nearer, and her perception shrank until it included just the two of them. Surely, he didn't mean to kiss her? The man filled her vision, from the golden highlights in his hair, to his intense blue eyes, to his contoured mouth.

Her blood surged, and despite her wariness, places within her that had lain dormant began to stir.

His eyes sparked as though he knew his presence affected her. He lowered his head and brushed her lips before she could protest.

The touch of his mouth on hers set her nerves aflame. She should be affronted by his actions, but his feathering kiss made her stomach flutter and her limbs turn languid. Molten lava poured through her veins as though a sleeping volcano had just awakened. The edges of her mind receded.

Bracing herself for another vision, she placed a hand on his forearm. A muscle moved beneath his hair-sprinkled skin, and his playful kiss changed to a deeper assault.

No, this is wrong. The man is a complete stranger.

She sprang back, her breath coming in short pants, her body trembling. If this was wrong, why did being with him feel so right?

Paz's mouth twisted in a wry grin as he took in her flushed face. "I hope I haven't offended you."

"No… I mean, yes. Don't do that again, or I'll change my mind about taking you along."

His eyes darkened to indigo. "Don't worry about me. It is others whom you should fear. Whatever happens, I will protect you."

What's with his delusion about protecting people? He might be the biggest nutcase she'd ever met, but at least he didn't act dangerous toward her. Well, he was dangerous in one respect. His kiss melted her best intentions.

She'd be wise to keep a professional distance between them.

****

Paz slid over on the seat, widening his distance from this woman who seduced his senses and compromised his will.

Ever since he'd laid eyes on her back at the studio, he was drawn to her like a glitter bug to sunlight. Those creatures on his home planet could bedazzle a mighty beast, and so Jen had the power to beguile him as well.

Acutely aware of her presence, he could barely think of anything else except sweeping her into his arms and into his bed. Desiring her was wrong. She belonged to a rung in society he couldn't abide: the rich, spoiled set who looked down their noses at honest laborers. Jen had offered him a job, though, so perhaps there was more to her than he might expect.

Certainly, her sense of compassion had surprised him, as did the way he felt when they kissed, as though they had been transported to a space between dimensions.

He'd only agreed to take the job she offered so as to accompany her to Florida. He needed to reach his safe house and reclaim his equipment. He couldn't afford the distraction of a woman otherwise. However, a more pressing reason to remain by her side had presented itself when he noticed her wristwatch. And that's why he'd had to kiss her.

Paz had seen a similar timepiece before. The symbol etched

on her watch face didn't quite match the other, but he recognized its runic form. This led to one conclusion.

Not only would Jennifer Dyhr play a crucial role in his mission's success, but they were destined to be together.

Chapter Three

Jen removed her seatbelt as soon as their Gulfstream G450 reached a safe distance aloft. She couldn't stand to be confined, plus their situation called for food and drink. She'd been running on low ever since six that morning, Tokyo time, and needed to refuel.

Paz sat directly across from her. His predatory gaze was another reason why she jumped up as soon as the pilot turned off the seatbelt sign.

The takeoff had brought a smirk to Paz's mouth. He seemed amused by the rush down the runway for some reason but didn't comment. His perceptive glance fell on her hands clutched on the armrests. Nothing escaped his notice.

Now was a good time to question him about her wristwatch. His promise to provide answers was the only reason she'd brought him along. They had hours before their first scheduled stop, and although she craved a nap, she didn't dare lower her guard. This man had a way of worming past her defenses. Hoping she wouldn't betray her nervousness, she smiled.

"Can I get you something to drink? You must be hungry, too. I'll see what snacks they have in the galley."

"Now that you mention it, I could use some nourishment."

He unsnapped his safety belt and stretched to his full height. In his borrowed jeans and T-shirt, he looked magnificent. His windswept hair and rakish grin reminded her of a cross between Sawyer on *Lost* and Nathan Fillion on *Firefly*. Sexy. Seductive. Dangerous.

Yes, she did watch those science fiction shows. She shared that secret with her staid, Republican father.

And to think her parents had once despaired for her future. Not only did she like dorky TV shows and Viking tales, but she'd refused to glamour up for their Palm Beach crowd. Yet, after persistent peer pressure, she'd finally succumbed.

Now she projected a sleek and sophisticated image, just like the models she hired. But underneath it all lurked the child who feared she didn't measure up. She hid that insecurity under a veneer of polish but yearned to really be herself.

Turning toward the rear, she strode down the aisle. The business jet her father had chartered held seats for up to twelve people. Four singles were located up front, each by a window, with one pair of seats facing the other. Further along, two double seats faced each other over a table with inset cup holders. A wood credenza took up space on the opposite wall.

She passed a partition toward an aft section with a divan facing two more single seats. The galley was beyond, with maple cabinets and stainless-steel appliances.

It must have cost her father a mint to charter this plane, she thought with an inward wince. No worries. He'd write it off as a business expense. Anyway, there wouldn't have been time to wait for the company jet.

She opened several drawers in succession and pulled out a couple of trays. Paz sauntered over to stand in the doorway. Her peripheral vision caught his mouth curving up at the view of her derriere. Heat flooded her veins. He made her lose her cool without any effort on his part.

She could imagine how her parents would react if she brought *him* home. Why, the man had the audacity to kiss her when they'd only just met! Remembering how his lips felt on hers made warmth coil in her belly.

She kept her back to him, acutely aware of his proximity. After placing the trays on the counter, she chose a selection of snacks. She didn't realize he'd come closer until his hot breath seared her neck.

"Are you going to tell me about this job you hired me to do?" He spoke in a low, husky tone that played her nerve endings like music.

"I will, but only after you tell me what you know about my watch. Does this symbol mean something significant?" She'd tried to find someone who could interpret the inscription, but no one in her circles had the requisite knowledge.

"It means a great deal. To prove what I'm about to tell you, however, I have to kiss you again."

Before she could say no, his hands found her hips, and her nerves jumped as warmth penetrated her clothing from his touch. Her body responded instantly, and she dropped the bag of chips in her grasp. Intending to brush him off, she turned toward him instead.

His piercing gaze captured hers. Whatever he saw in her eyes made his expression brighten. His head descended, and he claimed her lips. An undeniable craving for more melted her resistance.

He tilted her chin and varied his slant. Unable to stop herself, she parted her mouth, allowing his tongue access as though he'd breached her mental gates. Her defenses crumpled further when she sniffed his sea heightened scent and felt the rough scrape of his bristle-roughened jaw.

Fiery bolts shot through to her core like Cupid's arrows as the universe shrunk to encompass them alone. Mist swirled around the outer edges of her consciousness, folding her in its embrace.

She'd known it was dangerous bringing him on board, but oh my. A vision of him naked popped into her head, and the thought of his being aroused on her account made her throw caution to the winds. She wrapped her arms around him, pressing him close as she relished the feel of his hard body against hers.

A buffet of turbulence jolted her back to reality. What was she doing? Heat crept up her skin as she stepped away.

"I told you not to do that again. I'll retract my offer of a job if you keep hitting on me." The engine whine surged as the jet lifted. She gripped the counter to steady herself.

He didn't budge, his cobalt eyes narrowing. "The prophecy says we must be together. It may not be what either of us wants, but there is no denying Fate."

Oh, but I do want you, buddy. And judging from the bulge in your pants, the feeling is mutual. "What prophecy?"

His mouth quirked up at the edges. "The one that claims you and I have to join forces to fight evil."

Here he goes with his delusional nonsense again.

She jabbed her finger in the air. "The only reason we're together is because I offered you a job. We should discuss your duties. They do not include seducing me."

He lifted an eyebrow. "If that's true, why did you kiss me back and put your arms around me?"

His knowing smile made her stutter. "T-That was a momentary lapse. It won't happen again."

"Won't it? You felt it, too, the connection between us. I knew it the moment I saw your watch. Your destiny is written there, and it's linked to mine."

"That's absurd."

She thrust a tray at him. She'd stacked it with a turkey sandwich, bag of chips, grapes, and a water bottle. She could use something stiff to drink, but it wasn't a good idea right now. She needed to keep her wits around this guy. Otherwise, she might believe his ridiculous stories.

It occurred to her that he might be a con man sent by her cousin Clifford to undermine her confidence. Aunt Alba might have told Cliff about her self-winding watch and her visions. In that case, she'd better stick to business for the rest of the trip so as not to reveal anything more of a personal nature.

****

Sitting at a table across from Jen, Paz munched on crunchy potato chips while she outlined his duties as a model. Her descriptions of fittings, trunk shows, and runway walks filtered through his brain like subatomic neutrinos.

If Jen truly was the woman meant for him according to the prophecy, they'd have more important things on their minds. And if not, he'd be on his way as soon as they touched down in Florida. He never meant to take the position she'd so kindly offered.

Too bad, because he'd never met a woman so responsive, and he had been with many. Paz had a reputation in the different star systems where he repaired the space comm nets. A carefree guy who could whisper words of love in any language, he stuck with casual relationships. It avoided the risk of rejection, an emotion he knew all too well thanks to his father.

He glanced at Jen, wondering if she'd scorn him if she knew the truth. She'd finished her turkey sandwich and patted her mouth dry with a paper napkin. He followed her movements with his eyes, wanting to taste her again and hating himself for his weakness.

"You're not listening, are you?" Her mouth formed a pout, which only made him desire her more.

"It's a lot to absorb." He perused her with a lazy smile. Pleased by how her face flushed and her pupils dilated, he decided to drop a hint at his origins to see how she responded. "I don't understand this runway business. Is it like an aircraft runway? Your terms can be confusing."

Jen tightened an earring. "You're the one who's confused. Sometimes you act like you're way smarter than me, and other times you seem like you're from outer space."

His grin broadening, he pointed to her earrings. "Those are nice kewa stones. Or I should say, diamonds. Did a boyfriend give them to you?"

She rolled her eyes. "No, they were a gift from my parents. And I'm single, if that's what you're asking." She pointed to an LCD monitor on the wall that showed their route. "I'd better put these trays away. We're flying near the Dragon's Triangle. It's best to be buckled down just in case."

"Dragon's Triangle? What's that?"

"It's a region in the Pacific where airplanes and ships have mysteriously disappeared." She stood and collected their trays. "You've heard of the Bermuda Triangle off Florida's coastline? Most people don't realize this area has more anomalies. Japan declared these coordinates a danger zone for shipping."

"Is that so?" He pressed his lips together, his impassive face guarding his thoughts.

"Japan sent a research vessel to investigate in 1952. It vanished without a trace. A myth blames the disappearances on an undersea dragon." Jen shrugged, while Paz admired the wisps of hair floating about her face. "Most likely, natural phenomena are to blame. Still, we could run into turbulence even though it's a clear day."

Paz studied the view after she turned down the aisle. Fluffy white clouds reflected the late afternoon sunlight. The billowing pillars of moisture floated in a sky of azure blue. Flying this slow enabled him to appreciate the sight.

Never mind the beauty of nature. He'd rather examine the propulsion system on the turbine-powered jet in more detail. It amazed him how the pilots got these heavy machines off the ground without anti-grav engines.

Although Kaj was the team's engineer, Paz had received cross-training in multiple skills. He was more than just a telecom expert in real life, too.

SattCom Networks may employ him as a repair technician, but that was because it suited his needs. He liked the travel benefits and the lower rank which hid his true ambitions. Certified as a comm system design engineer, Paz had the skill and education to develop network architecture on his own.

That's what he worked on in his spare time. His new system would revolutionize the space nets, but too many obstacles prevented him from building a prototype. The Trollek invasion was one of them. His duties as a Drift Lord took precedence over his private life. This had been his curse ever since his innate abilities had been discovered.

He wondered if the Dragon's Triangle hid another dimensional rift like its infamous cousin off the coast of Florida. That could account for his arrival here. Spontaneous tears in the space-time continuum were happening more often. They'd started when the Trolleks learned how to force open the barrier between dimensions.

Now the evil creatures invaded Earth through these rifts. The Drift Lords, trained to fight them, sought to seal the breach before the dimensional drift widened enough to cause a catastrophic energy blast.

Paz's mouth tightened into a grim line. He didn't like being near another possible rift. He liked it even less when he sniffed the ominous portent of burning filaments.

His muscles tensed. *Cors particles.*

Not only was the material produced at a rift horizon, but also when the Trolleks spatial shifted from one place to another. His ability to detect these particles was what made him a Drift Lord. Smelling it here could mean only one thing.

He shot to his feet as a crash sounded from the galley.

"Jen, what is it?" His heart raced as he scanned for a weapon. By Odin's grace, if only he had his T-6 laser pistol. Wedged between the table in front and the credenza at his back, he didn't see a thing he could use.

"I dropped a dish," she called. "Do you hear that odd buzzing noise?"

"Come here. Now."

Too late. A Trollek vectored into sight beside him.

An ugly humanoid with a hook-shaped nose, malformed ears, and beady eyes—he wore a leather tunic cinched with a wide belt, military grade trousers, and boots. Regular trooper, then. Not a specialized assassin.

Jen's shriek told him she had her own problems. More than one must have arrived.

Paz gulped in dismay. He hadn't polarized himself against their spell in the last twenty-four hours, but it looked as though capturing him wasn't their goal. The brute charging him with an axe had murder in his eyes. At least they knew better than to fire disruptors in a pressurized cabin.

He'd worry about how they'd found him later. Issuing a battle whoop, he attacked.

He deflected the beast's swing with his arm then followed through with a kick to the gut. Crouching, he twirled, then came up elbow at the ready. His blow to the thug's jaw had no effect. The Trollek merely grunted, eyes intent on his prey.

Assessing his adversary, Paz stepped back. He had no wish to have that beefy hand grab him.

To be touched by a Trollek meant to fall under his spell and become his mind slave. Although Paz was trained to resist, he'd still succumb to their influence in the end. He'd heard about the means they used to break a Drift Lord, if they were even interested in taking him alive.

Jen's screams tore at him. From the corner of his eye, he saw her across from the galley where another assailant grasped her forearm. She brought his hand up and bit it. With a howl of rage, he slugged her. She staggered back against the bulkhead.

How had she not been confounded? Were they trying to capture her, but not him? Without being able to spell her, they couldn't spatial shift out of the aircraft and take her with them. If they realized that, he and Jen would both be toast.

Jen dodged aside when the beast swatted at her again.

"Come with me, human. Cease your struggle."

"Get off our airplane." Her twist had come undone, her raven hair streaming down her back.

"How do you resist my touch? You should be mine already."

"What are you talking about? Who are you?" She cast Paz a desperate glance.

"Your Drift Lord cannot help you. We will subdue him, just as we did his friend." The Trollek sneered. "The one called Kaj screams like a stuck pig. Fighting us is useless."

Paz's blood ran cold at the mention of his missing colleague. He ducked when the axe swung at him again. He couldn't help Jen until he dealt with this guy.

He hopped up on one of the seats, kicked the axe out of the brute's hand, and rained a series of blows on his thick head. It was like attacking a punching bag. His thrusts barely made an impact.

Leaping down, he meant to go for the gut when a hand from behind clamped onto his wrist. Horror dawned on him as he realized he'd been touched.

"*Smark*," he cursed in his native tongue.

In the instant that followed, he thought about his team and how any surviving members would be disappointed at his failure. He thought about his father, who'd receive notice of his death, and wondered if the old man would even care. And he thought about his lost dream and how his invention would never see reality.

With fury born of desperation, he lashed out, a flurry of fists and feet, battling the two of them while wondering how his mind remained clear. He should be reacting sluggishly, fighting the chemical their touch produced in his body.

His first assailant drew a dagger. Paz sucked in his gut as the blade slashed the air in front of him.

Oh, no. The other guy had yanked out a disruptor. But he didn't aim it at Paz. Instead, he plunged toward the flight deck and fired an energy bolt at the door. The *riff* followed through with a kick that demolished the barrier and shot the pilot and first officer in the back of their heads.

Paz got a glimpse of their slumped bodies inside and Jen's terrified face over by the galley before the big Trollek stabbed at him again. Since the aircraft kept its flight pattern, he assumed the autopilot was engaged.

Did the beasts intend to land the plane? Paz would rather go down fighting than be captured and tortured. Since they couldn't confound Jen, they'd have to find a safe landing site if they meant to take her with them.

He wouldn't allow that to happen.

The Trollek nearest him yelled something to his comrade. He stuck his dagger into its sheath before pulling a silver ball from his pocket. Light gleamed off its metal surface as the beast tossed the object down the aisle.

An EMP grenade. Paz's heart skipped a beat.

In the next instant, both Trolleks hit a button on their armbands and vanished in a shimmer of air.

They'd vectored out, leaving him and Jen behind. Reacting automatically, Paz flung himself at Jen.

A flash of brilliant white light erupted inside the cabin.

The EM pulse lasted just a few seconds but that's all it took to kill the power.

In dead silence, the aircraft tilted nose-down and plummeted toward the earth.

Chapter Four

Jen screamed as the jet lost power and plunged downward. Thrown into the aisle with the plane's sharp pitch, she slid toward the flight deck.

Anything that wasn't tied down boomeranged around the cabin. She ducked as a serving tray flew by and bounced off a seatback onto the deck. Oxygen masks dangled overhead. Grappling for a handhold, she dug her fingertips into the nearest seat cushion. With a white-knuckled grip, she hauled herself sideways.

Gravity yanked at her. Her arm muscles strained as she gained on her target. Sweat popped out on her brow. With a final surge, she flung herself onto the seat. Her hands trembled violently as she fumbled to fasten the harness. The buckle eluded her slippery fingers. Gritting her teeth, she managed to snap the straps in place.

Not that it would do much good. In a few more minutes, they'd be finished.

Gasping for breath, she yanked the mask over her nose. Her heart pounded a staccato beat as though it meant to leap from her chest. Her breath came in short, hard bursts, while a wave of dizziness assailed her.

Outside, they'd descended through the clouds. The ocean rushed to greet them. Her mind shoved aside images of the impact to come. At least it would be fast.

Sadness overwhelmed her at the loss of all she wanted to do yet with her life and at the grief her parents would feel. The blow of losing a daughter would bring them endless pain, despite the problems Jen had caused over the years. Well, at least they'd meet in the afterlife, if one existed.

She gripped her armrests, clearing her mind and giving herself up to God. They were in His hands now. A brief thought flickered in her brain that she should assume crash position, but why bother? She might as well meet her fate with open eyes.

Paz's face loomed in front of her, giving her a jolt. The last she'd seen of him, he'd been aiming in her direction but then that brilliant flash of white light had erupted.

"Give me your earrings." Despite their imminent death, his voice remained calm but authoritative.

"What?"

"I need your kewa stones. Diamonds."

Oxygen deficiency must be making him daft. "You're confused. Put a mask on." She hadn't seen what happened up front except that the thug who'd attacked them had breached the cockpit. Maybe the pilot, if merely stunned, would recover in time to gain control of the aircraft.

Paz crouched beside her, his powerful thighs holding him in place against the jet's steep angle.

"Listen to me. I can align the diamond crystals to transmit power from my comm unit." He tapped his wristwatch. He must have put it back on when he'd changed clothes at the film studio. "If I get the frequency right, I'll be able to interface my modulator with the ignition sequence for the engines."

"Huh?" Jen didn't understand a word he said, but she unscrewed her earrings and handed them over.

Paz sped toward the flight deck. Noticing how he breathed well enough on his own, she cast her mask off. Perhaps they'd dropped low enough for the pressure to equalize.

Wondering what he planned to do, she unsnapped her seat belt and followed him. She stumbled down the sharply pitched aisle, gripping the seat backs for support. A glimpse of the pilots' slumped bodies ahead reinforced her worst fears.

She swallowed against a rising tide of panic. Maybe this was just a nightmare. Her psyche detached, seeking defensive maneuvers and an analysis of her plight.

Who were those ugly men with deformed features? How had they appeared out of nowhere and then disappeared into thin air? What sort of blast had they set off to kill the engines?

This was real all right. Numb with the certainty that they were about to die, she sank into the seat nearest the flight deck, fastened the safety strap, and prayed.

The aircraft shuddered, its vibration increasing with the rapid rate of descent. Her teeth clamped together when they hit an air pocket. Her stomach heaved and then dropped. She tightened her grip on the armrests, biting her lip against the urge to scream.

The jet shook so hard it rattled her bones. Surely, they'd break up in midair. Would the breath be sucked from her lungs in the thin atmosphere? Would she experience instant blackness? That would be better than being crushed on impact.

She caught a blur of movement from up front. Paz had tossed the pilot's body aside and taken his seat. Foolish man. Did he plan to cobble together a power source as though he were switching telephone lines?

He yanked back on the control column, gripping it with two hands. It bucked with the craft's movement, but he maintained his tight hold. His arm muscles bulged with strain, as he wrestled it back. The plane's nose inched upward, and then the world tilted.

Jen squeezed her eyes shut, certain they were going into a spin and would crash within minutes.

Her head reeled. By the grace of God, the deck beneath her feet stabilized. When she opened her eyes, she gasped. Paz had miraculously managed to level their attitude although they continued to sink.

Gravity could be a bummer.

"Jen, come here. I need your help." He didn't break concentration but continued to peer forward.

The plane banked left and then dipped right, as though he were testing its maneuverability. He must have had some flying experience but maybe not in a jet.

"You have to keep the nose steady while I restart the engines." He glanced over his shoulder at her. "Now, please."

"Okay." After undoing her harness, she staggered forward.

"Good girl. Get the copilot out of his seat. Just put him on the floor behind you."

She swallowed hard, wondering what type of weapon would scorch the first officer's head. His body felt like a lead weight as she dragged him sideways to the deck. After hauling him out of the way, she stepped over his still form to reach the copilot's chair. She fastened the restraint, aware of the plane's erratic motion and how the deck tilted and heaved.

A console sat between her and Paz, its array of levers and buttons looking like the space shuttle's command center. She stared at the blank monitor screens.

He noticed the direction of her glance. "The EM pulse zapped the electronics. We'll have to fly on visual, but don't worry. The aircraft has backup systems for emergencies like this."

"That's good to know. Now what?"

"See what I'm doing?" Paz nodded at his hands, taut on the wheel. "Just hold your column the same way and keep the horizon in a straight line."

"How long can we stay in the air?" *And who's gonna land the damn thing?*

"The manual systems are still working. We can always glide her down if necessary. See those dials over there? They're standby indicators for altimeter, airspeed, and attitude."

Yielding the controls to her, he pressed something on his wristwatch and then held it close to his mouth. "Paz to anyone. Come in."

Was he nuts? Maybe the lack of oxygen had gone to his brain.

The plane seesawed, and she struggled to maintain a level attitude. Her palms grew greasy with sweat.

He fiddled with the dial and tried again. "Paz to Zohar. Sire, are you there? Can anyone answer?" No response. He shot her a wry grin. "Well, it was worth a try."

"Don't tell me, that's some sort of radio?"

Noting her skeptical glance, he shrugged. "It's a comm unit. I thought maybe I could raise my team from up here, but I guess not."

The jet dipped to the right. Jen adjusted their attitude, her heart thumping wildly. She muttered prayers that she hadn't remembered since childhood.

Please, please, let us survive.

Paz took his space-age wrist radio and set it in his lap. Before she could blink, he'd popped it open and picked at the circuits. Her diamond earrings rested in his lap.

Focusing out the window, she kept to her task and tried not to notice how the plane kept descending. Without power, she struggled to maintain an even position relative to attitude. Ocean stretched in every direction below like a vast blue carpet.

The engines coughed, died once, and then sputtered into life. "All right, I'll take it now," Paz said.

Happy to comply, she yielded the controls.

"We need to find a place to bring her down just in case my frequency modulator stops transmitting. I can do a water landing if necessary, but it would be nice to find a piece of land."

"There," she cried, pointing as a shape took form on the horizon. "Is that an island?"

"We'll see." He surveyed the console. "There should be a manual throttle here somewhere. Ah, here it is. Let's give this a try."

He pulled back on the black lever, and the airspeed slowed. The nose dipped to a few inches below the horizon, and they began a controlled descent.

"Supposing that's a rock up ahead, it will still give us a place to gain ground if we have to land on water.

Can you swim?" Paz spared her a glance.

Jen bit her lower lip. "Yes, but I'd expect there are flotation devices aboard."

"Let's wait and see if we'll need them first."

As their altitude above sea level decreased, the chunk of land enlarged into a sizable island with sandy beaches, a mountainous interior, and signs of civilization. She and Paz could summon help, assuming they got down in one piece.

"That strip of sand on the far side is our best bet, but it could get rough." Paz grinned at her. "You're doing great, by the way. Just swing in there, and you'll be fine."

"Swing? Do you mean hang in there?"

His shoulder rose then fell. "Right. I get the slang terms mixed up sometimes."

"You think?" This day couldn't get any stranger. If they survived, he owed her a bucketful of explanations.

A muscle in his jaw clenched, as he scanned the console with narrowed eyes. "Here, this should extend the flaps and lower the landing gear."

A moment later, various thuds and thumps rocked the craft. They dropped further, their airspeed reduced. Paz approached the beach heading into the wind, fighting to keep the wings straight.

The ocean rushed at them. That strip of sand ahead looked so tiny that Jen's breath came in pants. She gripped the armrests, her knuckles white. They were coming in too fast and too high!

Paz killed the power just before touchdown. Jen's teeth clattered together as they bumped the beach, bounced into the air, and bumped again. Sand spewed in all directions. Then the jet skidded along the narrow strip toward a tangle of trees ahead.

"We're not stopping." She stared forward with horrified fascination, her heart threatening to jump out of her chest.

"Hold on." Paz pressed on the brake pedals. His hands gripped the wheel, arm muscles bulging with strain.

They tipped sideways, and a terrible rending noise tore the air. Jen's blood froze solid as part of the wing ripped off with a horrendous scraping sound. The deck tilted, and then suddenly, they stopped. Her side of the jet dipped toward the sand.

She breathed in a couple of rapid, shallow breaths—stunned they were still intact. A grove of bamboo stood dead ahead. If they had not stopped, they would have been skewered.

Dear God, we made it.

She sat motionless, unable to budge, her body trembling.

"Get out." Paz jabbed his thumb toward the exit.

"Fire is a risk since we weren't able to dump the fuel. Plus, we need to vacate this site."

His grim face told her there might be other reasons for haste. What if the natives were hostile?

One thing at a time, Jen. Get your ass out of here.

Paz collected the parts from his wrist device, unsnapped his harness, and rose. Jen followed suit, but she gathered her wits enough to grab her purse while he popped the escape hatch. Her cell phone was inside. Maybe, by some miracle, it would work in this remote location.

"Come on, we can't waste time." Paz signaled to her from the open hatchway.

She staggered toward him. Peering outside, she was glad to note they didn't need the emergency chute. They could easily jump the short distance to the ground. Holding her long skirt, she leaped after Paz onto the beach.

He caught her in his muscular arms and gently eased her down. His tousled hair, determined jaw, and ocean blue eyes had never looked better.

"Thank you. You saved our lives." On impulse, Jen rose on her tiptoes and kissed him.

She'd only meant it to be a brief expression of gratitude, but Paz's gaze intensified. He swept her into his arms and gave her a passionate kiss that left her breathless.

"We're safe now." He broke away with a regretful expression. "At least, for the moment. But we shouldn't linger."

"For the moment? What does that mean?" The memory of

those ugly men who'd attacked them returned with full force. "You know who assaulted us, don't you? When are you going to tell me what's going on?"

"Let's summon help first. I need to put my comm unit back together. If we can hook it into a local network, you can call your people."

"I have my cell phone." She patted her purse.

His hand clamped onto her arm. "We should scout around first. Our landing probably attracted attention, and we don't want the wrong people to find us."

"You're right." She glanced around with sudden nervousness. Waves washed onto the beach, while the late afternoon sun cast brilliant sparkles onto the sea. The sand ended at the edge of a jungle. "Hey, do you still have my earrings? I'd like them back."

He reached into his jeans pocket, where he must have stuck them after they'd landed. "Thanks. We wouldn't have made it without them." Paz handed the pair over. "I wonder…"

"What?" She kept pace as he aimed for the trees.

"Some things are meant to be. This place, our landing here, might be one of them." He sniffed the air, his brow creasing. "This can't be the same island where Nira and Zohar found themselves after they fell through the mirror. The captain didn't detect any cors particles.

But I do."

****

Jen stopped a few feet ahead and faced him. "Listen, I'm due for an explanation. Tell me why all this is happening."

Paz thought she looked amazingly beautiful with her hair streaming down her back, her brown eyes blazing, and her hands propped on her hips.

His glance dipped to her cleavage, exposed as a dress strap slid off her shoulder. She adjusted it, her face flushing as she noticed his glance. He liked the long dress. It showed off her curves to perfection, but unfortunately it wouldn't serve her well on a trek through the jungle.

She was right. He owed her explanations, not only because he admired her courage during a life-threatening situation but because knowledge might enhance their survival.

The crisis wasn't over yet.

"Okay, let's regroup for a few minutes." He led her into the brush where he checked a fallen log for vermin before plopping down. Sweat trickled down his back, and his skin itched. Scratching at a bug bite, he cursed their lack of weaponry and provisions.

Maybe he should return to the aircraft to salvage what he could. With some of the onboard circuitry, he could piece together a makeshift PIP. Then he could pinpoint the source of the cors particles.

The distant sound of waves reached him amid the tangle of vines and jungle undergrowth. The sun radiated blinding rays but fortunately the canopy acted as a filter. Nonetheless, they'd get dehydrated fast. He needed to acquire water, food, and weapons.

Jen sank onto a black rock, one of many strewn about the foliage. She moved with grace, like a longnecked *liema* on his home world. And like a forbidden fruit, he was tempted to taste her again. The imprint of her lips had emblazoned onto his memory like a branding iron.

Her luscious mouth formed into a pout. "Well? Talk fast, because I'd like to reach a town before dark. And I should try my cell phone to call my father. He'll be frantic with worry."

"Wait." His raised hand forestalled her action. "If anyone is tracking us, your signal could be triangulated. Let me explain first what we're up against. You need to understand the danger."

He stared at a lizard scampering under a dropped palm frond and hoped it was just that: a creature of the ground, and not a shapeshifter like he'd encountered before. Jen didn't realize half the threats facing them.

He took a deep breath then began. "We were attacked midair by beings known as Trolleks. They come from another dimension."

Jen gaped at him. "Another what?"

"You heard me." He regarded her with an unwavering gaze. "Let's start at the beginning. The earliest sentient people on Earth were humanoids we call the Originals. They predated your known ancestors."

"Hold on. My ancestors? What does that make you?"

His mouth curved in a mirthless grin. "I'm from the planet Morata in the Zood System. The Originals seeded more than this world. Other intelligent life exists out there." His gesture encompassed the heavens.

Her jaw dropped. "Shut up! You're pulling my leg."

"That isn't physically possible when you're over there and I'm here." Really, some of the slang terms didn't make any sense.

She straightened her spine. "Tell me the truth. I deserve that much."

"I am." He flashed his sexiest smile. "Let me finish my story. Descendants of the Originals took different paths. One group lived close to nature on this world until mankind encroached on their territory."

Wisdom imbued her expression. "Don't tell me. Those were the Trolleks."

He nodded. "Humans persecuted them until they were no longer comfortable here. During a natural rift between dimensions, they passed through to another place with pristine forests and fertile fields."

"What do you mean by a rift?" She lifted her nose, as though doubting his every word.

"You'd mentioned the Dragon's Triangle where strange anomalies occur." He tilted his head. "Imagine a cosmic energy grid underlying the tectonic plates. The grid lines are called ley lines. The points where they intersect are known as Vile Vortices. Twelve such locations exist around the world. Rifts occur at these sites."

"Huh? I don't get it." A breeze rustled the tree branches, and a flurry of leaves dropped onto their heads. Jen combed her fingers through her hair while he watched, mesmerized. He'd like to filter through her tresses and feel the silken texture.

Shaking his head to dispel his wayward thoughts, he continued. "When the dimensional plates grind against each other, the resultant pressure forces open a door between dimensions. Normally, the event horizon at this natural rift produces a substance called cors particles. When their mass reaches a certain level, the resultant pressure forces the rifts to close. This time, however, the Trolleks have devised a means to force open the rifts and keep them from shutting down." "That's not good," she said in a dry tone.

"You're catching on." He beamed his approval, pleased to see her eyes brighten in response. "With the portals remaining open, the accumulation of cors particles will breach the point of no return. The dimensional drift will widen, causing a massive shock wave that alters reality in all dimensions. It will destroy everything in existence."

"Oh. You're talking about Doomsday… the end of the world." Jen glared at him as though unable to wrap her mind around the concept of annihilation. "What's your role in this? You can fly an airplane, fight bad guys, and turn my earrings into wireless transmitters. Who are you?"

"I am a Drift Lord." He puffed out his chest. "Our league formed many eons ago when Trolleks first began invading Earth. We are tasked with repelling their forces."

"How can you stop them? What are you planning to do?"

"We have to locate their rifts and shut them down. In our last battle, my team was attempting to destroy their jamming device so our sensors could detect the portals."

He didn't tell her how he'd ended up injured, or how he had the innate ability to detect cors particles.

She might think him as freakish as his father.

"These Trolleks, what do they want?"

"They mean to turn humans into mind slaves."

"Weren't they happy on their own world?"

"They resented being forced from their homeland and felt this was their rightful place." He thought it best not to mention the enemy's plan for genetic manipulation of the human race. Jen might already suspect he was missing a few actuators, and that additional info could fuel her skepticism.

Then again, she acted as though she believed him.

"How could the Trolleks appear out of nowhere?" Her fearful gaze darted at the jungle surrounding them.

He picked up a small rock and twirled it with his fingers. "They can maneuver vectors within the spacetime continuum, parallel shifting themselves from one location to another."

"You said they capture humans. How?"

"They transport people who've been confounded. Trolleks secrete a chemical substance that directly alters the human brain. They transmit it through touch."

"My ears buzzed just before they attacked us."

His eyebrows lifted. "Nira Larsen gets the same sensation whenever Trolleks are nearby. She wears a wristwatch similar to yours and she's also immune to the confounding spell. Very likely you're one of the six sisters mentioned in the prophecy."

"What are you talking about? I don't have any sisters." Jen scrubbed a hand over her face. "This is too much."

A flare shot into the air delayed any further explanations.

Paz tossed the rock aside and leapt to his feet. "Let's move. They've found our aircraft. We don't want them to find us."

Chapter Five

Jen watched her footing as she dodged fallen coconuts, tree roots, and rocks embedded in the sandy soil. It wasn't easy in a long dress. She had to be careful not to snag the fabric on trailing vines and branches, or it would slow her down.

She wasn't ready to believe Paz's wild tale, although circumstances supported his story. It sounded like something out of a science fiction novel: alien invaders, multiple dimensions, and sentient life on other planets.

Could it be possible these rifts accounted for the vessel disappearances in the Bermuda Triangle? And who was Nira Larsen? How was her watch similar to Jen's? And what did Paz mean about six sisters in a prophecy? Jen had no siblings.

Then again, she'd always been curious about how her timepiece was not only waterproof but kept running over the years without a battery. After seeing what Paz's wrist unit could do, she wondered about the true purpose of hers.

Thinking of his device reminded her of the need to call home. "I should try my cell phone. Will it work, or were the components zapped by the EM pulse?"

"Let's find out. Did you have it turned off during flight?" At her nod, he said, "Then it might still function. Go ahead but make it quick."

She fished the phone from her bag and thumbed it on. A few musical notes sounded, raising her hopes. The screen blinked on, showing the system logo but then it read, *No Signal.*

"Well, the good thing is, it still works. The bad thing is,

we're out of range of the network." "Give it to me. I can reassemble it into a PIP." "A what?" She handed him the phone.

"Portable Intel Platform, or a mobile data unit. I'd hoped to salvage parts from the aircraft but that's no longer an option. What else do you have in your bag?"

Jen rummaged inside. "A Swiss Army knife." She demonstrated its uses before he snatched it from her fingers. "Notebook and pens. Makeup. Scarf. Breath Mints. Sunglasses. Comb. Business cards. Calculator. An eBook reader." Not to mention her birth control pills, the real reason why she needed to keep her purse.

"Perfect, I'll take those electronic devices." His eyes gleamed as he collected her booty. "Let's find a place in the shade where I can work. You don't have any snacks in there, do you?" His dimpled grin disconcerted her.

"Sorry. We can always search for some bananas if we get hungry."

"That's the spirit." Perching himself on a rocky ledge, Paz used the tools in the penknife to disassemble her gadgets. He spent several minutes working in silence, his face taut with concentration.

Jen leaned against a knobby tree trunk and studied him. Golden highlights in his hair glinted in a beam of sunlight. A stubborn lock fell across his forehead. He raked it back with stiff fingers, a motion he did often as though he preferred to see things with clarity.

Why, then, did she catch him wearing a guarded look when he thought no one was watching? Perhaps his confidence was tempered by an element of reserve.

Her brow beaded with perspiration in the jungle heat. A chittering noise came from a nearby tree, while something slithered among the dead leaves on the ground. Jen didn't like to think about what might be lurking in the bushes, so she focused on Paz instead.

"What's it like to be a Drift Lord? Do you really work in telecom in your down time?"

"Yes, that's my real job. Being a Drift Lord is sort of like your Army Reserves. We're called to duty only when a rift occurs." He scratched his jaw. "Hey, you got any fire starters in that sack of yours?"

"You mean, like a lighter? I have matches if you need them. I take them from restaurants and keep a pack in my purse for emergencies."

"Supernova! I just need to weld these two wires together and that should perform the trick."

Her mouth curved upward. "It's *do* the trick, Paz." She glanced heavenward. "If you're from up there, how did you learn English?"

He lifted his chin. "I'm the team's Communications Officer and Linguistic Specialist. I speak many languages, but I also have an implanted translator." He pointed to a spot behind his ear. "We need to get you one. I left all of my equipment in Florida. That's why I have to get back there."

Before she could ask him the rest of the questions hovering on her tongue, he snatched the matchbook from her hand. "Thanks. We should keep moving. I hear voices."

She straightened, brushing debris off her dress.

She, too, heard a murmur from somewhere off to the right. As she scanned the treetops, she picked up a trail of smoke in the distance.

"Hey, look. That smoke might be coming from someone's chimney. It could lead us into town."

"All right, but I should finish putting this unit together. It'll give us an accurate fix on our location. We'll need our coordinates if we want to summon help. Give me your scarf so I can carry these parts." He dumped the components onto the piece of fabric Jen gave him and tied the ends together.

She prepared to move out. Her skin itched, and she yearned for a change of clothes. Her current state of dress made her a moving meal ticket for the friendly insects.

Jen traipsed through the undergrowth after Paz as he sought

to put distance between their position and the beach. Probably anyone with tracking skills could follow them. They weren't making any effort to cover their trail.

Why did he suspect the natives might be hostile? Were they related to the thugs who disabled their plane? How could he know that? And where was the rest of his team? How had the man ended up bruised, naked, and confused on her film set?

Sweat trickled down her back and between her breasts. She craved water, air-conditioning, and telephone service. They did have electricity on these remote islands, didn't they?

God, she hoped the inhabitants weren't primitives with face paint and spears.

With each step, her fears escalated and so did her sense of the surreal. This couldn't be happening to her.

She must be trapped in a nightmare. But when she stumbled on a root, and Paz's firm grip steadied her, she swallowed her doubts. Like it or not, she was stuck with him as her partner for now.

After what seemed an interminable trek but had only taken a half hour, Paz called a halt beside a cluster of ferns. Jen rubbed her arms, scratched from fronds and sharp-bladed plants.

"I'm going to finish compiling the PIP. You hear that sound of rushing water? Follow it to the source if it isn't too far but come back if you hear anyone nearby. We need to locate fresh water to avoid getting dehydrated."

Without waiting for her reply, he settled onto a flat-topped boulder, unfolded the scarf in his lap, and got to work on assembling his device.

When she didn't respond, he glanced up. "What?"

She propped her hands on her hips. "Are you going to tell me what to do the whole time?"

His lips compressed, and his gaze darkened. "Unless you have survival skills and know how to deal with nasties as well as other dangers, I suggest you let me call the slots."

"It's call the shots, tiger. Get your slang straight."

He reminded her of a wild animal: clever, resourceful, and deadly. An aura of power emanated from him that radiated strength and prowess. She'd known the man only a few short hours but had faith in him to get them out of this fix.

He'd just finished his project when she returned to report on a nearby waterfall tumbling into a freshwater pond. She'd taken her time, relieving herself after ascertaining no one was watching, and then washing her hands and face in the pool.

Paz stood and panned his PIP around like Spock with his Tricorder. "We're on Togura Island. It's part of the Izu Archipelago south of Japan in the region known as the Dragon's Triangle. Our arrival here cannot be a coincidence."

"You've said that before. What do you mean?"

Paz's eyes glittered as he regarded her. "I smelled cors particles on the aircraft just before the Trolleks vectored into view. The odor is strong on this island, and my improvised PIP confirms it. There's a rift here."

"O-kay." Too weary to absorb his words, she signaled for him to follow her toward the water.

The gushing sound grew louder as they wove through the trees, their shoes scrunching on dead leaves. Overhead, a green parrot flitted from branch to branch. A loud screech from higher up spurred her to walk faster.

She stopped at the water's edge, spray from the waterfall wetting her face. The pool's surface glistened in the dappled sunlight. A pleasant nutmeg-like scent pervaded the air.

Paz aimed his device at the water, fiddled with the controls, and smiled triumphantly. "It's clean. We can drink."

After quenching their thirst, they headed toward a cluster of life signs on his device. It led them toward the east and away from their landing site.

Vines dangled in front of her nose. She brushed them aside, wary of cobwebs. Overhanging branches made her pulse quicken. She feared spiders or snakes dropping on her head.

A shudder racked her shoulders. She'd never been a nature

fan and didn't intend to start now. The sooner they reached civilization, the better.

All this talk of rifts and Trolleks confused her. Fatigue seeped into her bones, discouraging any further inquiries.

Her heart leapt when they emerged at the jungle's edge where a small village hugged the coastline. A dirt road ran through the main street lined by pastel-colored houses on stilts. Chickens strutted in the yards where laundry was strung out to dry. Boats of varied sizes bobbed on the water. Likely the villagers made their living from fishing.

Paz held up a cautionary hand. "Let me do the talking."

He approached a couple of women repairing a long net. They had weathered faces and wore simple, loose-fitting clothes. Jen followed in Paz's wake, deferring to his expertise.

If he had so many skills as a Drift Lord, why wasn't he doing more than repairing telecom equipment? Even if he dealt with advanced communications systems, it wouldn't explain his complacency.

Every nugget he revealed about himself led to a greater mystery. Did he really want a job as a male model, or had he used that as an excuse to tag along? Her lips thinned. Sooner or later, she'd coax him to talk.

Right now, he engaged in conversation with the citizens of this peaceful village. They spoke in a foreign tongue incomprehensible to Jen.

Residents converged on the newcomers, staring with overt curiosity. Aware of how disheveled she and Paz must appear, Jen felt her face heat under their scrutiny.

Paz's mouth turned down as he translated for her. "They don't have any phones or radios here, but there's a larger town to the north where we may be able to access a line to the mainland. We can rent a ride in one of their trucks to get there along the coastal route."

"That's a good idea. These shoes aren't made for hiking." She stooped to brush sand from between her toes. The abrasive grains irritated her skin. Blisters would form if she didn't wash her feet and get decent footwear.

One of the women, missing a couple of teeth, rattled off a series of sentences. Paz's response came back laced with anger.

"What is it?" Jen plucked at her skirt, hoping the air would cool with the descending sun. The smell of dead fish brewed in the heat.

"A group of men stopped by here earlier asking about us. They'd spotted our aircraft and were headed toward our landing site." He paused. "They had guns."

"Oh." She swallowed. "Trolleks?"

He shook his head. "Sons of these folks. Lord Morar of Shirajo Manor pressed them into service."

"Pressed them? You mean, he forced them to work?"

His jaw tightened. "The Trolleks turned them into mind slaves. The men do whatever they're told, and they were ordered to intercept us and bring us to their master."

"Did this warlord send those goons to disable our jet? Does this mean we've landed right in his lair?" Her pitch rose as she realized their jeopardy.

Paz's expression hardened. "I believe so."

"Then let's hire a boat and get out of here."

"These are local fishing boats. If we want to hire a seaworthy vessel, we'll have to go to Kamaji, the town on the north coast."

She swept her arm in a semicircle while the breeze whipped hair into her face. "This island has only two towns plus an enemy fortress?"

Paz made an inquiry to the residents. A gaunt man in a tattered shirt muttered something in response. The Drift Lord gave a resigned sigh before speaking in English to Jen.

"This guy claims the interior is too mountainous to traverse and has a volcano that rumbles whenever the gods get angry. The south coast is rocky with cliffs, so they can't fish off that side. Plus, a deadly sea serpent lives there and swallows boats whole."

Jen rolled her eyes. "This just keeps getting better. Then we'll hitch a ride in a truck, go to the larger village, and hire a boat to take us off this damn island."

Paz's intense gaze bored into hers. "I'm not leaving yet. It's my job to determine the source of the cors particles, locate the rift, and shut it down. Unfortunately, I believe the Trollek stronghold is where we'll find our answers."

"No, thanks." She slung her purse strap over her other shoulder. "I'll take these people up on their kind offer for transportation, and you can do your hero thing."

Paz gave a snort of laughter. "Do you really think you'd get far without me?"

She lifted her nose. "I can try."

"You'll end up getting yourself killed. The Trolleks are onto you now, and they'll take you any way they can—dead or alive. If you want a chance at survival, you'll have to stick with me."

Jen glared at him while her blood chilled at the truth of his statement. She couldn't even understand these people without his help. But to head straight into the lion's den? What did he hope to accomplish?

She asked him after they garnered a ride to Kamaji on the dirt road paralleling the coast. They rode on the flatbed of a pickup truck amid a tangle of tools and a closed metal box. The ride was a series of bumps that jostled them against each other.

"Are you thinking of breaking into the Trollek compound?" Her nose clogged from the dust kicked up in their wake. "We could be walking into a trap."

"They'll be expecting us to escape the island." His eyes glimmered in the late afternoon sunlight. "Look, even if I locate the rift, I don't know how they're keeping it open. We have to shut down these portals to stop their invasion. That's our team's main objective, but we need more intelligence. How are they keeping these rifts open against the pressure from the cors particles?"

"It must take a lot of energy."

"Exactly. I can't pass up this opportunity to learn more about their technology."

"How many inter-dimensional rifts are there?"

"We don't know. The Trolleks activated a jamming device that blinded our sensors. We spent several weeks trying to locate their signal. Finally, we found it in a warehouse near Drift World."

"The adult role-playing theme park in Orlando?"

"Correct." He nodded, a lock of hair falling into his face. With an impatient gesture, he thrust it back. "Our last mission was meant to destroy the jammer. I am unaware of the ultimate outcome."

He glanced away, but not before she caught the flicker of pain in his eyes.

"Who else is on your team?"

"We started out as seven, but we lost three men." He drew a deep breath. "Rayne got killed, Kaj went missing, and Dal was poisoned. A traitor among us worked for Zohar's political opponents from home and betrayed us to the Trolleks. Zohar Thorald is our captain," he explained.

"That's only six, including you."

Paz nodded, his gaze distant. "Yaron is our medic and the seventh team member. At the last count, only three of us were left. This doesn't include Lord Magnor, a Tsuran swordsman who joined our team unofficially as did Nira Larsen."

"Tell me about this woman."

Paz focused on the shrubbery bordering the road. "She's an expert on Norse mythology and one of the principles in the prophecy. All of us were captured during this last mission. A Trollek pushed me into a pit housing the power source for the jamming device. I hit my head. That's the last I remember before waking up on the film set."

They hit a pothole, and the truck shook and rattled.

Jen's eyes widened. "Do you mean to tell me you started out in Orlando and ended up in Tokyo? Naked?

How is that possible?"

"The generator mechanism had sharp edges and moving parts. It tore my clothing as I fell. The ocean ran below. I must have been sucked into a spontaneous tear in the space-time fabric when I hit the water."

"Well, that would explain your confusion and bruises."

He touched the purplish wound on his head. He'd ripped off the bandage on the airplane. "As for why I landed in your location, that was Fate. I knew it as soon as I saw your watch." His gaze swung to her wrist. "Hmm, I wonder. Where would you be if you could wish yourself there?"

"Home, of course."

Paz gripped her hand, the heat from his palm radiating up her arm. "Go ahead. Visualize the place."

She gaped at him. "What are you saying? That I can whisk us there like magic?"

"It's worth a try."

"Huh. The sun must be baking your brain." Nonetheless, she squeezed her eyes shut and pictured her family's two-story white columned house in Palm Beach. When they hit another rut in the road, her eyes flew open. "We're still here."

"I guess so. Apparently, you're not ready to wield your power."

She withdrew her hand, confused by his words. Her dress rumpled under her legs, and she smoothed it out. Maybe she could get a change of clothes in the next village.

Idly she scratched at a bug bite on her shoulder, pondering their conversation. What wasn't he telling her?

Her toes ached, the skin between them scraped raw. A glimpse of sparkling sea to their right made her yearn to dip her body into the cool water. She wasn't cut out to be Nature Girl. Discomfited, she adjusted her position.

Paz's amused glance followed her movements. She had a momentary mental image of him massaging her feet. Her face heated again, or maybe it was just the humidity getting to her.

"Why did the Trolleks attack us? Were they after you?" She asked the question foremost on her mind.

"At first I thought the beasts had vectored in to capture me." He raised his voice to be heard over the truck's engine noise. "But I think my presence surprised them. One guy came at me with an axe, while the other *riff* grabbed you. If you hadn't been immune to their spell, he'd have taken you. I believe that was their prime objective."

"To capture *me*?" Jen's pulse accelerated. "How would they even know I was there?"

His eyes narrowed. "Your wristwatch allows them to track you. I suspect its special functions activated when we met. It has properties similar to the transport units the beasts wear on their armbands. We don't know how it works."

"Oh, that's just great."

"I do know one thing—kissing you saved me from being confounded. Zohar learned this from Nira. Our mingling transfers your immunity to me." He sidled closer, his gaze darkening. "In fact, we'd better do it again for safety's sake."

"What? You must be addled in the attic."

"Attic? I do not understand."

She circled her finger around her ear. "You know, nuts."

"Ah." He leaned closer until she could smell the scent of the jungle on him. "I am serious. Normally we polarize ourselves against the Trollek touch. It has to be done every twenty-four hours. My margin has long since passed."

"So, I have to kiss you to protect you." Her tone dripped with sarcasm.

"At the very least. The more intimate we are, the longer the protection lasts."

His mouth prevented her next question from forming as his head descended. She tasted the tang of salt as he brushed her lips with the slightest pressure.

The nerve of the man for making up such a story. And yet it held a kernel of truth. Just in case it had merit, she allowed him to plunder her mouth. He didn't go deep, just tantalizing her enough to want more.

And oh, did she want more.

The horror and stress of the last few hours returned with full force along with the realization that this man had saved her life.

Her arms wrapped around him of their own volition. She parted her lips and pressed her body closer. Her breasts ached as they encountered his broad chest. A vision of them naked together made her breath come short.

His strong arms hugged her against him while she relished his strength and power. The man might be confident, cocky, and arrogant to boot, but he sure could kiss. His mouth changed angles and hungrily devoured her.

They started to slide downward, and so did his hands. She felt a low ache in her belly, a surging need as he found her breasts. This might be the wrong time and place, but she couldn't help herself. Lust consumed her.

His thumbs brushed her nipples, and she moaned.

Paz kissed her once more and then withdrew. "I'd like to continue this, *leera*, but not now. We have a mission to accomplish." He helped her to sit upright.

Jen straightened her dress. "I just did that to protect you. Don't think I'm easy."

"A lady like you? Never." His smirk told her he thought otherwise. "Although, if the Fates are to be believed, you and I are meant to be together."

"Is that so?" Was that another excuse for him to kiss her? She tilted her head. "Why didn't any of this happen earlier, like at my showroom in New York? The Trolleks could have jumped in and grabbed me then."

"As I said, it was the confluence of our being together that raised their alarms. You can always ask those guys."

His deeper tone alerted her even as the truck slowed. A roadblock of angry armed Trolleks waited for them ahead.

Chapter Six

Paz would have preferred to enter Shirajo Manor on his own terms. Being escorted there by a squadron of Trolleks didn't bode well for their prospects. At least, he hoped they'd be taken to the base commandant and not summarily executed.

Jen trembled next to him as they stood by the road, with their hands raised, along with the pickup truck driver. Her face pinched and her forehead beaded with sweat.

A large, beefy Trollek wearing military gear inspected them one-by-one. When he reached the driver, he drew out his disruptor and shot the man point blank in the chest.

"Oh, my God." Jen's voice edged on hysteria.

"Search them, Menig Gwarp," the officer snapped.

"Yes, Leytnant." A Trollek with a missing front tooth approached Jen and leered at her.

"Don't resist," Paz warned her from the corner of his mouth. It might go in their favor if they appeared docile.

The stocky one called Gwarp took his time feeling Jen up while she focused forward and clenched her jaw. Paz curled his fists and reined in his impulse to punch the brawny *riff*. This was only a small humiliation compared to what was coming.

Menig was the lowest enlisted rank in the Trollek military force. Paz wondered at the size of their garrison and how they'd gotten here. Had they opened a rift on the island near where one naturally occurred when the dimensional plates shifted? If so, what was the advantage of this remote location?

He stared straight ahead, his mouth taut, as Gwarp patted him down. He'd find the answers in their command center.

"I just found one weapon, Min Drott," the enlisted rank told his officer. He displayed Jen's handbag, Paz's PIP that looked like a bulky cell phone, and their Swiss Army knife.

A quick search inside Jen's bag by the leytnant brought a sneer to his lips. "These items are worthless. The woman can keep them for now." He held onto the knife but tossed Jen back her handbag along with Paz's PIP. She stuck it inside her purse.

At the officer's signal, the guards herded them into the back of a small transport. Gwarp kept his disruptor trained on them as they sat in silence.

Jen bit her lower lip, her face white. He wanted to offer comfort but not while they were so keenly observed.

They drove across the island over a bumpy road that inhibited progress. An hour or so later, their vehicle halted at the base of a hill.

Forced out at gunpoint, Paz and Jen exited the ground transport and started up the slope—armed sentries flanking them.

Tall, shady trees lined the packed dirt road. A sweet scent entered his nostrils, but it was far from pleasant. It reminded him of dead people and the cloying odor that lingered after death. Massive stone lanterns stood at intervals along the way.

At the summit, they stood before an arched gate. Ancient wood doors were set inside the structure that had a peaked tile roof. As they approached, the doors flung open. Two armed humans regarded them impassively as they marched through. The men's eyes had the glassy look of confounded souls.

They entered the outer sanctum of the citadel. Stone walls surrounded the compound. Passing a grassy expanse of what might have been a moat in the old days, they followed a gravel path. Clearly the Trolleks had confiscated someone's property, perhaps a retreat for Japanese nobility.

In the distance rose the five-tower structure that housed the main keep. It had a stone foundation, blue tile roof, and whitewashed walls. Multiple towers surrounded it, making for a huge complex.

He tried to keep note of their route, but an array of twisting paths, gates, baileys, and stairs challenged his sense of direction. The compound must have been designed on purpose to befuddle intruders and allow for ambushes along the way.

Confuse and Conquer: A brilliant strategy.

He grasped Jen's hand as they trudged up another hill, a stone wall on one side and a white building rising on the other. After a switchback, they reached another gate nestled into a structure that looked as though it housed residences. The doors remained closed at their approach.

The leytnant yanked on a cord that rang a bell. He leapt back as the doors opened outwardly. More guards waved them through.

Jen glanced at him, her eyes anxious. "What if they separate us? How will we find each other?"

He squeezed her hand. "We'll work it out. In the meantime, the Trolleks won't harm you. You're too valuable to them."

He hoped he was right. At least his words gave her the strength to straighten her spine and move on. She stopped quaking and held her chin high. He gave her credit for accepting the situation with courage.

Despite her pallor and exhaustion, she still looked lovely with her delicate features, tousled black hair, and wide-eyed gaze. He cursed his inability to protect her.

They might not harm Jen right away, but Paz didn't have any illusions about his own fate—a torturous death.

The Trollek's words from the aircraft played in his head. *"The one called Kaj screams like a stuck pig. Fighting us is useless."*

A chill racked him. Kaj's locator beacon had stopped transmitting while he patrolled the Vile Vortices. When the engineer didn't respond to comm signals, his team had feared the worst. Now Paz knew for certain Kaj had been taken.

He could only imagine the torments to which his comrade had been exposed. Paz would soon be up close and personal to them himself.

Gritting his teeth, he returned his attention to their route.

Should he attempt to escape, getting through this maze would be paramount. He could probably tap into a satellite to get an aerial view if he kept his mobile data unit.

"Jen, give me back my PIP," he gritted between closed teeth as they crossed a second moat.

She didn't spare him a glance but surreptitiously handed it over. He stuck it in his pocket, grateful their wrists hadn't been restrained.

Beyond an intersection stretched a wide expanse of grass with gravel on either side. They turned left, sticking to the path. After rounding a corner, they faced a steep set of stairs.

Jen held up her hem as she climbed the stone steps, a resigned look on her pale face. A wall abutted one side, with overhanging trees shading the other. Her feet dragged, and she faltered before the summit.

Without warning, the squadron commander yanked a shock stick from his belt and jabbed her in the gut.

"Keep moving, human." She screamed, doubling over.

"Don't touch her." Paz launched himself at the officer.

The Trolleks descended on him in numbers. Their blows pummeled him to the ground while he fought to protect his head. Electric jolts to his mid-section stole his breath and brought his arms around to guard his stomach. More jolts scrambled his nerves and made his vision blur with pain. He lay on the ground, twitching and unable to command his limbs.

"Stop it, you'll kill him," Jen cried. He heard her howl of pain follow but was helpless to defend her.

One beast kicked him in the kidneys. He took the hit with a grunt of agony. The next bolt of energy to his lower spine sent him over the edge of consciousness.

****

Jen had quelled her urge to panic, but seeing Paz get hurt brought her simmering hysteria to a boil.

"Don't hit him anymore!" She choked back a sob. "Can't you see he's down? You'll only injure him further."

"So what?" the leytnant snarled. "General Morar gave us orders to capture you. That pathetic human is just collateral."

She had to give them a reason not to kill Paz. "He's no ordinary man. Paz Hadar is a Drift Lord. He'll be more valuable to your leader alive than dead."

"A Drift Lord? *He's* one of the legendary warriors? If you tell the truth, I will ask for the privilege of interrogating him myself."

Jen studied her captor's brutish face. Whiskers stuck out from his taut jaw under a bulbous nose. His enormous ears looked like scalloped satellite dishes. Getting a whiff of his breath, she grimaced. He smelled like roadkill.

She held his gaze for what seemed like an eternity, and then the muscular alien signaled for his troops to lift Paz. They carried him on their shoulders, outstretched like a corpse.

Praying Paz was all right and that her kiss would protect him against their mind spell, Jen fell into place.

At the top of the stairs, she spotted the manor, rising in the near distance. Multiple towers surrounded it. She assumed that site to be their destination.

Prodded in the back with a painful jolt, she stumbled forward toward another gate. Instead of opening to a path again, this door led inside a building.

"Leave the Drift Lord here." Their commander indicated the wood plank floor in an empty room. The soldiers dumped him on the ground. "You four stay here and guard him until we get further orders. I'll take the woman to General Morar."

"What if she has the same power as the other one of her kind?" Gwarp said. He was the shortest among them with tufts of dark, spiked hair on his head. "We've heard rumors, Leytnant Bosk. If they're true—"

"She would have already killed us. See for yourself." Bosk squeezed her arm, making her wince in pain. "She's nothing but a puny female." The officer leered at her, his whiskers nearly poking her in the face. "Maybe the general will give her to me after he's done questioning her."

"Not if his wife has any say. Dr. Morar is likely to want this one for her experiments."

"Too bad, then there won't be anything left to enjoy." Grasping Jen's arm, Leytnant Bosk dragged her toward a spiral stone stairway. "Come, we have to get through this *maug* building before we can access the citadel."

She got a last glimpse of Paz splayed on the floor before Bosk pushed her upstairs. They strode down a corridor lined with various rooms, the doors all in the same oppressively dark wood as the floors and ceiling beams. The walls were painted white but had grayed over time. She gazed at the solid and antique looking wooden doors leading into the different chambers and didn't like to think of Paz sealed behind one.

How could she help him? Moreover, what power might she possess that could kill people?

Their footsteps echoed until they reached a narrow, steep staircase at the far end. Her legs trembling with fatigue, she watched her footing carefully as they descended.

At ground level again, Bosk marched her down another hallway with windows open to the sunlight. They emerged outside into the fresh air. She wanted to question her escort but had no breath left to speak as they climbed another slope toward the main complex.

Her heart sank as she realized they still had farther to go. She lurched ahead, afraid the Trollek would poke her with his electric rod if she slowed. The road curved a hundred and eighty degrees, returning the way they'd come. What sort of maze was this place?

Despair weighed her heart. Her parents would assume the airplane had crashed after it vanished from radar. No one would come looking for them. Meanwhile, she and Paz would either rot in some dungeon, or they'd be tortured by these monsters.

Dread seeped into her bones like an insidious mist, chilling her to the core.

"Who's Dr. Morar?" She struggled to match the leytnant's pace as they headed toward the immense white tower. "Why did Gwarp say she'd want me?"

He gave her an evil sneer. "According to Algie, you're one of the chosen. I don't believe in the legends myself."

"What legends? I have no idea what you're talking about."

"Then you'll meet your doom in ignorance. Keep moving."

They came to yet another archway under a second-story structure, and she had to crouch in order to proceed. Was this built on purpose, so an enemy had to squeeze through single-file? She had to admire the genius of the architect.

Laughter sounded from above. Did this place serve as a barracks for Trollek troops?

Hopelessly lost, she followed a narrow walkway lined with shrubs to a courtyard surrounded by warehouse-type buildings. The smell of cooking onions met her nose.

A man slogged past, carrying a barrel on his shoulder. He didn't even glance their way.

Her mind numbed as they climbed more steps, passed through more gates, and skirted more buildings. She didn't like the vibe from the place labeled *Tent Ten*. Armed Trolleks flanked its iron-plated door, in front of which drag marks scored the soil.

Finally, they entered a tall structure past a final stone arch. Inside, the interior reminded her of a cave with its lack of light and claustrophobic feeling.

They climbed to the fourth level. Jen surmised this must be the main keep. Her gut quivered. Whoever was in charge of this compound would be waiting for her beyond the next door.

They emerged into a great hall lit by fading sunlight filtering through long, narrow windows. Spears, swords, and axes hung on the walls. Utilitarian furnishings were arranged in various groupings, clearly lived in from the empty glassware and bowls of fruit on the tables.

At the far end was a massive stone fireplace. Bosk prodded her in that direction. Standing before the mantel was an imposing Trollek, his tunic decorated with medals and a fierce scowl on his face as he watched them approach.

Bosk beat his chest and bowed. "General Morar, I bring you the human female as ordered."

The military commander meandered over to inspect her. His nostrils flared as his beady gaze studied her from head to toe. She washed her face of emotion so her revulsion wouldn't show. He had broad shoulders, a muscled torso, and a nose that vied with Pinocchio for length. This beast had a wife? She wondered how they kissed, or if Trolleks even followed that custom.

If she ever got out of this, she should learn more about their culture. The old adage, *know your enemy*, still rang true.

General Morar expanded his chest. "This woman doesn't look like much of a threat."

"No, Min Drott. She knows nothing of the legends."

The general scratched his bristly jaw. "Then again, Nira Larsen looked like a redheaded nymph, and yet she killed the Grand Marshal. My wife wishes to take charge of this one. I see no reason to deny her. Where is the woman's companion?"

He didn't take his eyes off Jen as he spoke. She stared forward, chin held high, feeling like a prisoner of war. Her knees quaked, and her heart raced. Terror assaulted her in huge, pulsating waves. She'd never felt so alone.

Leytnant Bosk wiped a dribble of spit from his mouth. "We left him at the West gate. The Drift Lord gave us some trouble, so we subdued him."

"Drift Lord?" Morar's face lit with astonishment. "No wonder he resisted our troops in the aircraft. He must have been sent to guard this woman."

"If you need help with his interrogation—"

"I'll handle it myself." Morar compressed his lips. "Our liege was not happy when Prince Zohar's team destroyed the transmitter at Drift World and blew up our operations center. We must find out what his colleagues plan next."

Jen stood still as a statue, listening. *Prince* Zohar? Paz hadn't mentioned any royal titles to her. He'd be happy to hear his team had succeeded in blowing up the jamming device. At least that's what she figured Morar meant by the transmitter.

Surely the Trolleks would realize Zohar's team could locate the rifts now. But wait, the beasts were interested in what the Drift Lords planned next? That meant some of them had survived the last battle. Paz needed to know this; he'd be relieved by the news. If only she could see him.

"Were your troops responsible for attacking us mid-air?" she ventured to ask.

The general nodded. "My orders were to capture you once we detected your signal. We didn't expect to encounter any resistance. Our troops panicked and set off an EM grenade."

"What do you mean, you detected my signal?"

He glanced at the other officer and shrugged. "You're right, she knows nothing. Nonetheless, we'd better notify our other recruitment centers to monitor the frequencies. If we can capture the other women and break the circle, the king's advisor won't have to worry about the prophecy anymore."

Jen dared to look him in the eye. "Will someone please tell me what this prophecy is all about?"

General Morar ignored her. "I have to report to the Council, and then I'll question our other guest. Meanwhile, take our female prisoner to my wife. Algie has just finished with her latest test subject."

"I didn't hear any screams." Leytnant Bosk sounded disappointed.

Morar glanced at him consideringly. "This one knows you. She might be more cooperative in your presence. I'll tell Algie to let you stay and watch." He poked Jen in the chest. "What's your name, human?"

She didn't see the harm in telling him. "Jennifer Dyhr."

"If Bosk tells me you've been helpful, I'll make sure the Drift Lord gets a swift death when the time comes. Otherwise, it'll be more agonizing for him than you can ever imagine."

Jen's vision blurred, and she barely heard General Morar's parting words to his subordinate.

"I'll notify Algie you're on the way. She will be eager to get started. You are dismissed, Leytnant."

Jen needed to think of some way out of this before she and Paz were both tortured and killed. Pressing a hand to her head, she followed Bosk while two troopers brought up their rear.

How had she not noticed that incessant buzzing sound before? Her head ached like a thousand hammers were pounding her.

The prophecy… that was the key. Paz had connected her to Nira Larsen, and Nira had killed a man, or rather, a Trollek. *How? And what's my role in all this?*

If only she had some answers, she might know what to do.

As Bosk marched her away, she decided her best bet was to gain intelligence and bluff her way out of this situation through the power of superstition. If the troops thought she was a witch of sorts, she'd just have to provide the smoke and mirrors to accomplish her escape.

Never mind that the task seemed impossible. Never mind that she had no idea about the legends. And never mind that her stomach knotted when Bosk led her down the stairs, out of the keep, and toward the place known as Tent Ten.

Chapter Seven

Paz awakened with a pounding headache and the metallic taste of blood on his tongue. He tested his limbs. Everything moved on his command, albeit stiff and sore. He appeared to be lying on a cold, packed earth surface.

He opened his eyes to total blackness and felt a surge of panic. Had the beating left him visually impaired? Rising on an elbow, he grunted at the bodily aches that ensued. He stifled his response when a scraping noise sounded from behind.

"Who's there?" He held his breath, listening to the silence.

Hearing nothing, he sniffed the stale air, rife with the smell of burning filaments that indicated a rift. Had the soldiers brought him inside the citadel? Maybe he could find a wall to lean against if this was some sort of cell.

He'd just sat upright when a voice startled him.

"Welcome to the dungeon, my friend. If you're wondering why you can't see anything, it's because there's no light," the speaker's dry, raspy tone informed him.

"Who are you, and what is this place?" Thank the Creator he hadn't been blinded.

"My name is Smitty. It's short for Goldsmith. At least, that's what the Trolleks call me. My real name is Anga'ra Deylano Bo'org Vir."

Paz's mouth curved in the dark. "I'll stick with Smitty. Where are we?"

"Shirajo Manor. Why are you here?"

Aware that this could be a trick to get him to talk, Paz replied with caution. "I'm Paz Hadar. My aircraft crash-landed on the beach."

"And these savages picked you up? How come they didn't confound you? Are you human?"

"I could ask you the same."

"Their spell doesn't work on me. I'm a member of the dwarf kingdom."

Paz coughed on the word. "Dwarf? As in, little people?"

"We're not just any little people," Smitty said in a haughty tone. "Our realm isn't normally visible to humans, or to Trolleks either, for that matter. I had the bad luck to get caught when I was making a delivery."

"I had a companion with me. Is she here?" His heart lurched. What had the beasts done with Jen?

"Sorry, it's just us. So why did you say you're not confounded?"

I didn't. Yet what would it matter if he told the truth? Maybe he could gain an ally, if Smitty wasn't a mole.

"I'm a Drift Lord sent to dispel the Trolleks back to their dimension."

"We've heard of you." Smitty's voice quavered with excitement. "Your league began eons ago when the Trolleks first broke through the dimensional barrier. Whenever there's a breach, your warriors contain it. You come from a place far away, but your origins were here."

Paz adjusted his position with a grimace. His lower back ached. "You're well informed, my friend."

"This time, the Trolleks have launched a wide scale invasion that's affecting everyone. My kind might be interested in forming an alliance with you. We've stayed neutral up until now, but I suspect that will change after my report."

"Why are the beasts keeping you here? Is it because you're immune to their confounding spell? They can still get you to join their labor force with their blasted shock sticks."

A moment of silence followed. "They have used it, among

other methods. But what I do isn't ordinary labor. That is why they separate me from their human slaves. Plus, they fear if I escape, they'll face the wrath of my brethren."

"Does no one know what happened to you?" Paz knew how that felt. He was glad for the companionship, even if he couldn't trust the fellow yet.

A clanging sound deterred any further discussion.

"It's not mealtime yet. They must be coming for you," Smitty said in a low, warning tone.

Paz's muscles tensed. The door swung open, and a bright light blinded him. He flung up an arm to protect his eyes.

"Bring that one, Menig," a Trollek barked.

The enlisted soldier twisted Paz's wrists behind his back and clamped a set of manacles on him. He hauled Paz to his feet and shoved him toward the light. Paz stumbled blindly into a wall.

"Not that way, you pale-faced son of a snipeling. Try the door." The menig guffawed, swatting Paz on the shoulder blade.

His vision cleared as four troopers marched him through winding corridors and outside past several gates. The moon had risen in the darkened sky, and crickets sang their nightly chorus. Slaves trudged past, their eyes downcast, not even bothering to spare him a glance. He glimpsed the tall donjon that was the main keep before the guards prodded him into another building.

If only he could get free, he'd investigate the source of the cors particles. He'd already recorded the coordinates for the island on his improvised PIP, secure in his pocket. His captors must not consider him much of a threat if they didn't search him.

They halted in front of a set of heavy wooden doors. At the enlisted rank's knock, a gruff voice called for them to enter.

Paz swallowed, his bowels turning icy, as he caught sight of the long table with restraints and the instruments spread out on a metal tray in the interrogation room.

****

69

Jen passed through the doors to Tent Ten with quaking knees and a tumultuous stomach. What would they do to her in there?

Her Trollek guards snickered as they pushed her inside then shut the doors behind her. She swallowed past a sudden lump in her throat. What looked like a brightly lit operating room met her eyes.

A treatment table sat in the middle of the floor with various contraptions surrounding it. An IV bag hung on a pole, full of a clear liquid, and tubing reminiscent of a hospital ward protruded from the wall.

"Welcome, Jennifer Dyhr." A woman smiled at her from a computer console, but the smile didn't extend to her glacial blue eyes as she approached Jen's position. She had exquisite features and lovely blond hair cascading in waves to her shoulders. "I've been waiting a long time to meet you. I'm Dr. Morar, but you can call me Algie. Please, come inside."

Jen didn't budge. "I'm not moving until you tell me what's going on. Why am I here, and what do you want from me?"

The female, wearing a white lab coat, moved closer and regarded her with curiosity, like one might do for an amoeba under a microscope. Her nametag read *Dokter Algie Morar*.

"Sit on the table, Jennifer. I won't hurt you."

Jen couldn't believe this beautiful creature was General Morar's wife. She didn't possess any malformed features like the males of her species. Obviously, Jen had a lot to learn about their race.

Since they were alone and Jen's rubbery legs threatened to derail her, she perched on the edge of the treatment table, which was covered by a clean white sheet.

Her nose sniffed a coppery scent. "What exactly is this place? I've heard mention of experiments."

Jen's heart fluttered at the sight of a gutter bordering the table's edge. It ended in a spout below where a person's feet would go. A rust-stained receptacle rested under this spout.

Realizing its purpose, she fought against a wave of

dizziness. She leaned on her hands, the table's cold surface penetrating through the sheet.

Algie lifted a tourniquet from a nearby tray along with an alcohol swab. "I'd like to get a blood sample. If you do not resist, I will answer your questions."

"All right, but why me?" It might work to her advantage to pretend to cooperate.

Algie's rosy lips curved in a sly smile. "You're special, my dear." She applied the tourniquet around Jen's upper arm. "Make a fist, please. Good girl. You see, our king perceives you and your sisters to be a threat. I view things differently. I believe you to be our people's salvation."

She swabbed Jen's vein, then picked up a needle. Jen winced when Algie stuck her. Dark red blood oozed into a test tube.

"What do you mean by my sisters? And how am I special? How can I help save your people?"

Algie inserted a new vial. "Well now, where to start? We first became aware of your power when Nira Larsen walked into the employment office for Drift World, a theme park in Orlando and our central recruitment station. She was the first human to resist our spell. We had to find out what made her different."

"Go on."

Algie plugged in a third test tube, while Jen watched with growing alarm. How much blood was she going to take?

"At first, we feared Nira might have a mutated genetic trait. If she wasn't the only one among your kind to have this ability, we could lose our power to confound humans." Strands of blond hair fell into her face as she bent over Jen's arm. "We'd already begun testing people for certain proteins, but Nira's results showed a significant difference."

"How so?" Jen sat still while Algie withdrew the needle and applied pressure to her arm with gauze. "She possessed a strand of Trollek DNA. We've mated with humans before, but Nira's sequencing differed from other hybrid children. I suspect your blood will show the same trait."

"What? That can't be true."

Jen's face must have shown her horror because Algie laughed. Then her expression sobered. "Nira has other abilities, and so might you."

"If I have similar powers, how did I get captured?"

Algie fastened a strip of tape over the gauze. "It's simple, my dear. I suspect your talent hasn't blossomed yet. Tell me, can you read the symbol engraved on your wristwatch?"

Jen shook her head. "No, but I'd like to learn what it means."

"Nira Larsen can read runes. However, I'd rather the two of you do not meet each other in person."

Jen's fingers curled. "What do you know about my watch?" She didn't like Algie's last remark. It sounded ominously like a threat.

Algie's mouth tightened. "You and your sisters all have them. They have something to do with the prophecy."

"Yes, Paz mentioned it to me." She kept her voice even to hide her ignorance, hoping Algie would elaborate.

"Our king heard the prophecy from his advisor's lips. *The six daughters of Odin must unite with the six sons of Thor to utter the ancient words and prevent the coming darkness.* I don't put much credence in legends myself. My beliefs are, shall we say, more grounded than King Jorg's."

"What is it your king wants?" The information could be useful to Paz when they met up again. And who were those sisters everyone kept mentioning? Jen had no siblings.

"What our liege wants doesn't matter. I have the solution to our problems." Algie strode to the counter to place the test tubes in a holder.

"What problems? Help me to understand." She filed away a mental note about Algie's attitude toward her king. The Trollek scientist didn't sound very respectful toward her leader.

"As I said, other people among your kind have mixed blood. That's one of the purposes of our recruitment centers, to screen people for these genetic markers. I've been trying to find a more compatible match to our genetic code. It's possible your particular sequence holds the key."

"A match? For what reason?" Jen slid off the table and began pacing.

Finished labeling the vials, Algie shot her a pensive look. "I don't see any harm in telling you, since you won't be sharing this information."

Jen swallowed. What did that mean? Did Algie plan to kill her? She remained silent, while her heart pounded so hard it rattled her ribcage.

"Over the years, our reproductive rate has decreased." Algie dragged a manicured fingernail across the counter. "We discovered a defect in the Trollek male gene. The water on our world is responsible. We learned this after years of study.

"We can still have children when our females mate with human men, but it's diluting our bloodline. King Jorg ordered us to invade Earth, not only for your resources that are rightfully ours, but because our race is dying."

"What is your solution?"

Algie waved a hand. "I'm in charge of the SARB project. SARB stands for Stabilize and Reboot. Our objective is to make our male sperm viable again. To that end, we've been splicing our DNA into the human genetic code to find a compatible combination. Once we identify a stable string, we'll use it to repair the damage to the Trollek male genome."

Jen's stomach churned. "You've been combining Trollek and human DNA? Is that why you need blood samples?"

Algie nodded. "Our screening process identifies humans who already possess a string of Trollek DNA. Presumably, they're descendants of prior mating between our peoples. We've been injecting them with our DNA to find a stable sequence but so far have failed. Unfortunately, the human test subjects do not survive the studies. It's just a matter of hitting on the right sequence with the right serum. Your blood might be more compatible."

Jen's heart skipped a beat. "You're planning to inject me with Trollek DNA?"

"You'll be ensuring the survival of my species if we succeed." Algie's mouth twisted in a wry smile. "And if we don't, well then, King Jorg need not fear your part in the prophecy."

Jen didn't want to press her luck by asking for further explanations. Time was running out, and if she didn't escape, she'd be the next victim on that table.

Algie spoke into a comm panel on the wall. "You can come and get our guest now." She turned to Jen. "Leytnant Bosk will see to your comfort while we wait for these lab results."

Five minutes later, the officer pushed through the doors, his bulk stretching his uniform taut across his chest.

"Put her in the tower room that's shielded against vector shifts. We don't want her making any unexpected trips away from here."

How could I do that? Jen wondered at the strange remark but got distracted by the sadistic gleam in Bosk's eyes.

"When are you gonna work on her? Can I stay and watch?"

"Later. I need to run these tests first." Algie sauntered toward him and trailed her fingernail down his pock-marked cheek. "Be a good boy, and I might grant you permission to stay." Her sweet tone turned sour. "What's happening with her partner? Did he talk yet?"

"He's in Interrogation now. The general is personally handling the session. Too bad these walls are so thick, or we could hear his screams."

Jen's eyes widened but she remained silent. What were they doing to poor Paz?

Algie glanced at a security camera mounted on the wall. "Can you tell Oversergent Warok that I have an errand for him?"

"Yes, Min Dokter." Bosk beat his hand on his chest and bowed. "I will send for him as soon as I lock up this puny human." Wheeling toward Jen, he glowered at her, a dribble of spit on his mouth. "Come, let's get you secured."

Aware of the shock stick hanging off his belt, Jen had no choice except to meekly accompany him.

****

General Morar paced in front of Paz, who was strapped to a table in the center of the interrogation room. The Trollek commander's ugly face creased in a scowl, making his long nose curl downward toward his mouth.

"I thought you and your friends were dead. What a surprise to hear from my troops that Major Zune failed in his mission to capture your team. They destroyed the jamming signal transmitter and half of Drift World along with it."

Paz's heart swelled with joy and pride. Despite overwhelming odds, his friends had accomplished their goal.

"I'm sorry I missed the action," he replied, testing his bonds. The leather restraints held firm. "Zune pushed me into a pit housing the power generator, and I ended up across the ocean."

"Do your colleagues know you're alive? Have you been in touch with them?"

A surge of hope followed. His team was still intact!

"Does it matter?" Paz attempted a shrug along with a nonchalant expression. His gaze followed the shock stick the general kept slapping against his palm.

"It might, depending on how well we loosen your tongue. Cooperate, and I promise your death will be swift and painless. Where is their base of operation?"

"They'll have moved it by now." Sweat popped out on his brow. He bunched his biceps, pushing against the straps holding him down. They still held tight, digging ridges into his skin.

"Where was it before the raid on our facility?"

"We had a suite in a local hostelry." He named the resort. They'd long since left the location where one of their team members had been murdered. He doubted the Trolleks knew about their safe house.

"You have a ship in orbit, do you not? What is the frequency for the defense shield?"

"I guess Kaj didn't tell you much if you don't know that answer." He flushed with satisfaction, hoping he could hold out with the same bravery.

The general applied the shock stick to the nerve bundle on the side of his thigh. Agony burst into his brain like a solar flare. He screamed, unable to stop himself.

"You *will* talk, Drift Lord. If not to me, then to the Korporal here who knows how to use these instruments. When he starts cutting, you'll wish you'd spoken earlier."

"Go to Hel's dominion. That's where your kind belongs. But I guess your king already knows this. It's said he's either mad as a howler monkey from the voices he hears in his head, or else he communes with the devil."

A jab to his groin stole his breath and made pain explode into white stars behind his eyes. He struggled to gain air.

"Do not disparage King Jorg, human, or I may take one of those knives and gut you myself."

Go ahead. I would die quickly.

Paz spared a thought for Jen. If it weren't for her, he'd provoke the general into killing him. But while he still breathed, hope lived that he could free her. He didn't know what he'd do if they threatened to harm her.

"Why do you need the frequency for our ship anyway?" he asked in a hoarse voice. "We're not going anywhere until we defeat you."

The general guffawed so hard it shook his brawny body. "There is hardly anyone among your team left. Captain Zohar plots against us with Yaron of the Glade and the Tsuran swordsman known as Lord Magnor. Three against the mighty Trollek army?"

"Then why do you care where to find us if we're so small a threat? Do you mean to kill us for sport?"

The corners of Morar's mouth turned down, and his eyes blazed. "There's the prophecy. Our king gives it credence."

"Do you really believe in those old legends?"

"What I believe doesn't matter. I obey my liege's orders. And he wants to eliminate any chance of the prophecy coming true. Tell me, what is your team's next objective?"

Paz's lips tightened. The prophecy said that six sons of Thor and six daughters of Odin would prevent the coming darkness. With Kaj still missing, Dal in the hospital, and Borius and Rayne gone, their force had been seriously diminished. It didn't seem viable for the legends to be true.

He was taking too long to answer. The general jabbed him again, and rational thought fled in the explosion of pain that followed.

"I don't know," he said between gritted teeth. "I've lost contact with them. I thought they must all be dead."

"With our jamming signal deactivated, your ship sensors can detect our portals. Is that why you're here? To destroy this gateway?"

Morar didn't even give him a chance to answer. He stabbed the stick into Paz's side.

Even while a cry escaped his lips, a surge of triumph bloomed inside him. So, this island did harbor a portal to the Trollek dimension.

"That's not why I came here. When I was tossed into the pit back in Orlando, I must have fallen through a spontaneous rift in the space-time continuum. I lost consciousness. When I woke up, I was in Japan."

He tried to lean upward but the strap across his chest was too rigid. "Listen, General, these random tears are increasing. By keeping the rifts open, you're causing the dimensional drift to widen. The energy blast that will result from the buildup of cors particles will destroy everything, not just our world. If you believe your people will be spared, you've been fooled."

The general smacked him across the face. "Our king says we will be protected. Are you calling our liege a liar?"

"I'm just saying… if that voice King Jorg hears in his head

has promised him that his kingdom will survive the mass destruction, it's lying."

General Morar glanced at the other officer in the room and the enlisted soldiers guarding the door, then he leaned over Paz. "What do you know about that voice?"

Paz smirked. "Some say the demon Loki is manipulating your king. Loki wants to be released from his underground prison. In destroying our multiverse, he gains his freedom and his revenge against the gods who put him there."

Morar straightened, his mouth tightening. "I do not believe such nonsense. Our liege commands us to regain lands that are rightfully ours."

"So why does the prophecy matter to him?"

"You're not the one asking questions here." The general jabbed the stick into him repeatedly until shadows danced about the room and Paz's eyes rolled up in his head. "How did you come to be on this island?"

"I crashed here in an aircraft. You should know. Didn't you send those soldiers onboard to capture us?" Paz's voice came out a dry croak.

"Only the woman. We didn't realize you'd be aboard. Were you sent to protect her?"

Paz shook his head from side to side. His back hurt from lying supine, and his nerves screamed from abuse. He needed to change his position. Squirming, he grunted with frustration at being strapped down.

"You must have met up with the woman somewhere. Did you trace her through her watch?"

"I don't know what you mean. When I regained consciousness, I found myself near her. I was disoriented, and she took pity on me as a fellow American in a foreign country. At least, she assumed I was a compatriot by my accent. She offered me a ride home, that's all."

Another long jolt from the shock stick left him gasping for air. Paz knew this punishment was mild compared to what would come next. The korporal shifted his feet, impatient to get to work with the real tools.

"I'm not an idiot." The general's nostrils flared. "I know you and the woman are working together. How much does she know of your mission?"

His blood chilled. He had to divert the beast's attention from Jen. "She's just an innocent caught up in this fiasco. Let her go, and I'll tell you what you want to know."

"She's not going anywhere. My dokter wife has plans for her. And she is far from innocent. Jennifer Dyhr is a critical player in this game." His eyes hardened. "Cease your struggle. Fighting us is useless. You might as well talk and ease your discomfort. Where is the rest of your team? Are they on the island, or are their targets elsewhere?"

"I've told you, we lost contact. I didn't even know they'd succeeded in knocking out the jamming signal until you said so."

"You're as stubborn as the other Drift Lord. Korporal, I don't think your knives will work on him. Let's use the boratus worms. Do you know of these creatures, Drift Lord?"

"No, but I'm sure you'll tell me." He didn't like the evil grin that split the korporal's face. It made his elongated nose stick in the air like a space antenna.

"The little creatures bore into the nerve ganglia. You'll experience excruciating pain and beg for the mercy of death."

Paz tensed his muscles against the straps, then gave up in despair. "I can't give you the location of my mates if I don't know it."

The general stuck his face in front of Paz's, giving him a whiff of foul breath. "We mean to kill every member of your team and use the Earth women in the prophecy for our experiments. But first, you'll tell us about your ship in orbit. You'll reveal the shield frequencies for the Star Empire's defense grid. Then, and only then, will you die."

Chapter Eight

Jen languished in a tower chamber furnished with a toilet, a sink, and a hard cot. A sliver of a window high up on a wall provided light but not much fresh air. She'd fallen asleep, awakening in the morning when a guard brought her an apple and cheese and a mug of water. She'd gulped them down like an animal.

Her stomach knotted as she thought of Paz locked in the dungeon. What were they doing to him? Was he being tortured? Was he even still alive? Nausea assaulted her at the prospects.

Her own future wasn't much brighter. The notion of being injected with foreign DNA as one of Algie's guinea pigs made her shake uncontrollably.

If the Trolleks had wanted help finding a solution to their male sterility problem, why hadn't they asked instead of attacking the human race? Had revenge for past wrongs so blackened their hearts? Was their king truly mad, or did he listen to urgings from someone—or something else?

She couldn't deal with the whys or wherefores now. What mattered was getting out of here.

Algie had mentioned her power. Like Nira, Jen supposedly had abilities that defied and threatened the Trolleks. How so? What could she do against their fearsome army?

An odd notion popped into her head. She rubbed her brow, aching from that incessant low buzzing sound. What if it wasn't the Trollek force she could influence but the human slaves instead?

No, hadn't one of the soldiers called Nira a witch because she'd killed one of them?

Jen bit her lip, pacing the small space while the wood boards creaked underfoot. Sweat ringed her neck, and the heat made her clothing stick to her body. Perhaps it didn't affect her hosts. She had no idea what their home world was like.

From their fierce appearance, one might think the Trolleks would be savages like their ancestors, but they were intelligent and cunning beings. What would they *not* expect her to do?

She strode to the door and pounded on the wood panel. "I want to see your leader. Take me to him. Open the door."

It swung open and a Trollek soldier faced her with a scowl and a drawn weapon.

"What is it, human?" His scornful gaze raked her, his small eyes set above a hooked nose like a summer squash.

"I have news for the general. If he provides better amenities than this hole in the wall, I'm willing to talk, but only to him."

She was betting the lowly enlisted soldier didn't know Algie's plans for her. He probably had no idea why she'd been imprisoned there and not enslaved like other humans.

"Wait here. I will consult my superior." The menig shut the door in her face, and she heard the click of a latch.

She sank onto the single cot and waited. If only her head would clear. Closing her eyes made the noise worse. It felt as though thousands of mini jackhammers danced inside her brain.

Buzz. Buzz. Buzz.

It would drive her insane. What had brought on this torment?

She buried her head in her hands and moaned. It had started in the jet just before the Trolleks jumped in. Could it be caused by the rift Paz claimed was in the vicinity? Or were the Trolleks the source of her problem? Hadn't Paz mentioned Nira experienced the same effect? Likely just being in the beasts' presence brought on the sensation.

Footsteps outside scattered her thoughts. Leytnant Bosk busted open the door.

"What is it, human?"

She leapt to her feet. "I wish to see General Morar."

"What for?" His whiskers twitched.

"I have information to share, but I'll only tell him in exchange for better facilities."

"You'll tell me what you know. I won't have you bothering the general." He kicked the door shut behind him then strode forward, yanking his shock stick from his belt. His eyes seemed to shrink further into his head as he regarded her like a carrion bird might its prey.

"Hurt me and incur the dokter's wrath. I'm her special project." Jen lifted her chin.

"So why do you want to see her husband?"

"That's between us."

She had in mind the notion to plant seeds of mistrust between the general and his wife. Algie didn't seem particularly obedient to their king. She obeyed when it suited her needs but had her own agenda.

With a growl, Bosk raised his stick. Her heart pounding, Jen backed up against the wall. He could do what he wanted here, and no one would be the wiser. Those electric shocks would hurt but didn't leave permanent damage.

She gritted her teeth against anticipated pain. The leytnant had been itching to torment her. She feared he hadn't done so sooner because he'd been working on Paz. Where was the brave Drift Lord who'd risked his life to protect her? Was he chained in the dungeon, still being tortured, or dead?

"Don't come any nearer," she warned the officer.

His stick got her in the stomach. Through an explosion of pain, she sank to her knees.

"Confess, witch. You have nothing to tell the general. You merely seek a means to escape."

He jolted her on the chest, and she collapsed to the floor. Her body twitched, shards of agony igniting her nerves. She bit her tongue, tasting blood.

"Nice sash you're wearing, Leytnant. Was that a reward ribbon for capturing me and Paz? Where is he, by the way?"

"Probably begging for death." Bosk grinned, exposing jagged teeth. "General Morar left him with Korporal Nagt, our chief interrogator. He gets a particular delight out of carving recalcitrant humans until their skin hangs in strips. But he'll probably try the boratus worms first."

Jen wanted to close her ears, but compulsion made her ask, "What's that?"

He snickered at her lying on the floor and kicked her with his boot. She grunted as he connected with her ribs.

"Nasty creatures about this long." He spread his fingers an inch wide while she struggled to breathe against the soreness. "They crawl in through the nose and attack the nerve ganglia."

Her gut quivered. She couldn't imagine such a horror. "Does anyone survive?" she asked in a small voice.

"Unfortunately for them, yes. The worms don't last long in the host's body heat. When they die, they release a longer-lasting toxin." His grin widened. "It's the greatest pleasure to hear the victims scream."

"Bastard. I hate you." Tears leaked from her eyes at the thought of what Paz must be enduring. They barely knew each other, and yet that connection he spoke of was undeniably true.

"You'll hate me more when I'm through with you. If it weren't for the dokter's orders, I'd have taken my satisfaction from you already." Drool dribbled down his chin. "What are her plans for you? She hasn't shared them."

"Sucks for you, buddy. Guess you're not important enough."

He slapped her. "Provoke me again, human, and I'll say you caused trouble and needed to be subdued."

Her glance fastened on the sash slung across his torso at a diagonal. If only she could tie it around her ears to block that incessant buzzing noise. Her head pounded in synchrony with the throbbing points of pain throughout her body. Or better still, she'd like to wrap that piece of fabric around Bosk's thick neck.

He pummeled her again for sport, and her vision dimmed. As her head lolled back, she imagined the cloth snaking up his shoulders and twisting around his neck. With every ounce of energy, she squeezed it tight, her imaginary fingers tightening the noose from behind.

Choking gasps sounded followed by silence.

Awareness seeped back into her mind. Staring at her eyeball to eyeball on the floor was the leytnant, dead as a battery out of juice. His tongue dangled from his open mouth. Her glance shifted to his neck. He'd been strangled by his own sash.

Shock froze her in place. Good God, had she done that? How was this possible?

Guilt flushed her face and made waves of heat and cold skitter up and down her spine.

She took a couple of rapid, shaky breaths. *Worry about it later. Use this opportunity.*

Caution made her glance toward the closed door. At any moment, the sentry might burst in to check on them. He'd see his superior on the floor. Jen didn't want him to realize the guy was dead until she'd had the chance to get far away.

With a grimace, she unwound the sash and then wrestled with the Trollek's big body to put the ribbon back in place. Done with that unpleasant chore, she grabbed his shock stick from where he'd dropped it on the floor.

She turned the rod in her fingers but couldn't determine how to operate it. Nonetheless, the thing might have its uses. For extra measure, she confiscated the dagger from the beast's boot and stashed it between her breasts.

"Help! Someone help me!" She leveraged to her feet and retreated to a spot by the door. "The leytnant is sick. He's collapsed to the floor."

The door opened outwardly, so she couldn't hide behind it when the sentry came in. Fortunately, he was alone and unsuspecting. She bashed the shock stick into his temple as he entered. It was like hitting a brick wall. He turned toward her and snarled, raising his hand to strike.

Jen cast aside the useless rod and drew the dagger. As he

stepped toward her, she lunged forward and aimed for his throat. The knife sank into his flesh. A stunned look crossed his expression, and then he slumped to the ground.

Her hands bloody, Jen stared at him. She had just killed a man.

Not a man. A Trollek.

Two Trolleks, to be exact.

Left alive, they would have beaten or tortured her and Paz to death or given them over to others who would do the same.

Paz. She had to find him. Their only hope of escape was to stay together.

She rushed to the sink, washed her hands thoroughly and shook them dry. Then she flew out the door and down the stairs.

****

Paz rolled on the hard dirt floor, curled in on himself, and groaned. He'd just regained consciousness back in the dungeon and wished he hadn't. Every cell in his body flared with pain. He reeked of sweat and vomit, his body's defense against the invasion. He shivered with horror at what they'd done to him.

He hadn't talked, revealing nothing after the korporal inserted the squiggly creatures into his nostrils while he lay strapped down and helpless to resist. Instead, he'd resisted the way he had been trained with his mind.

As pinching, shooting pains traveled along his nerves, he had envisioned Jen, her wavy black hair unfurled, her dewy brown eyes wide, a sexy smile on her lips. He'd heard his own screams in the background as though they belonged to someone else. He'd also heard the korporal's persistent voice in his ear, urging him to spill information from his tongue. The noises washed over him, unable to touch him in his private place.

Blessedly, he'd passed out amid promises of worst torments to come.

He must have been granted a reprieve to wake up here.

"Some water?" Smitty's gravelly voice said.

He lifted his head, noticing a lantern in the corner. The guards must have left it there by mistake.

Smitty knelt beside him, holding out a dented pewter mug. Paz accepted his offer and drank greedily. The dwarf had to have saved his own ration for Paz. He vowed inwardly to make it up to the fellow later.

"Thanks." His thirst quenched, he pushed away the mug.

"What did they want?" Smitty's eyes gleamed in the dim light.

"Information. I didn't talk."

"Used the worms on you, did they?" Smitty shook his head while Paz struggled to a sitting position. "I'm sorry to say I took one look at those nasty things and fainted. That's all it took to get me to cooperate. You won't tell anyone, will you? As far as you know, I withstood days of torture before I cracked."

"Don't worry, my lips are sealed."

The dwarf thrust his chin forward. "It takes courage to face each day in this place, and I've been here for months."

"Yes, you're very brave, Smitty." Paz gave him a curious glance. "What do they want with you, anyway?"

Smitty glanced away. "We used to create magic objects for the gods in the old days. Now the Trolleks force me to turn bricks into gold. They need it for commerce in your world."

"Really? I thought alchemy was just a myth. You happen to have any tools on you?"

Smitty gave him a sly grin. "As a matter of fact, I stole a chisel. I've been digging a tunnel. It's slow going, and my back is killing me. Now that you're here, you can help."

"I'll do better than that. We can use your tool to bust the lock on the door. It's pretty rusty."

"And pretty secure. I already tried." Smitty stroked his bearded jaw. "There's a wooden bar on the other side. We wouldn't be able to lift it, even if we were able to dislodge the lock. And the only way they provide food is through that hinged door on the bottom."

"Hmm." Paz considered their options. He could pretend to be sick or dead and have Smitty summon assistance. But the guards might be wary of that old trick.

He could attack next time they came to drag him out for interrogation, but he wouldn't have much chance against their shock sticks without a weapon of his own. Besides, he couldn't wait that long. Who knew what they were doing to Jen in the interim? He couldn't even go there. Thinking of her being interrogated would derail him.

"I have an idea. Isn't pure gold very malleable? What if you turn the door into gold, and we kick it in?"

Smitty shook his head. "Too thick. Wouldn't work."

"Can you change the lock into a thin layer of gold so I could punch it out with your chisel?" He rose and hobbled to the door to peer at the circular mechanism. "I think I could reach my hand through there. I might be able to move the bar on the other side."

Smitty raised an eyebrow. "If you fail, you'll bring the guards down on us. Two of them are stationed in the wardroom beyond the outer door."

"You'll say I forced you to do it, and I'll take the blame."

"If we succeed, we'll still have to deal with the guards."

Paz tapped his chin. "Let's wait for mealtime. That's when they'll open the outer door and be vulnerable."

"How do you plan to get off the island?"

"I'll swim if I have to." His brow wrinkled. "We can worry about that later. Do your thing on the door lock, my friend."

Smitty held up a hand. "I still think tunneling is the best option. There's less chance of getting caught." "Fine, you can stay here and dig after I leave." "Nuh uh." Smitty glared at him. "If you go, I go. You're taking me with you. And I'll only use my gift for something in return."

"Are you crazy? I'm not bargaining. Either you're with me or you're not."

"That's the way it works, bozo." Smitty stooped over to rub his toe. He wore short boots with pointy ends. "Ow, my arthritis is acting up. This dampness just aggravates it."

Like you aggravate me. "If I bring you along, there are two conditions." Paz folded his arms across his chest. Two could play the same game.

"What's that?" Smitty eyed him suspiciously.

"I still have to locate the rift. Do you know anything about it?"

The bearded dwarf nodded. "There's some sort of transfer station near the main keep. I pass it on my way to the forge. Trolleks are always coming and going there, new faces each time."

"I have to find Jen and then check that out before I leave."

Smitty's mouth tightened. "We've gotta be out of here before they sound the alarm."

"Let's just do it." Paz's patience was strung taut.

Smitty gave him a sly glance. "I'll take your belt buckle. It'll make a nice addition to my collection back home."

"What?"

"You heard me. I want your buckle in exchange for my turning the lock into gold. Give it to me! Give it to me!" Smitty hopped from foot to foot.

"Be quiet, you'll alert the guards." Paz slid the buckle off his belt and handed it over. "There, are you happy?"

Smitty stuck the shiny item into his baggy pants pocket. Then he lumbered toward the door.

"This requires concentration. Don't interrupt."

Waving his hands in front of the door lock, Smitty squeezed his eyes shut and recited a string of unintelligible words. Dust glittered in the air and settled on the lock. Before Paz's astonished gaze, the mechanism changed to gold.

"Good work. Now where's that chisel?" Paz asked.

A solid *thwunk* was all it took to push out the soft metal. It left a hole big enough for him to wriggle his hand through. Twisting his body, he reached upward. His fingers felt the solid wood bolt on the other side.

"Ugh, it's heavy." His muscles strained as he strove to dislodge it. Pain flared along his nerves as a thousand pinpricks stabbed his flesh. He broke off, sweat beading his brow.

"Don't quit now," Smitty urged. "You're probably feeling the toxin left over from the worms. They've dissolved in your body, but their poison takes longer to wear off. Keep going."

Gritting his teeth, Paz tried again. This time, he managed to lift the bolt. It fell with a heavy thud to the dirt-packed ground. The hinges creaked when he pushed the door open.

"Come on. We'll wait for the guards to bring our meal. Then we'll make our move."

Smitty waddled after him out of their prison to the dingy lane between cells. "Good thing these old places don't have surveillance cameras."

"So we hope. Keep your voice down."

They crept toward the door at the far end, staying in the shadows. Hours passed while they waited, crouched against the walls. Paz caught himself dozing off a couple of times, twinges of pain waking him.

Finally, a rattle sounded followed by a couple of clunks. The dungeon door banged open, and two guards trudged through. The first one carried a tray with nourishment. The second Trollek held a laser carbine.

Smitty jumped on the first one's back and hammered at him with his chisel. Paz attacked the armed guard and kicked the weapon out of his hand.

With a snarl, the Trollek lashed out with his fists. Paz blocked his blows. He leapt and spun, kicking out and landing a foot in the beast's solar plexus. The Trollek grunted.

As the beast doubled over, Paz jabbed his elbow at the guy's nose. The Trollek dodged and lunged at him. Paz's muscles ached, and his lungs burned, but he fought back until the right opening came and he snapped the beast's neck.

He glanced at Smitty. The dwarf had floored the other fellow. Not bad for a little guy.

Paz gestured toward the open door. "Come on. Let's go and find Jen."

Chapter Nine

Paz ran into Jen by an outdoor courtyard where confounded humans carried supplies from building to building. His gaze took in the torn strap on her dress, the bruises on her face, and the needlestick on her arm. Rage swept through him followed swiftly by concern.

"Jen! Thank the stars. I was coming after you. Are you alright? What did they do to do?"

"Nothing worse than what they did to you. Algie wanted a blood sample. I took the bandage off. It was itching me." Her mouth tightened when she noted his hunched posture. "Can you walk okay? You were being beaten when I saw you last."

He imagined he wasn't a pretty sight. His body ached all over. "I'll be all right. Who hurt you?"

"No worries. I took care of him." She glanced away.

He tilted her chin toward him. "What is it?"

"I-I killed him. I couldn't help it. Bosk would have hurt me." Her eyes flooded with tears.

"It's okay, Jen. You can tell me later. We'd better get out of here."

Sunlight glinted off her diamond earrings, and he realized morning had arrived a number of hours ago. Paz wondered why the Trolleks hadn't taken her jewelry. Maybe they preferred gold, or like him, regarded the gems as worthless kewa stones.

A throat cleared behind them. "Aren't you going to introduce us?"

"Oh. Sorry. Jen, this is Smitty." He waved the dwarf forward.

"He was in the dungeon with me. I promised to take him with us when we escape the island."

Jen gave his friend a wan smile. "Nice to meet you."

Smitty grinned, exposing a row of tiny white teeth. "Don't let my size fool you. I'm second cousin to King Tiberius of the Dwarf Realm, and I hold the rank of Chief Courier."

"O-kay." Jen's eyebrows lifted as she regarded him.

"You can only see me because I got caught. Normally, we're not visible to humans."

Paz poked him. "You're free to go on your own if you want. You might be better off without us, especially if you can turn invisible."

Smitty kicked a pebble on the ground. "I can't. They cut my hair. It blunted my powers, all except for the one thing they needed from me." His eyes brightened as he examined Jen. "Nice, shiny stones you're wearing. I like them. Give them to me!"

"Stop it, Smitty, they belong to her." Paz glowered at him. "I have to find the source of the cors particles, remember? Take us to that transfer station you mentioned."

"What, we're not leaving?" Jen gazed at him askance. "At any moment, the soldiers will sound an alarm that we've escaped. We'll never get through all those gates in time, if we can even find our way to the exit. We have to go now."

He compressed his lips. "I will not forsake my mission. You and Smitty can head for the main gate. I'll catch up to you later."

"I don't think so." She lifted her chin in that stubborn manner he recognized. "It's all for one and one for all, boys." At their puzzled looks, she explained. "We're in this together. You stay, we stay."

He gritted his teeth. "So be it. Smitty, lead on."

They evaded detection as they wound through a series of twisting paths and outbuildings. At the sight of one set of heavy iron doors, Jen gasped and clutched his arm.

"That's Tent Ten. It's where they took me."

"Keep moving." He didn't ask questions. They'd exchange stories later—if they made it out of here.

He needed to find the rift and determine how the Trolleks kept it open. He'd already decided he would not destroy any of the portals until he'd identified the main gate from their world to this one. If it linked to a worldwide network, then taking down the primary might topple the rest.

"There's the transfer station." Smitty drew them into the shadow of a wall where they watched a number of Trolleks coming and going through an arched door into a nearby building.

A siren wailed. The soldiers took off at a run for the keep.

Paz spoke in a low tone. "They must have discovered our escape. This is our chance to get inside."

He waited until the Trolleks stopped pouring from the open door before they scuttled inside. Past several arches and empty rooms, they came to a place with a loud ratcheting noise and a vibration underfoot. The odor of cors particles was so strong it roiled his stomach. He stifled the bile rising in his throat.

Two rounded, raised platforms consumed most of the chamber. Each one had an arched canopy supported by four columns. Cables snaked every which way across the floor. One column at each site held a control panel.

Using his PIP, Paz recorded the readings on each console for the last set of coordinates.

"Look," Jen said, pointing, "there's an opening in the floor."

He strode over to where she'd indicated. Through a gap, a spiral stone staircase led to a lower level.

"Wait here, I'm going to see where this leads. You and Smitty stand guard. Yell down to me if you hear anyone coming."

Without waiting for a response, Paz descended the stairs. A huge mechanism stretched along a cavernous hall at the bottom.

His ears hurt from the deafening noise. How did the Trolleks tolerate it? They didn't care for loud sounds, but then again, you couldn't hear it from outside due to the thick walls.

The device appeared to be automated from the lack of any workers. Was this the generator that powered the portals above?

Paz deployed his makeshift PIP to snap images with the

camera function. He took photos at a broad angle and then took some closer views.

Halfway down the great hall, he paused. Set in an alcove off to the side was a control console. Eager to salvage what information he could, he opened drawers until he found a stash of blank data crystals. He popped one in the slot and sat in the chair.

The monitor screen remained blank. He tried voice commands to bring up the files. When that didn't work, he typed on the old-fashioned keyboard. A list popped up, and Trollek symbols scrolled across the screen. *Smark,* the files were encrypted.

Aware he was on borrowed time, he clamped his lips together. From the intense odor of cors particles, he surmised one of the portals upstairs was a dimensional rift. The other might serve to transfer Trolleks from here to another location on Earth. His concern was the former, but he didn't have enough information to understand how it operated.

He couldn't just blow this thing up like the power source at Drift World. An explosion here might not close the gateway and might even widen it. He needed Kaj's engineering expertise to analyze the data.

Swiveling in his chair, he stared at the mass of cables twisting overhead. There was something about this setup he wasn't getting. Reluctant to linger, he copied the contents of the hard drive onto the data crystal before removing it and placing it for safekeeping in his pocket. He'd work on breaking the encryption later. Meanwhile, he returned the monitor screen to its original state.

He'd just started up the spiral staircase when he froze. Guttural Trollek voices sounded from above. Soldiers must have found them.

"Paz, come up here," Jen's voice called. "They're friends."
Friends? Impossible.

He raced up the staircase. At the top landing, he peered

around the corner. Two armed Trolleks stood talking to Smitty. One of them caught sight of him.

"Do not fear us. We work for the Viden cause. We will help you." The speaker's long nose had a downward tilt. Coarse brown hair curled around his head.

The Videns were a faction among the Trolleks who espoused science instead of warfare as the path to peace. But why should he trust them? He emerged into the chamber.

"If you're on our side, tell me what powers this rift."

"We'll help you escape because we may need you later, but we won't help you destroy our access to this world. Dr. Morar still seeks the answers we need to solve our problem."

"What problem?"

Jen strode over and clutched his arm. "I know what he means. I'll tell you later. Let's just leave." Her fingers dug into him.

He understood. If they didn't accept this offer now, they'd lose the chance.

"Very well. What's your plan?" He detached himself, standing ready in case he had to act.

"A supplier is unloading food stocks a few doors down," the second Trollek said. "You'll hide in his cart. We'll escort the vehicle to the exit, and then you're on your own."

"Why are you helping us?" Jen waved a hand in the air. "I thought Algie wanted to keep me here."

Paz threw her a look of exasperation. Did she mean to sabotage their escape?

Hook Nose spoke. "The dokter has your blood sample. Further experimentation might kill you. We feel it is better to keep you alive until she has positive results."

"Aren't you working together?"

"To a certain extent." He hesitated as though about to say more but then decided against it. "We must go. Another group is scheduled to arrive, and a reception committee will be coming to greet them. Remember to act confounded."

The two Trolleks ushered them outside. Paz did his best to instill a glazed look on his face. He nudged Jen to do the same. Smitty waddled along beside them, his head downcast.

They followed the path through another archway. Up ahead, a cart was hitched to a couple of donkeys standing in front of a storehouse. Empty burlap sacks filled the rear. A man came out of the building. He wore baggy clothes and a blank expression.

"Hobbs will be returning to his farm in the highlands," the first Trollek told them. "You'll want to get off before he heads into the mountains. Now get inside, cover yourselves with those sacks, and lie still." He slipped Paz a knife. "Here, you might need this."

Paz took it then gripped his arm. "Thank you, my friend. May I know your names?"

The Trollek's large ears stiffened. "It is best if we remain anonymous. Be off with you. The farmer nears."

Paz hopped into the cart and hauled Smitty onto the flat surface. Jen landed after them, aided by the second Trollek. Their friends tossed the sacks on top of their bodies along with some stray leafy greens. They settled down as the entire cart sagged under the weight of the driver.

"Move on, human," Hook Nose commanded the fellow.

Paz figured the man was under orders to obey any Trollek rather than just the kabak who'd confounded him. As they rattled down the gravel drive, he ignored the discomfort of lying on a hard surface, smelling sun-warmed compost, and being shaken side to side. They still had to get through the checkpoints and clear the exit.

Then he had to come up with another plan. With this slow method of transportation, it would take hours before they reached a turn-off road to the mountain passes. At that stage, they'd strike out on their own.

He'd stick to his original idea of heading to the fishing village of Kamaji and hiring a boat to the mainland.

With minimal movement, he patted his pocket. Stored in his

PIP were the coordinates for the two gateways in the chamber they'd just left. If one brought in Trolleks from the home world, where did the other one go?

He suspected it might lead to another recruitment center like the one at Drift World. If so, that might be their next destination. He hoped Jen wouldn't mind another detour.

****

Jen hung back while Paz negotiated with Hiroshi Jin Kolami, a man of mixed descent and owner of the largest junk in Kamaji. The thin, dark-haired fellow accompanied his speech with animated gestures. He spoke in a native dialect, and Paz responded in kind. The Drift Lord amazed her with his ability to speak different languages.

Kolami pointed to Paz's wristwatch, and Paz shook his head. Narrowing his eyes, the fisherman pointed at Jen. Paz shook his head again. Were they bartering for the price of passage? It would be stiff for the three of them.

She stood at the side of a dirt road. A couple of chickens waddled past as she swatted insects and worried about Trollek soldiers discovering their route.

Smitty wandered toward an old woman selling dried fish and stringy vegetables. As they exchanged words, his face reddened, and his voice rose in anger. He, too, could speak their native tongue, making her feel as awkward as she had growing up in her socialite mother's shadow.

Feeling out of her element, she meandered over to Smitty. "If you're negotiating for supplies, I could really use some decent clothes and sturdy shoes."

Smitty cast her an annoyed glance. "Would you like anything else? Some pretty baubles maybe or a new handbag? What have you got in there, by the way?" He pointed to the purse she'd managed to retain.

Jen's face brightened, and she pulled out her enameled

business card case. Maybe she could be useful after all. "Here, see if she'll take this as payment."

The woman's weathered face crinkled as she grabbed the metal case and bit on it. She shook her head and thrust it back at Jen.

Smitty intercepted the object. "I'll take it. Look, I can see my reflection in its shiny surface." He peered at himself, grinning in childish delight. "I want it!"

Jen's mouth curved up. "All right, it's yours." Anything to pacify their new ally. "How about a comb?" she asked the old woman, pulling one from her bag. "Or a notebook and pen? A lovely scarf?" She waved the fabric at the old woman who kept shaking her head. Jen's heart sank. What else could she offer?

Taking out her designer sunglasses, she dug further inside her bag. The woman muttered excitedly.

"She'll accept those." Smitty pointed to her dark glasses.

"What? These cost me over two hundred dollars!"

"Give them to her." The dwarf bounced on his heels. "She'll get you a set of clothes and some slippers for your feet. She says you have tiny feet like a proper lady. You've just bought us a stash of food, too."

The woman hobbled off with her prize. Jen was startled by a tug on her arm. Paz stood next to her.

"Jen, I need your earrings," he said in a low tone.

"Why?" She stared at him.

"We have to buy our passage on Kolami's junk. He wants the diamonds. It's the only thing of value we have to offer him."

"I could turn some of these stones into gold." Smitty kicked at a pile of pebbles on the ground.

Paz compressed his lips. "Not a good idea. I told him we were shipwrecked on the other side of the island. Having pieces of gold on us would make us suspicious. We're ragged enough to fool them but not for long." He turned to Jen. "I'll get you some new kewa stones, bigger ones."

"But my parents gave me these," she said with a pout.

"I'm sorry, but it's the only way."

With a heavy heart, Jen sighed. "Oh, all right." She unfastened the earrings and handed them over.

Paz strode away, his boots sinking into the sand.

Jen scratched her arm. Dust and mosquito bites covered her body. That's what she got for wearing a sleeveless dress, but who knew?

Next time I travel, remind me to choose more practical clothes.

The old woman returned, handing Jen a pair of drawstring pants and a faded blouse and giving Smitty a sack of food. Jen changed in a nearby hut but carried her new slippers as she emerged onto the beach. The junk was anchored a short distance offshore. They'd have to paddle out in a flat-bottomed sampan.

She cast a last glance toward the curving road as they boarded the boat. No sign of the Trolleks. Could their escape have been orchestrated? If so, to what end?

Heck, it didn't matter. The sooner they left this place behind, the better. She donned her new shoes—pleased they fit.

Paz helped her and Smitty climb the rope ladder onto the junk. As Jen set foot on the scrubbed wood deck, a couple of crewmen who were already onboard sauntered over to consult with their captain. Jen gazed with awe at the masts overhead and wondered if the ship was motorized. She'd been boating before but not in a sailing vessel.

"Where are we headed?" Smitty poked Paz on the shoulder. "I need to get back to my people."

"Taiwan. We can get transport to Hong Kong from there."

Jen clicked her tongue. "Oh, crap. We forgot to ask about a telephone in the village." She consulted her watch. "It's five o'clock. We've been missing for over twenty-four hours. My father must have mobilized a search mission by now."

"The Trolleks may have provided evidence of our demise." Paz noted her questioning glance. "They recruit mind slaves and send them home to wait for further orders. These sleeper agents may be more widespread than we've thought. They'll follow instructions and no one else will be the wiser."

"So, they could have claimed our aircraft crashed into the sea and sank with no survivors?" Tears pricked her eyes at his nod. "My dad won't give up. He won't believe I'm gone." She tightened her resolve to connect with her parents and spare them the pain of loss. "Can you ask Kolami if he has a radio? You could try to contact your team again, too," she added as extra incentive.

Smitty stepped between them. "Let's find our bunks first. This thing weighs a ton." He lifted the sack with their food stores. "I hope they have some good ale onboard. Wouldn't trust their water if I were you. Awful tasting stuff in the dungeon."

Jen regarded him curiously. "You didn't tell me how you ended up there, or why the Trolleks captured you."

"Later." Paz gave her a dimpled grin. "I'm with Smitty. Let's go below where we can't be spotted from the deck."

One of the crew led them down a rickety companionway. He stopped at the bottom and spoke in a rapid dialect. Paz turned to the others to translate.

"Jen, you and I are assigned to the captain's cabin since we paid for our voyage. Captain Kolami will share quarters with his first mate, that's Kano here. Smitty, you'll bunk in crew quarters with Rafu and Senichi. They'll explain your duties."

The dwarf's cheeks puffed out. "What duties? And why am I stuck in crew quarters while you get a luxury suite?"

Kano pushed open the nearest door, and Jen peeked inside. She gasped at the closet-sized space with a short, single bed, a bureau, and a tiny porthole. Luxury? Ha!

"We're working our way through this passage," Paz explained in a patient tone. "It was the only way Captain Kolami would agree to take us. I'll be assigned duties, too. Jen, I hope you can cook. You're in charge of the galley."

Her jaw dropped. "You've got to be kidding."

"No, I'm not. And I wouldn't be exaggerating if I said our lives depended on it. There's nothing stopping these guys from stealing everything we own and tossing us overboard."

Chapter Ten

The first mate rattled off instructions and swept his hand toward the cabin. His narrow face pinched, and his shoulders hunched. Jen surmised he wasn't pleased by their hesitation to budge from the companionway landing.

"Kano says to move our butts inside," Paz translated. "He has to help get the sails unfurled while the tide favors us. He mentioned it's the custom to pray to the gods for deliverance from sea monsters at the start of every voyage. We should do the same."

"Sea monsters, huh?" Jen arched her eyebrows. "If they're so superstitious, how come they let me aboard? Aren't women supposed to be bad luck on sailing vessels?"

"Diamonds can be persuasive." Pressing a hand to the small of her back, Paz urged her to enter the tiny space. "Smitty, we'll catch up to you later."

"Don't forget about me," Smitty called as he trailed Kano down the dark corridor. "I'll hold you responsible if anything bad happens."

Shutting the door behind them, Jen faced Paz. A wisp of hair floated across her face, and she blew it away. "I can't stay in here with you. There's room for only one person on that bed. Nor can I cook meals for the entire crew. I barely know how to boil water."

"Then you'd better learn fast. I don't trust these fellows. If they like your cooking, they'll be more apt to honor their word and protect us from pirates."

"Pirates?" Her pitch rose. "Are you for real?"

His expression grim, he nodded. "I know these aren't the accommodations you're used to, but it's better than a Trollek prison cell. Now tell me, what did they do to you?" He tested the mattress, which sagged under his weight.

Jen plopped down beside him and let her shoulders sag. "I'm too tired to talk about it. Do I have to start dinner right away?"

"Tomorrow morning. Kolami said we could have tonight to acquire our sea legs."

A series of thumps sounded overhead, and shouts reached her ears. It didn't appear they'd get much rest.

Her nose wrinkled at the mingled smell of tar, fish oil, and stale human sweat. The ship rolled, and her stomach lurched. Oh, great. If she got seasick, they'd surely throw her overboard for shark meat.

Paz put an arm around her and tilted her face toward his. "We'll be fine, Jen. I promise." And before she could protest, his mouth closed on hers. He brushed her lips with a feathery touch, then murmured in her ear. "I need protection against the Trollek spell again, just in case. It's been more than twenty-four hours since the last time." He stroked her arm, sending shivers along her skin.

She slid away and stood in a huff. "Is that all I mean to you? Our kisses are only a means to pass on my immunity?"

"Of course not." His eyes darkened. "Make no mistake, Jennifer Dyhr. I want you as a man desires a woman."

"Oh." Was he just saying that to appease her? "Well, don't think because we're sharing a cabin that we are sharing this bed. You'll sleep on the floor."

He eyed the wood planks with skepticism. "We can both squeeze onto the bunk. You needn't be afraid of me, *leera*. We won't do anything that you don't want to do."

That's what spooked her. She'd like nothing more than to lose herself in his strong arms. Her face burned as his knowing smile battered her defenses.

"Look, if it helps, I'm still sore." He rubbed his lower back for emphasis. "I just want to get some rest."

Guilt washed over her. He could have made a run for it on Togura Island and yet he'd come looking for her. Without his intervention, she wouldn't have made it out of the fortress.

She lowered herself onto the thin mattress. "You're right, I should be more considerate. I'm sorry. Did they hurt you very badly?"

He glanced away. "I've been treated worse. They didn't use the worms on you, did they?"

"No, they weren't trying to worm information out of me." She chuckled at her own wording."

"You were fortunate." He stretched out on the cot, closing his eyes. Through the bristle covering his jaw, she noted discolored skin. How many more bruises covered his body?

"Tell me what torments you suffered." She crawled over him and lay on the other side against the wall.

Facing his back, she fought an urge to lift his shirt and examine him. She'd never felt this way about a man before, wanting to care for him. Why did Paz Hadar bring out her nurturing instinct? It must be their situation. They depended on each other for survival.

He curled his knees up, making her wonder if he was still in pain. Her treatment must have been mild in comparison to whatever happened to him.

"Morar questioned me about the *Protector*'s shield frequency and the Star Empire's defense grid. He talked about the prophecy and your role in it. He also mentioned my team members are alive and that they'd succeeded in blowing up the jamming device."

"Oh, yes. I meant to tell you I'd heard they survived. That's good news, right?" She rested her hand on his shoulder, needing to reassure herself that he was whole.

"The general wanted to know what our team planned next. I didn't tell them anything, not even when they put those creatures up my nose." His voice slurred as tendrils of sleep seduced him.

He fell silent, his breathing becoming slow and regular, while she stared at the dim outlines in the cabin. The meager light from the portal was diminishing, but she didn't have the energy to light a lantern. Her eyes drifted shut while she thought of the horror of having worms crawl up your nostrils.

Someone screaming jolted her awake.

"Hush, you'll draw attention to us." Facing her, Paz shook her back to consciousness. "You're having a nightmare."

"Omigod, I killed him." Jen couldn't see anything in the dark. Her heart raced, and her breaths came short.

"You're safe now. We're on the ship, and I'm here to protect you." His soothing voice calmed her.

Awareness flooded back. "Oh, thank God. I thought I was back there and Bosk was hitting me, and I-I…" Her voice broke off.

"You what, Jen?" Paz asked gently, stroking her arm.

"I… one minute I was looking at his sash, thinking how I'd like to wrap it around his ugly neck, and the next minute, he was dead. Strangled by the fabric *wrapped* around his neck."

Silence met her words, while the horror of what she'd done overwhelmed her. She had no doubt she'd been responsible for the act, but how?

"Say again. You thought about using his sash to strangle him, and it happened?" Paz spoke very precisely as though aware of her fragility.

She nodded but then realized he couldn't see her motion. "Y-Yes. I took his dagger. The guard came in. We fought. The knife ended up in his throat."

Hysteria bubbled near the surface. She hadn't had time to react before, but now the terrifying implications hit her. What kind of monster was she?

Paz patted her arm, and his reassuring touch evaporated her worries. She sniffed his masculine essence along with a hint of the sea. He leaned closer, his breath fanning her face.

"Do not fear your power." He nuzzled her ear. "You'll learn

to control it. It's part of your destiny." He made a series of nibbling kisses toward her mouth.

She kissed him back, wanting to feel alive, needing to feel cherished. She'd only wanted to get away from Bosk. It wasn't as though she was a bad person. If she believed Paz, this was meant to happen. They were part of something greater.

"Ow!" Paz jerked away.

"What's wrong?" Had she touched him where he'd been hurt?

"Nothing I can't handle." His voice sounded strained. "It's a residual effect of the boratus worms. Body heat kills them, but they leave behind a toxin. It'll dissolve eventually but until then, every now and then I get a twinge."

Maybe she could distract him. His presence aroused her. She wanted to forget her nightmare, their perilous plight, and the unknowns ahead.

With this man, she didn't have any pretense. The aloof, sophisticated image she showed the world wasn't necessary with him. She'd already become someone else, and it empowered her.

She reached up and pulled his head down, kissing him full on the lips. Tasting his surprise, she flicked her tongue across his mouth in invitation. Boldness hadn't been her strong suit before, but now she embraced it. Turning into him, she entwined her legs around his, and let her passion loose.

"Jen," he murmured, tangling his fingers in her hair and sealing his mouth to hers.

Their tongues danced a duet as they melded together. She writhed against him, unable to get close enough to sate her lust. Bolts of desire shot through her, startling her in their intensity. Her perception narrowed, as it often did before one of her visions.

As her mind's eye cleared, she saw them naked on a celestial plane where nothing else existed.

Soon they were both disrobing in real time, tossing their tattered clothing to the floor. Their bodies touched, skin to skin. She moaned into his mouth, lashing her tongue out, lathing him, and drinking in his essence.

****

Paz accepted her offering without knowing why she wanted him. Well, he knew why. His physique had always attracted women the universe over, but Jen didn't seem the type who'd tumble into bed with a man she'd just met. Likely she needed comfort, and he was only too happy to oblige.

Despite her sophisticated appearance, she hadn't turned out to be the spoiled lady he'd expected upon his first glimpse of her. She'd proven herself to be resilient, level-headed, and adaptable. Rather than complain about their peril or her own physical discomfort, she had sought to analyze their prospects. He appreciated her sense of logic and her ability to gauge a situation and move on.

Whatever her motives for opening to him, he'd give her an experience she wouldn't forget.

His hands roamed her body while he ached to be inside her. He worshipped her breasts, caressing first one and then the other, flicking his thumb across her nipples until they peaked in salute. His fingers tickled their way down her flat belly to the sensitive region between her thighs. She broke away from his mouth, arched, and cried out when he touched her *there*.

"Oh God, Paz, don't stop."

He obeyed, scraping his fingertips along her tender inner thighs, ending up right where she wanted him. He spread her feminine folds, exploring her, dipping his finger in where his shaft wanted to go. Her wetness spiked his desire tenfold.

Unable to wait any longer, he rolled atop her, wriggling his hips so she could feel his arousal and know how hard she made him. Her legs opened in response, and her body jerked as she neared her release.

By Odin's grace, he couldn't get enough of her. His mouth claimed hers as reason fled him. He wasn't even aware of the pinpricks of pain that still plagued him. Lust energized him, driving him mad for her.

"Are you sure?" His voice came out a dry rasp. He still had

enough presence of mind that he could stop, if she so chose. An animal he wasn't. He'd abide by her wishes.

"Yes. Don't talk. Just do it." She yanked his head back down and kissed him.

His muscles clenched as he readied himself to enter her. He probed her opening, his breathing fast and heavy. His heart hammered and his blood surged.

He slid inside, meaning to be gentle to allow her to accommodate him. He didn't know how much experience she'd had and wanted this to be memorable.

She bucked under him, covering his buttocks with her hands and pressing him closer. Her fingernails dug into his ass.

That was all the incentive he needed. He plunged deep, his breath mingling with hers, his mind consumed with her scent and her taste. The spiral to completion captured him. She came first, convulsing under him, her shudders gradually diminishing. In one final, glorious insertion, he joined her over the edge.

After his respirations slowed, he rolled off, facing her on his side. His index finger traced a pattern on her arm. She lay on her back, eyes closed, blatantly naked for his perusal were there enough light to see.

He liked the dark when he had sex. Somehow, he felt it hid his true nature, the part of him that made him a Drift Lord. The part of him that his father despised, calling him a freak.

His ability to detect cors particles had manifested with puberty. Those so blessed, or cursed if you will, had to attend Drift Lords Academy, their own career choices put on hold. His father had spared no words about how disappointed he was over this development.

When Paz had gone off-world to take a job as a field technician, Alain had really blown a fuse. He'd expected both of his sons to join the family business. Paz hadn't been home since. Nor did he keep in touch with his older brother, Renslow, an uptight donik who didn't deviate from the rules.

Jen's soft breathing sounded beside him. He sifted his fingers through her hair, relishing the silken texture.

She came from a moneyed family just like him. She wouldn't be happy settling down with a drifter who moved from star system to star system for his real-life job. Nor would she like the place he called home, a tract in the Red Flatlands on the planet Morata. He loved the wide-open space and the privacy. The isolation would drive her mad.

Once she grew to know him, she'd turn away for better prospects. Wealthy women were like that. Whatever he and Jen had together wouldn't last.

He needed to clear her from his mind and focus on his mission. As for the prophecy, likely it meant they'd have to work together to ensure their survival and the continuance of humanity. He believed in it to that extent. It could even be why the sexual chemistry between them was so strong.

But after his team defeated the Trolleks, he'd go his own way. Destiny or not, Jennifer Dyhr wouldn't want any part of his life then. Regret tasted bitter on his lips. Too bad. He could have gotten used to having her around.

****

Jen lay on her back, staring at the ceiling in the dark, while utterly aware of Paz's movements at her side. The handsome warrior was everything she'd want in a man, in terms of the physical sparks between them. But what about the rest?

As a Drift Lord, he was courageous, resourceful, and skilled. She knew very little else about him except that he worked as a telecom repairman in his spare time. How did he react under normal circumstances? Did he exhibit the same verve, or did he become complacent like many men and look forward to a beer and a sports game?

Assuming she returned to her former life, would he fit in with her swirl of social activities, high fashion events, and fun-loving friends? Or would he stand out like a sore thumb, awkward and out of place? She felt that way in their current situation. The opposite might be true on her turf. Paz reminded her of a diamond in the rough. Did he want to be polished, or would he rather remain below his true potential?

Let's say he accepted the modeling job and met her expectations. What then? They'd have great sex and he'd make fantastic eye candy on her arm. But soon he would get bored and leave her. It would be foolish to put energy into a relationship that wouldn't go anywhere.

She rolled onto her side, scrunching her half of the thin pillow under her head. She couldn't deny the sensual attraction between them. Regardless of his lot in life, the man was a hunk. If she yielded to her impulse to live in the moment and enjoy him, she needn't worry about the future.

Certainly, getting pregnant wasn't a concern. Was that even possible with an alien? Despite his extraterrestrial origins, Paz had descended from the same seeds of humanity. She supposed it could happen if she weren't on the Pill.

She'd share his bed, but that's all. She wouldn't invest her emotions in a bank that would close its doors in the end.

The deck pitched and rolled, and she swallowed against a swell of discomfort. Sleep would be a welcome distraction. Her eyes drifted shut, and she dozed despite the queasy feeling in her stomach. Paz must have slept too, because the banging on the door woke them both.

"Wake up, you lazy humans," Smitty's voice called. "These men want breakfast, and so do I."

Jen opened her eyes to find Paz regarding her with a sexy grin on his face. Heat rose from the tips of her toes to the roots of her hair. She was unaccustomed to waking up next to a man. Her last boyfriend, Jake the Jerk, had insisted on going home after they had sex. She hadn't known until later it was because someone else waited for him.

She sat bolt upright before realizing she had no clothes on.

"Be right there," she hollered to the closed door.

Scrambling over Paz who watched her with a raised

eyebrow, she grabbed her bundle of clothing and hastened into the tiny lavatory. She washed up as best she could, rinsed out her underwear and hung them to dry, then tossed on the pants and loose blouse. She didn't want to go without her undergarments, but they had to be clean.

"Good luck," Paz called as she flew out the door.

She was just as glad not to spend time with him alone after last night. It would distract from her cooking duties, and she wasn't in the mood to discuss their relationship issues.

Smitty waddled ahead of her toward the galley. When he showed her the miniscule space where she'd be expected to cook, her mouth dropped open.

"Are you kidding? How can I get anything done here? There's no space even to move." She glanced at the gas-fired stove, the cupboards, and the single stone countertop. It was stifling hot and dimly lit besides.

Smitty gave her a beatific smile and rubbed his stomach. "We're all counting on you, lady. The captain said he wanted the food ready by eight o'clock. I'm to help you get what you need from the stores below."

"Oh, yeah? What happened to the sack of food you bought from the old woman in the village? If you have fresh produce, I can use it."

Smitty shook his head. "It's mostly smoked fish, and there's not enough to go around. Besides, I already ate half of it. You can scrounge up something here."

Jen searched the cupboards to take stock. Other than rice, many of the ingredients were unfamiliar. She doubted these Asians ate eggs and toast for breakfast. What should she serve them? Seaweed and sushi aside, she could stir up some sort of fried rice concoction for the four crew members.

"The men are talking about you." Smitty shifted from one foot to the other as he watched her with his observant eyes. "They're torn between sharing you for their pleasure or throwing you overboard if you don't carry your workload." He paused while she figured out how to turn on the burners. "I wouldn't take a swim in these waters if I were you."

She glanced at him before filling a pot with water to boil. "What do you mean?"

Smitty scratched his bearded jaw. "Giant jellyfish inhabit this area. Captain Kolami says they can get up to four hundred and fifty pounds. They've been known to capsize trawlers larger than this vessel. Their stings can kill you, if you're unlucky enough to annoy one."

Jen added canned vegetables to a jumbo fry pan, turned up the heat, and stirred. The smell of food combined with the motion underfoot made her stomach roil. Sweat broke out on her brow. No matter how bad she felt, she'd have to finish cooking this meal. She lifted a bag of rice from the cupboard.

"Rumors of sea monsters crop up everywhere." Jen found a measuring cup for the rice. "Have jellyfish been sighted here?"

"Fishermen have caught them in nets along with fish poisoned by their toxin."

"I didn't realize such things existed." Jen stir-fried the vegetables until they were aromatic and tender. After turning off the burner, she used a cloth to lift the frying pan from the heat. Steam clouded the air. "How could they grow so huge?"

Smitty shrugged. "Could be global warming that heats the water, or pollution from dirty river run-off. Captain Kolami thinks over-fishing of other species allows more plankton to grow for the Nomura jellyfish to feed on."

"Well, that's just great. It gives me another thing to worry about besides pirates." She added rice to the boiling water, stirred it, and put on the lid. "Where do I serve the meal?" She took out a pile of dented metal plates from the cabinet.

"I'll take the food to the officer's mess, but then I've got my own chores to do. I suggest you figure out what you're going to make for lunch." He gave her an assessing glance. "You might want to get some fresh air. You don't look so well. Just keep a lookout for a large scaly tail."

"What, there's more than giant jellyfish, sharks, and pirates out there?" Jen found a tray to put the plates on. "Are you scaring me on purpose?"

After the rice finished cooking, she scooped it onto the plates and topped each lumpy mound with a portion of wilted vegetables. She handed Smitty the laden tray before pressing a hand to her stomach.

Smitty's eyes held a gleam of mischief as he regarded her. "The sea serpent even scares the sailors. Your Bible mentions the creature, calling it Leviathan. *His sneezes bring forth light. From his mouth, burning torches burst into flame making sparks of fire leap forth. Out of his nostrils come smoke. He makes the deep boil like water in a pot.*"

The dwarf glared at her. "This area is dangerous. Why else do you think it's called the Dragon's Triangle?"

Chapter Eleven

"Come on, Smitty, I'm not that gullible. Go take your fish tales to the crew." Jen waved him off. The deck heaved. So did her stomach.

She rushed to the sink and vomited her guts out. Surely, she'd die on this voyage. If a sea monster didn't get her, the crew would toss her overboard for failing her duties.

With a moan, she sank to the floor and huddled in a corner. Shivering despite the sweat on her face, she wrapped her arms around her knees in misery and listened to the creaks and groans of the ship. Men shouted from above, competing with a splash of waves. The vessel rolled, and the side-to-side motion combined with the smell of old grease and tar made her retch again.

"Jen, what's the matter?"

Paz's voice roused her from her stupor. She'd lost track of time, unable to think of the next meal and not knowing what to serve anyway. Most of the food stores were foreign to her.

She lifted her head. "I'm seasick. Kill me now."

He crouched beside her and swiped the hair from her face. "Nonsense, you'll be fine. It just takes a few days to get your sea legs."

"My father has a boat. I've been out on it many times, and it never bothered me."

He wet a cloth and handed it to her. "I've been on every ship in our fleet, and some designs affect me more than others."

"You're part of a Navy? I thought the Drift Lords acted on their own."

A shadow crossed his face. "Not that kind of fleet, although we work with Imperial Space Command when necessary."

Then what did he mean? Too wretched to care, she washed her face with the cloth he'd kindly provided.

"What's there to drink on this boat besides ale? I couldn't stomach it the way I feel."

"I'll find something. Smitty gave me the key to the storage locker. He said you could use assistance. Wait here."

"Oh, like I have anywhere to go."

She wanted to laugh at her own humor but lacked the energy. Paz's concern warmed her heart. He returned with an armful of canned goods and a stack of fresh vegetables.

"The crew buys produce from farmers who live on the mountain." Paz dumped his stash on the counter and began sorting the items. "The volcanic soil is rich for growing crops, but it's dangerous to live there. The mountainside shakes when the gods get angry, or so rumor goes. Authorities from the mainland have warned people to leave, but they need to earn a living. They're paid regularly to bring supplies to the manor."

"The crew might believe that, but I don't. You saw the farmer who owned the cart we escaped in. He'd been confounded." Jen pushed to her feet. "Look, I can take over here. You should go back to scrubbing decks or whatever job you have."

His hair hung in stringy clumps, and his shirt was drenched in sweat. Nonetheless, his manly appearance sent a thrill through her, especially with the devilish grin on his face.

"Not yet. I have a drink for you. It'll settle your stomach."

"Man, I could sure go for a ginger ale." She took the concoction he'd mixed, pinched her nose at the fishy smell, and downed it. Her mouth puckered. "Ugh, what was that?"

"You don't want to know. Why don't you go lie down? I'll whip something up for lunch."

She didn't want to get him in trouble. "Do you have time? Seriously, I have no idea what to make. I don't understand what half this stuff is."

He set to work at the counter separating slimy things that looked like tentacles. Her gut clenched, and she leaned over the sink.

"Come on, I'm taking you to the cabin." Paz turned her around to face him. "You'll do neither of us any good if you don't recover your strength."

Realizing he was right but feeling bad that she'd left him with her burdens, she preceded him down the narrow corridor, using the walls to steady her footing as the ship dipped and rocked. The dingy interior and confined space made her cringe. Once inside their cabin, she collapsed on the bunk.

"I'll bring you some broth when I have the chance," Paz said, a tender expression in his eyes that she hadn't seen before. "You'll be all right in a while."

Friday morning passed in a blur. Paz returned as promised with a bowl of chowder and pressed the spoon between her lips. She managed to keep it down, and feeling more stable, fell asleep. Jen barely heard the creaking noise later when Paz sank onto the mattress beside her.

By Sunday, Jen awoke with a clear head and was able to resume her chores. Paz had worked like a demon so he could carry out her duties until she was well. He showed her what to do in the galley, and she managed to put together the next few meals without further mishap. They were both so tired by the end of each day that nothing was on their minds except rest.

A violent pounding on their door woke them early Tuesday.

"Open up," Kano shouted. "The captain wants to see you."

What was wrong? Jen dressed hastily while Paz threw on his clothes. Then they headed up the companionway after the first mate. Jen squinted in the sunlight. She'd been outside only a couple of times, wanting to avoid the crew, and was unaccustomed to the brightness.

The sails billowed in a stiff breeze while the ship plunged into the waves. Jen marveled that the motion didn't bother her anymore and lifted her chin as the captain approached. He wore a scowl and hunched shoulders—not a good sign.

Smitty ambled their way from the other direction, his face grimy, and his battered shoes all wet.

With animated gestures, the captain exploded into speech. The other three crew members crowded around with mean looks on their faces.

Paz cleared his throat, prepared to translate. Despite his bedraggled looks, Jen felt comforted by his presence.

"Captain Kolami says someone stole the diamond earrings from where he stashed them," Paz informed her and Smitty. "Since he trusts his crew, he claims it's one of us. We are to produce the stones immediately or suffer the consequences."

Jen spread her hands. "But we don't have them. Smitty?"

The dwarf puffed out his chest. "Don't you dare think such a thing. I've been working like a slave and getting no thanks for it. It's an outrage, a person of my stature forced to hammer nails, swab decks, and clean latrines. This guy just wants to renege on our deal before we reach land."

Paz exchanged words with the captain who drew a nasty curved knife. At Kolami's nod, one of his crew hefted a piece of rope and swung it menacingly.

"The captain plans to give me fifty lashes if we don't give up the earrings. Smitty, he'll cut you up for shark meat. Jen will become a prize for their efforts."

Jen's face blanched. "The double-crossing pirates."

A large swell lifted the boat. The vessel dropped with a resounding splash and then lifted again. A sudden shadow blocked the sun.

What was that?

Her heart pounding, Jen scanned the waves. The current rippled and danced, white foam topping the crests. Water splashed against the hull as the bow drove through the sea. Sails with bamboo battens snapped in the wind, straining the supporting braces.

The sun spilled tangerine light across the water. In early morning, it looked like a golden orb in a clear blue sky. Despite the glorious sunrise, goose bumps prickled her skin.

A thud hit the junk, which shook violently and keeled to the side.

"Uh-oh, that's not good," Smitty muttered.

Jen staggered as the deck heaved underfoot with another bump from below. A tail flapped out of the water and then disappeared.

"Did you see that?" Hysteria rode her voice.

The thing had been huge. Oh, God. Maybe that talk about sea monsters had been true.

Another thud rocked their vessel. The captain shouted orders, and his crew rushed to a locker on deck and withdrew rifles from inside.

"I'd say our hosts are the least of our worries right now." Paz pointed out to sea.

Everyone turned. A series of humps rose out of the water and then dipped below the surface. The creature had to be enormous although its full length remained hidden.

"Do they have lifejackets on board?" Jen scuttled to a nearby chest and threw it open. Fishing gear. Oh, like they could reel in this thing. It might choose them for lunch, not the other way around. At a loss, she returned to her companions.

"This way." Paz gestured for her and Smitty to follow. "I thought I saw a harpoon on the quarterdeck."

The three of them hustled in the direction he'd indicated.

"I should have known we couldn't defy fate," Smitty muttered. "Jormungand knows we're here. He means to destroy you."

"What are you talking about?" Jen's pulse throbbed in her temples. Why couldn't they just find a safe harbor already?

"As descendants of the ancient gods, you are his sworn enemies. The Midgard serpent hails from the giants and is a spawn of Loki. *Kimmlebush*, I shouldn't have come." Smitty cast a fearful glance at the water.

The sea boiled and churned, and a great tail rose up to swat them. Jen grabbed the nearest rail as the ship tilted, hung in the balance, and then righted itself. This wooden rig wouldn't hold up for very long under repeated assault.

"What do we do?" She gazed at Paz, her head reeling.

The sailors advanced toward them, aiming their firearms.

Captain Kolami halted in front of her, his eyes blazing. He rattled off some words and Paz translated.

"You have brought doom upon us. We should not have allowed a woman on board. Over the side with you. That may appease the creature."

Jen gasped. This was a no-win situation. What did they call it on Star Trek, the *Kobayashi Maru* scenario?

As she saw it, they had three choices: to be murdered by the crew, drowned in the ocean, or eaten by the sea monster.

The good thing was, she didn't have to make a decision.

The bad thing was, the serpent made it for her.

It chose that moment to rear its ugly head. Two round yellow eyes glared at them from above a yawning mouth filled with sharp, jagged teeth. The creature looked like a cross between a dinosaur and a snake. Its long, winding body made seemingly of pure muscle twisted to the surface.

Jen opened her mouth to scream, but her voice was swallowed by the monster that gulped the entire ship down its throat.

Wet blackness surrounded her as she tumbled into free space. Her breath escaped her lungs.

This is it. I'm going to die.

And then she was rolling and landing on a squishy, spongy surface. A body knocked into her and ricocheted off. Another thud sounded nearby followed by a curse.

"Paz? Is that you?" Jen sniffed in the dark. There appeared to be breathable air, but it stank something foul.

"Yes, I'm here." His deep voice sent a rush of relief through her.

"Where is here?" Sounds of trickling water met her ears along with an ominous creaking noise. "Wait, I still have my purse." She'd strapped it on under her shirt so none of the crew would try to steal it. "I have an emergency penlight."

She took it out and shone it around, propping herself on an elbow.

"This looks like a cavern, but I don't think we're in any cave," Smitty's voice rasped from somewhere in the gloom.

"I thought the creature ate us." Paz struggled to his feet, staggering when the ground trembled beneath them.

"The sea serpent swallowed us," Smitty clarified. "We're in its stomach. Lady, shine your light farther afield."

Jen did as instructed, her eyes widening. She and her pals had landed on a ridge, presumably a ripple in the creature's innards. Below them sat the junk, its masts broken. The ship listed ominously toward a vast pool of sloshing liquid.

As the bow dipped into the pool, the liquid bubbled and spurted. The crew were nowhere in sight.

"This isn't good." Paz glanced at her, his face grim.

"Why? There's air in here, and we're still alive." She pushed a strand of damp hair off her face.

"But not for long. See the junk? It isn't just sinking. It's dissolving."

"Huh?" She could barely discern the ship's outline. His eyesight must be sharper than hers.

"That's acid, not water. Stomach acid, to be precise."

"Oh, Lord."

"By Thor's hammer, do something." Smitty waddled over to them. "Get us out of here."

A rumble sounded, and the ground underfoot shook.

"I second that." Jen placed a hand on the nearest wall to steady herself. Grimacing at the slimy surface, she jerked back when it quivered under her fingers. "Listen, maybe we should tickle it?"

Paz glanced at her as though her mental threads had unraveled. "What would that accomplish? We're not in its lungs. It can't sneeze us out." His gaze darkened. "You may be onto something, though. If we irritate it—"

"It might spew us out, like in the biblical story of Jonah. He was swallowed by a big fish, and after he prayed to his god, the creature vomited him out."

"We could pray to the gods." Smitty nodded vigorously, his eyes glistening with hope. He sank to his knees. "Mighty Odin, hear our plea. Deliver us from the evil servant of Loki so your chosen ones can fulfill the prophecy."

Jen rolled her eyes. "Like that's gonna work. I meant we should do something practical. We can give it heartburn."

Paz swung his gaze toward her. "We are in the belly of the beast, nowhere near its heart."

"Heartburn is what you get when you eat something that upsets your stomach. It's a burning sensation in the esophagus." She pointed to the ship, tilted at a precarious angle, twenty-five percent gone into the swirling depths. "We have plenty of timber. Not all of the wood is wet. We can build a fire."

In two steps, Paz reached her. He grasped her in his arms and kissed her straight on the lips. "You're brilliant. I can generate a spark with my PIP. Wait here." He loped off, using his handheld device to illuminate the way.

"Be careful! The entire junk could slip under the surface at any time."

As though to emphasize her words, something cracked and tumbled off the ship into the acid, spewing a lethal spray into the air.

She cried out in horror. Paz had just boarded the slanted deck. He leapt back, shielding his face with his arm. Her beam didn't reach that far, and she lost sight of him.

Her heart lodged in her throat. "Paz, are you alright?"

No answer. Had he crashed through the decking? Was he even now lying unconscious or trapped inside the doomed ship?

"Hold on, I'm coming." With a grimace of determination, she stepped forward.

Smitty's pudgy arms wrapped around her from behind. "You're not going anywhere. The Drift Lord ordered us to stay here."

She fought against him, but his arms were surprisingly strong. "Let go of me. He needs my help."

"No, you're not leaving me alone."

Jen stomped on his instep. He cursed but tightened his grip. She grabbed his pinky fingers and bent them back. With a howl, he released her.

She spun around with her fists clenched. "I'm going after him and don't you stop me."

A large groan sounded. As both of their heads turned, another quarter of the ship sank into the vile pool. Paz would die in there if she didn't hurry.

She stumbled over a series of spongy ridges toward the sinking junk.

Just then, Paz's head surfaced. The ship's deck had risen with the tilt, and he peered over the side rail. She'd never been so happy to see his handsome face.

He thrust one leg over the edge, followed by the other. Then he jumped from the ship toward a patch of relatively dry ground.

He raced toward her as a plume of smoke curled up from inside the wooden hull.

Reaching her side, he prodded her to move on. "I set a fire. There's still plenty of broken wood that's dry enough to kindle. We'd better return to the ledge and hope the smoke doesn't kill us before the creature coughs us out."

As they picked their way over the undulating surface, Jen worried her lower lip. If this ploy didn't work, they'd end up being digested same as the ship. Grit irritated her lungs, and her throat constricted. Maybe they'd suffocate first.

The ground bucked under them. She clutched at Paz for support.

Compressing his mouth, he took her arm and guided her along until they stood beside Smitty. The bearded dwarf acknowledged them with a glum nod.

Her pulse pounded in her ears. Fluid sloshed somewhere, and a droplet fell on her wrist. She shook it off, grateful when it didn't eat into her flesh. It must have only been water.

Only water. Good Lord, they could still drown.

They might be deep under the sea, meaning even if the creature spit them out, they'd be too far beneath the surface.

She turned to Paz to express her latest fear, but a roar of flames from behind stopped her.

The junk's wood had ignited. Smoke clouded the air, making her cough and choke. Their environs tilted and swayed. What if the creature spewed them out along with a plume of acid? They wouldn't be any better off. How could they protect themselves?

She posed the question to Paz, but before he could answer, a light opened far in the distance. Ripples cascaded along the moist walls of their cavern. Then an inrush of seawater headed their way like a tidal wave. It passed below their ledge, spraying the junk and dousing the fire. When the tide subsided, a faint luminescence flickered like fireflies in the dark.

"*Smark*, the beast has swallowed more food." Paz indicated the tiny pinpoints of light. "Those types of fish are usually found deep under the ocean. The serpent must be feeding along the bottom. And now the fire will go out from all that fresh intake of water."

Jen's heart sank. "It's still smoldering. Maybe we've upset the beast's stomach, and that's why it swallowed more water."

"What if the food is spoiled? That might make the creature regurgitate," Smitty said, offering them a new option with a hopeful expression.

"True," Paz said, stroking his jaw. "You know, I read that mercury has been poisoning fish in the sea here. Is gold just as toxic?"

"Gold is inert." Smitty's brow wrinkled. "If ingested, it'll just pass through the digestive system."

Paz referenced his PIP. "Gold doesn't dissolve in nitric acid like most other metals. That's where your term, acid test, comes from. It refers to a test that will determine if an item holds any real value."

"What about stomach acid?" Jen's spirits soared as she caught on.

"Gastric acid consists of hydrochloric acid plus potassium chloride and sodium chloride. And gold reacts to chlorine."

Jen wondered how Paz had become so familiar with chemistry. "Why are you asking about gold anyway?"

He pointed to Smitty. "Tell her about your gift."

Smitty shuffled his feet, staring at a spot on the ground. "I can turn inanimate objects into gold. That's why the Trolleks were holding me. They need gold bars to buy goods in your world." He waggled a finger at her. "Don't tell anyone, lady. It's our secret."

"Of course, but I don't see how this relates to our situation. Are you thinking of turning the ship's remains into gold? That could work if the metal acts like a lead weight in the monster's stomach."

"Or it could dissolve in the gastric acid and sicken the beast. But further action on our part may not be necessary." Paz coughed, waving away a plume of smoke.

So, the wood still burned. Only a portion of the junk still showed, the rest gone. Bits of debris scattered around the area.

Another ripple passed along the ledge, making her feet stumble and fear shoot through her. What if some sort of valve at the far end had opened, and they were about to proceed to the next phase of digestion?

Smitty's sudden cry made Jen's pulse spike. The ridge crumpled where he'd been standing, and he plunged down a slippery slope toward the churning, boiling pool below.

Paz didn't hesitate. He leapt down from their foothold to the lower surface and charged toward Smitty, still sliding, his arms flailing. Paz grabbed a nearby beam and used it to vault himself over and beyond the hapless dwarf.

He landed upright, cast aside the wood beam, and spread his feet. Smitty flew in his direction. Paz stooped and caught the little guy with barely a stagger.

That's when the beast gave a huge bellow, opened its mouth, and belched them out. Jen's legs flew into the air. Her body tumbled, and along with a flume of water, she rushed down a tunnel toward a wide gap with light beyond.

She got a glimpse of spiked, uneven teeth that started to come together, and a moment of panic hit her.

In the next instant, the serpent upchucked her out to sea level.

Gasping and choking, she kicked to keep her head above the surface. A wave battered her face, and salt water trickled down her throat and stung her eyes.

She sputtered and coughed. The effort made her sink. With a gasping breath, she kicked upward and treaded water. Her arm muscles quickly tired. Another wave swamped her, making her senses reel and disorienting her. Which way was up?

It was daylight, so she followed the sun's rays.

Blinking and sucking in short gasps of air, she managed to keep her face free of the water. How long could she last before fatigue sapped her energy and she sank into the depths? Would drowning be painful?

Sunlight glared into her upraised face, blinding her. She squinted, imagining her lungs burning for oxygen while her muscles gave way. Her body would sink, her limbs paralyzed by fatigue. Should she suck in big gobs of water to quicken her demise? She'd die alone in the vast ocean.

Tears of despair filled her eyes as she visualized the end, her respirations slowing with lack of oxygen, her consciousness fading. She'd become another nameless victim of the sea.

Through her blurry vision, she glanced around for Paz and Smitty, but the crests obstructed her view. Waves lapped and swelled and dipped, and she struggled to maintain her balance without being knocked over as water beat her from all sides.

Bits of wood drifted her way, remnants of the junk.

"Paz, can you hear me?" She could barely hear herself. Her voice came out a raspy whisper.

No one answered. Not even a seagull flew overhead. Another swell washed over her. Salty brine filled her mouth. Kicking to the surface again, she spit it out.

Her chest heaved. It was getting harder to breathe. Her arms and legs felt heavy and trembled from exertion. Maybe she should just let go.

So much for her destiny. So much for her dreams of expanding her business worldwide. So much for finding true love and having a family.

Did any of that count at this point? Her parents were what mattered, and so were the friends she'd leave behind. They'd all think she'd died in a plane crash anyway.

Her consciousness detached from her body, as though it were someone else about to drown. Another flow of salt water flooded her mouth and stung her nose as a swell impacted her. She gagged and coughed, breathing in short, frantic pants.

She couldn't fight the waves any longer. Her muscles, strained beyond endurance, froze with fatigue.

Her legs, which she'd been kicking in a slow rhythm to keep her head upright, floated uselessly downward.

She slipped below the surface, hoping the end would be fast. Her lungs cried for air, the pressure building inside her chest. She couldn't hang on for much longer.

She'd have to inhale, and then would begin the gasping, choking, painful finale.

Just as she opened her mouth, ready to give herself to the Almighty's embrace, strong hands gripped her and hauled her to the surface.

Chapter Twelve

Paz gripped Jen by the back of her shirt and swam upward, his heart pounding in fear that he was too late. Breaching the surface, he dragged her onto the floating piece of mast he'd found and flipped her onto her back. Smitty hung onto one edge, his breaths wheezing gasps punctuated by splashes as waves crashed against them.

Jen's eyes were half shut, and her mouth gaped open. Her face was pale as a newborn babe.

With trembling fingers, Paz pressed the side of her exposed neck. By Odin's grace, a weak pulse still beat but it was erratic. He needed to breathe life back into her.

"Is she dead?" Smitty croaked.

"Not yet." Holding onto the log, he bent and sealed his lips over hers as he'd learned at the Academy. He blew in a lungful of air.

Come on. Wake up. Respond to me.

When she still lay motionless, he sucked in a deep breath and repeated the action. Her limp body made him more afraid than he'd ever been in his life. They'd been through so much together in a short space of time. She couldn't quit on him now.

"Don't you die!" He gave her another frantic breath then bent over her silent form with a muted cry.

"Keep trying." Smitty waved a feeble hand. "Sometimes it takes a while. She won't leave us. She's vital to the prophecy."

Paz covered her mouth again, remembering the kisses they'd shared. He hadn't sought her sweet lips merely for protection against the Trolleks. He'd be lying to himself if he used that excuse.

He wanted more from her, everything she had to offer. When had this Earth woman come to mean so much to him?

Her mouth moved under his, and suddenly she lay on her side, gasping and choking. Paz supported her while she coughed and spit up salt water. When her lungs cleared, she drew in deep, shuddering breaths.

"It's good to have you back." Paz gave her a sardonic grin when she finally had the strength to gaze at him.

"Thanks. Is this what it takes to get you to kiss me again?" Her frail attempt at humor ended in another coughing fit.

It was then he noticed she still had her handbag, fastened by a sturdy shoulder strap diagonally across her body. He shook his head. Leave it to a woman never to let go of her valued possessions.

He felt his trousers pocket. The PIP was still there, but without its waterproof housing, the electronics would be useless.

That was the least of their problems.

He glanced around, glare from the sunlight off the ocean nearly blinding him. Waves swelled and receded, pushing them to and fro as they clung to their bit of flotsam. Everywhere, the sea stretched to infinity. Not a single vessel came into view.

His legs dangled underwater. He dared not think of sharks. They were fortunate the temperature was warm enough that hypothermia didn't pose a threat.

Jen blinked at him through waterlogged eyes. "You both made it." Surprise registered in her voice. "How did you—"

"I was still hanging onto Smitty when the creature burped us out. Lucky for him, since our dwarf friend can't swim. I saw this beam floating among the bunch of debris and retrieved it."

A wave splashed them. Opening her mouth, Jen gasped like a grounded fish. "My back hurts. I can't lie here like this."

She slipped into the water, clinging to the log with both arms like him and Smitty. A slimy strand of seaweed floated by along with pieces of wood, remnants of the junk.

Hours passed. The sun arched overhead, crossing from one horizon to the other. But still they hung on, desperation fueling their efforts. They couldn't stop being vigilant. Exhaustion was their enemy, and they'd fight it as long as there was breath in their bodies.

An attempt to summon saliva to soothe his parched throat failed. Paz pressed his cracked lips together, tasting encrusted salt. His mind drifted, and his consciousness ebbed away.

He forced his eyes open, unwilling to yield to blissful sleep from which he might not awaken. He was a Drift Lord. Drift Lords stayed stalwart to the bitter end.

Maybe he'd been regarding their situation the wrong way.

When he'd wanted a means to speed the space comm network, he didn't think about how gargantuan a task it would be to overhaul the relays. He'd considered the end effect first and then developed the architecture to make it work.

Think of the solution and not the problem.

An insane idea popped into Paz's brain. He swallowed, his tongue thick. "Jen, listen. Remember what I told you about your wristwatch? It works like a Trollek vector shift device."

Ignoring him, she glanced over his shoulder, and her eyes widened. "Look out!"

He turned just as a big wave crashed over them. Losing his grip, he tumbled into a frothing, hissing sea of foam. His lungs burned for a breath. He hadn't had time to suck in any extra air.

Before the current could pull him under, he blinked to clear his vision and kicked toward the surface. He broke free but floundered in a trough. A wall of water sloshed over his head. He waited until it passed, filled his lungs, and then searched for his friends.

The log floated several feet away, Smitty and Jen barely hanging on. With every swell, it moved farther from him. His arms ached as he paddled in their direction. His heart banged against his ribs in protest.

He gained on the mast, cast a leg over, and got a grip. His fingers touched Jen's outstretched hands. She gave him a wan smile, seemingly too tired to speak. Smitty inched over, looking a sodden mess like the rest of them. His beard glistened with droplets of moisture. His short fingers crawled across the wood until his hand covered theirs in commiseration.

"Oh God, Paz. We almost lost you." Jen's brown eyes soaked him in, while damp strands of hair clung like seaweed across her face. "We're not going to survive the coming night, are we? Once it's dark, we won't be able to see each other." Her lower lip trembled. "I never thought it would end this way."

A shiver ran through him. She already looked like a corpse with her pale, wet face and bluish tinged lips. Her body temperature must be dropping. Helpless to do anything about it, he entwined his fingers with hers.

"I'm sorry. I shouldn't have dragged you into this."

"It's not your fault." Her voice quaked. "Those Trolleks might have come after me somewhere else if not on the jet. I just wish we'd made it to the mainland. I could have caught a commercial flight from Hong Kong. They wouldn't dare expose themselves so overtly by attacking me in front of other people."

"Their interest in you just reinforces how special you are." His voice deepened. "Use your gift. Get us safely to dry land."

"Lady, I'll reward you handsomely if you deliver us from this accursed water." Smitty shook himself and droplets flew everywhere.

"I don't know how! Tell me what to do, and I'll try it." When neither of them offered any helpful advice, Jen's eyes drifted shut, and her head lowered to rest on the mast. Her dark hair splayed across the wood.

Paz's fingers twitched. "Focus, Jen. Our lives are at stake. Envision us in Hong Kong."

She squeezed his hand. "I've been there before. Fascinating city full of fabulous shops." A smile played across her mouth. "They have the most amazing fabrics."

Water splashed his face and trickled into his ears. He heard a rushing noise right before his body was sucked into a swirling vortex. His vision somersaulted as a haze of spinning lights disrupted his sense of balance. Had a wave capsized them?

A heavy weight pulled at him from the depths, instilling in him a sense of dread. Whatever creature dwelled there, he didn't want to meet it.

Jen's palm gripped his along with Smitty's clammy hand, but he could see nothing. At least he could still breathe, so he wasn't drowning. A force wrenched him free, and he tumbled through space. The sensation was similar to the way he'd arrived in Japan. Could this be another rip in the space-time continuum?

In the next instant, he landed on a soft surface. A thud followed by a grunt at his side sounded like Smitty.

Recovering his senses, he rolled to his feet. They'd arrived on a grassy slope. Jen lay a few feet away, where she was just beginning to stir.

He sniffed the air, detecting the faint scent of cors particles. Already fading, it was overshadowed by a sweet scent that must be coming from the white flowers on a nearby bush.

Jen's head lifted, and she peered around them. Paz's glance followed hers toward the glittering cityscape and bustling harbor stretched out below their hilltop. With a cry of surprise, she scrambled to her feet.

"How is this possible? We made it to Hong Kong, and we're not even near the coast."

"I believe you brought us here." Paz gave Smitty a hand to rise. Once upright, the dwarf brushed off his clothes with a snort of relief. They all looked wet and bedraggled.

"Me? How so?"

"You activated your watch. I told you it is a vector device like the Trolleks wear."

A joyful look on his face, Smitty clapped his hands and jumped up and down. "I'm free! I'm free! Well, guess I'll be going now."

He turned away but Paz grabbed hold of his ragged shirt. "Not so fast. I think you have something that belongs to us."

Shuffling his feet, the diminutive man gave Jen a sheepish look. "Captain Kolami had no right to them. He would have fed us to the sharks and taken whatever else you had in that sack of yours."

Jen propped her hands on her hips. Paz was glad to see the color returning to her cheeks. "What are you talking about?"

"Here, these are yours." Reaching into his pocket, Smitty withdrew her diamond earrings and displayed them on his palm. "They're very shiny. I like them. Why don't I keep them as a token of our friendship?"

"You're the thief who stole them from the captain's cabin?" Jen's eyes blazed. "The crew would have murdered us because of you." She held out her hand. "Give them over, Smitty."

With a grimace, he complied before turning to Paz. "I guess I owe you a life debt, Drift Lord. I promised you a reward if we reached dry land. A dwarf always keeps his word."

His small eyes darted around, his gaze falling upon some nails scattered by the roadside. He scooped them up and rolled the nails in his hands while muttering an indecipherable chant. When he opened his fist, a gleaming golden armband lay in his palm. Straightening his spine, he offered it to Paz.

"Wear this bracelet at all times. You will need it in the coming cataclysm." After Paz took it, he tilted his head, and his face brightened. "I can hear them. They've come for me."

Paz's pulse spiked. "Who? The Trolleks?"

"No, my people. They can hear me now. My powers must have returned. By Thor's hammer, that means I can go home." He grinned broadly. "Peace be with you, my friends. I see many children in your future."

Paz held up a hand. "Wait. What did you mean by the coming cataclysm?" He ignored the personal message. "Will your people help us against the forces of darkness?"

"I'll speak to them on your behalf. In view of what happened to me, they may listen. Farewell."

In the blink of an eye and a brief shimmer of air, he was

gone. Paz snapped the arm bracelet around his bicep and covered it with his shirtsleeve.

Jen shook her head as though she couldn't quite grasp what she'd witnessed. "I don't understand any of this."

In several short steps, Paz reached her side. He pressed a hand to the small of her back, wanting to reassure himself that she was safe. "Look below. What were you thinking about just before we ended up here?"

Wrinkles creased her brow. "Hong Kong. I can't believe I transported us. It's incredible. I'll have to figure out how this watch operates, but not now." She pointed to the city. "I recognize those tall buildings. That's the district with the glitzy hotels. How do we get down there? Omigod, Paz, we've actually reached civilization."

He strode toward the road. "We snitch a ride."

"You mean *hitch* a ride. I need to call my parents. Will that thing you made work here?"

He shook his head. "Unfortunately, my PIP wasn't shielded, and it got wet. I'll have to destroy it. We need to find lodgings while we determine a plan of action."

"My plan is to hop on a commercial jet and fly home."

Paz waved a hand. "Dressed like that? We look like a couple of slaves from the hovels at Anriat. We need to get cleaned up and acquire new clothing."

Her shoulders slumped. "I suppose you're right. We're a mess. They'd never let us on an airplane like this. I'm dying for a drink of water, too."

They followed the road and came to a tourist site with a restaurant and an overview of the city. A tram on a steep set of tracks led down the slope to the metropolis below.

Outside a gift shop, Jen found a banking station and inserted a plastic card. Out spurted a stack of paper bills he recognized as currency. She bought tickets and they rode the tram down the hill.

"I'd better call my credit card companies," Jen mused as they emerged onto a bustling street. "They knew I was in Japan, but they might question charges from Hong Kong. I need to find a telephone."

Paz peered at a confusion of sights that reminded him of Fararra, the pleasure planet with resorts, eateries, shopping emporiums, and entertainment complexes. Tall skyscrapers competed for attention with old-style street markets. The roar of bus engines and motorcycles vied for decibels with a construction jackhammer.

He sniffed roasting meat as they strolled along the sidewalk. They paused to buy a couple of soft drinks from a vendor and gulped them down. The fluid hit his empty stomach like a tsunami. They needed food, among other things.

A trolley rumbled past. People jostled them from all sides. He viewed the hilly, narrow side streets bustling with workers and crowded with vendors. Stalls offered cameras, embroidered linens, kimonos, brocade purses, and jade figurines. Other vendors sold livestock, fresh produce, and colorful birds in cages. Various smells lingered in the air, not all of them pleasant.

Having been around the galaxy, Paz had seen just about everything, and this swell of humanity rivaled the best. It would make an interesting cultural study some other time.

"Look, there's an Internet café." Jen nudged him. "I can make a plane reservation home. My passport is still in my purse. What about you?"

He shrugged. "I have a few things to do before I leave town. Let's go inside and contact our people."

The Trolleks had found Jen once already and could be tracking them again. He didn't want to alarm her, but it was a risk staying out in the open.

They entered the Internet café next to a shop selling jewelry made out of animal horns. Jen paid for their time while Paz cursed his lack of credits.

If only he hadn't lost his uniform. He'd had a stash of currency in his pocket. Captain Zohar had brought a number of kewa stones from his home world, Karrell, where they were common as sand. Here they were known as diamonds. Their leader had sold some and distributed the cash among their team members. Paz needed to replace his funds.

He swallowed his disappointment when he failed to raise his team online. Either they were observing radio silence, or something bad had happened. Although the Trolleks were their most potent threat, Zohar's political enemies couldn't be ignored.

As Crown Prince of the Star Empire, Zohar had to earn back his people's regard after his father's disastrous reign. The traitor who'd betrayed him to the Trolleks had worked for a group of insurgents who challenged Zohar's rule and called for a republic. Zohar might have cut off the snake's head by learning who led their movement, but now he had the tail to subdue.

Paz turned to Jen. Stranded without identity papers, credits, or any equipment, he still needed her assistance.

While she busied herself at another computer, he looked up the coordinates he'd seen on one of the control panels at the portal in Shirajo Manor. The location led to a place called Manga World, a local theme park. Likely it served as another Trollek recruitment center.

That would be his next target, assuming he could convince Jen to stay. Or maybe he shouldn't. Despite the signs indicating otherwise, perhaps she wasn't the woman meant for him. Working together to defeat the Trolleks was only one interpretation of the prophecy. Being together as soulmates was the other, like the love Zohar and Nira had found.

Paz didn't conceive of how he and Jen could ever feel that way about each other. Too many obstacles divided them. Maybe it would be wise to let her leave.

And if the prophecy proved to be true, it would find a means to keep them together.

****

Jen wondered why Paz was giving her such an odd look when she turned away from the keyboard. "I booked a flight for tomorrow, although the weather prediction is iffy. There's a storm at sea that might change direction last minute."

She rolled her shoulders, feeling sweaty and grimy and desperate for a meal, a shower, and a change of clothes. Once the water had dried from her skin, it left an itchy salt deposit.

Paz raised his eyebrows. "Then we should secure lodgings for the night. You've notified your parents?"

She smiled, remembering her father's response to her online message. "Yes. My mother felt that I was all right. No one had found any wreckage from our airplane. I suspect they were looking in the wrong place."

"So, you're really leaving."

Did she detect a note of regret in his voice? "I told my father I'd catch a flight as soon as I wrap up a few details, just in case I couldn't get a reservation right away. He'd postponed the vote with the Board of Directors, so it's not critical that I rush home."

"Too bad you booked a flight, or you could have joined me. The coordinates from Togura Island lead to a theme park called Manga World. I suspect it may be a Trollek recruitment center. I'm going to check it out if you want to come."

Are you crazy? Like, why would I willingly walk into another place crawling with those creeps?

"That's okay," she said aloud. "I'd rather return to the States. How will you get to Florida?"

"I'll need a passbook for a flight unless my comrades pick me up."

"You mean a passport." She shook her head. "How will you ever manage without me? Were you able to contact your friends?"

"No one answered. You can always stay and keep me company."

The heated look he shot her way sent pinpricks of desire through her. "No thanks. It must be upsetting to not reach your team. Do you think they're on radio silence or something?" She'd seen enough sci fi movies to make a guess.

"It's possible." He gave a nonchalant shrug, but she saw the gleam of worry in his eyes.

Other patrons glanced their way, doubtless wondering why they lingered. They headed outside to the crowded street. Hong Kong bustled with humanity, a mélange of mixed races.

"We could pick up some clothes and other items before we find a hotel," she suggested with a hopeful lilt.

"Let's find something to eat first."

Typical man. However, she could use the energy boost from a meal. They veered toward the vendor stalls. She grimaced as they passed a guy selling scrawny looking dogs tied to a post. Nearby, fresh red meat hung from hooks overhead, flies feasting on the blood oozing down.

"I can't believe they eat dogs and cats here. I've lost my appetite." She covered her mouth with her hand and hastened past.

They strode by another stall with jellied delicacies that looked like fisheyes, and her stomach lurched. Produce vendors sold bean sprouts, onions, and cabbage while seafood purveyors offered live snails and crabs. She scooted quickly by a man hawking some sort of disgusting green juice squeezed from leaves.

A double-decker bus rattled past. She swiped her brow, beaded with sweat. It was hot and humid, and lights blinked on around the city and on the hillside as dusk arrived. Toward the harbor, fully sailed junks, small motorized sampans, and ferries plowed back and forth.

Fascinated by the sights and sounds, Jen wished she had her sketchpad and cell phone. What a goldmine for business contacts, from boutique owners to designer showrooms to shops selling beautiful fabrics and threads. Ideas gelled in her mind for accessories such as belts and bags.

Her thoughts scattered when they passed a vendor selling live lobsters in a tank and whole dead fish that stared at her from a bed of ice. The briny smell brought the taste of salt to her tongue.

Instantly, her memory flashed to their harrowing experience at sea, but then her brain segued to another time and place.

Her vision receded from the narrow lane in the Hong Kong

street market. She blinked away the white haze that swept around her and found herself strolling along a wharf by the North Sea.

The wind whipped a tunic dress around her ankles. She braced against the storm-driven sea breeze. The biting cold air raised goose bumps on her flesh.

Paz's tap on her shoulder jerked her back to reality. "Are you okay? You looked as though you were parsecs away."

"I'm fine. And you're right, we should get a hotel room before it gets too late."

"I have to eat first." He pointed to a dish with an enticing aroma. "That looks decent."

After downing a bowl each of fried rice noodles with cooked shrimp, eggs, and scallions, she and Paz shopped the clothing stalls. They selected jeans, tops, running shoes, socks, and clean underwear, and took turns changing behind a flimsy curtain.

Jen, still craving a hot shower but feeling more presentable, bought some accessories and twisted her hair into a knot.

"Let's get a hotel and then check out the shops that are open late. You can buy electronics and put together another scanning device."

"Excellent idea, *leera.*"

He offered his arm, and she took it with gratitude and perhaps something more that she didn't care to examine.

As they headed down the street, she perused the storefronts. Her eye for design caught on the textiles in a display window. "Wait, let's go into this place for a minute."

Inside, she gushed over the rolls of fabrics. Imagine what she could do with this material! Paz followed her up and down the aisles as she mentally designed her creations.

A small woman with gray hair approached and chattered in a foreign tongue. As Jen gazed at her blankly, Paz translated.

"She wants to know how she can help us."

Jen nodded in comprehension. "Please ask if they ship stuff overseas."

While he got the particulars from the woman, Jen strolled down an aisle to examine the bolts of brightly colored fabric.

The chime at the front door tinkled as another patron entered. Jen's head whipped around. An attractive brunette had stepped inside. Why, then, did her sense of alarm escalate?

Could it be because she heard a sudden low buzzing in her ears?

Chapter Thirteen

Paz turned his head as another customer entered the shop. The woman had wavy chestnut hair that tumbled about her shoulders, lovely features, and alluring blue eyes. A perfumed scent wafted about her as she meandered toward them. She wore a sexy wrap dress and fancy high heels.

Breaking off his conversation with the sales lady, Paz hovered by a collection of buttons while waiting for Jen to make her selections. He tapped his foot impatiently, eager to move on and find a hostelry for the night.

A hand on his arm startled him. "Excuse me," said a woman's soft voice. "Do you speak English?"

The brunette's scent drifted into his nostrils. He inhaled deeply, his loins stirring. That alone should have alerted him, but his mind suddenly vacated. He turned toward her, absorbing her beauty and wanting to lean forward to taste her plush lips.

Alarm bells rang in his head. His training sprang into play, and he jerked back.

"Sorry, I can't help you."

"Please, sir. I'll just take a few minutes of your time." She reached out an imploring hand.

He backed away, fighting the tantalizing scent that drew him toward her. His pulse accelerated, and his palms grew sweaty. Through the fog in his brain, he knew he needed Jen.

Wheeling around, he staggered toward her. He grasped her by the shoulders and yanked her against him.

"Kiss me," he grated, then mashed his mouth to hers.

Despite the roughness of his treatment, Jen's mouth softened under his, and her lips parted. He flicked his tongue out, invaded her, and drank in her essence. Her body pressed against him, her leg rubbing along his inner thigh. Moaning into her mouth, he cupped the back of her head and explored her depths.

The sales lady's angry tirade restored his senses. Breaking off the kiss, he stared into Jen's stunned face. "Trollek," he croaked. "Run."

Her eyes widened. At that instant, the brunette reached into her purse with a snarl.

"You won't get away this time, Drift Lord. General Morar has a special punishment in mind for you."

He cursed under his breath. As long as Jen wore her watch, the beasts could track them, but he didn't know how to get around that problem without a set of perimeter rods.

Paz pushed Jen past the buxom Trollek. Together, they rushed out the door into the bustling crowd. A streetcar came to a screeching halt ahead.

He grabbed her hand and raced toward it.

Passengers stood in line by a sign. Paz skidded to a stop at the rear behind a woman carting shopping bags. A bus rattled past, emitting hot blasts of exhaust fumes.

Water ran in rivulets along the curb while dark clouds scudded overhead. The breeze stiffened, tossing his hair about his head. They needed to find shelter, a safe place where the Trolleks couldn't vector in to attack.

He caught sight of the brunette rushing in their direction as they boarded the trolley through a back entrance. He didn't see any place to pay. He hoped Jen would have the correct coins.

People crowded the aisles after the seats filled. He steered Jen toward the front end, his heart racing.

His sense of smell knew exactly when she entered the tram car. The allure of her scent set his nerves aflame. He had a nose numbing spray to help him resist their pheromones, but the dispenser was back in Florida with the rest of his equipment.

The trolley lurched ahead and rumbled down the street. People bumped elbows. Hot, sweaty bodies pressed close on all sides. At the next stop, patrons up front dropped coins into a machine before hopping out the exit.

Glancing back, he noticed the Trollek gaining on them, a fierce look on her face. She touched one person after another and muttered something in their ear. Swallowing a lump in his throat, Paz recognized her intent. All of those in her immediate vicinity turned to stare at him.

His muscles tensed. Tugging Jen after him, he shoved at the nearest fellow in his haste to reach the door.

"She's confounding people behind us. We have to get out of here."

"Where can we go? They'll find us again." Jen's panic-stricken voice matched the expression on her face.

"We'll worry about it later. Move."

Only a few more feet to go. He shouldered people out of his way and dragged Jen toward the exit, reaching it just as the trolley shuddered to a stop. Ignoring the coin machine, he leapt into the street with Jen beside him.

A whistle blew, and the driver yelled at them from his window. Great, now they'd have the authorities on their tail.

He dashed through various alleys and lanes, blindly charging ahead while gripping Jen's hand. His breath came in short, hard bursts. When he felt they'd finally put enough distance between themselves and the Trollek, he paused for air.

Jen held her middle and hunched over, gasping for breath. "This damn watch. It's pointing them right to us. I'm taking it off." She wrestled with the band, but it stayed clamped to her wrist. "I have to learn how to operate this thing. Maybe I can get it to work again. Take us to Florida."

Squeezing her eyes shut, she folded her brow in concentration. Nothing happened.

A straggly dog hobbled down the alley. It stopped to pee alongside a wall.

Jen's eyes blinked open at the disturbance. A Chinese man with a wrinkled face scooted down the alley after the mutt and swung a large net. The mangy dog yelped and limped away.

"Oh, no. He's not aiming to catch that poor thing for dog meat." Jen stepped into his path before Paz could stop her. "Please leave that animal alone. Paz, translate."

The man spouted angry words while attempting to sidestep her. Paz uttered a retort in the man's native tongue.

"He wants to sell the dog at market. Says it won't bring much because it's skinny, but the bones would be good for soup."

"That's horrible." Jen cried out when the man bumped her hip and charged past.

The canine dodged an overflowing trashcan, slipped on a puddle, and careened into a wall. It whimpered as the fellow approached. The meat monger made clucking noises while swinging the net in the air.

Jen moved forward and tugged on the man's arm. "Stop, you can't have him. Dogs are to be protected, not eaten."

The man swatted at her, and she let go. Paz stepped in, lifting the man as though he were a sack of buttons and tossed him aside. The man, still gripping his netting, rolled to his feet and ran off in the opposite direction.

"Thanks." Jen brushed off her hands and then smoothed her hair. Her twist had come loose, and disorderly waves trailed down her back.

She glanced at Paz to see the gleam of battle receding in his eyes, replaced by disapproval.

"That was foolish, Jen. The man could have been a Trollek mind slave sent to distract us. What's that animal to you?"

His gold armband reflected the light from a streetlamp. There wasn't any moon in the darkening sky. Slate clouds gathered, heralding the approaching storm. The wind whipped a swirl of dried leaves down the lane.

Jen lifted her chin. "The poor thing is homeless and prey to anyone with a stall in the street market. You know very well how it feels to be hunted."

"Amen to that, sister. Thanks for saving my sorry arse." The voice came from below and had a British accent.

Jen glanced around but the alley was empty except for them. "Who said that?"

"It is I, your friendly mutt. You may call me Dik. It's short for Dikibie." The dog's mouth moved, and intelligence shone in its wide, brown eyes.

Jen's jaw dropped. "Y-you can speak? What are you?"

"I am a descendant of the Originals left behind to aid the Drift Lords."

Paz thrust her behind him. "Be careful, he's a shifter." He addressed the dog. "You're a Gatekeeper? We were told your kind had been eradicated."

"Pray, may I ask by whom?"

"Askr, the last of your kind. He informed us the Trolleks had sent pfrells to annihilate you. The old man claimed to be the only survivor until the nasty creatures got him, too."

"Askr lied. I'm sure you realized the demon Loki possessed him. There are more of us, although we're few in numbers. I recognized your armband. The dwarfs would only bestow their magic on one who was worthy."

Paz's lip curled while Jen stood by in stunned disbelief. "Prove your power. Turn into a bird."

"Unfortunately, old chap, a curse has left me in this miserable body. I need your help to regain my human form. If you do this for me, I'll help you in return. What do you need?"

Jen spoke up. "How about a quick ride home?" She glanced at Paz when he grunted. "What? You wouldn't require a passport."

The dog pawed the ground. "Very well. Once I regain my natural state, I'll provide you with a ship that will take you to any port."

"Just what do we have to do to earn this reward?" Paz's tone dripped with sarcasm.

"Get me a drop of dragon blood. It will break the curse and restore me to my rightful form. You'll find Fafnir the dragon in a cave up on the peak. I'll catch up to you when you've achieved your objective."

Paz glared at the animal. "How do we know you're not possessed by Loki's spirit and this isn't a trick?"

Dikibie bared his teeth. "If Loki wanted me to eliminate you, I would have done so already, Drift Lord."

Paz stooped to face level with the creature. "If you're telling the truth, where are the Trolleks holding Kaj? Why haven't your fellow Gatekeepers rescued him?"

The dog gave a barking laugh. "We have our limitations. I'll give you five days. If you don't have the dragon's blood by then, consider our agreement cancelled." With a sniff, he turned away and dashed into the distance.

Paz snagged Jen's arm and walked with her toward a brightly lit avenue. Questions hovered on her tongue, but she felt too weary to ask them.

"I'm still planning to leave tomorrow." She shook him off, not caring about any magic ship or dragons or shapeshifters. Her flight was already arranged.

"You can't go." He gave her a disarming smile.

"I'll need the immunity you can convey to me."

"Is that the only reason you want me to stay?" She turned her head so he couldn't see the hurt in her eyes.

"Of course not." His voice softened as he strode by her side. "I want to do a lot more than kiss you, *leera*. But we have to keep moving for now. Besides, you need me as well. Are you forgetting you're a target for the Trolleks? They can find you wherever you go. You're not safe without my protection. As soon as we finish here, I'll accompany you home."

He was right, and she knew it. Nonetheless, she'd still take that flight tomorrow even if it meant leaving him behind. The Trolleks wouldn't dare accost her on a commercial airline.

"Let's find a hotel," she suggested. "We can debate this issue later." The gusts picked up, chasing them down the street. She sniffed impending rain in the air.

A high-rise hotel adjacent to an indoor shopping mall drew her attention. She pulled Paz inside and strode across the elegant lobby with crystal chandeliers. At the reception desk, an older woman in a shabby dress spoke English to the clerk in a voice loud enough for her to overhear.

"I have the money, I tell you." The woman scratched her head of scraggly gray hair. "Don't tell me you're sold out."

Jen's heart sank. Great, now they'd have to look for another place to stay.

A young man signaled her over from the next console.

"Hello, I'd like a room for one night, please." She braced herself for a negative reply.

"How many adults?"

"Two of us. My, er, husband and me." Her face flushed. She hadn't considered how they would present themselves.

"We have a room with a king size bed available."

"Fine, we'll take it. We're in between flights and had an unexpected delay." That would account for their lack of luggage.

After she wrote down the requisite information, offered her credit card, and took the keys, she glanced at the woman still arguing with the other clerk. Why was he giving her such a hard time? Because she looked like a bag lady come in from the cold?

Feeling sorry for the woman who'd said she could pay, Jen walked over. "Excuse me, I couldn't help overhearing your conversation. Can I help you?"

The lady's rheumy eyes looked her over. "This stuck-up fellow says the place is full. I should sue for discrimination. I have the money, but he says I'll have to wait for a cancellation."

"That's absurd. We just booked a standard room, so there has to be more in reserve. Look, mister, would you like me to tell your supervisor how you let a paying customer go?"

The man pursed his lips and pressed a few keys on his keyboard. "I see a junior suite with two queen beds has just opened up on the fourteenth floor. Will that do?"

The woman winced. "Oh, my. It's more than I wanted to

spend, but I'll take it." She rummaged in her worn handbag and withdrew a small wad of cash.

Jen turned away, but the older lady stopped her.

"Wait, dearie. Maybe you'd like to trade and take the larger suite instead, since there are two of you?" Jen's eyes widened but she nodded. Probably the woman wanted to save money by trading for the less expensive room. "That would be great, thank you."

"My name is Edith, by the way."

After making the switch and obtaining the proper keys, they left the reception desk. Paz stood by scanning the lobby with narrowed eyes.

The gray-haired woman poked Jen, startling her. She hadn't realized she'd become so sensitive to being touched by strangers.

"Listen up, missy. I noticed your watch."

"It was a gift from my parents." Jen glared at Edith with suspicion. She hadn't just been touched by a Trollek, had she? The beasts seemed to send beautiful young females across the dimensional barrier, but there could be exceptions.

"From your true parents, you mean. You're Two of Six. You'll need to interpret that inscription to fulfill the prophecy."

"What?" Jen rubbed her ear. Had she heard the woman correctly?

Edith's eyes glowed with fervor. "You must unite with your sisters. Each one of you is special in your own way. Together with the Drift Lords, your powers will save us from the coming darkness. It is foreseen."

"Did Paz put you up to this?" She glanced at him, but he wasn't paying them any attention. Leaning against a post, he watched the exterior doors with an alert expression.

Getting no answer from Edith, Jen turned her head. The old woman had gone. She stared at the empty space where Edith had been a moment before. Had she imagined their conversation?

Jen approached Paz. "Did you see where that woman went? I wasn't finished talking to her. She just vanished."

He shook his head. "What was that all about? I thought you were helping her get a room."

"I did, but then she started rambling about me being two of six and I need my sisters to fulfill the prophecy."

Paz gripped her arm. "She said what?"

"I have to join my sisters and unite with the Drift Lords to prevent some disaster. Her name is Edith."

Paz scrunched his eyes. "Hmm, where have I heard that name before?"

"You know her?" Jen gaped at him.

"It'll come to me. Let's go upstairs. We're too exposed out here."

The front doors rattled as the wind increased. After settling into their room, they headed to the shopping mall to acquire more supplies. Paz bought electronics and a switchblade while Jen added new outfits, backpacks, and other essentials to their meager stock. Then they dined on steamed dumplings and beef stir-fry at a restaurant before retiring for the night.

Rain pelted down outside, battering the windows in their suite—a bedroom, bath, and small sitting area. She shut the drapes, but her hands froze on the cord as the familiar white haze blurred her vision.

Suddenly she stood on a wharf with a shawl around her shoulders and a Viking ship bobbing on the waves. The wind blew cold, freezing her fingers and the tip of her nose.

A man's heavy hand rested on her shoulder. "Come inside, Jorunn, before the gale gets stronger." He spoke in a foreign tongue but somehow, she understood him.

"We can't escape the tempest." Her voice quivered, and her gut clenched with fear. "The town isn't prepared."

"Odin will protect us." The husky man made a fervent sign above his forehead. "Don't the gods keep the sea monsters away?"

"Yes, but that's because we ring our church bells whenever there's a sighting."

He adjusted the fur over his shoulders. "Do you really think that scares them?"

"Rumor has it that loud noises make them recoil. They remember the sound of Thor's hammer zinging through the air."

"I don't see the connection. Anyway, waves cannot be scared away. We'll be inundated. We should have gone to higher ground."

Rain splashed her face as the clouds moved in.

Another gust hit her, cool air-conditioned air.

She blinked, back to reality once again. She whirled around, signaling Paz. "I know how to keep the Trolleks away."

He'd turned on the television like any human male. Holding the remote, he glanced at her. "What do you mean?"

"I just had another vision. I was standing on a wharf and a storm was coming."

His mouth curved. "Have you looked outside?"

"Just listen, will you? The townsfolk rang church bells to keep the sea monsters away. It worked because it reminded the creatures of Thor's Hammer swinging through the air. Maybe it'll keep the Trolleks away from us, too. Otherwise, they might jump in while we're sleeping."

He stared at her for a long moment. "I've wondered about your role in the prophecy. These visions… do you have them often?"

"Not so much. They bring me to the Viking era."

His lips tightened. "My defensive perimeter rods are in Florida with my other equipment. They prevent anyone from vector shifting within range." He pointed to the clock on the nightstand. "That device is also a radio, yes? I'll change its frequency to one only the Trolleks can hear. I can have it transmit a loud signal that won't bother us."

Without waiting for her reply, he got to work, taking the radio apart and using the tools he'd bought to make adjustments. Observing him, Jen admired the frown of concentration on his brow, the hard planes on his face, and the wide set of his shoulders. Was there nothing this man couldn't do when it came to electronics?

"Do you really just repair communications equipment when you're not a Drift Lord?"

"Yes, that is my job."

She heard the challenge in his voice and didn't question him, but it disturbed her that he was so accepting of his lot when his skills qualified him for much more.

Striding to the nearest queen-sized bed, she gave a weary sigh. She'd unpack the goods in her bags before taking a shower.

She had just finished sorting through the pile of makeup, toiletries, and clothes when Paz straightened.

"It's done." He stuffed his tools into one of the backpacks. As the wind howled outside, he pointed to the window. "Sounds nasty out there."

A weather report on TV drew his attention. His brow wrinkled as he listened. "Jen, I hate to tell you, but flights have been canceled. The storm is expected to hit here directly, and the airports are closed."

"Oh, no." Her heart sank. "I thought we were supposed to get just a few rain bands."

He lifted an eyebrow. "Not anymore. We'd better call the front desk and ask for an extension. *Smark*, and I'd wanted to check out Manga World tomorrow."

Jen called her father while Paz went in the shower. Her dad wasn't happy about the delay but told her to stay safe. She wondered how that was possible when she couldn't trust anyone except Paz.

****

Paz's loins stirred as he watched Jen emerge from the washroom. She wore a towel around her torso, her loose hair damp down her back. He'd put on his briefs but now they felt taut. Part of his anatomy swelled as he glimpsed her deep cleavage, long and shapely legs, and bare feet. By Odin's grace, it took all his willpower to restrain his need for her.

She caught him watching, and her face flushed.

"Turn around. I have to put my nightshirt on." She stopped by the far bedside, a pout on her lush mouth.

"Don't bother on my account." He gave her a lazy grin.

Her chin lifted. "You just want insurance against the Trollek touch."

Females were all alike. They needed reassurance that his desire was for them alone. While his technique had earned him many happy memories, this time he hesitated. He didn't want to mingle with her just to satisfy his lust. He wanted to lie with her because she was a beautiful woman whose resourcefulness and courage would warm any man's heart.

With several quick strides, he reached her.

Paz tilted her face toward him. "It's true that I'm dying to taste you, but not only because you offer protection."

He stroked along her prominent cheekbone, across her chin, and over her lips. Her scent invaded him, enticing him to lean closer until their mouths almost touched.

"I can't get enough of you." His voice came out a husky rasp. "I want to explore you all over, to find the hidden spots that drive you wild, and to watch you as we break the crest together."

He grasped her, yanked her close, and melded his mouth to hers. She moaned into his kiss and thrust her leg between his thighs. His frenzy grew. He plunged his tongue inside her, claiming her for his own. Even if she cast him aside later, she'd remember their mingling.

He kissed her until his breath came short. Her hair felt moist under his fingers. Breaking off, he stepped back.

"Let me dry your hair. Turn around."

When she faced away from him, he unwound the towel from her body and ministered to her hair. His pulse beat a staccato in his neck as he viewed her bare bottom, straight back, and slender shoulders. When he'd dried her hair enough so it wasn't dripping wet anymore, he tossed the towel aside.

His hands found her breasts, and he caressed her gently.

"Oh, God, that feels good." She swayed against him.

As her nipples swelled, he brushed his thumbs across them. With an answering moan, she reached back and grasped his shaft. Her touch on his sensitive skin drove him wild. He kissed her hair, her neck, and down one arm. Then he spun her around to plunder her mouth while nudging her toward the nearest bed.

She wasn't the sort of woman for casual encounters, and never the type he thought he'd end up with some day. Yet he could no more stay away from this woman than a bee could avoid nectar. Why she wanted him didn't matter. Likely because he was there, offering comfort and security, and that's probably all it meant to her. For now, it was enough.

****

Jen tumbled onto the bed alongside Paz, aware of where this was leading and not caring. She'd meant to get a good night's rest, but with the typhoon trapping them, time lengthened and offered opportunities.

She ran her hands over her warrior's well-defined muscles, savoring the hardened planes of his back, the firm contours of his arms, and the width of his shoulders. When he rolled on top, she spread her legs, a warm languor stealing through her. Surrendering to the right person could be so divine.

As his mouth blazed a trail of kisses down her front, she writhed under his ministrations. He tickled her inner thigh, stroked one finger across her there, and then planted his lips on the spot. She gasped, unable to think clearly, as her spiral to ecstasy blocked all else from her mind.

Then he was atop her, probing her entry, and easing himself inside. His mouth found hers again, and their breaths fused as they found a common rhythm. Her perception narrowed until she was only aware of her body racing toward a climax. They floated in a weightless plane where nothing else existed. She felt cocooned in a place of light and warmth and something indescribable but infinitely pleasurable.

Her explosive release came as a cataclysm of delight. His finale followed, his breathing labored until he sagged on top of her. Their sweaty bodies pressed close until he rolled off to sprawl on his side. He kissed her shoulder then splayed out flat on his back, naked and spent.

After her pulse rate slowed, she leaned up on an elbow to regard him. He'd closed his eyes, and for a rare instance, she glimpsed the man with his guard down. She couldn't help brushing a stray lock of hair off his forehead. He always appeared so strong and capable, but even strong men needed a good woman to care for them.

Was he the right man for her, or was he merely a convenient hunk whom she needed for protection? Actually, that worked both ways. But did their connection extend to anything more?

His sexy dimples, scruffy jaw, and devilish gleam were enough to turn her on. His magical mouth and hands added to the equation, driving reason from her mind when he touched her. But could sex sustain a lasting relationship?

She already knew the answer.

If you fall for him, you're destined for heartbreak.

Chapter Fourteen

Two days later, Paz allowed Jen to go first through the turnstile at Manga World.

"I'm an idiot for coming along," she said, waiting for him on the other side. "I should have caught another flight instead of going with you."

Paz grinned as he joined her. "Fate intervenes when it is least expected. Little did you know the storm would close the airport, and that flights would be booked solid when it reopened. You're meant to be with me."

At a wide plaza, Jen snatched a guide map in English from an information kiosk. Bending her head so he couldn't read her expression, she studied the colorful diagram.

She hadn't said a word about their lovemaking all day yesterday when the storm had raged outside their hotel window. Presumably, he'd just been a handy body offering comfort.

That might not be such a bad thing, considering how he'd never wanted attachments from the women he met at various ports. But even if he cared enough for Jen to admit it, an attractive, worldly woman like her wouldn't settle for a man who lived such an unsettled life. His innate ability made him a Drift Lord. He couldn't deny the trait that had condemned him to this role.

Plus, she didn't approve of his regular job. Being a repairman who fixed space comm relays wasn't good enough for her. He'd noticed how her nostrils flared when she mentioned his work. Her disdain might not be as obvious as his father's, but he sensed it nonetheless.

Striding back and forth with his hands clasped behind his back, he considered revealing his dream. He hadn't yet built a prototype, but he knew his invention would work. That wasn't the problem.

His new system would challenge the monopoly propagated by his employer. Because his design was non-proprietary, it would support competing platforms. More importantly, his revolutionary project would bring interstellar communications into real time, eliminating the current lag. Imperial Space Command would be interested in the advantages it could bring them. So would their enemies.

One wrong move on his part could see his research stolen or destroyed. Better Jen should regard him as a low-level worker, the image he'd chosen to project, than to expose her to further danger.

She'd drawn her black hair into a bun at the nape of her neck. She wore a pair of slim fitting jeans with a smoke patterned tank top and a stone-gray sweater she'd rucked up at the arms. Sturdy but stylish boots added sex appeal.

Paz gritted his teeth and glanced away. The woman could wear a sack, and she'd look magnificent. His body stirred, wanting her again, craving the silky smoothness of her skin and her womanly scent.

To distract himself, he adjusted the backpack straps across his shoulders. They'd each stuffed their meager belongings into a sack. He wished he'd had time to buy more serious weapons but at least he had a blade.

His nape prickled. Jen's wristwatch would be a beacon to the Trolleks. General Morar might already be aware of their location.

"What's wrong?" Jen adjusted her sunglasses while tourists strode by them with determined expressions. "You look worried."

"I feel like we're being watched." He peered around, his eyes narrowed. "What is this Manga? The figures on those signposts look like children."

She tilted her head. "I'm not a big fan myself, but it's a respected art form in Japan that has become popular in the States. Comic books and graphic novels are its mainstay."

"Then it's a type of literature?"

"I suppose so. You can buy it in magazine or book formats. There are many long-running series that have been translated into different languages. It's a very stylized form of art. The characters are distinctive with their large eyes."

She waved the brochure. "I recognize some of these character names from the stories. Then there's Anime, which is Japanese animation based on Manga. That's represented here as well."

Paz watched a family of four heading toward a food vendor. "I don't understand why children are permitted in this park." His forehead creased. "The Trolleks don't usually confound the young. Maybe I'm mistaken about this location being a recruitment center."

Jen's lips pursed. "Parents bring their kids here, but many of these rides have height restrictions. You have to be an adult to go on them. All it takes is one touch from a Trollek to subvert someone, right?"

"True. The beasts confound people and then send them home to wait for further orders."

"Orders to do what?"

He shrugged. "Perhaps to bring forth the disaster called Ragnarok."

Her face blanched. "That's the darkness we're supposed to avert according to the prophecy?"

He nodded, falling silent as someone jostled them. They shouldn't talk about these things here. Park guests strode by, chatting happily. They looked normal, likely because they hadn't been confounded yet, but it was better to be cautious.

"I've studied Viking history to inspire my designs, you know." Jen kept her voice low as they moved on. "Ragnarok was the final battle between the giants and the gods. The giants were the original inhabitants of our universe, and they got angry when the gods relegated them to the underworld."

Paz glanced at her. "The Trolleks are like the giants, forced from their homes. Now they, too, gather allies in preparation for battle."

Her intelligent gaze met his. "They're doing more than confounding people at these recruitment centers, though. Algie has plans of her own, and I don't want to be part of them. Let's finish our business here and leave. Dad expects me to catch the first available flight home. He wasn't happy about another delay until I told him I'd met a man."

Paz's eyebrows shot up. "Did you now?"

She elbowed him. "Don't get ideas, Drift Lord."

He sobered. "Our objectives are two-fold. We have to confirm the Trolleks are recruiting humans at this locale. That'll be your goal. Drift World was set up as a role-playing adult theme park. Guests attended an orientation session to learn about their pretend jobs. As each person entered, a Trollek shook his hand."

"So, you want me to scout for Trolleks? It shouldn't be too hard to recognize their ugly faces."

"Not if they're dressed up as theme park characters. And remember, their females look normal." His glance skittered away.

"Okay, what aren't you telling me?"

"General Morar knows we're in Hong Kong. He's probably put out an alert for us."

She glanced around. "It's not like we're hard to notice among these Asians. We're obvious targets in that case."

He met her level gaze. "If we split up, I can't protect you."

Her face eased into a soft smile. "Don't worry about me. I can take care of myself. What will you do while I'm looking for their recruitment station?"

"I hope to find the portal from Togura Island. If it has a reverse function, I'll return to Shirajo Manor and take more readings of the inter-dimensional gate."

"Are you crazy?" She gaped at him, her eyes wide.

His mouth tightened. "I have to determine how they are keeping the gateways open. My last scan was inconclusive. This time, I'd like to get a reading from inside the rift itself."

He'd fine-tuned his scanning device to collect particles at the quantum level. The data he'd acquired before might still prove useful, but there was nothing more accurate than direct observation.

His scalp crawled. Only one way existed for him to determine how the Trolleks maintained the rifts, and that was to step through and take readings on the other side. He hadn't told Jen his entire plan because he didn't want her to worry. He might end up being trapped on Jak'tar—the Trollek home world.

"Look, if you're spotted, I want you to leave." He gripped Jen's arm, concerned for her safety. He hated leaving her alone but had to use this opportunity to his best advantage. "Do not engage the enemy. Find out where the Trolleks are confounding people, and that's all."

He checked his chronometer. "We'll meet outside the front entrance to Manga World. If I'm not there by five o'clock, assume I'm not returning and take the next flight home."

Maybe he should have let her go and not involved her. She could have gone to the airport this morning instead of staying behind with him. Was he being selfish in wanting her company? Keeping her here had put her in jeopardy.

She'd be in danger anyway, fool.

Once her airplane touched down on American soil, the Trolleks could come after her. That is, if Algie still wanted Jen for her experiments. And if not, likely General Morar would still hunt for his escaped prisoners to save face.

"Are you sure we shouldn't stick together?" Jen regarded him with a forlorn expression as he handed her back the map.

His mouth curved in a mirthless grin. "You don't want to go where I'm headed, leera. Stay safe." He pulled her into his arms, gave her a lingering kiss, and then headed off.

****

Jen watched him leave with a sinking feeling. After struggling for so long to be self-reliant and independent, she disliked the sensation. Paz's absence left a hole in her heart in a space she hadn't known existed.

Dread pitted her stomach at the thought of him entering General Morar's fortress again. Yet she knew him well enough by now to realize he wouldn't back off from his goal.

It struck her as uncharacteristic, with his skill set, that he'd settle for a complacent job fixing telecom equipment. Could there possibly be more to his work than he cared to admit?

Maybe he'd been dragged into his role as a Drift Lord, but the man appeared to be a natural born warrior. It seemed incongruous for him to work for a corporation without exhibiting the same initiative as he did now.

Or perhaps she just wanted him to be more than what he seemed in real life. She shouldn't judge him, considering how he'd proven himself in all the ways that mattered.

As a tender lover, he couldn't be beat. He faced adversity with courage, determination, and resourcefulness. They'd only known each other a short time, but she trusted him with her life.

Then why was it so hard for her to accept who he was outside of being a Drift Lord? Was that the only part of him that appealed to her?

With a grunt of self-disgust, she studied the map to gauge the best place to start her hunt. The park was divided into several themed sections surrounding a broad lake. These appeared to be based on genres.

Pirates, Ninjas, and Samurai adventures occupied one corner with a stunt show as its highlight. Modern Fantasy with vampires, werewolves, wizards, and such stood on the opposite side of the lake. A popular ride there was the Dragon Dive Bungee Jump.

The Science Fiction area had a Rocking Robot Roller

Coaster and an Asteroid Shooting Gallery, among other attractions. Was this different from Superheroes? That appeared to be a separate site while Romantic Comedy brought up the rear. She counted five sections total. Where to start?

Jen tapped her lip as she contemplated the most popular attractions as noted by the wait times on a digital board by the information kiosk. Fortunately, all the signs were in English as well as the local language.

She'd expect the Trolleks to wear costumes that blended in with a themed show or ride. Monsters usually appeared in fantasies or as hostile aliens in science fiction. Through a process of elimination, she decided they could pass for pirates, dark fantasy creatures, or evil aliens.

So where might they lure their human recruits? Scratch the family attractions, since the Trolleks only confounded adults.

She narrowed her choices to thrill rides with height restrictions, scary 4-D shows, or adults-only rides. The brochure gave a one-liner description of each numbered point on the map.

Sweating from the heat and an attack of nerves, she proceeded down the main street bustling with people rushing in one direction or another. Gift shops, confectionaries, toy stores, and boutiques tempted guests to empty their wallets.

Jen appreciated Paz's trust in her to complete her own mission. Not wanting to let him down, she considered which attraction might involve personal contact between a staff member and a guest.

She rubbed her temple. A troubling dream of Aunt Alba had plagued her last night. As before, they stood in a cemetery. Her aunt had crouched in front of a headstone, mouthing words Jen couldn't hear. The dream had left her with an unsettled feeling.

Or maybe the discomfort came from the low-grade buzzing that sprang into her head. Trolleks must be close, trolling as it were for victims to confound.

She hit pay dirt inside the Goblin Forest Flight, where attractive females dressed like wood nymphs with glitter on their faces and crowns of leaves greeted each guest in two separate lines. Jen approached the turnstile that would allow her entrance to the ride. A hostess smiled at her in a way that made Jen feel like a butterfly about to be pinned to a board.

"Welcome to the Goblin Forest, mistress. Please insert your index finger into the scanner to receive your boarding pass."

Jen's heart thudded as she complied. Something inside scraped her fingertip. Startled, she jerked her hand out. A paper popped from the machine. The attendant held it out, and when Jen reached for it, the woman grabbed her arm for a quick squeeze.

"Congratulations, visitor. Have a pleasant ride."

Jen snatched the ticket, berating herself for being caught unawares. Her pulse pounded in her ears.

"Beware the enchantment of the ghost walkers," the hostess exhorted. "They may tempt you to linger in the forest." A sly smile curved her mouth. "Listen to the recorded message. It will tell you what you need to know to escape."

Shaken, Jen pushed through the turnstile and took a seat on a bench next to three other people. A safety bar lowered in front of them. Ahead of the track loomed a dark tunnel. Would they emerge safely at the other end?

The bench lurched ahead and seemed to rise into the air as they entered a magical land beyond the tunnel. They soared, dipped, and twirled through a colorful landscape with giant mushrooms, huge green plants, and goblins popping up to scare visitors.

Trees reached for guests with grasping branches. A waterfall sounded ahead, and her heart leapt at their sudden plunge toward a pool below. They lifted at the last moment, soaring into the air again, their feet dangling.

The bench tilted dizzily as they flew over a swamp with knobby cypress knees and prickly plant spines. Music drummed in the background. They ascended a grassy slope and then skimmed across a forest.

A goblin king rose at the far end, a snarl on his face. He blocked their progress forward. As their bench hovered, a Manga warrior popped up to battle him. A brief combat ensued and then the goblin sank from view. The victorious caped hero addressed the guests in a mechanical voice.

"You will be rewarded generously for helping us vanquish the evil king. When your ride comes to a stop, step through the exit and receive a special gift. Then go home and tell everyone you had a great time. Remember to visit our other theme parks around the world." He repeated his message in various languages.

Jen gulped. *Around the world?*

Paz's theory was correct. Trolleks were acquiring mind slaves through popular tourist attractions. Who would suspect a nefarious purpose to favorite vacation spots around the globe?

Wait a minute. Didn't they also test blood samples of humans at these sites? Individuals who showed certain protein markers became subjects for Algie's experiments. But how did they go about it in this place?

She probed her fingertip, the one she'd stuck into the scanning device at the ride's entry. Her skin seemed a bit red. Had they taken a scraping for DNA analysis? Why go to the trouble of drawing blood when that method might be more expedient?

A disembodied voice spoke from a loudspeaker as their bench glided to a stop. "Some of you may be selected for a special promotion. Please go along willingly. Your companions can meet up with you at home."

She exited at a brightly lit platform, where an attendant shuffled them through to an adjacent gift shop.

Jen strode down an aisle with goblin dolls made in Japan. They looked suspiciously like Trolleks with their long noses, shaggy hair, and toothy grins.

"Excuse me, miss, do you speak English?"

She glanced up. A westerner covered from head to toe in a safari jacket, cargo pants, boots, and a hat approached.

"Yes, I do."

He bustled to her side. "Tell me, did you notice anything strange about this attraction?"

"In what manner?" *Talk about strange, aren't you hot as hell in that outfit? You're even wearing leather gloves. Are you afraid of germs or something?*

"Do you see how these folks behave after they get off the ride? It's like they're robots. You're different. You have an alert look on your face." His brown eyes examined her. He had a scar on his upper cheek and looked to be in his mid-forties.

"I'm sorry, I'm not following you." Was this a test to see if she was confounded? If so, she'd failed miserably.

"You're from the States, aren't you? I can always tell a fellow citizen. Talk to me."

Her eyes rounded. "About what?" Who was this man, and how much did he know?

"Things aren't right in this place. They do something to people here. Folks have gone missing, too."

She surveyed his attire, realizing he'd covered himself on purpose. He had left no exposed areas for a Trollek to touch.

Her pulse pounded in her throat. "Who are you?"

He withdrew his wallet and flashed a badge. "I work for the U.S. government. We're concerned about certain anomalies."

What? Could they be aware of the Trollek incursion?

"I-I can't talk now." She peered past him, afraid he'd impede her own investigation.

"Then take my card. Call me later. Seriously, I could use your input."

She stuffed the card into her pants pocket, hoping no one had observed them. Further down the aisle, a tall, thin Asian browsed a display of fake swords and shields.

A staff member dressed as a goblin with a pointy green hat hurried up to the guy. His overly large ears and hands alerted Jen. Alarm frissoned up her spine.

"Sir, congratulations, you've won a free photograph. Kindly step behind that curtain."

Without hesitation, the fellow obeyed. From the corner of her eye, she noted the man in khaki watching.

Her body trembling, she made a beeline for the exit and the bright sunshine outside.

A firm hand on her arm stopped her. "Just a minute, mistress. You've been chosen for our special promotion. Please follow that gentleman."

Jen's heart skipped a beat. Dear heaven, what now?

She glanced toward the door, where freedom beckoned. If anything went wrong, Paz wouldn't be available to assist her. She'd have to rely on herself and her unknown power. She quaked at the notion of unleashing it again, of losing control.

She'd have to take that risk. Paz had assigned her this job, and by God, she'd follow it through.

Willing her face to appear impassive, she stepped past the black curtain as indicated. On the other side, she faced a large space with partitioned cubicles. Another staffer gestured her toward cubicle number three. She entered the area where there was a scent of antiseptic and a single chair facing forward against a gray background.

A pretty blonde entered immediately after her. True to their deception, she carried a camera with a large lens. "Before I take your photo, may I see the hand you put into our scanner? I'm afraid it might have left a smudge."

Jen turned her palm over, hoping the Trollek wouldn't notice her tremors. If she were confounded, she'd be in a calm state, receptive to commands. She lowered her gaze to appear docile but couldn't help her sharp intake of breath when the blond grasped her hand.

"Let me just clean that for you."

Jen felt a cool, moist swipe on her skin followed by a sharp prick. She bit her lower lip to keep from crying out. Had she been stuck? Sure enough, from her peripheral vision she saw dark red oozing from her fingertip. So they did take blood samples here after all.

"I'm so sorry, there must have been a splinter in the wipe. Here, press on this gauze with your other hand while I snap a headshot." That task done, the Trollek beamed at her. "It will just take a moment to process. Please wait here."

On her way out, the female flicked a privacy curtain down. Jen didn't know if a hidden security camera might be aimed at her, so she resisted the urge to examine her finger. She waited as ordered, her spine stiff, expecting at any moment for a bunch of armed Trolleks to burst inside and grab her.

How did they know who to waylay after the ride? The scanning device that presumably took a DNA sample must give quick results. Those humans who possessed genetic compatibility to the Trolleks would then be targeted for further testing. And if they showed the protein markers, they'd be candidates for Tent Ten.

That raised a host of other questions. How did the Trolleks transport the fated guests from this theme park to Togura Island, assuming that held the closest facility for Algie's scientists? Had Paz been correct in guessing the portal at Manga World had reverse functionality?

Moreover, what happened to the people who never returned home? Weren't their families concerned?

She thought about the government agent, if that man's identity was real. What if some of the confounded guests who'd been sent back to lead normal lives were diplomats, holding positions in high places? Maybe their behavior had alerted the intelligence agencies.

Yet that wasn't likely, since you couldn't always tell an individual had been confounded. Maybe it was the missing people who'd raised alarms. Either way, any investigation would be dangerous and would have to be deeply covert.

A chill shuddered through her. It appeared she'd stumbled onto something a lot bigger than she and Paz had expected.

Chapter Fifteen

Paz regretted leaving Jen to her own resources, but he had no choice. After parting from her at Manga World, he followed his nose to where the smell of burnt filaments was strongest.

The olfactory trail of cors particles led him, as he'd thought it might, to a door labeled *Staff Only* in the back of a souvenir shop at a Flying Wizards attraction. From there, he bet it would take him into a series of underground utility tunnels like at Drift World.

He eyed the staff members, mostly Asians. A uniform would help disguise him in case security cameras were trained on the staff door.

He selected a taller than average man as his target and signaled him. "Excuse me," he said in English plus sign language. "Can you direct me to the men's room?" When the guy jabbered back, Paz frowned. "Sorry, I don't understand. Would you mind showing me the way?"

Outside, he lured the fellow behind a planter and subdued him with a Morabi nerve jab. A few minutes later, he walked into the store wearing the man's uniform and headed for the private door. If the design of this place was anything like Drift World, a room below would hold the portal back to Togura Island.

He descended a concrete staircase into a series of utility corridors. Wondering which way to go at a junction, he adjusted his backpack across his shoulders. He'd feel a lot better with a stash of weapons. All he had for defense were his own hands and a pocketknife.

Paz missed the weight of his personal dagger. That treasured item, given to him upon graduation at the Academy, had been lost along with his clothing in the ocean. He'd lost more than his belongings in that final battle. Adrift without his team on an alien world, he felt isolated and alone.

If he hadn't met Jen... it frightened him how much he needed her. Whenever he grasped her hand, he felt stronger, more capable, and able to accomplish any task. How did she do that to him? And why was he thinking of her when his mind should be on his mission?

Hearing voices coming from around the corner, he slid into a recess and sucked in a breath. A couple of beasts stomped past wearing military-cut trousers and belted tunics. They carried laser carbines. He was definitely in the right place.

Should he follow them? They might merely be on patrol. He needed to find the transfer station.

A couple of human staffers came into view from around the corner. They escorted a small group of guests who stared straight ahead in a blank manner. Paz waited until they passed and then dashed forward to take a position at the column's rear. He mumbled a noncommittal reply when one of the employees shot him a question.

His muscles tensed as they approached a door flanked by two armed Trolleks.

Their entourage halted. The guy in the lead exchanged a few words with one of the soldiers. The beefy Trollek surveyed the unhappy lot of visitors, six men and two young women. He said something that made his friend chortle. Then they stepped aside to allow the group passage.

Paz's heart pounded in his chest as he sauntered by, head lowered. Would they notice he was too tall for an Asian? That he was a lot more muscular than these puny humans? That he wore a backpack and they didn't?

Evidently not, because his presence didn't raise any alarms. They were used to unquestioned obedience from their mind slaves, including the staff members among them. He fixed his face into a mask so as not to betray his excitement when he saw the apparatus ahead. An archway formed over a raised circular platform, its canopy supported by four columns. One post held a control panel.

At a barked command from the lead staffer, the guests stepped upon the dais. Paz carefully observed the code punched in by the fellow at the touchpad. The air under the archway shimmered, and in the blink of an eye, the people vanished. Paz wrinkled his nose. The chemical smell of burning filaments that accompanied vector shifts pervaded the air.

When the other employees turned to leave, he waved them on, stooping as though to fix his shoe. Hopefully they wouldn't notice his boots under the uniform's pant cuffs.

He'd have to wait until the reception committee met the victims on the other side. He pitied them if they were destined for Tent Ten. None of those folks would survive.

Didn't anyone ever miss them? He supposed their companions at the park were confounded, too. They'd be sent home with the excuse to tell everyone their friend or family member had been called away. But what happened when they never returned? Surely some people must make inquiries.

Anyway, he couldn't think about that now.

After a sweat-inducing interval, he stepped onto the platform, punched in the code he'd seen the Trollek input, and gritted his teeth for the bone-jarring sensation of a vector shift. The room tilted, lost focus, and rematerialized into the chamber at Shirajo Manor that held two portals.

Paz let out the breath he hadn't realized he'd been holding. No one occupied the room. In two quick leaps, he made it onto the larger platform. Cables snaked from the basement, which housed the generator, to receptacles on the arch itself.

He took out the specialized scanner he'd constructed in their hotel room, cobbled together from the electronics he'd acquired at a consumer store. Taking a reading from the other side of the dimensional rift should give him the information he needed. Along with the copied data from the room downstairs, it would tell him how the Trolleks forced open the gates.

Poised to go through the barrier, he swallowed hard. He'd only been to the Trollek home world once before, and it hadn't been a pleasant experience. They had guards on the other side and weapons aimed at the gate. He didn't have any sonic grenades to toss through this time to disable the enemy. He'd just have to make this visit a quick one.

Remembering the activation code, he keyed it on the control panel. The disorienting sensations that followed were much worse than a simple spatial shift between locations on the same plane. He felt an instant of disembodiment, where he appeared to be weightless in a void.

Another presence loomed from the depths. He sensed its anger, its challenge at his invasion. It pulled him down, siphoning his energy. He resisted by strength of will, picturing himself on the other side.

Then he was there, facing a contingent of guards who fired at him as soon as he stepped across the threshold. He merely had to wait until the scanner light turned green, meaning it had completed its job. Come on, he thought, dodging laser beams.

From the corner of his eye, he glimpsed woods in the background and two moons in the sky. He smelled wood fires and the fresh scent of rain.

A loud ratcheting noise came from a construction off to the side. He couldn't see past its housing, but it made a steady *gud-a-lump, gud-a-lump* sound. Cables snaked from the thing to the archway. He looked up, noting the bits and pieces of metal imbedded in the arch. A frown creased his brow as he tried to make sense of it.

Light reflected off an array of mirrors facing the gate. They reminded him of radio satellite dishes on Earth aimed at space the way they were laid out in even rows.

He dove sideways as a laser bolt sizzled past. His move put

him in the path of a disruptor beam which he barely dodged. Ozone tinged the air along with cors particles.

Suddenly, the barrage of fire stopped. A quick glance told him the troops were gathering to rush him.

He was running out of time.

The light on his scanner turned green.

He whirled, punching in the return code. A hot, blazing pain stabbed his leg, making him falter. He squinted as lights flickered around him, and the world spun. In the next instant, the room back at Shirajo Manor sprang into sight. As soon as his vision cleared, he staggered off the platform.

Searing heat burned his leg. He gasped, sweat dotting his brow as he limped forward. His glance dropped to his thigh.

He'd been hit.

Fortunately, he still wore the staff uniform over his own clothing. The double layer of fabric had taken some of the brunt from the laser. He grimaced at the scorch marks, not wanting to imagine what his flesh looked like beneath. At least the hot beam had cauterized the wound, so he wouldn't bleed out.

He gritted his teeth against the agony. He'd been hurt worse. He would deal with it later.

He stored his scanner in a pocket as he dragged himself toward the opposite platform. Each step felt like a mile. He climbed onto the dais while shards of pain made his breath hitch. Pressing his lips tight, he reversed the code from before and ended up back at Manga World.

Somehow, he made it through the utility corridors and up the stairs to the surface while avoiding detection. That final effort nearly undid him. He hesitated before entering the gift shop, his chest heaving. The Trolleks might be looking for an intruder at Shirajo Manor, but not here. Although, they'd trace where he'd gone soon enough.

He glanced at his chronometer. Nearly time to meet Jen. He must have spent more time down in the utility corridors than he realized.

Inside the shop, he snatched a kimono-type robe, a fake gray beard, and a wizard's hat with an attached wig and paid for them with cash Jen had given him. In a nearby restroom, he exchanged his staff uniform for the disguise. The robe would hide his leg injury.

Outdoors in the afternoon sunshine, he put a blank look on his face as he headed for the exit. It wasn't easy. Whenever he put any weight on his leg, his gut lurched and his head swam. If only he had a hypospray from his medkit.

Just get out of here. See if Jen is safe.

He clenched his jaw, dragging himself forward, once again cursing his lack of equipment and the situation that had landed him there. How would he make it to Florida now when he could barely walk?

****

Jen paced outside the front gate where Paz was due to meet her. She hadn't waited around for the results of her finger prick, slipping away from her cubicle and back into the gift shop when no one was looking. She'd hastened toward the exit, glad to escape unhindered.

She tapped her foot impatiently, anxious for Paz's safe return. Where was the man?

Peering over her sunglasses, she scanned the guests streaming through the turnstiles. Asians mixed with westerners, but she saw no sign of her handsome warrior.

An old man dressed in a kimono and a pointy hat hobbled toward her, his robe swishing with each slow step.

He nudged her as he shuffled past. "Let's move. We'll take the tram into the city."

Her jaw dropped. "Paz? I never would have guessed. But why the tram? It makes too many stops. The subway would be faster."

"It's too far to walk, and I can't do the steps."

"What do you mean?" Her eyes narrowed as he limped forward. "What happened to you? Did you get the info you needed?" She knew that would have been his priority.

"Yes, I did. How about you?" His lips pressed together.

Jen didn't like his pale complexion but deemed it unwise to question him where they might be overheard. "I have news, but we'll talk later."

His face pinched as he climbed aboard the tram. He sank into a seat with an audible sigh.

She bit back her concern to gaze out the window. Tenements whizzed past, laundry strung out on balconies to dry. A stiff breeze made the fabrics billow like so many sails. Kids tossed a ball on a concrete lot, their lone playground. They dodged puddles on the ground, remnants from the storm.

Debris scattered the area, tree branches and broken awnings and trash. As they got closer toward town, hilly streets bustled with people laden with shopping bags. Vendor stalls that had been folded away for the tempest now thrived with customers.

"Where should we get off?" Jen asked Paz.

He didn't respond. He'd closed his eyes and slumped in his seat.

"Paz, what's wrong? You don't look so good."

"I've been shot." His voice quaked. It appeared to be an effort for him even to speak.

"Dear Lord. Where—?"

"My leg." A groan escaped his lips as their tram hit a pothole.

"We need to get you to a hospital."

"No way. Take me back to the hostelry." Before they'd left, Jen had reserved their suite for a couple of extra nights just in case they needed a safe place to stay again.

Her pulse raced. There went her hope to exchange information and then catch a flight home. She figured Paz could find someone in Hong Kong to provide him with a passport. But her warrior was in no condition to go anywhere.

She considered their only other option.

"That dog, Dikibie, said he'd give us a ship if we got him a drop of dragon blood. Do you believe him?"

"Even if I did, I'm in no shape to fight a dragon."

"We have to get you fixed up."

"No medics. I wouldn't be able to explain the scorch mark."

"Scorch mark?"

"I got hit by phase weapon fire."

She swallowed, panic tightening her throat. "What should we do?"

"I'll treat my wound in the hotel room."

Fortunately, he managed the short walk from the tram stop to their hotel. Jen got curious stares from strangers as she guided the feeble old man, her arm around his waist for support.

Once inside their suite, Paz slipped the backpack from his shoulders, tore off his disguise, and collapsed on the bed.

Jen disengaged her purse and pack and then rushed to his side. He lay sprawled out and unconscious.

"Paz, wake up." Frantic with worry, she shook him.

On the nightstand stood the radio he'd remodeled to emit a high frequency signal to repel the Trolleks. At least they wouldn't be disturbed by the beasts in here.

His face looked so pale. She surveyed the crescent of his lashes, the strong angles of his jaw, and the perfect shape of his mouth. She missed his dimples when he flashed a sexy grin.

Her breath caught in her throat. Would he be all right?

She'd come to think of him as her warrior. Someone who was there for her, who would fight to protect her, and who worried about her safety. Someone whose kisses turned her knees to jelly and sent her heart into a flutter.

Her heart. He'd captured it despite her resistance.

He was the last man she'd expected to want, an alien from outer space, a foreigner on home soil, and a man who had no real ambition to rise above his station. And yet he was so much more. He had courage and valor and many unusual skills. Didn't he realize his own worth? Was she wrong in thinking he might be hiding something from her?

If this was the entire package, maybe she could convince him to reach for a greater goal, but first he had to survive.

She stared at the scorch mark on his pants, wondering what to do. A lie sprang to her lips, and she reached for the phone.

"Hello? Do you have a doctor on call? My, er, husband has injured himself and needs immediate medical care. We'd like someone who can come to our room."

"Yes, ma'am, I'll send someone straight up," the front office clerk said in fluent English.

Jen replaced the phone then rushed around to straighten the room and hide away anything that looked otherworldly.

At the sound of a bold knock, she flew to the door and peered through the viewport. A short, dark-haired Chinese man holding a leather satchel greeted her with a solemn nod when she swung the door wide.

"Hello, I am Dr. Wong. I understand someone is injured?" He spoke with a lilt in accented English.

Jen led him inside. "Yes, it's my husband. Foolish me, I dropped my curling iron onto his leg. It's left a terrible burn mark. I hope you have something to treat it."

"I'll do my best." After setting down his bag, he approached the patient. His mouth curved down in dismay as he separated the burnt edges of Paz's jeans and peered at the wound. "That is a large injury, miss."

Jen held her breath. Would he question her story?

"We need to cut his pants away." He withdrew a pair of bandage scissors from his bag and proceeded to cut through the fabric. Watching him brought to mind a vision of the fabric sash wrapped around the officer's neck at Shirajo Manor. Jen swallowed. She didn't want to be reminded of that now.

"Shall I remove his boots?" she asked.

"Not yet. Let me examine the gentleman first." Dr. Wong exposed Paz's thigh just as he began to stir.

The doctor reached into his bag and withdrew a prepared syringe. He injected Paz in the arm.

"What's that?" Jen had never been very useful in the sickroom department and sometimes preferred ignorance to knowledge. That wasn't the case this time. She'd do whatever it took to heal Paz.

"An analgesic for the pain." He studied the wound while Paz's eyes blinked open, stared blurredly at Jen, then closed again. "I need to clean the site, debride the dead tissue, and then treat him with antibiotics."

Jen saw him hesitate. "That's fine. Is there a problem?"

His gaze scrutinized her. "I am surprised you did not take this injured man to a hospital, but I understand insurance can be a problem."

"We can pay, if that worries you."

He nodded in acknowledgment. "I would like to recommend one more remedy, but it is costly."

"What's that?" She wished he'd get on with the treatment already instead of talking.

"Dragon Balm. It has been used in China for generations."

"What does it do?" She didn't know much about Chinese medicine except their techniques often worked.

The doctor removed supplies from his bag and set up a sterile field. "The ointment speeds recovery and prevents infection, as well as providing pain relief. One ounce costs a hundred and fifty American dollars."

She blinked. "What? You've got to be kidding."

"It is very rare and made from a secret family formula. Rumor says it comes from real dragon spit." He peered at her. "Also good for wrinkles and joint pains."

"Ah, sure." *Like snake oil claims of old?*

She couldn't tell from his expression whether Dragon Balm was a genuine medication or a scam. If it made Paz worse, she could always complain to the management and get some antibiotic cream on her own. Then again, traditional Chinese medicine was a respected and valid practice.

"We'll take one container. Do you accept credit cards?"

Dr. Wong grinned broadly. "I have a mobile credit card reader. Very modern." He laid out his instruments on a sterile pad and then donned a pair of Latex gloves.

Jen turned away while he cleansed and debrided the wound. "You say this ointment comes from an old family formula?"

He focused on his work. "Ra Mat, a local herbalist, developed it in the late 1870's. His sons built Dragon Balm Gardens up on the hill as a tourist attraction. Now his great-grandson Shlom owns the property."

Her interest piqued. "This medicine has been around for that long?" It had to have some therapeutic effects.

"Some say a dragon trapped underground is the source of its secret ingredient. Many have tried to find this beast but failed." He lifted his head to regard her. "I believe the rumor was created to spur business. No matter; Dragon Balm works. Attempts to analyze its components have not proved fruitful."

Falling silent, she paced the floor. Dikibie the dog—and she felt like an idiot calling him that—had demanded a drop of dragon's blood from a creature who lived on the mountain. Was there truth, then, in the doctor's tale?

Paz couldn't travel in his current condition, and she had no idea where to get a false passport even when he recovered. If there was any kernel of truth in what the Gatekeeper said, she should follow it through. Jen didn't see that she had a choice.

Torn between wanting to do the right thing and longing to go home, she considered what would happen when she arrived in New York. She'd check in at work, catch up on mail, and confirm their plans for Fashion Week. All of that seemed so mundane compared to invaders from another dimension.

And if that had proven real, why not a dragon?

"How long until he recovers?" she asked after the doctor had finished his work and she'd settled their bill.

Paz lay slumbering peacefully, his wound clean and bound. Dr. Wong had helped her remove his boots and the tattered remains of his clothes. He rested under the sheet in his underwear.

"For his injured tissue to heal completely, six to eight weeks. For your man to get back on his feet, a day or two. Twice a day, clean the wound, apply the ointment, and put on a fresh dressing as I showed you. Advise your husband to take it slow."

Jen felt warmed by his use of the word, husband. "Thank you so much, doctor. And please, keep this visit confidential between us. If anyone asks—"

"Yes, I know. He had a serious burn from a curling iron." Dr. Wong winked before turning on his heel and departing.

Jen shut and locked the door, then spun around. With Paz settled, she could take care of herself.

She showered and washed her hair, changing afterward into her sole nightshirt. Another trip to the shopping mall was in order should they have to stay here much longer.

In the meantime, she called the airport just in case Paz made a miraculous recovery and she found a black-market vendor for fake passports. Flights were still backed up from the storm, and one of the runways remained closed.

She called her dad, reassured by the hearty sound of his voice. "It's going to take me a few more days to get there."

"I'm sorry to hear that, Jennifer. Where are you?"

"We're still in Hong Kong. All the flights are booked."

"I hope you're not delaying your return because you've shacked up with that guy you mentioned. Our company is facing a serious challenge, and you're needed at home."

"I know, and I'm sorry."

"You don't understand. Your cousin Clifford is attempting to compromise your shares with false accusations."

Her grip tightened on the receiver. "Exactly what is he saying about me?"

Robert Dyhr cleared his throat. "I can't tell you over the phone. Your mother and I must speak to you in person before you confront the Board. If you don't show up soon, they'll accelerate the vote and approve the merger without you."

"Why can't I just send a proxy?"

"It's a personal issue. You need to reassure the directors of your position and quell Cliff's influence."

"I'll get there soon as I can."

"Let me send our company jet this time."

"That won't help. The airport is having issues. Besides, Paz lost his passport."

"Oh, great. How well do you know this guy? I hope he isn't taking advantage of you."

Jen gritted her teeth. "You can check him out for yourself when I bring him home." Static sounded on the line.

"What? You're bringing him here?"

"You heard me." She'd love to see the look on her parents' faces when she introduced them to Paz.

More static. "This connection is bad. Why don't you buy a cell phone with an international plan? I need to be able to reach you."

"I'll think about it. Gotta go, Dad. Love you." She rang off before he had a chance to question her further.

After replacing the phone in its cradle, she sat on the free bed and folded her hands in her lap. Facing down dragons seemed easy in comparison to facing the music at home. Maybe she should ask Paz if a permanent place on his team was available.

Then again, what skills did she have to offer? Her fashion sense? Nor could she turn her back on the career she'd worked so hard to build.

A moan from Paz drew her attention. A few quick strides took her to his side. She sank down next to him, stretching out lengthwise.

His warmth penetrated her skin, providing a sense of comfort. He made her feel useful, even when she stumbled along not knowing her way. His lovemaking made her feel special, especially when the shy, plain girl inside craved approval. And his strength made her feel protected, even when she was the one caring for him.

She stroked his arm, relishing the solidness of his muscle

and the maleness of his hair-roughened skin. Burying her face in his shoulder, she prayed for his swift recovery.

Right now, getting him better was the only thing that mattered.

Then they had a dragon to slay.

Chapter Sixteen

It took two days for Paz to be back on his feet enough for them to attempt a trip to Dragon Balm Gardens. He still walked with a limp, but the wound was starting to fill in. It hurt like hell as the effects of the ointment wore off. He hoped to buy a few more pots of it at the park.

They didn't know what to expect so took along their full gear to be prepared. Aware this was another tourist attraction, he didn't want to take chances. Who knew what scourge would lurk in the shadows?

He would have scoffed at the notion of a dragon if the talking canine hadn't mentioned one first. If the creature truly existed, they would get the dragon's blood and bring it to the shapeshifter. Hopefully, he would keep his promise to reward them with a ship.

It all sounded absurd, but so did everything else about this mission. He'd ceased to wonder at the mystical aspects and just focused on his immediate tasks.

He glanced at Jen, who stood beside him in line at the ticket booth. She could have caught a flight home later this afternoon but refused to leave him. His heart swelled at her loyalty, knowing how important it was for her to get to Florida. She'd argued with her father as a result of the delay.

Guilt assailed him, but he brushed it aside. Even without his influence, Jen was involved in this battle. If not for him, she'd be dead by now.

And vice versa. He had little recollection of getting back to the hotel from Manga World. She'd taken charge of his care, waiting on him and treating his wound as the healer showed her. Her steadfastness, devotion to duty, and adaptability broke every preconceived notion he'd had about spoiled, rich women.

He wouldn't call the females he normally dated ladies, but Jen suited the term. She carried herself with confidence, looked fabulous in anything she wore, and took charge when necessary without blinking an eye.

Normally he avoided women with a lifestyle similar to his cool, distant mother. But Jen was different. She had heart, and somewhere along the way in their short relationship, she'd stolen his. Her gentle touch bespoke her true nature, and it belied the worldly image she presented.

He supposed her job required her to appear as sleek and sophisticated as her models, but inside hid a woman with vulnerabilities like his own. Maybe they were more alike than they realized.

Hoping to still accompany her home via a commercial airliner, he'd left their room earlier to hunt for a passport. His inquiries drew the wrong kind of attention. Instead of making contact with a black-market dealer, he saw one fellow signal an enforcer. *Police officer*, he corrected himself.

He got away and slipped inside an Internet café in an attempt to contact his team again, but no one responded to his hail. They must be observing radio silence.

Worry gnawed at him for Kaj's safety. He should have tried to gain more intelligence from General Morar on where his friend was being held.

Frantic to return to Florida to retrieve his equipment and contact his friends, he'd returned to the hotel. They'd had no choice except to go the route involving magical beings and myths.

His chronometer now read thirteen hundred hours on Saturday afternoon. The air was hot and heavy and scented with a sweet floral fragrance. Thunder rumbled in the distance. He hoped they could complete their business at Dragon Balm Gardens and leave before it rained.

While he'd recovered in their hotel suite, Jen had visited the adjacent shopping mall again and mailed several purchases to her New York showroom. He liked how her eyes lit up when she described clothing items. She wore jeans with a V-neck top and short boots in antiqued brown leather.

He wore a navy shirt tucked into a fresh set of denims with a leather belt. She'd selected the brass buckle herself to replace the one he had given Smitty. Shopping for him seemed to delight her, and who was he to deny a woman pleasure on his behalf?

After Jen paid their entrance fee, they passed through the turnstile. She pointed to a vendor stand just beyond where they stood.

"Look, Paz, the symbol on that sign matches the logo on your tube of Dragon Balm."

He adjusted his backpack. "Maybe that old man sells the stuff. Let's buy some now. We might be in a hurry to leave later on."

They strode over. Jen frowned at the different sized containers and the labels written in Chinese. "How do we know which one to get?"

He addressed the vendor in a native dialect. "I need the ointment for treating burn wounds."

The older man gave a gap-toothed grin from under his wide-brimmed hat. "These jars contain topical analgesics, good for muscle aches and pains. Also useful for the chest if you have bad cough. For more concentrated salves, you have to get prescription from healer and visit herbalist."

Paz translated to Jen. "He says I'd need an order from a healer for a higher strength balm and would have to get it filled at an herbal shop."

"Does this stuff have any antibiotic properties?"

He asked the vendor, who regaled him with the balm's many benefits. "All of these formulations work to some degree for the same problems," he told Jen. "I'll try the red jar. He says it's stronger than the white and may be all I need."

Paz bought several small pots with their leftover cash as people streamed past them on either side. With his peripheral vision, he kept watch for any suspicious movements, but no one paid them any particular interest.

He stashed the wrapped jars in his backpack. Now what?

Directly ahead were statues in colored plaster of historical figures and creatures of mythological origins. A diorama from Hong Kong's past stood by a cluster of yellow flowers and tall leafy plants.

Tropical shrubbery graced the paths which looked to be as winding as Shirajo Manor. What was it with these places and their mazes? He admired the genius behind the defensive tactic. It was certainly an effective method to trap your enemy.

Jen pulled a printout from her pocket.

"What's that?" He waved a hand at it.

"While you were gone this morning, I went to the hotel's business center and looked up dragons on the computer."

"What did you learn?" His mouth curved in appreciation. Whatever knowledge she had gained might prove useful.

The humidity caused the hair to curl around her face. She brushed a stray lock off her forehead. He watched her graceful movement, entranced by her slender wrist. He'd like to take her palm and swirl his tongue over her sensitive flesh.

"In Norse mythology, Fafnir was a giant who disguised himself as a dragon to defend his treasure. One of the items he guarded was a magic ring that brought its wearer unending wealth. However, the trickster Loki had taken that ring from the dwarfs who created it. The dwarfs were metal workers who made magical items for the gods."

"Like our friend, Smitty?"

She nodded. "The dwarf who originally guarded the treasure cursed the ring that Loki took. Now instead of creating wealth for its wearer, it would bring death. A descendant of Odin named

Sigurd killed Fafnir and stole his treasure. Sigurd ate the dragon's heart in order to understand animals. He bathed in the creature's blood to become invulnerable except he missed a spot on his shoulder."

Paz grimaced. "Sounds gruesome."

"Let me continue. Sigurd was in love with a Valkyrie named Brynhild. The Valkyries were virgin maidens who served Odin. They could fly and carried the souls of dead warriors to Valhalla."

He scratched his jaw. "Nira told us some of these stories but I don't recall this one. What is Valhalla?"

"It's Odin's Hall where the chosen dead lived in honor while they prepared for the final battle at Ragnarok, the end of all times."

According to the prophecy, Ragnarok was coming again. Loki wanted to bring chaos and destruction to the multiverse in revenge for the gods banishing him.

Paz kept his dark thoughts to himself. "You've certainly done your homework."

Jen beamed at him. "Listen to the rest. To mark his engagement to Brynhild, Sigurd gave her the magic ring he'd stolen from Fafnir without knowing it had been cursed."

"What happened?"

"He set off on a journey to a foreign court, where a magic potion made him fall in love with the king's daughter. When Brynhild found out he'd betrayed her, she persuaded one of the king's sons to kill Sigurd. The fellow pierced him at his weak spot on the shoulder. Brynhild repented and killed herself on his funeral pyre."

He tilted his head. "And what does this tale of woe have to do with us?"

"How can Fafnir be here if he's supposedly dead?"

Paz shrugged. "I guess we'll find out. Maybe this dragon has no relation to Fafnir in the myth."

"Well, if a real dragon exists, where would it hide?" She swept her arm to encompass the array of statuary, colorful wall murals, and lush plants.

Stone stairs took guests up and down the eight-acre hillside property. According to the guide map they'd been given with their tickets, faux caves, shrubbery, hidden alcoves, and picturesque ponds wound through the acreage.

"What about the house?" He pointed to a three-story palatial structure that stood atop a hill beyond a grassy slope.

The impressive building had a white lower level, red upper stories, and a curved tile roof. A green-covered mountain rose in the background. The scent of pine filled the afternoon air.

Bending her head, Jen consulted their brochure. "The Ra Mat family mansion is on the historic register. It has over five hundred relics and was built in the Chinese Renaissance style."

"There could be underground passages in a house that size."

"I suppose."

Moving on, they passed the statue of a man with a goat head and a painted tiger poised on a bright blue boulder. Paz winced at the gaudy colors. Apparently, others appreciated the art forms more than him, judging from the burgeoning crowd.

A spicy scent tickled his nose. He suppressed the urge to sneeze, swatting at an insect that droned by his ear.

The path took them on a circuitous route past a seven-story high white pagoda. A series of steps led to the entrance. Chinese lettering ran down the varnished wooden door.

"What's inside that place?" He stopped beside a mural featuring an azure sky and fluffy white clouds.

Against this placid background, two dragons spewed cords at each other. The cords made a symbol in the center that looked a bit like the mansion on the hilltop.

Jen perused the pamphlet. "The pagoda contains Buddhist relics and the ashes of monks."

Further along, they came to a scary statue of a husky man with big eyeballs, a wide sneer, and a muscular body. He carried a curved blade and looked as though he could come to life in an instant.

The next path wasn't much better. Paz glanced in horrified

fascination at ancient punishments depicted by grindstones to press a person to death, body stretchers to pull limbs apart, and tools to cut out tongues from gossipers and to sever hands from thieves.

"Ugh, this is awful. How can they show this stuff?" Jen scurried by the brutal scenes of torture.

"Some artist had a sick mind." Paz took the lead up a staircase alongside an artificial cliff where plaster monkeys sprawled in various poses.

At the next level, he halted to scour the landscape and to sniff the flower-scented air. No cors particles. That was a good sign. It meant the Trolleks didn't have a portal in the vicinity.

"We're not accomplishing anything. We need a plan." His leg throbbing, he lowered himself onto a boulder with a groan. Sweat made his shirt stick to his back.

Jen seemed impervious to the heat and the climb. Her chin jutted with stubborn persistence, while her stance indicated confidence. Despite his fatigue, he wanted to pull her into his arms and kiss her senseless.

"What if the secret ingredient for the balm really is dragon spit?" he said, feeling a bit lightheaded and trying to focus.

"If that's true, how did the dragon get here and why does it remain?" Jen withdrew a water bottle from her backpack and took a drink, reminding him to do the same.

He glanced around. "It would be ages old by now. Where would it hide for so many years?"

"Don't dragons always live in caves?" Her eyes brightened. "Maybe that's what happened in the first place. The original member of the Ra Mat family trapped it here."

Paz slurped water down his chin in his haste to drink. "So how do we find it? Let me see the map." His energy restored, he stashed the bottle in his backpack and unfolded the brochure.

Squinting at the diagram, he studied the terrain as he would a battlefield. There had to be a tunnel running from the house to the dragon's lair. The creature would have to be fed and watered.

His ears perked up. He'd heard the wind and the chatter of guests and the tinkle of chimes. But now as he listened acutely, he picked up the sound of a trickling stream.

He stood abruptly, clutching the map. Despite the fake rocks, this entire park sat on a real mountainside.

"I'll wager there's a brook that goes underground at some point to supply the dragon with drinking water."

She adjusted her sunglasses. "So what? Even if we find where it disappears into a crevice, we can't enter there."

He pointed to a nearby mural depicting flying creatures by a set of heavenly gates. "One of these displays might hide a door."

"Where it could be discovered by landscapers? Why wouldn't it be somewhere on the real mountainside?"

"The irony. I'll bet the Ra Mat brothers built this place for the sole purpose of disguising their activities. Just like Shirajo Manor, the winding trails and twisted paths were designed to confuse the enemy and protect their secrets. Confuse and Conquer. I shall have to relay this strategy to Prince Zohar."

"*Prince* Zohar? I thought you said he was your team leader."

Jen had meant to question him about this earlier. Hadn't it been General Morar who'd mentioned the royal title?

She hadn't thought to bring up the subject in their hotel room when she'd described to Paz all that had occurred to her at the Trollek fortress, including what she'd learned from Algie.

Paz straightened his spine. "Zohar Thorald is Captain of the Drift Lords and Crown Prince of the Star Empire. When we vanquish the Trolleks, he will assume his rightful place as emperor. Nira Larsen has agreed to be his bride. They have many problems to overcome, including political dissidence at home."

"Oh." Jen didn't ask where Zohar's home was located. She could barely grasp the concepts of ancient myths coming to life and aliens from other worlds. It behooved her to meet Nira as soon as possible.

Paz strode toward the sound of the water. Jen kept pace, observing how he favored his injured leg. The exertion must be hurting him. He'd pinched his lips together, a frown creasing his brow. Stubborn man. He should let her find the stream while he rested, but she wouldn't dare suggest such a thing. It would injure his pride.

At the park's far border, a brook cascaded down a series of rocks. Beyond a perimeter fence, woods led uphill toward a summit. Was that the same peak where they'd landed after their sojourn at sea?

If so, it wasn't any coincidence. She'd learned that fate played a hand in how things were meant to be. If only she knew how to use her watch to take them to the places they wanted to go. That was the first item on her list to ask Nira to teach her.

"Here's where the water goes underground." Paz tracked the stream with his finger. Instead of emptying at a pool, it disappeared into a crack between two rocks.

"That doesn't help. Where can we find an entrance?"

He gestured to a shaded area with a bench under a leafy oak tree. "Over there."

The small grotto squeezed between angled walls was painted cobalt blue with plaster casts of dragons on either side. Rope-like cords spewed from their mouths as on the other display they'd seen. The cords joined in the center to form a similar symbol resembling the mansion on the hill.

Jen's heart accelerated. "Wait a minute. Show me your Dragon Balm jar."

He took one from his sack, and she pointed to the label. "Look, this logo matches that drawing on the wall."

His eyes gleamed. "These murals must be clues. I'll bet they're scattered throughout the garden. Maybe this one hides the entrance to the passages below. It's closest to where the stream vanishes into the mountain."

"Then we're on the right track. What next?"

"We'll search for a door."

He put away the jar and then approached the recess for a closer examination. Jen, adjusting her backpack, followed at his heels.

Twigs and dead leaves covered the ground. When she'd kicked them away, a swirl of inlaid stones drew her attention. Shaped in a semi-circle, the ends curled inward. She bit her lower lip, concentrating. Surely that wasn't a natural formation? It looked too perfect, like combed Japanese serenity gardens.

While she contemplated what it meant, she withdrew a couple of energy bars from her sack and offered one to Paz. They munched for a few minutes in silence.

Paz stuffed his empty wrapper into a pocket and moved toward the grotto walls. He pressed his hands around the enclosure. Nothing happened. A scowl marring his features, he pushed at the faux jade flowers cemented into the rear wall. His shoulders hunched as he prodded the solid surface.

Jen wrinkled her nose. "Do you smell that? Come over here. Ugh, it reminds me of the dead lizards we used to find in our garage at home."

She glanced down. How could they be so stupid as to overlook the obvious? "Paz, the entrance is right here beneath our feet."

"You may be right." He started to kneel, but his face went white. "Would you mind?"

Jen crouched and used a stick to brush aside the loose dirt by the fixed stones. A metal handle poked up from the earth where she'd cleared the soil. She tossed aside the piece of wood and yanked on the bar. Her arm muscles bunched. Finally, with a cloud of dust, a square section of ground lifted up. She propped the lid open, weighting it with a couple of heavy rocks.

Paz peered at their surroundings. "No one is around. We're clear to go."

"Give me your flashlight." She aimed the light at the hole. "There's a set of stairs. You should stay here while I scout below. I know your leg is bothering you."

"I've had worse. I'll be fine."

"Are you sure?" At his sardonic look, she gave up trying to convince him otherwise. "Okay, then you can take the lead. Age before beauty."

Paz raised his brows. "Are you saying I'm too old for you?"

She rolled her eyes. "It's another slang expression, Paz. Move on before someone comes this way." In preparation for the climb, she fished in her pocket for a scrunchy and tied her hair into a ponytail.

The foul smell brought bile to her throat as they descended. At the base of the stairs began a tunnel. Sensors must have been planted because electric lights mounted on the walls flared on at their approach.

Paz put away their flashlight and brought out his PIP. "There's a whole network of passages down here. One branch leads toward the family mansion." As they came to a fork, he stopped.

One path led upward, the other down. Paz signaled they should take the lower road.

Jen watched her footing as they descended deeper into the mountain. The damp air was cool, but it felt good after the heat of day.

A deep rumble came from somewhere ahead. The resonance made her nape prickle. What was that unearthly sound?

Her sense of dread increased. She didn't want to find what creature waited for them in the dark.

Chapter Seventeen

Paz called for a breather after they'd traveled down a particularly steep incline. His thigh burned as though hot tar dripped onto his flesh. He gritted his teeth against the pain. If he didn't apply some salve, he couldn't go on.

He sank to the ground, leaning against a rocky wall. A steady dripping noise sounded in the underground chamber, where a dank, foul smell made his nose wrinkle.

He laid his sack down and rummaged inside for a jar of Dragon Balm and a fresh bandage.

"You shouldn't have come," Jen chided, regarding him with concern. "You won't be strong enough to fight that monster."

"Don't worry, I'll manage." He laid out the supplies.

"Here, let me do that for you." She plucked the Latex gloves from his hands and proceeded to treat and redress his wound.

He thought it looked better. Indeed, the ointment seemed to accelerate healing, but his leg wouldn't be one hundred percent for a while.

When she'd finished, Jen packed away his medical stores. He'd never had a woman fuss over him before and appreciated her care. But now wasn't the time to think about what she meant to him.

Once the welcome numbness from the salve seeped into his skin, he prepared to explore further. First, he took a reading on his PIP. "Two thermal figures are showing dead ahead on this route, one small and one huge."

"The dragon and someone else?"

"Apparently so."

Paz leveraged to his feet and slung the backpack straps across his broad back. Wishing he had a laser weapon, he motioned for Jen to follow in his wake.

"Wait." Her eyes appeared luminous in the reflected light. Wisps of hair had come loose from her ponytail and floated about her face. Pale, anxious, and tired, she still looked amazing.

She reached him and grasped his face, planting a kiss on his mouth. "For good luck. It's an old Earth custom."

He smiled, tracing her cheekbone with his finger. "I like that one, *leera*. You can show me more later." His voice sobered. "Do you have the vial?" They'd brought a container in which to capture the dragon's blood to bring to the canine.

Jen nodded. "It's in my bag." He took point, switchblade in hand.

As they progressed through a series of passages that appeared to be natural formations from the mica imbedded in the rock and the occasional stalactite, a roaring noise came from ahead. It echoed against the underground chambers and made the ground vibrate underfoot.

"Uh-oh. If that's the creature, it sounds angry." Jen's voice quaked. "Do you think it knows we're here?"

"I'm not sure. If it's distracted by company, we may be a surprise."

They approached the next bend carefully. Paz's eyebrows shot up as he peeked around the corner. An enormous reptilian creature battered its tail against a bamboo gate. On the other side stood a short Chinese fellow poking at its belly with a long pole.

"How come your drool has dried up?" the man said in fluent English. "You haven't given me enough to fill this bucket. Ra Mat Shlom will not return to the surface empty-handed."

"Grrr." The dragon growled, his eyes fiery slits. "I am getting old and still you mistreat me."

Paz exchanged glances with Jen. Should they have expected anything less than a talking beast?

"You will split into this receptacle or pay the price." The Asian magnate glowered at the hapless creature.

To emphasize his request, Ra Mat Shlom replaced his pole with a spear and jabbed the dragon. It screamed and recoiled.

"You feel the sting of the pepper wasp poison, do you not? Fill this bucket now, despicable reptile, or I will do worse."

"Starve me or torment me, I do not care." The dragon's nostrils hissed steam. "It is time I die."

"Then you'll never learn where your people live."

"You will never free me, so what does it matter?"

"Legend says the one who chooses the correct ring will be your liberator. Do you not care to see if this story is true?" The man laughed, a harsh sound in the hollow cavern.

Fire whooshed from the creature's mouth but didn't touch his caretaker. "You lie. No human exists who can resist temptation. Who do you bring me next to feed my wrath?"

"Those two unfortunates spying on us." He whirled around at the same instant as a net descended on Paz and Jen.

The heavy rope knocked the blade from Paz's hand. His legs folded, his limbs twisting with Jen's as the net clamped tight. It encircled them and swung them into the air.

"An effective trap, yes?" Shlom, wearing a business suit, approached them with the swagger of a man accustomed to running his own industrial empire.

He carried the spear with which he'd stuck the dragon. Paz's gaze fixed on the droplets of blood at its tip. By Odin's grace, if they could get hold of that, those few drops would serve their purpose. They needn't confront the beast at all.

"Who are you? Did my dear friend, Wo Is Mi, send you to steal my formula? None of his agents ever return." Shlom snickered, his dark eyes appraising them.

"We're not here to steal anything. Cut us loose and we'll tell you why we came." Paz wagged his hand past the rope.

"Oh, you will talk. They all do."

Shlom pushed a knob on the tunnel wall and a grinding noise

sounded. Their net hoisted on a pulley before being dragged overhead toward the dragon's enclosure. Paz gripped the rope to steady himself. A section of the gate near the top slid aside. The cable jerked their net into the dragon's lair then stopped.

Paz watched the gate seal shut with a sinking sensation in his gut. He felt as helpless as a pig on a spit over a fire.

A breath from the dragon aimed a crackle of flames their way. It heated the air directly beneath them. His skin warmed as he wriggled to untangle himself.

"Stay still." Jen's voice rose in pitch. "You're making us swing more. Listen, maybe we can reason with the creature. It's trapped here just like us."

"Sure, go ahead." Doubtless many others had tried the same tactic and failed. "Do you still have a Swiss Army knife in your handbag?"

"Yes, you gave me a new one, remember?"

He grunted with the effort of movement, their bodies pressed close. "Just turn around a bit, will you?"

Another blast from the dragon singed the ropes and heated the air, making it hard to breathe.

Shlom's cell phone rang. He jabbered to the caller in his native tongue and then hung up. "I have to go. You find out who they work for before you eat them, Faffi. Understand? And no more talk of dying."

The dragon bared his teeth. "I will be happy to obey you this time, master. Thank you for the treat."

Shlom hefted his bucket filled with dragon slime and turned away. He took a different path than Jen and Paz, presumably one that led toward his mansion. Shlom must be the remaining descendant of the Ra Mat family, Paz figured. That meant the tales were true. This creature's spit was the secret ingredient in Dragon Balm.

Jen shrieked as another hot blast hit them. "Wait, we can help you," she called to the dragon. "If you're related to Fafnir, you'll understand when I say we're part of the prophecy."

"Ah," Paz cried. Jen's latest movement had twisted his leg. A jabbing pain shot through him as he attempted to ease his position. "Jen," he gritted between clenched teeth, "do you think that's wise? A descendant of Odin killed Fafnir and stole his treasure. If the legends are true, *you're* a descendant of Odin, too."

"The original Fafnir must be long dead." She addressed the dragon. "I am Jennifer Dyhr and I bear Odin's blood, the mighty God who created this world. I've come to make amends for our ancestor's actions and to set you free."

The dragon roared his ire. Steam wafted their way, but the flame just missed them. "Fafnir lived many ages ago. I am named after him. Your kind murdered him."

"I am truly sorry. As I said, we are here to make amends."

"What did you say about a prophecy?"

"Ragnarok comes again. This warrior came from the stars to prevent the great cataclysm."

"You lie." The beast's nostrils flared. "Humans cannot be trusted. You are thieves and brigands."

"I'm telling the truth. We've come at the behest of a Gatekeeper, one of our allies. He has been cursed into the shape of a dog. Only a drop of your blood can turn him back into his human form."

"Your lies amuse me." The dragon sputtered with laughter. Drool dripped down his chin, pooling on the ground.

Ra Mat Shlom would love to collect that, Paz thought irreverently. While Jen engaged the dragon's attention, he manipulated himself to access her purse. If he could get her pocketknife, he'd cut them loose.

He didn't have to bother. In the next instant, the dragon blew a thin flame at the knot holding the netting in place, burning it through. Suddenly he was free, tumbling to the earth. He landed with a thump on his side and a jarring bump to his sore leg that left him breathless.

"Thank you," Jen said to the dragon, giving Paz a quick concerned glance. She scrambled to her feet.

"I will merely eat you alive, human, rather than roasting you first. But you may take my test like all the others."

His large tail swept by as he turned to retrieve something from behind. The smell of sulfur in the air made Paz's nose wrinkle. He pushed himself upright.

The dragon whipped around to face them, holding two small gold bands in its claw. "One of these will bring you all the wealth you'd ever desire. Choose the right one, and you live."

Paz remembered the story. A dwarf had cursed the ring stolen from him so that its wearer would suffer an early death.

He leaned forward to examine the gold bands. One of them shone brightly like the nuptial rings he'd seen in jewelry stores. The other was dull with a dent here and there.

"The humble person would choose the dull ring," Jen pointed out, "like in the Indiana Jones movie with the chalice. You know, the Holy Grail."

"What are you talking about?"

"The greedy person would probably choose the shinier ring." Straightening her spine, she pointed to the dragon's claw that held the dull ring. "That one."

The dragon grinned, its pupils dilating and its nostrils flaring.

"No." Paz grasped Jen's wrist. "It's the other one with the polished surface. Think about it. The wearer is doomed to die. No one wears it for long. It's the shinier one."

"Choose, humans." Steam spouted from the dragon's nostrils. It stamped its feet in impatience, and the ground under them trembled.

Paz locked gazes with Jen. Her expressive brown eyes changed from doubt to trust.

"Very well. I agree with my partner."

His heart warmed. He liked how she referred to him. More than that, he liked how she trusted his choice with her life.

The dragon snorted and clawed at the dirt. Paz's pulse jumped. Had he been wrong? Would they be swallowed into its great mouth or fried to a crisp where they stood?

"You are correct, humans." The dragon cocked its head, its large eyes scouring them. "According to legend, the one who picks the right choice will free me."

"We'll do our best," Jen said in an earnest tone. "How did you come to be trapped here?"

Her hair had come loose and rained down her back. Even with smudges of dirt on her face, she looked magnificent. A surge of pride at her bravery swelled his chest.

She held her hands behind her back, clasping something in one fist. The vial! She must have taken it from her backpack after they tumbled to the ground.

Jen ambled toward the spear wound on the dragon's side. It oozed blood onto the beast's scales. She must be aiming to collect a few drops.

No, he wanted to shout. *It's too risky.*

"One of the original Ra Mat brothers captured my egg and brought me here. After I hatched, they raised me. I have been here my whole life."

"That's horrible. May I call you Faffi? I'm sorry you've been alone for so long. We'll help you get free." She neared the creature's side. It hung its head and didn't notice her approach or else it didn't care.

"She's right." Paz stepped forward into the dragon's line of vision. "How many ways out of here are there? I presume one tunnel leads to your keeper's house, and the other path we followed leads to the gardens above. Are there any other routes?"

The dragon shook its head, nearly knocking Jen aside. She recovered quickly and moved a few paces closer.

"You poor thing," she crooned. "May I pet you? We should be friends if we're going to help each other."

Before the creature could protest, she laid a hand on its scales. With her other hand, she scooped some blood into the vial where it had oozed down from the wound.

The dragon shrugged her off. "I let you live. That is my favor to you. Now keep your promise to set me free, or I'll change my mind."

"You've grown too big to take out through the tunnels," Paz mused, scratching his bristly jaw. "And that gate must be fireproofed if you haven't brought it down by now. Nor do we have any explosives. There must be another way." He thought about the training exercises he'd performed and how his team had accessed enemy facilities. "What about the water?"

"What do you mean, human?" the dragon thundered.

From the corner of his eye, he noticed Jen stashing the stoppered vial in her bag. "Where do you get drinking water?"

Fafnir's nostrils flared. "I will show you. Do you wish to keep the gold ring you have earned?"

"No, thanks, not when it comes with a curse."

The dragon secured the rings inside a flap on its great body and then stomped off. The ground shook with its footsteps.

Paz grabbed Jen's hand and scurried after him. The beast ducked into a tunnel, his drool dribbling in his wake.

"Shlom should bring his dipper in here," Jen whispered at Paz's elbow. "There's plenty of dragon spit for his formula."

"Too bad for him." He grimaced. "This place stinks."

The slope declined, and Paz winced as his legs compensated. The constant trauma wasn't helping his wound.

Jen let go of his hand to zip along as though the cooler temperature enervated her.

She made a great partner. He glimpsed her profile, his heart quickening at the sight of her delicate features, feminine curves, and determined stride. How he'd like to lose himself in her sweet embrace.

Stop it, he ordered himself. *You can't afford distractions.*

Down, down they went. The rush of water grew louder and became a splashing, tumbling roar.

When they broke out of the tunnel, Paz stopped and gasped. A river flowed in front of them beneath a short bank. The water dropped out of a hole at the right side of the underground chamber and disappeared into blackness at the opposite end.

The dragon snorted. "Here is where I drink."

Fafnir led them by a small culvert where the water diverted into a pool. As they watched, Faffi lowered his head and slurped the liquid into his mouth.

With water dribbling down his scales, he raised his head and glared at them, his eyes narrow slits.

"So, humans, where is your way out? If you tricked me, I shall eat you now." To emphasize his threat, he blew a small flame into the air.

Paz pointed to the far side of the cavern. "That has to lead somewhere. I'd expect the water flows down the mountain toward the base. We only need to follow the current."

Jen poked him. "How do you know that passage doesn't narrow farther along? Or, the stream may continue underground with no outlet. We should look for another tunnel leading to the surface."

"My PIP didn't show any other routes. This is our best chance." He addressed Fafnir. "We'll build a raft. Didn't I see some bamboo stalks leaning against a wall in that cavern earlier?"

"My caretaker gives me those sticks to chew on."

"We can lash them together with rope from the netting."

"Are you saying we should ride the water, human?" The dragon's breath seared them with heat.

Paz gave a firm nod. "That's right."

A tongue of flame lashed at them. "You wish to kill me. I am not a fool."

Grabbing Jen's arm, Paz scuttled backward. "You're wrong, we're trying to help you escape."

"Dragons cannot go in the water. It would quench my fire and melt my bones."

Paz gaped at the beast. "Who told you that?"

"Ra Mat Shlom has warned me." The dragon's eyes glowed red. "You try to deceive me. I will eat you now." It opened its mouth, showing a display of jagged teeth.

Jen jerked her hand out of his and raced to the water's edge. Stooping, she scooped some liquid into her hands and then splashed it onto the beast's scales.

"Look, nothing happened! We're telling the truth. Shlom has lied to you to keep you imprisoned here. You could have escaped through the river at any time. Let us prove it. If we use a raft, you'll barely get wet."

"Faffi doesn't go near the big water."

Jen sashayed toward the creature, while Paz feared for her safety. "I understand that you're afraid." She petted him on his huge body. "So are we. And if we're willing to take the risk, why wouldn't a brave, handsome dragon like you?"

Fafnir shuffled his feet. "You think I am handsome?"

"I do, and when you reunite with your people, maybe you'll find a mate who feels the same."

The dragon lowered its head until its eyes met hers. "How will I find my kind? I was stolen as an infant. Dragons are things of legend now. Maybe I am the last one."

He sounded so forlorn that Paz almost felt sorry for him. "When you're out in the sunlight, you'll be able to fly," he said. "You can soar high and far to search. At least you'll be free."

The beast nodded, its head inadvertently knocking Jen back a few feet with a *whump*. She landed against a wall, her backpack taking the impact.

"Very well, humans. I have nothing to lose."

The next few hours saw Paz fastening the bamboo poles into a raft using the ropes from the netting. Jen used her penknife to cut them into even lengths, aided by the dragon's short bursts of flame. It was brutal work, especially in the noxious atmosphere. A musty odor combined with the beast's stench made his stomach churn.

After finishing their rough craft, they tied it to Fafnir's tail and let him drag it to the riverbank. Paz unfastened the leading rope from the dragon and knotted its end around a sturdy boulder. It took some heavy maneuvering to get the craft poised over the water's edge.

He dropped it onto the current, watching the mooring line go taut. Good, it would hold for now.

While the dragon used its teeth to hold the raft in place, he and Jen lowered themselves over the edge. Once they had secured themselves, it was Fafnir's turn.

"Easy now," he cautioned. "Your weight could capsize us."

The great beast hesitated, snorting steam.

"Come on." Jen extended her hand. "We're here for you. You can do this."

Paz glanced at the rope. "I'd hurry if I were you. That won't last much longer."

The dragon crouched and rolled onto the raft. The whole contraption dipped into the water but then rose again to bob in the current. The rushing water strained their cable to its limit.

Already wet, Paz tied a safety line around himself and Jen and anchored it to a knot he'd created for that purpose.

"Ready?" He signaled the dragon to burn through the mooring fibers. His heart pumped rapidly as he remembered their last dunking in the sea. They'd been spewed from a serpent's belly that time. Was this ride destined to be as wild as that one?

Time to find out.

The last few fibers split apart, and the current slammed them downstream.

Chapter Eighteen

Jen clutched the safety line as their raft dipped, swirled, and plunged through a series of dark passages.

Hey, it's no worse than a water plume ride at a theme park.

Yeah, right. She clenched her teeth to keep from screaming.

Sitting beside her, Paz swayed as they skimmed down a slough. He bent with the motion like a piece of supple fabric, whereas she held herself rigid, her heart galloping, and her breaths shallow. Terror filled her at the thought of slipping into the cold depths.

If only she could wish them somewhere else, but squeezing her eyes shut and praying for deliverance had no effect.

How did the damn watch work, anyway? She needed to learn how to control the vector device as soon as possible. That would be one of her first priorities if they survived.

Paz's presence loaned her an iota of confidence. His courage facing adversity never faltered. He'd expect nothing less from his partner.

When did it happen that she felt lost without him?

Water sloshed her face and soaked her clothes. They whooshed around a curve, danced on the current, and then slewed down a tunnel toward a roaring noise that made her pulse leap. She didn't even have time to take a breath or warn Paz. In the next instant, they were sailing through the air over a waterfall.

Miraculously, their craft landed right side up, bounced, and crashed onto the current with a spray of foam. The water calmed, and they floated toward the opposite bank of an underground lake. Glowworms on the ceiling illuminated the cavern.

Jen pushed her sodden hair out of her face. "We have to be near the outlet, but I don't see any daylight."

Fafnir snorted. "If we are trapped here, I will fry you before I eat you. This had better end soon."

Paz gave Jen a reassuring pat. "Just hold on. It can't be much longer."

Was that a note of doubt she heard in his voice? She glanced in the direction the current was pushing them. The river disappeared into another dark passage.

"Maybe we should get off at the opposite bank and try to find a way out of here on dry land." Her voice sounded hoarse in the echoing chamber.

"That might not be a bad idea. Unfortunately, we have no oars, and we're picking up speed."

Something rammed into them from below and nudged them toward the opening at the far end. The ceiling narrowed overhead, and Fafnir had to duck as the water sluiced them onward.

They entered another tunnel, careened around a curve, and raced down a slope.

"Look, there's light ahead," Jen cried.

The current slowed, and the flowing river narrowed into a stream heading toward a growing brightness.

When they burst into the fresh air and late afternoon sunlight, she threw her arms around Paz.

"Oh, thank God. We made it." She buried her face in his neck.

They came to a jarring halt against a rock barring their progress. The brook meandered on, presumably toward an outlet by the sea.

Paz disengaged himself, and Fafnir burned through the rope they'd used as their safety line.

The dragon didn't wait for their thanks. He leapt to the riverbank and turned his fiery eyes on them.

"You have kept your word, humans. I owe you a debt, but I repay it by not consuming you. Pray we do not meet again."

He flapped his wings, and with a mighty bellow, lifted into the air. By the time they reached dry land, he was a distant speck in the sky.

Paz turned to Jen. With her hair plastered to her head and droplets of water running down her face, she looked like a pale waif caught out in the rain. She shivered in her wet clothes, her teeth chattering.

He drew her into his arms to share his warmth. "Are you alright?"

She nestled her head on his shoulder. "I'm not cold, just glad to be alive. You?"

He grimaced. "I'll be fine, although I could use another application of Dragon Balm."

She sprang back, her eyes wide. "Omigod, do you know what we just did? We took away the source of the secret ingredient. Ra Mat Shlom won't be able to produce any more of the miracle drug."

"Likely Shlom will keep manufacturing it anyway. Who'll know the difference?" He took out his PIP but like their backpacks, it was soaking wet. Neither one of them had thought to pack their supplies in waterproof materials. "Great, this is useless. Where are we?"

Jen peered at their surroundings. "I think we're on the other side of the mountain. What do we do now?" She checked the vial. Fortunately, it was still intact. "I'd better keep this in my pocket for safekeeping."

"Dikibie said he'd meet us at the entrance to the gardens."

"Ugh, I hope there's a shortcut. I don't relish walking around while sopping wet."

He stepped closer, putting his hands on her shoulders. "You did good, *leera*. I can think of no one else I'd want by my side." Bending his head, he kissed her.

****

Jen's blood warmed as she stood in his strong embrace. She let him plunder her mouth, tasting salt on his tongue and sniffing the lingering scent of hemp on his body. Mist swirled around her, turning into the all too familiar white haze blocking reality from view.

When it cleared, another vision met her eyes.

Wind whistled at the wharf where she stood in the arms of her husband, a Viking warrior. He patted her hair and murmured soothing words into her ear. About to leave on a long journey, he'd provisioned their dwelling for the winter, but she'd left the safety of their hut to see him off.

Her belly prevented their bodies from fully touching. She looked down at her pregnant form with a sense of fear.

"What if you're not back in time? I cannot raise a babe without its papa."

"You're strong, wife. You'll be fine. If you doubt my word, consult the Book of Odin. The All-Father has recorded his wisdom there. You who share his blood need not be afraid. Our babe will have the gift and will pass it on."

"But I am afraid for you..."

"Jen, what's wrong?" Paz's sharp tone snapped her back to reality.

She must have frozen, because he'd broken off their embrace. He stood a few paces away, staring at her with concern.

Jen gazed into his steadfast blue eyes. "I had another vision. I was on the wharf again, and I wasn't alone. M-my husband was there, about to sail off on a Viking ship. He mentioned a Book of Odin."

"What do you think it means?" Paz wrung out his shirt. Droplets of moisture spewed everywhere.

Hopefully, the warm air would dry out their clothes soon enough.

Jen shrugged. "Who knows? Let's talk about it later. We need to fulfill our bargain with the dog."

"It may be too far to walk, especially in our condition. Let's find a road and ditch a ride."

Her mouth curved in amusement. "You're still getting it wrong. It's *hitch* a ride, tiger."

Dragon Balm Gardens had closed for the day by the time they made it back to the park entrance via public transport. No one would stop to give them a ride in their bedraggled state, but they'd found a bus. They exited at the designated stop, the sole visitors at seven o'clock in the evening.

Loitering by the ticket booth, Jen observed the setting sun glint off the harbor and the spectacular cityscape below. Her shoulders slumped. If they had to stay at a hotel again, they'd have to go shopping for more supplies.

She glanced around, wondering why the Trolleks left them alone. General Morar had unfinished business with Paz, and Algie wanted Jen for her experiments. Was the enemy holding off for some reason?

A breeze lifted the hair on her arms and brought a floral scent her way. All she'd cared about before meeting Paz was how she looked in front of the mirror and what impressions her fashions made on the world.

Now as her glance slid toward the silent warrior at her side, she thought about what he could teach her. Weapons and combat skills. How to infiltrate enemy territory. What weaknesses to exploit among the Trolleks, if any.

Her brow wrinkled. Why did that last thread stimulate a figment of memory?

Arf, arf.

Her head lifted. A small dog bounded in their direction.

"Dikibie, this way." She clapped her hands, skidding sideways to intercept him. He scooted past, dodged an oncoming bus, and aimed downhill. Not the Gatekeeper, then.

"Maybe we should just go to the airport," she said with a resigned sigh. She barely had the energy to move, let alone haggle with airline personnel. Nor did Paz have a passport.

Frantic barking came from her left, and she whipped around. A familiar mutt scampered toward them, a pretty brunette on its tail. The woman had murder in her eyes and a weapon in her hands.

"Come here, Dikibie." The female waved her gun. "You're not getting away this time."

The dog zigzagged toward them. "Stop her," he said. "She means to kill me."

Paz thrust Jen behind him. "It's that Trollek woman we met in the fabric shop. She's got an immobilizer. Stay out of range."

Jen gazed around but they were quite alone. The bus had moved on, disgorging no one. Birds twittered overhead and leaves rustled. An insect buzzed her ear.

Paz's eyes narrowed at the same time that Jen noticed the Trollek's attention changing to them.

"Ah, look who we have here. General Morar will be pleased." She swung her weapon at the Drift Lord.

Paz attacked in a flying leap, kicking the immobilizer from her hand. She responded with a roundhouse kick. He dodged the blow and brought his elbow up toward her nose. She twirled, rebounding with a thrust, and aimed at his gut. Paz parried but wasn't fast enough. Her next kick caught his injured thigh.

He grunted, his legs crumpling. Jen stared, horrified, as he went down. The woman leapt forward, stooped, and grasped his forearm.

"You will obey me. Heed your kabak."

"I don't think so." Leaning on his elbow, Paz sneered at her. "I'm a Drift Lord. Your spells don't work on me."

He swept his arm behind her ankles and yanked her off her feet. She tumbled to the ground.

Jen spotted the gun where she'd dropped it and scooped it up. The metal piece felt heavy in her hand. It had a long barrel, but where was the trigger?

"You, daughter of Odin."

Jen spun toward the source of the voice.

"It is I, Dikibie. Did you obtain the dragon's blood like I asked?" The scraggly dog tilted its head, peering at her with large, somber eyes.

"Yes, we did." She moved out of range of Paz and the Trollek.

Torn between wanting to conclude her business with the Gatekeeper and helping Paz, she tucked the weapon into her waistband. Getting home was paramount once Paz defeated his adversary. Thankful he still possessed some immunity to the Trollek mind spell, she focused on the shapeshifter.

"Part the fur between my shoulder blades," Dikibie instructed. "Take the blood and dribble it onto my bare skin."

Jen withdrew the vial from her pocket, yanked off the stopper, and did as directed.

Nothing happened for the first few seconds. She jerked back when the air around the dog suddenly rippled.

The ripple turned into a mini cyclone that swirled around the creature from its feet upward. Higher and higher the dervish flew until an older man stood before her in his naked glory. A bearded man, with a wrinkled face and a thin body.

A pontifical look on his face, he stretched his arms toward the heavens. "At last, I am free."

Jen's face colored. Spying a seagrape bush, she stalked over and plucked a couple of large, round leaves. "Here, you might want to use these until you get some clothes. Now, about our reward…"

"My thanks, mistress." Holding the leaves in place, he combed through his hair with his other hand. His fingers produced a folded paper. "Here is your prize. Go to the water's edge and announce where you want to go. As soon as the ship unfolds, climb aboard."

"That's it? A piece of paper? You've got to be kidding."

He puffed out his chest. "Do you question my gift?"

Afraid he'd withdraw the offer, she snatched the item from his hand. "No, of course not. Thank you for your generosity."

He sniffed the air, as though he hadn't quite lost his canine sense. "We'll meet again, daughter of Odin. It is prophesied in the book."

She gripped his arm before he turned away. "What book? I've heard one mentioned before."

He cast her a sly glance. "Seek your sisters. Together with the Drift Lords, you will defeat the coming darkness. So it is written. So shall it be."

"Wait, it's written where?" Jen called after him. He'd already started down the hill, giving her a not very tantalizing view of his bare butt.

"Hey, miss!"

Jen whirled around. *Now what?*

From the corner of her eye, she saw Paz still holding his own against the Trollek female. Huffing up the road from the opposite direction was the man she'd encountered at Manga World. She recognized the scar on his cheek when he got closer.

"What are you doing here?" she demanded.

Pausing to catch his breath, he thumbed toward the woman slicing her arms and legs though the air as she leapt and kicked at Paz. "I've been tracking her. I could ask you the same thing."

"Let me see your badge again."

This time she leaned forward to read it carefully. It gave his name as Agent Grant Monroe and said he was with the United States Bureau of Anomaly Research.

"What kind of agency is that? I've never heard of it."

His keen gaze regarded her. "No one has, lady. We like to keep it that way. Usually, we're sent out to debunk stories about alien abductions and UFO sightings, but this time—"

He stumbled back as Paz flew past them, thrown by the Trollek female. She wasn't even breathing hard while Paz looked pale with fatigue.

"Who is that guy?" Monroe pointed to Paz who picked himself up and lunged at the Trollek.

"He's my partner." Her voice held a note of pride. Despite his wound and their recent exertions, he fought like a true warrior.

Munroe's gaze swung to the weapon tucked into her waistband, and his eyes narrowed. "Where did you get that?"

"It belongs to that woman. She dropped it."

"May I?" He extended his hand.

Jen stepped back. "What do you want with her?"

"We have questions to ask." He took out a device from his pocket and frowned at it. "Tell me about your friend."

Jen bristled at the implied threat in his tone. "Look, if your business is with that woman, we won't stop you. Just keep in mind that we're on the same side." And with those words, she took out the immobilizer and tossed it to Paz in one of his free moments.

He shot the Trollek. She slumped to the ground. Then he aimed the weapon at Grant Munroe.

"Who is this fellow? Is he confounded?"

Like before, Monroe wore clothing that covered him from head to toe. Clearly, he knew what Trolleks were capable of doing to people.

He flashed his badge. "I'm an agent of the United States government. We should talk. I know your girlfriend isn't vulnerable to these creatures, and we'd like to know why. As for you," he squinted at his device, "I'm getting an anomalous reading. Who are you, and why were you fighting that alien?"

Paz's eyes glittered right before he fired the weapon. "Sorry, I don't have time to answer questions."

Jen gasped. "Did you kill them?"

"No, immobilizers only stun. They'll be out for a few hours. We should hide them." Grunting at the effort, he dragged their unconscious forms into the bushes. "There, that should solve the problem for the moment."

"You can't let Monroe wake up next to that Trollek. She might confound him when he's too groggy to resist."

"You're right, but we don't want Agent Monroe to capture her either. It sounds as though his agency believes the Trolleks to be aliens. Best they should stick to that belief."

"You think it's better they should think aliens from outer space are invading us rather than evil trolls from another dimension?" She glanced at him askance. "What about your team?"

His mouth curved into a sexy grin. "We're helping humanity. We don't need interference, especially if your people are provoked into what you term a witch hunt."

"I'm afraid it's too late if our government has caught onto the game. Anyway, we can worry about it later. I got the magic ship from Dikibie."

"Supernova! That's good news." He tucked the immobilizer into his belt. "I'll separate these two. Then when they wake up, they won't be near each other. Too bad I don't have my gear. I'd put a locator on the Trollek in case we needed to track her later. She might lead us to General Morar." He slung the female over his shoulder with a grunt.

"I should check your wound." Jen indicated his leg.

"Not now. Let's move on." He clenched his jaw as he lugged his burden down the hill.

They found a spot enough of a distance away and left the Trollek woman propped against a tree, so it looked as though she'd fallen asleep. Then they caught a tram to the waterfront.

Junks and sampans crowded the harbor as they strode along the walkway, looking for a quiet spot where they could unfold Dikibie's ship.

"Do you think this will work?" Jen stopped at a food vendor selling fish burgers after a detour at a public restroom. She ordered two meals to go and gave Paz his share.

"If not, we go to Plan B." He stared at the water while chewing.

Jen ate too fast, distracted by his determined profile, chiseled jaw, and unruly hair. He looked even sexier when disheveled. His attempts to wash up hadn't been much more successful than hers. At least the warm breeze helped to dry their clothes.

Much to her surprise, televisions flickered among the vessels in the harbor. She wondered where they hooked up to electricity. The aroma of garlic and onions wafted on the night air from cooking fires on board the boats. It mingled with the smell of fish and fuel.

"What's Plan B? Find a black-market dealer to provide you with a passport?" Jen tossed her trash into a nearby can.

Paz followed suit. "That's the idea. However, with a government agent breathing down our necks and a Trollek right behind, it's not the best option."

They continued along until they came to a dimly lit space just beyond a woman washing laundry at a street faucet.

"This looks like a good place to try our luck." Jen stood at the edge of the pier and withdrew the folded paper from her jeans pocket. "Dikibie said to mention where we want to go. As soon as it inflates or whatever it does, we should climb aboard."

"That piece of paper is supposed to turn into a ship?" He gave her an incredulous glance.

"Yep. Cross your fingers. I wish for us to go to Manhattan." She held the paper in both hands with her arms outstretched.

Paz faced her, his eyes blazing. "I thought you'd said you lived in Palm Beach. Aren't we going to Florida?"

She lowered her arms and met his stormy gaze. "I live in New York. My parents are in Florida. I need to check my mail, pay my bills, and contact my friends. Plus, it's almost Fashion Week. I have things to do at the showroom. Dad has postponed the critical vote, so I don't have to return to Florida just yet."

She didn't like the way his mouth tightened, as though she'd betrayed him.

"Look, I know you're anxious to meet up with your team. You can contact them from my place. You don't even know if your safe house in Florida exists anymore."

He pursed his lips. "True. However, Nira Larsen resides in Florida. It is imperative for you two to exchange information."

She'd forgotten about Nira. He was right. She had much to learn. "Okay, how about if we stop in Manhattan for one night at least? It would make me feel better to settle things there before confronting my cousin and the Board of Directors."

"Very well, but keep in mind that our enemy isn't far behind." He raked stiff fingers through his hair.

"It could be a moot point. This piece of paper hasn't done anything." She waved Dikibie's gift in her hand.

"Try again. Maybe it needed us both to agree."

"We wish to go to Manhattan," she announced in a firm tone.

As though the magic understood they meant it this time, the paper unfolded, jumped from her hands, and landed as a fully sailed motorized junk on the water.

A ramp extended to the dock.

Excitement making her heart race, Jen scampered aboard. As soon as Paz joined her, the ramp retracted. The ship creaked and swayed on the rippling current.

Then with a shuddering vibration, the engine started and the ship chugged out to sea.

Chapter Nineteen

As they sailed out of Hong Kong's harbor, Jen stood on deck watching the towering skyscrapers recede in the distance. Victoria Peak jutted toward the sky while lights twinkled on throughout the city like a theme park electrical parade.

A stiff breeze whipped her hair about her face, sending a shiver down her spine. The fresh sea air reminded her of the underground tunnels beneath Dragon Balm Gardens and how they could have been buried down there forever.

She took a deep breath, admiring the glittering skyline. Too bad they'd lacked the time or leisure to explore more of the city with its narrow alleys, shops, and crowded stalls. Nor had they made it to Kowloon or the outlying territories.

How many of those residents had visited Manga World and been compromised by the Trolleks? Were the invaders truly establishing sleeper agents throughout the world, individuals waiting for their command? That was a truly frightening thought, and one possibly shared by her government—judging from Agent Monroe's presence.

A green and white Star Ferry crossed the water in front of them. Their junk maintained a steady pace, navigating among the barges, freighters, and other ships clogging the harbor. She wondered about the route they would take and how many days they'd be at sea. Did the magic extend to providing food and water?

She turned toward the deck, scanning for Paz who'd disappeared below to do a quick reconnoiter. He meant to search for weapons in case unexpected visitors arrived. Was their ship visible to others? Or was it like a ghost ship, apparent only to them?

Since they'd be entering pirate territory, she hoped they had defensive capabilities. Not that Paz couldn't fight off any intruders. Her stalwart warrior seemed able to handle anybody, although their last fight had taken its toll. His wound hadn't fully healed, and their ordeal with Fafnir had exhausted him. She'd better see if he was all right.

The vessel dipped and swayed as the swells increased and they ploughed into the open sea. Wind rushed past her ears. Overhead, the three sails billowed like air-filled pockets. She steadied herself on posts and protuberances as she made her way to the hatchway leading below. At least an actual stairway rather than a ladder led down into the depths.

Her mouth dropped open as she hit the bottom landing. Unlike the fishing vessel run by Captain Kolami, this junk had a beautifully appointed interior. She couldn't have chosen more elegant fabrics herself for the upholstery in the main salon.

Peeking inside the spacious area, she took note of the teak cabinets and tables, the sofas with turquoise and gold pillows, and the polished dining room set.

"Nice, huh?" Paz sauntered into the room, hands in his pockets. "There's a fully loaded larder and a choice of cabins. It's a lot better than I expected."

His face creased into weary lines, his features testimony to what he had suffered. Her body stirred. The grubbier he looked, the more he appealed to her. Jen's parents probably figured they'd meet an American who was down on his luck. Wouldn't they be surprised when she showed up with a battle-hardened warrior in tow?

How would she introduce him, if she could convince him to meet her family? As a male model she'd hired for her showroom, or as a telecom expert who worked on space relays? Then they'd think he belonged to NASA or some other science agency. That wasn't such a stretch. Maybe they could come up with a plan together.

In the meantime, why not take advantage of this time alone? They'd hit the ground running in New York. Paz would want to contact his team while she dove into work. At least she'd sent Sandi a quick email from the Internet café. Sandi had everything under control for Fashion Week. Thank God for highly paid assistants who were competent at their jobs.

Jen stumbled as the deck underfoot lifted and fell. Paz rushed forward and grasped her elbow to steady her. Warmth shot up her arm where he touched her.

"Are you okay? You're not going to be seasick, are you?"

"I hope not." Jen shrugged him off and gazed at cabinets holding crystal wine glasses and porcelain dinnerware. They must have some sort of glue on the bottom to keep them in place. "Whoever decorated this room had exquisite taste. Look at those drawer handles. They're shaped like fishermen casting a line."

"I can think of other details I'd rather study."

She ignored his husky innuendo and strolled over to examine the label on a statuette. It was the Chinese goddess of mariners, Tien Fei. Well, at least it wasn't a fertility goddess. She didn't need that complication.

Jen cast a sly glance at Paz. He watched her from under his thick brows, a smirk on his face as though he knew the direction of her thoughts.

She turned away, pretending to admire the decor. What course would he take when they were back on shore? His team still had to destroy the generators keeping the rifts open, but that wouldn't end their mission. They still had much more to accomplish.

"We should get cleaned up," she said, convinced he'd be around town for a while. "Then we can grab a snack. I'm hoping we can find a good bottle of wine stashed somewhere."

His smile broadened. A gleam entered his eyes, one that made her feel special because she only saw it when he looked at her. Her appetite spiked for this man who aroused her like no other. She couldn't wait to feel his hard planes against her skin and taste his lips on hers.

Proceeding into the hallway, she glanced at a row of closed doors. "These are the cabins, I presume?"

She pushed one open and strode inside, impressed by the teak trim, wide bunk, and writing desk. A quick inspection showed a private bathroom with a shower and a closet holding a selection of clean clothes. What fabulous fabrics. She stroked a silk kimono, admiring the embroidered dragon on its back.

"Should I be jealous of the clothing?" Paz's teasing tone induced her to turn toward him. He leaned against the doorframe, studying her with an intent expression she recognized.

"That would imply you cared where my affections lie. Do you?" She sashayed toward him, her body craving his touch.

His gaze darkened to indigo. "I care enough that I want nothing or no one else touching you except me. I want to see your flesh bared before my eyes so I can feast on your beauty."

A lump clogged her throat. "You're just saying that to seduce me."

His eyes became liquid pools as he regarded her. "You surpass any of the stars in the universe, *leera*. I'm surprised you don't have suitors falling at your feet."

She laughed. "My feet stink. They'd chase away just about anyone right now. I need a shower."

"Me, too. Maybe we should share."

A glimpse at the facility discouraged that idea. It was adequate but tiny. She'd barely fit inside, let alone be able to wash her hair. She would have to shave her legs at the sink.

"I think not." She pressed her lips together. "Besides, I'm hungry. Those burgers weren't much of a meal. I need energy if we're going to, uh, you know."

A slow smile curved his mouth. "All right, I'll meet you in the galley. But afterwards—"

She cut him off with a dismissive wave. "Yes. Afterwards."

****

The sea must have calmed because during dinner, Paz barely felt the ship's motion. They'd put together a meal from the ship's stores and found a bottle of wine to accompany it. A leisurely dinner put him in a languid mood.

Too well-trained to let his guard down, he patrolled the deck while Jen washed dishes. A cooler wind prevailed, blasting his face and lashing his hair into his eyes. It was growing long but women liked it that way.

Sometimes when he worked in deep space on the relays, he didn't see a groomer for months. That only attracted women more when he made port. They liked his rugged image, and he was happy to oblige them with a rough and ready tumble.

He stuck his hands in his pockets and stared out to sea, a black void as dark as interstellar space. He'd meant what he said to Jen about her being a shining star in his universe. Around her, he felt like a moth to a butterfly. She was the exact opposite of the type he usually sought when planet-side, but he'd come to realize she projected an image, too. Inside the sleek, sophisticated businesswoman was a girl who doubted her own worth.

Paz understood those doubts, harboring the same ones about himself. And that's what scared him. Jen resonated with him on a deeper level than any other woman. They had more in common than either of them could admit aloud. Yet they still differed enough that she'd turn away from him someday.

Jen was goal directed and expected the same ambition from others. His warrior role earned her respect but not his everyday life. Once the danger subsided and the glamour wore off, she'd look for someone else more in line with her social status.

For now, though, he had her all to himself. If she cared to amuse herself with him, he wasn't about to deny them both the pleasure. He would fulfill her fantasy of bedding a Drift Lord and warrior of the Star Empire.

He'd walked away from relationships before. He could do it

again. They merely had to fulfill the prophecy and vanquish the Trolleks. Then he could leave when Jen had no further use for him.

He didn't put credence in the part where he and Jen were meant to be together. It seemed unlikely that things would work out that way. And yet why then did the prospect of living without her fill him with such regret?

****

Jen cleared the dishes while Paz patrolled the deck and made sure no one approached their vessel. They had no defense against Trolleks vectoring in, but perhaps the Gatekeeper had enhanced the magic to repel them. She didn't want to worry about that now.

In the small but adequate galley, she washed the dishes, dried them, and put them away. She'd made a casserole with canned chicken, peas, mushroom soup, and Parmesan cheese. Their stores had labels in English, which didn't surprise her, considering how the ship probably catered to its occupants. Too bad its special properties didn't extend to having fresh food onboard along with a chef and a steward.

She sensed Paz before she felt his hands on her hips from behind. He smelled like sea salt and fresh air.

"What's for dessert?" He nuzzled her hair, his hot breath wafting by her ear.

Jen's nerves surged into overdrive. "That depends. Do you think we are, um, free of any distractions for a few hours?"

"I didn't see any other vessels in the vicinity, if that's what you mean. And I don't think the Trolleks will be a threat while we're on this junk." He ran his fingers along her arms, tickling her skin. "Did I tell you how great you look in that sarong?"

No, he hadn't, but she'd seen it in his eyes when they met in the galley after she'd showered and changed. He wore jeans and a short-sleeved shirt. He had shaved but left a hint of a mustache and beard, just enough to give him a rakish look.

Jen turned around to face him directly. Their bodies nearly touched. Her breath hitched at his proximity and at the way his heated gaze probed hers.

"Why don't you show me what you had in mind for dessert?"

His mouth curved up in a disarming grin. "Your cabin or mine?"

"We'll use your digs, Drift Lord."

"Digs?" He squared his shoulders, straight and broad.

She couldn't wait to trace their wide breadth. Jen met his smoldering gaze. "Your place. We'd better save the talking for later. Things are getting lost in translation."

Inside his cabin, she kicked off her sandals. He locked the door as a precaution before turning toward her with a predatory gleam in his eyes.

"Lie down," he ordered. "I'll inspect your feet. Didn't you get blisters on our trek across Togura island?"

"They're better now. I put some of that Dragon Balm on my toes back in the hotel room." Her eyes widened. "What about your leg wound? I'm sorry, I should have—"

"I'm fine." He propelled her toward the bunk, yanked the coverlet down, and indicated that she should stretch out.

Jen lay on her back, feeling awkward. Her dress had hiked up and she yanked it down, settling onto the mattress.

She should be tending to him. He'd been injured. But obeying his commands gave her an erotic thrill. She waited for what he would do next while her body tingled in anticipation.

He sat at the edge of the bed looking like a cat about to drink its fill of milk. That made her think of a lapping motion and what he could do with his tongue. She squirmed, her skin so sensitized that when he took her foot in his hands, she jumped.

"Easy, I'm just going to massage your foot. Try to relax. You're too tense."

No kidding. Good God, what man had rubbed her feet before? None in her lifetime. Who would have guessed her brave warrior had such tender skills?

She moaned in pleasure as Paz rolled his thumbs up and down her sole, kneaded the ball of her foot, and squeezed each toe in turn. He rubbed her heel, stimulating her circulation, and applied pressure up the side of one foot and down the other.

"Aaahh." She closed her eyes.

The man might be a superb lover, but she reminded herself that he'd probably practiced his skills in every port he visited. Nonetheless, he made her feel like she was the only woman he wanted. However long it lasted, she wanted to savor that feeling of being special.

There seemed to be no barriers between them. They'd shed the trappings of society the instant the Trolleks had dropped that EM grenade in the airplane.

Fleeing for one's life can do that to you.

Unafraid in his presence, she lay open to his lavish attention. She didn't let her guard down easily, and Jen hoped she wasn't setting herself up for heartbreak later.

He switched to her other foot while she moaned and wished he would satisfy the ache between her legs. Obviously, he intended to take his time, because after finishing with her feet—which felt sublimely warm and tingly—he rotated her ankles one at a time. Then he pushed her dress up to mid-thigh level.

"You could be one of your own models. Your legs are perfect." His low, deep voice thrummed along her nerve endings like a room full of sewing machines working in tandem. The sound brought her joy and comfort.

She cast him a skeptical glance. "I'm not tall enough and I'd have to lose weight. Models are stick thin."

"You're lovely just the way you are." He massaged her calves and ran his knuckles up and down her lower legs.

Her thighs sagged open. She couldn't help herself. Streaks of heat imploded toward her core.

Did he really mean what he said, or was that one of his lines? No one had ever admired her looks until college, when she'd transformed herself into her mother's ideal of the perfect woman.

Either her chin was too angular, or her forehead too high, or her posture wasn't straight enough. She'd grown up with criticism on her appearance all through her youth. Even the men she'd dated had found something wrong, but they could overlook her defects because her family was rich. She'd never felt truly appreciated until Paz came along.

His fingers reached her thighs, and her perception narrowed.

"Oh, yes. Go there." He circled her inner flesh but still didn't stroke her where she wanted it the most. If he didn't do it soon, she would combust.

She wriggled her hand at him, letting him know she wanted to return the favor. He brushed her arm away.

"Later. We have all night. I want to do this first." With those words, he pushed her dress up to her stomach.

As she lay there, he drew her panties down and tossed them to the floor. Genuine admiration shone in his eyes as he regarded her half-naked form lying exposed before him.

"Stars, you are so beautiful. I can't wait any longer."

He lifted her hips with his hands and lowered his head between her legs. The first stroke of his tongue was like a lick of fire. It shot sparks through to the cauldron bubbling inside her.

Reason fled, and her concentration centered on one spot only. He flicked his tongue in a side-to-side movement right where it made the most impact.

She cried out, arching her back.

He kissed her swollen, sensitive folds then suckled her until she thought she'd die of pleasure. When he dipped his tongue down to taste her wet readiness, she gasped in passionate abandon. He probed and teased while she yearned for release. One more stroke in the right spot was all it took.

She jerked, her climax swift and violent. Spasm collided upon spasm until she lay sweaty and satiated flat on her back, legs spread open for his proud male perusal.

"Oh God, Paz. That was amazing." She waited for her breathing to regulate.

"I know." He stretched beside her, his long length pressing against her. His arousal bulged from his jeans. "Your scent drives me wild. I want to taste you all over. That wasn't enough." He nuzzled her hair, spread out on the pillow.

A shiver of delight ran through her as she imagined his hands on her breasts. She rolled sideways in his direction. "I want to feel you next to me, without these clothes between us."

His mouth twisted in a wicked grin. "Do you always give your men such orders?"

"Only you," she said truthfully.

"Then I must obey." He rolled off the bed and stripped away his clothing while Jen divested herself of her sarong.

After he resumed his position at her side, Jen splayed her hand on his chest, enjoying the silky feel of his hair. She didn't want to rush things.

He'd tormented her into submission. Now she would do the same to him.

Chapter Twenty

Paz sucked in a breath when Jen touched him. The mere contact of her hand on his chest electrified his skin. If he'd been aroused before, an explosion became imminent at the least provocation. Cupping his hand behind her head, he brought her face closer and brushed her lips with his. Her tongue flicked out in response, a teasing probe that only inflamed him more.

She pressed herself against him, squashing her soft breasts against his chest and entwining her legs around him.

Hounds of Hel, he could lose himself in this woman. Mist swirled in his vision, blocking out their surroundings until he was conscious of nothing but their naked bodies twisted together. Jen's labored breaths matched his own in a rapid, staccato tempo. She writhed against him, her mouth glued to his.

"Ah, *leera*, you drive me wild," he whispered when they came up for air. How could he let her go after he'd finished his mission? No other woman captivated him like she did.

Jen reached down and grasped his privates in response. He sucked in a sharp breath, replying in kind by caressing her breasts. Pleased to hear her gasp of pleasure, he brushed his thumbs across her nipples as his impatience burgeoned. She moaned and thrust herself further into his hands. He savored the feel of her lush softness.

Paz nearly lost it when her fingers scraped up and down his sensitive flesh and brushed across his slit. She must feel the moisture oozing from him, stimulated by her touch. His body tensed. He couldn't hold off much longer.

She swung atop him, her black hair spilling forward, her brown eyes blazing. In a heartbeat, she impaled herself upon him. Such exquisite torment! Her tightness enclosed him.

Jen thrust herself forward and back again, setting a rhythm, her eyes wide open, and her mouth parted. He stared up at her, passion clogging his throat. A maelstrom of ecstasy swept him in its path, hurtling him into a cyclone that burst through the clouds. He spurted into her with a triumphant cry as bliss overwhelmed him. Her release came subsequent to his, accentuating his finale. A haze wrapped around his mind, languid with satisfaction.

She collapsed beside him. He lay on his side, awed by how she made him feel.

A flare of alarm blossomed in his head as he thought of Nira, who possessed some Trollek DNA. The mythologist presumed this resulted from a Trollek and a human mating in the past. It was this inherent trait that fueled Jen's vector device. Could it also be why he felt so drawn to her?

Hybrid offspring of Trolleks and humans weren't unknown, but they'd never shown powers like the six women in the prophecy. As incredible as it sounded, Odin—king of the Norse gods—must have lain with a human female. Their progeny had then bedded a Trollek down the road. The prophesied women could be their descendants.

Regardless of her origins, Jen was bound to Paz. They had a destiny together. But was that all? Were they hardwired for each other merely to serve a greater purpose, or was there more substance between them? And if so, did danger serve as the cement to their relationship? Would Jen turn away from him once life returned to normal?

He couldn't answer that question until his team vanquished the Trolleks. And until then, survival came first. Otherwise, none of them would have to worry about a future because there wouldn't be one.

****

The ship's motion woke Paz hours later. Jen lay curled asleep at his side, stark naked, her hair splayed across her face. He brushed the strands away and drew a sheet over her before rolling off the bunk.

The deck tilted. He staggered as the ship rocked underfoot. It was moving a lot more than last night.

He squinted at the clock on the desk. Its luminous dial read 07:00 hours. Eager to check their status, he made quick work of washing his body and throwing on his clothes. He opened the curtains and dim light streamed inside.

"What's happening?" Sleepy-eyed, Jen leaned up on one elbow.

"It feels stormy. I'm going topside to check the weather." Creaking noises and a steady, dull thud punctuated his statement. "Hear that? Something must have come loose in the wind."

She groaned. "I need some coffee."

"Me, too." He cast her a wry grin. "I have become too accustomed to your Earth cuisine."

Paz liked everything he'd tasted here, especially their seafood. His villa being on a desert planet, he didn't partake of delicacies from the ocean often except when on assignment, and only then when he visited a seaside port. He'd miss the abundance of fish when he returned home.

Jen sat, stretched, and slid to her feet. Her face flushed when she noticed him gazing at her nude body. "Stow it, tiger. It's too early in the morning."

"It's never too early where you're concerned. However, I'd better see what's making that banging noise."

"I'll meet you on deck." Jen gathered her clothes in her arms as he turned away.

Outside, dawn cast a dismal gray across the ocean. Angry clouds gathered overhead, scudding across the sky on a chariot of wind. He could almost imagine Thor riding his great steed through the heavens and throwing his infamous hammer.

Thunder rumbled in the distance, while the sea tossed waves

against each other in protest. The ship rolled side-to-side and plunged in and out of troughs, the deck dipping and tilting. Sprays of water crashed over the rail while a cool breeze tossed his hair into his eyes.

The banging sounds drew him to a hatch that had come undone. He'd just fastened it shut when his ears detected a mechanical sound over the wind. His brow furrowed when he spied a motor launch speeding in their direction.

Who would be approaching in such stormy weather? Squinting, he studied the horizon but didn't make out any land masses. That left one alternative: this craft had to originate from a larger ship. He strode toward the stern, noting a trawler barely discernible far out on the waves.

Jen's scent reached him before she did. He turned his head, giving her a quick onceover. She'd dressed practically in jeans like him with a belted top and running shoes on her feet. She wore her hair in a twist and had applied a touch of gloss to her lips and shadow to her eyes. Even with the casual clothing, she exuded grace. Her swanlike neck lifted as she regarded him.

"What's that boat doing here? Who are those men?" She gripped his arm, undoubtedly noticing as he did the swarthy men congregated on the launch's deck. They didn't look friendly.

The sails flapped overhead. Should he and Jen store them for inclement weather? Not being a sailor, Paz had no idea. He'd figured the ship would steer itself under all climactic conditions, but maybe the magic had failed since they were visible to their pursuers.

Jen's grip tightened. "Can we outrun them?"

A wave thrust her against him and sprayed saltwater over the deck. "I don't know. We could try to increase throttle speed."

"Go ahead."

"Um, I'm not familiar with archaic sailing vessels."

"I thought you said you'd worked in a fleet?"

He thrust his jaw forward. "My family has investments in a merchant fleet, and I have indeed been on ships of every design… spaceships, that is."

"Oh." A look of determination entered her eyes. "Well, I wouldn't count on magic to defend us against pirates. I'll handle the bridge."

"Do you know what a throttle looks like? Because I can—"

She dismissed him with a wave. "I've been boating before. My daddy has a yacht, and he made Mom and me take safety classes. If there's a way to make this heap of wood go faster, I'll find it."

Jen turned away but a voice from a bullhorn froze her in her tracks.

"Yo, there. Heave to, and you won't be harmed."

She spun, grabbing Paz's arm to steady herself when the deck tilted again. One of the riffs fired a warning shot across the bow. As their launch drew closer, Paz observed the automatic weapons in their hands and the murder in their eyes.

He gnawed on his lower lip, worried for Jen's safety. They might keep her as a prize or traffic her as a sex slave. He'd heard such things existed on this planet.

No way would he let that happen.

The sea boiled and frothed, making it difficult for the pirates to narrow the distance between them. They tossed over a grappling hook while he debated how to meet this new challenge.

"Jen, go below. Increasing speed won't help us now. Lock yourself in one of the cabins. I'll hold them off."

She gave him a doubtful glance, loose strands of hair whipping about her face. "What, you against all six of them and maybe more? I know you're a fighter, Paz, but even you can be outnumbered."

"Please, Jen. It'll only distract me if you're on deck."

She shook her head. "There has to be another way." A thoughtful look entered her eyes as the pirate vessel scraped against their hull. Ropes were tossed over the railing. In a few minutes, they'd be boarded.

Jen strode to the open deck where the sails flapped madly in the wind. She stiffened and gazed upward, ignoring the wind and spray lashing at her. Her chin lifted, but she didn't break focus. She moved her lips as a cloud glided overhead and a curtain of rain fell from the sky.

Aware the intruders would shimmy up those ropes at any moment, Paz approached her. He couldn't hear what she was saying over the roar of the rain. A sheet of gray shrouded his view.

His head turned as a loud cracking noise tore through the air. Something hurtled past, followed by howls of surprise.

He couldn't tell what happened until the cloud moved on, and the rain lessened. One of the sails had ripped loose, propelled by the wind. It had collapsed onto the motor launch with the men aboard. The weight of it covered the small vessel like a blanket, so tightly as to smother any life within.

He stared in horror. Before he could surge forward, a large crest lifted the craft, severing the rope holding the grappling hook in place. The launch washed away and disappeared among the waves.

He turned toward Jen, whose face bore a satisfied smile.

Had she been responsible for that accident? A sick feeling told him she'd known exactly what she was doing. Did this mean she'd gained control of her power? It chilled his blood to think what she might do without understanding her abilities.

"It worked."

He bristled at her triumphant tone. "What worked? What did you do?"

He swiped at his dripping wet face. A light rain continued, soaking his clothes and pelting his skin. They should go inside until the storm passed.

"I'm not exactly sure, but I wanted that sail to chase them away." Confusion entered her eyes.

"Let's go into the galley to debrief." He spoke in a harsh tone, but her actions warranted it. She'd just dropped a canvas sail on a boatload of men. What if someday she hurt innocents by mistake?

Allowing her to precede him down the companionway, he gritted his teeth. If only he could resist her allure, it would keep him focused on his job. He couldn't deny the effect she had on him, though, and that's where he failed.

****

Jen leaned back in her chair after finishing a breakfast of sardines and rice. They'd stopped in their cabins to rinse off the saltwater and change into a set of dry clothes. Now she faced Paz across the salon table—dismayed by his silence.

She didn't understand how he'd gone from the sensitive lover of last night to this taciturn man whose suspicious glare made her feel guilty. Where was her teasing, affectionate warrior? Had she turned him off with her act on deck, or had it started earlier in their cabin?

She'd sensed his withdrawal this morning and wondered if he'd regretted their lovemaking. Perhaps it complicated his mission. Or maybe he just didn't want to get involved any further with a woman who would hinder his carefree lifestyle.

He'd confessed to casual flings in the outposts he visited. Did a fear of commitment keep him from intimacy, or were other issues at stake?

"We need a plan for when we reach shore," she said to break the ice. Her stomach knotted, and it wasn't from the ship's movement. She wanted to earn back his regard.

"You're damn right, but first tell me what happened up on deck." His eyes blazed as he surveyed her.

She shrugged. "Remember the incident at General Morar's fortress?"

"You mean where you strangled Leytnant Bosk with his own sash?"

She gripped her hands together so tightly her knuckles whitened. "I-I didn't actually strangle him. It just sort of happened."

"Right, just like Nira thought about how she'd like to get a Trollek's paws off her, and the next minute, he's dead?" He leaned forward, his lips thinned. "If you possess a similar power, you have to learn how to control it."

"I know that, and I'm trying to understand. Look, maybe my interest in fashion design is part of my legacy. What if our powers involve manipulating molecules at a very basic level? It could be related to Odin's shapeshifting ability but in a different way. Like, I can twist fabrics to do what I want."

He nodded slowly. "And your visions?"

"Part of the whole. When I stood on the deck, I saw myself on a Viking ship. We were defending against attackers. Those visions, while a link to the past, must serve some purpose in the present."

"Perhaps. I'd suggest you curb your gift until you learn more about it. You can tell Nira about the visions, too, when you meet her." His face relaxed. "So where do we go from here?"

Her gaze slid over his powerful shoulders. *Back to bed?* She wanted to feel his arms around her again, to relish his comforting embrace.

Bad girl! Focus on the mission at hand.

"Let's suppose you're able to reach your team. What then?"

He hunched forward. "We destroy the rift generators and seal the rifts." They'd exchanged information on what each of them had discovered so far, Paz during his last trip to Togura Island, and Jen at the ride in Manga World. "Once we've shut down their gateways, we'll deal with the Trolleks remaining on Earth."

"What about the people under their mind control?"

"We're hoping Nira's blood will provide an antidote. She's able to nullify the spell in humans, but we don't know how. We have to be careful; since the federal authorities are involved, the tentacles of the invasion must reach far and wide."

Concern creased her brow. "What's your next move?"

"Zohar should have been able to identify the portals with the jamming signal gone. That'll pinpoint our targets. I have data about the generators keeping the inter-dimensional gates open. We need to devise a means to take them out."

She tilted her head. "This all seems very factual. What about the prophecy?"

"I'm hoping Nira has had some success in locating your other so-called sisters."

"While your team is shutting down the rifts, what are we supposed to do? Follow up on a vague prediction about a coming cataclysm and locate the mythical rune to prevent it?"

"That's right."

"Do you know how absurd that sounds?"

He jabbed his finger for emphasis. "We're on a magic ship that unfolded from your pocket. We met a dwarf who turned a nail into gold, a serpent who swallowed us then spit us out, and a dog who changed into a man. Oh, not to mention a dragon who's afraid of water. What would you call those?"

Jen grinned, grateful they were on the same page again. "I guess my life has been unbelievable ever since I met you."

"I'm sorry about that."

"Why?"

"Because it was my presence that activated your power and put the Trolleks on your trail."

They locked gazes, studying each other's faces. Jen's glance dropped to his mouth, perfectly contoured for kissing. She reached across the table and grasped his hand. "I wouldn't trade knowing you for anything, Paz."

A responsive gleam entered his eyes, but it was quickly replaced by firm determination. He slid his hand free and leaned back, folding his arms across his chest. "What do you plan to do once we reach shore?"

"Go home, get into some decent clothes, and do my nails. They're a mess." She examined her fingertips with a grimace. "Then I'll check my mail, call friends and pay bills."

It sounded so odd to talk of mundane chores. Would her life ever be the same again? Did she want it to be?

She lightened her tone. "You can contact your team from my apartment. Then we'll head to the showroom where I'll introduce you as my latest male model. It'll be a good cover for you."

Her staff would fall all over him, especially when they learned he was straight. She'd have to stake her claim right away.

"I don't want to stay long in New York," he reiterated.

"I know." She was dying to have him try on her outfits. If he played along, she would design some fabulous jackets to fit his physique. And to see him strut down the runway—well, she wouldn't be the only one panting at the prospect.

"General Morar may pick up our trail again, especially if your timepiece acts as a locator beacon," Paz reminded her. "You need to consult Nira on how to block the signal."

Jen took a drink of orange juice. They'd found some nonperishable packs among the food stores. "I need to talk to Nira about Algie's experiments, among other things."

Paz drummed his fingers on the table. "We know the Trollek scientist is injecting humans with Trollek DNA to find a stable recombinant strand. What if she gets to the point where her test subjects survive?"

"Then I suppose the Trollek DNA would replicate inside those people. She has a sample of my blood now. That may give her the element she needs. My so-called sisters... our serum could give her the key to complete her plans."

She and Paz both fell silent, contemplating their tasks ahead. Their relationship problems were minor in comparison but there was no question they had to work together to succeed.

Otherwise, Ragnarok faced them, whether from the Trollek invasion or Algie's experiments or the evil demon Loki who aimed to bring about the end of time.

Chapter Twenty-One

The enchanted ship deposited Jen and Paz at a deserted wharf in Manhattan where they scrambled ashore. As soon as they stepped foot onto land, the ship collapsed into a folded piece of paper that wafted into Jen's hand. She stuck it in her purse, which she had miraculously preserved through their adventures.

A long walk brought them to a curb where Jen hailed a taxi. She rattled off instructions to the driver, and they proceeded to wind through a myriad of streets into the heart of the city.

"We should get out before we reach your place to see if anyone is watching," Paz said, peering out the window.

Jen agreed and told the fellow where to let them off. She paid the man then grimaced at the diminishing funds in her wallet. At least it was Monday, so the banks would be open.

On the sidewalk, Paz gawked at the sights surrounding them. Buses belched toxic fumes as they roared past. Yellow taxicabs shuffled one behind the other in nonstop traffic. He craned his neck to trace buildings that reached toward the sky, while his nose sniffed garlic from a nearby eatery. Pedestrians crowded the street, rushing to and fro. Despite the many metropolises he'd visited, this one had its own unique character.

Jen nudged him with her elbow. "Will you stop acting like such a tourist? You'll attract attention."

"You're right." His training kicked in. *Blend with the natives.* He slouched and glanced at blotches on the ground from old chewing gum. A woman pushing a baby carriage jostled past. He jumped as though touched by a Trollek.

"What's wrong with you?" Jen cast him an annoyed glance.

He dodged a fire hydrant as they moved on. "Danger lurks in big cities. General Morar's agent found us in Hong Kong. He can find us again. How far to your lodging from here?"

"Not much farther."

Smells of roasted chicken drifted their way from a restaurant they passed. "Should we pick up some groceries?"

"You know, I don't really do the cooking thing too well. Let's just stop at my place, deflate for a minute, and then we can go out to grab a bite."

"All right." He had no idea what she meant by deflate but grabbing a bite he understood. Besides, he was eager to see her residence. It would reveal more about her.

They approached a wide expanse of grass and trees that pleased his eyes. Trails ran through the park, crowded with joggers, families, and young lovers. A massive concrete structure rose to their left.

Jen pointed out the sights like a tour guide. "That's the Museum of Natural History, and this is Central Park. My place has a view of the park although it's not much."

They walked a couple of more blocks in silence while he absorbed his surroundings. He liked the green spaces. Being surrounded by tall buildings made him feel closed in.

"What's your home like?" Jen turned her curious gaze on him. "Do you have a house, an apartment, or what?"

He pictured his sprawling estate, imagining her surprise if he told her its acreage. "My world is a desert planet. Rivers are underground. My property sits on a plateau and overlooks a stark landscape of reddish-brown earth and pillars that point like fingers toward the sky. I miss the clean air and natural beauty but most of all the quiet."

"I'd think an interstellar traveler like you would be drawn to the cities. They must be fabulous."

A wistful smile crossed his face. "You have no idea of the wonders out there, but I prefer the peace of deep space. It's vast and silent, and stars play like concerts of light far away."

"Sounds lonely to me."

He shrugged. "Nobody bothers me. That's what I like about my job."

Jen pursed her lips as though his answer didn't please her. Doubtless the bustle of the city and the hectic lifestyle stimulated her. They were polar opposites in that regard.

She turned down a street lined with sturdy buildings the residents called brownstones. The odor of sun-warmed trash drifted their way. Spindly trees stood at intervals down the sidewalk surrounded by protective fencing. Steam hissed from round cylinders in the road. Every now and then, a heavy truck lumbered past.

A white delivery van was parked up ahead, the name of a flower shop emblazoned on its side. Jen turned into the building opposite, where a uniformed man greeted them with a grin. He had gray hair, a stocky body, and a discolored front tooth.

"Miss Dyhr, how are you? I haven't seen you for so long that I was worried."

Jen gave him a hug. "I had a business trip abroad, and then I took some time off. Sammy, meet my friend, Paz Hadar."

They shook hands as per the American custom.

"I figured you'd be back soon because you got a delivery on your doorstep today." The older man beamed at Jen.

She narrowed her eyes while Paz stiffened at her side. "What delivery? From whom?" she said, her tone sharp.

"A huge bouquet of flowers. I didn't see the card." Sammy glanced speculatively between the two of them.

"Let's go upstairs," Jen told Paz, leading him to the elevator.

"This isn't a good idea. Someone might be waiting for us." If his makeshift PIP hadn't gotten wet in Fafnir's cave, he could have scanned for life signs in her corridor.

"No one knows we arrived today. I didn't even know when we would get here." Her glance dropped to her watch. "This thing has become a liability, but I couldn't take it off if I tried."

"We should have gone directly to Florida. We've no

protection here. The Trolleks may have picked up our trail as soon as we stepped off the ship."

The elevator door opened, and they emerged into a carpeted hallway. Paz spied the floral arrangement on the ground in front of a closed door ahead.

Jen rushed forward, stooped, and snatched the card sitting on a stick in the midst of the floral bouquet. Her handbag shifted, and she adjusted its strap across her slim shoulder.

"Don't touch anything," Paz warned. "The doorknob could be booby-trapped. For that matter, the flowers themselves could be tainted with poison."

"Too late. The card says, *This is a taste of what's to come if you resist us. Your friends are next.*" She gazed at him in bewilderment. "What does that mean?"

He examined the door for signs of tampering. "We'll find out soon enough. Stand aside." Hearing nothing unusual from beyond, he twisted her key in the lock and pushed the door wide.

Jen gasped at the wreckage inside. Someone had trashed her apartment. The contents were broken and strewn about the carpet. His mouth tightened at the look of stunned shock on her face. She needed to face reality. The Trolleks would stop at nothing to track them down.

"Oh. My. God." She stepped across the threshold, her eyes wide. "Who would do this?"

Paz sniffed. "Cors particles. They couldn't have been here that long ago."

She whirled toward him. "Then why the flowers? And if they vectored into my apartment, why aren't they waiting here for us?"

He gave her a mirthless smile. "Because it's a lesson. They want you to know that they can get to you anywhere. They can get to anyone. Who do you think delivered the bouquet? Their mind slaves. The Trolleks can bend people to their will."

Her face paled. "I have to get to my showroom."

"No, we have to go to Florida, but likely they have people

watching us to see if I'll lead them to my team." He tapped her arm. "Take what belongings you need. We have to leave."

"You can use my computer to contact your friends."

But after he verified her apartment was clear of any lingering intruders, he discounted that idea. Her computer had been zapped by disruptor fire. Its melted ruins congealed on her desk.

While Paz stared out the window toward Central Park and kept an eye on the flower shop van still parked outside, Jen filled a zippered tote with clothing and cosmetics.

She joined him when she'd finished. "I love this apartment. It may not be much, but for a one-bedroom in New York, it's pretty spacious." She swiped at a tear running down her cheek. "We can't stay here now. It's not safe."

He liked how she said *we* but felt bad about how her world had been turned upside-down. Feeling partly to blame, he resolved to make things right for her. "I'm sorry, Jen."

He pulled her into his arms and traced a tender finger across her luscious mouth. His head lowered. He couldn't help stealing a kiss. Jen's arms wound around him in response and she clung fast, pressing her mouth to his with desperate insistence.

"We should move on," he said after a few minutes of savoring her sweetness.

He gently detached her, aware that her sad gaze would forever be emblazoned on his heart. He gritted his teeth, reminding himself they were on a mission.

There wasn't time for sentimentality.

Jen recovered her composure. "We should use the fire escape. Sammy won't see us leaving then and neither will the guys in the van."

"Good idea."

When they reached the ground, Paz followed Jen down a side street. She walked with purpose, her stride fast and her expression determined.

Carrying her bulging tote bag, he matched her brisk pace.

"How do we get to Florida from here? The Trolleks will instruct their agents to watch the airports and all departing flights."

"I could ask my dad to send us a private jet."

"That wouldn't lessen the risk. The beasts could vector onboard."

"Bus or train?"

"Too public. We could use the Chinese junk again to sail down the eastern coastline. The magic protected us from their spatial shifts en route from Hong Kong."

She shook her head. "Another sea voyage isn't my first choice. We'll decide later." They halted at an intersection. "In the meantime, I need to get a replacement cell phone at a phone store. You can shop for electronics and buy whatever you need to make another PIP. I know a place near Broadway and 47th Street, but we'll have to take another taxi. And I should stop at an ATM to get more cash."

Upon his nod of agreement, she stepped to the curb and waved vigorously. One of the yellow ground vehicles veered over and squealed to a stop. Jen slid into the backseat and Paz followed. The swarthy driver glanced at them expectantly.

"Let us off a block away from 47th Digital," Jen said.

The hired vehicle swung into traffic. As they passed sidewalks mobbed with people, shops, and eateries, Paz absorbed the visual onslaught. They'd gone from Tokyo to Hong Kong to New York City. How could Jen not get tired of the noisy crowds?

He was right to believe they weren't suited. She could never live in a place separated from her friends and isolated from society. Yet privacy was crucial to him. His estate held more than his residence. It held his laboratories and his testing ground. His blueprints were finished. He had only to build the prototype he needed to demonstrate his theories.

He imagined Jen in his kitchen, protesting that she didn't cook and they had to go out to eat. Go out where? The nearest dining establishment was miles away.

Yet the thought of returning home alone filled him with a

yawning emptiness he'd never experienced before. Besides, Jen could be an asset in different ways. She knew how to get a business off the ground, how to market her designs and how to establish a network of contacts. He could use someone with her experience. His lack of aptitude in this direction inhibited his progress.

Being a Drift Lord was infinitely easier than coping with business affairs. His father wouldn't agree, but then Paz had been a disappointment to him ever since they'd discovered his abilities.

"Let us out here," Jen told the driver, while Paz wondered how he'd lost himself in thought so completely that he had blocked out their surroundings.

Fool, you're going to get us killed or captured if you keep losing focus.

It was her influence. The sooner he rejoined his team and she met with Nira Larsen, the better for both of them.

Jen fumbled in her purse for cash, paid the driver, and exited. Paz followed suit, and they strolled down the street.

At a cellular phone store, Jen paused. "Wait here while I get a replacement for my phone. It was insured so there shouldn't be any problem. Then I'll take you to the electronics place."

He hovered on the sidewalk while she went inside. Loud music boomed from a food market next door. His bones vibrated from the bass. Down the broad avenue, flashing neon signs made a light show from the sides of buildings. People shoved past: workers intent on their destination, mothers pushing baby strollers, young women giggling as they shopped.

Jen emerged after what seemed an interminable wait. They continued down the block. She detoured inside a bank building to acquire funds while he loitered outside. Resuming their walk when she returned, he sniffed a divine aroma further along.

He gestured. "Where is that smell coming from?"

"The Hershey store. It's a popular brand of chocolate."

"As in chocolate chip cookies? Those are Zohar's favorite treat." He waggled his eyebrows. "Can we go inside? I'm hungry."

"Oh, all right. I could use a Reese's or two."

"What is a Reese's?" He trailed her into the emporium.

"It's milk chocolate coated peanut butter."

"Pee-nut butter." He cocked his head. "I am unfamiliar with this foodstuff." Jen bought a pack and gave him one.

The confection melted on his tongue, a heavenly combination of salty and sweet. "Give me another. I like this pee-nut butter."

"We missed lunch. Maybe we should grab a sandwich. Candy will only make us hungrier."

They bought hot dogs and chips from a street vendor then continued along their way as soon as they'd finished eating.

His spirits soared when he spied the electronics store and glimpsed the window displays. Those components would be more than adequate for him to build a new device.

Giddy with excitement, he browsed the aisles and gathered an armful of goods. Most were primitive constructs by his standards, but he could use the parts for his purpose.

Jen dragged him from the store after she paid for his items.

"Thank you. I will pay you back later once I get more kewa stones." He flashed her a grateful grin.

She waved a hand. "Don't worry about it."

Outside, a motored scooter roared past followed by a rumbling truck. Food smells from cafés mingled with fumes from a bus chugging down the road. People chattered and bumped elbows as they ambled along the sidewalk.

Despite his complaints about the assault to his senses, Paz could easily get lost exploring the sights and sounds of this great city. He glanced at the faces with their different colored skin and facial features and marveled at the diversity. He'd long felt a fondness for Earth, but now his heart swelled with warm affection for its people.

Despite their conflicts, the citizens of this innocent world would stand fast against a common enemy. He'd studied their history. They may not believe it of themselves, but faced with annihilation, they'd come together as never before.

It might be time to make them aware of the true threat that existed. A united front could be the only way they would expel the Trolleks for good. The American authorities had already recognized something was amiss, so it wouldn't be hard to convince them.

He glanced over his shoulder, his scalp prickling.

They'd been made.

But who was tailing them—the Trolleks or the Federal agents?

If the latter, he'd like to inform their people that his team was on the same side, but this directive must come from Zohar. His first order of business was to contact his commander. He had an idea how to go about it.

Not wishing to alarm Jen, he didn't mention their shadow. Besides, she was already aware they were being tracked by her wristwatch device. Ceding to her familiarity with the city, he accompanied her to a section of town called the garment district.

"Your name is on that building." He pointed to large lettering that said, *Jennifer Dyhr Designs.*

She gave him a proud smile. "That's where I have my showroom. We rent the first two floors."

"We won't stay long, will we?" He realized it was important to her peace of mind to ensure the safety of her colleagues.

"No. I just want to check in and regroup before we leave for Florida."

Jen breezed inside with Paz in tow. The receptionist, a pretty, young brunette, jumped from her chair at their arrival.

"Miss Dyhr, oh my gosh, we weren't expecting you today."

"I would have called ahead, but I just bought a new cell phone, and it isn't charged yet. Let me introduce you to our new model. This is Paz Hadar."

"Nice to meet you." Paz nodded a greeting while sniffing for cors particles. He didn't smell anything unusual in the cool air-conditioned interior.

Tension ebbed from him as he relaxed. He'd been half afraid

a reception committee of confounded staff members might be waiting for them.

"I'll notify Sandi you're here." The receptionist pushed on her earpiece and spoke in a low tone while Jen removed her cell phone from the box and hooked it up to an electrical outlet.

"Jen, where the hell have you been?" Sandi, the petite assistant, rounded the corner a few minutes later and rushed forward. "I was worried sick about you."

Jen gave her a quick hug. "You got my email from Hong Kong, right? I'll tell you the details later." Jen signaled for them to move on. They passed various workrooms and offices that he peered into curiously.

Jen waved to her colleagues and fielded a few greetings along the way.

Sandi whispered something in Jen's ear. Jen muttered something back. They both glanced his way. Sandi giggled while Jen's mouth curved in a sly smile.

"Good to see you again, Mr. Hadar." Sandi adjusted her clipboard. "I gather you're new at modeling. I'd be, like, happy to teach you what you need to learn."

"We'll show him the ropes later." Jen laid a hand on the blonde's arm. "What's been going on?"

"Omigod, we've been crazy busy. You wouldn't believe the nine-one-one's today. Denise called. She needs ten major outfits sent to London by the weekend for Kate's press tour."

"You can handle it. I have to go to Palm Beach."

"What? You just got here."

"There's a family matter I have to settle. I'm bringing Paz along. I'll finalize arrangements for our trunk show while we're there, plus I can introduce him to people on South Beach. He could use the connections. Is Ted around? I found some fabulous fabrics in Hong Kong. I shipped some samples here."

"Hey, Jen. It's great to have you back!" A redhead approached with a sheepish grin. "Sorry to interrupt. Sandi, did you ever find where we can get silicone nipple covers?"

"I already placed an order." Sandi turned back to Jen. "Chelsea is due here in ten minutes. She'll be, like, ecstatic to see you. She has five clients to dress for upcoming events and wants options. I hope you don't mind that we're giving her a sneak peek at the new collection."

Sandi's layered hair fell over her ears as she studied her notes. Her dark lipstick and heavily mascaraed eyes made a sharp contrast to her pale skin and hair.

Paz held up his shopping bag of electronic gear. "Uh, ladies, is there somewhere I can work while you're talking?"

"Sure, hon, go to the third door on your right," Sandi instructed him. "It should be quiet in there."

Paz walked away, glad to escape. He was glad, too, to see the color restored to Jen's face and the firc in her eyes. She'd been away from home, had come back to see her apartment trashed, and needed to reestablish a sense of order. Being among friends who cared about her and her work environment should help calm her.

He entered a room with a long wooden table, obviously a conference room. Broad windows showed a view of the brick building next door. A couple of old-fashioned radiators sat by the wall, silent in the summer heat. An air-conditioning unit hummed quietly in the background.

Setting out his supplies, he got to work. He became so engrossed that he didn't realize Sandi stood outside in the corridor until he heard her voice speaking to someone else.

"I meant to reach you earlier, but I couldn't get away. They're here, but not for long." A pause. "Yes, I'll try to stall them. And my kabak, they don't suspect a thing."

Chapter Twenty-Two

"Did you get delayed by that monsoon? I heard it tied up flights from Hong Kong." Ted spoke in his usual effeminate tone.

The styling associate regarded Jen from behind his nerdy black glasses. He had a tall, thin frame, dark hair, and a disarming smile. Dressed in a buttoned dress shirt and bow tie, he looked like a preppy graduate.

"Actually, we did catch the edge of it." Jen flicked a lock of hair off her face. "Our flight was cancelled. That's how we got stuck there."

"I thought you were filming in Tokyo?"

"It's a long story, Ted."

He pursed his lips. "You missed all the weather reports. There's been flooding in Venice, a volcanic eruption in the Caribbean, and an earthquake in Mexico. Some say this season of natural disasters heralds worse things to come."

"Oh, yeah? Doomsayers have predicted meltdowns before and nothing has happened." *Not yet.* "If I were you, I wouldn't watch the Weather Channel so much."

After consulting with Ted, she called her parents to tell them she'd reached New York. Then she entered a workroom to sort through the racks of men's clothing. She'd have to rush production of her new designs if Paz would model them.

Could she convince him to return here once his team sent the Trolleks back where they belonged? Or would he lift off for his next port of call to resume his day job? How did he manage to take a leave of absence for so long from his telecom company?

They must know he was a Drift Lord. Maybe giving him time off was a mandatory thing, like for jury duty.

She fingered the soft material of one shirt, spots wavering before her eyes. Oh, no. Her mind started to segue into another vision.

"Jen, darling, I'm so glad you're here." Chelsea, a celebrity stylist from LA, strode through the door and jolted her back to reality.

They air-kissed and exchanged pleasantries.

"Thanks so much for letting me in before the show. I know you've been out of town and have lots to do, but I've got so many events coming up for my clients. Give me options, darling."

Chelsea wore heeled boots, black skinny jeans, and a cranberry top with a low neckline. Gold hoops dangled from her ears. Her highlighted blond hair spilled in waves to her shoulders. Although her makeup was expertly applied, the bags under her eyes said she could use more sleep.

Jen was happy to accommodate Chelsea who appreciated her designs. However, she didn't have time for this right now.

"I can get you started, but then I have to run. Sandi will be able to assist you."

The blonde walked in as though on cue. "Jen, don't tell me you're running off so soon. You're the best person to describe your new line."

Chelsea started browsing through the racks. "I'll take this black sequin number," she gushed, not giving Jen the chance to make a graceful exit. "It's like water, so fluid."

"It moves like liquid, too." Jen beamed with pride. "Your client will adore it."

"We're doing this campaign in LA for Hal Weissman. It'll be a fabulous choice."

"We can have Rachel walk for you if you want."

Rachel was one of their in-house models. The long-legged young woman lounged in a corner on a white lambskin covered armchair reading a fashion magazine.

"No, that's okay." Chelsea stopped at a fuchsia silk dress with puffed sleeves. "This one is stunning. Do you have, maybe, a size six?"

"Sure." Sandi scribbled on her clipboard. She'd refused Jen's offer of an iPad. She still liked to do things by hand.

"Omigod, I must have this dress." The stylist fingered a sheer black chiffon. "Can you do it in metallic? No one will see the genius of this detail from the red carpet." She paused at the next garment, her jaw dropping. "Oh, my. I'm obsessed by this long floral gown with the drapey back. I love it."

Jen gave up on her plans to leave as her zeal took over. "Check out the blue gown with the beaded top. When the light hits the bead work, it's awesome."

"I can't wait to place these dresses. They're fantastic."

"Sandi can show you the accessories. Be careful with the shoes. Ankle straps can be your best friend or your worst enemy. Make sure the shoe complements the dress."

Sandi held up a hand. "You'll stay, won't you, Jen? I have a hundred other things to do."

Before she could reply, Paz poked his head inside the room. "Jen, may I have a word?"

"Sure, what is it?" She recognized the urgent note in his voice.

"In private."

"Okay. Ladies, please excuse me." She led him into their small kitchenette and poured herself a glass of water. "Want one?"

"No, thanks. Listen, Sandi has been compromised."

She choked on her drink. "What do you mean?"

"I overheard her speaking on her cell phone. She said, my kabak. That's the word for a Trollek master."

Jen felt her face drain of color. "No, it can't be. You must not have heard correctly."

His jaw tightened. "Her orders are to delay us. We must depart at once."

She nodded at the shopping bag in his hand. "Did you have time to assemble your equipment?"

"Not totally, but it doesn't matter. We have to go. Now."

She bit her lower lip. This couldn't be happening. "The Trolleks wouldn't dare attack us so openly. They'd have to take down everyone in this place."

"Not true. Their confounded humans will do the job for them. They're probably outside already, waiting for the signal to come inside and snatch us."

"I have to get my purse and cell phone."

"Then do it."

She'd just obtained them when Sandi located her and Paz on the first-floor corridor.

"Here you are. Chelsea is filling out her order. I'll make sure the dresses are shipped on time." The blonde's glance flickered between the two of them. "I thought we might go over your schedule for the rest of the week. It's lucky you came back on a Monday."

"Of course," Jen said in an airy tone. "Why don't you go get the appointment book? I need to put the dates into my iPhone. Look for us upstairs. I didn't finish giving Paz the grand tour."

As soon as Sandi left, Jen signaled for Paz to accompany her in the opposite direction. She sought out Ted, who glanced at her in exasperation from behind his desk.

"Jen, I'm glad you're still here. Diane just called about our runway show. I told her you'd phone her back."

"You deal with it. Listen, do you still have a car parked in New Jersey?" Always wary of possible disasters, Ted kept his car in a long-term lot outside the city.

"Right on. Why?"

"I want to borrow it. I'll pay you for the mileage, but I need the keys and location fast. And tell no one."

He scrunched his dark brows. "Sure. What's up?"

"Urgent family business." She smiled reassuringly at Ted. "I might be gone for several days, but I promise to bring the car back intact."

Ted stood to hand her the keys. Jen swung around to his side of the desk, lifted the key ring from his palm, and gave him a kiss smack on the lips.

"What was that for?"

"Insurance." Jen winked at him. "The directions, please?"

After Ted scribbled the location of the parking lot, she and Paz scrambled out. She'd almost forgotten the tote she'd brought from her apartment. She grabbed it from her office before they slipped out the rear exit into an alley.

The coast was clear. No one lingered in the narrow lane filled with trashcans.

"What was that all about?" Paz fell into step beside her as they headed toward an avenue bustling with pedestrians.

"I wanted to give Ted some immunity, just in case. I can't believe the Trolleks got to Sandi. They'll be expecting us to take a flight or train to Florida. Hence the car. We should be okay if Ted keeps his mouth shut."

"How do we get to New Jersey from here?"

"We have to take a bus from Port Authority."

"I've assembled most of my gear," Paz said, his face grim. "After I make a few more adjustments, I think I can block them from tracking us. My signal will create enough noise so they won't be able to distinguish your frequency."

"You'd better finish your work. They may have agents patrolling the bus station."

"We should get disguises. They'll be on the lookout for people of our description."

They bought sunglasses and baseball caps at a souvenir store along with *I Love New York* T-shirts. Then they ducked inside a café to order coffee. Paz fiddled with his gadgets while they sipped their hot drinks and ate apple pie. He made quick time of finishing his new PIP from a pile of components.

They changed into their tourist outfits inside the restroom. Catching a bus wasn't a problem and soon they'd entered the Holland Tunnel on their way to New Jersey. Rush hour traffic crawled at a slow pace. She prayed Ted had kept their secret and not been forced into betraying them.

After locating the parking lot as per his instructions, Jen used her credit card to pay his fee in advance so as to reserve his space. It was the least she could do for him in return.

A fleeting worry gnawed at her. Either the Trollek agents or the Feds might trace her credit card transactions. She cast aside that concern. Too many other issues faced them.

The sedan's interior felt like an oven after baking under the hot afternoon sun. She settled into the driver's seat and strapped in. The leather upholstery heated her sticky back.

She'd drive while Paz tried to contact his team. Her plan was to pick up the Auto Train in Lorton, Virginia. The Trolleks would be watching the train stations in Manhattan. They'd never think to look there. By Wednesday morning, she and Paz should be in Florida.

Or so she hoped.

$$****$$

"We have to stop in Orlando for a debriefing with my team." Paz gripped the steering wheel, driving their borrowed Acura from the train depot in Sanford, Florida.

He had been elated to get a response from Zohar when he'd scanned the emergency frequencies with his new PIP last night. His commander had been relieved to hear from him and had ordered Paz to join his friends for a strategy session. Their conversation had been terse. Zohar seemed reluctant to say more until they met in person.

Jen hadn't slept well on the train. She'd had one of her recurrent dreams, something to do with Aunt Alba in a cemetery. Nor had they had a good night on Monday, stopping at a motel on the road and worrying about the Trolleks picking up their trail.

She cast her soulful gaze in his direction. "I thought we were going to Palm Beach. I told my parents I'd be bringing you home to meet them." Her lower lip thrust out in a petulant pout.

"I don't mean to disappoint you, but it's critical that I exchange information with my colleagues and see what orders Zohar has for me. You should come, too. Nira is in town. Besides, it'll be time for lunch soon. We'd have to stop anyway."

It would be nearly noon by the time they reached the safe house in southwest Orlando.

Jen straightened in her seat. "Will you drive me home if I go with you first? The Board meeting is rescheduled for Friday afternoon, and Dad wants to clue me in beforehand."

"That shouldn't be a problem unless Zohar objects, but he might forbid me from pursuing personal issues until our mission is complete."

"Then we'll have to convince him to let you go. It's less than a three-hour drive to Palm Beach. I won't keep you long." Her frown deepened. "I could use your support."

Surprised by her admittance, he shared his concerns. "We've located the rifts. We have to determine how to destroy the generators keeping them open. My intel should help."

"Can't your spaceship just fire on them?"

"It's not as simple as that. And there's been an unforeseen complication." He hesitated, his mind still absorbing the news. "The *Protector* is gone."

Her eyes rounded. "That's your ship? How?"

He gripped the steering wheel as he headed west on I-4. "Seems one of the prince's enemies from his home world destroyed it. Fortunately, no one was aboard, and we have the two shuttles. But we're stranded here for now until we can get word out."

Her face brightened momentarily then she shuttered her expression. Did the thought of him being stuck here please her?

"Tell me about your team. Who will I meet?"

His mood lifted at her intent to accompany him. He'd felt bereft at the thought of her heading home on her own. He wasn't ready to part from her just yet, if ever. He shoved aside that troubling thought for later.

"Zohar, our team leader, has been reluctant to assume his rightful place as ruler of the Star Empire. He is afraid of becoming like his father. The former emperor fell under the spell of a Trollek female and married her. It was a dark time in our history." He frowned at the memory of the persecutions.

Jen gave him a sympathetic glance. "And now?"

"Nira restored his confidence. Zohar will make a worthy king, but he still has many enemies."

Those enemies had colluded with the Trolleks and corrupted one of their team members, turning him against them. This faction had destroyed their ship. They fomented rebellion in the Empire. The Trolleks weren't the only threat to galactic peace.

"Who else is on your team?" Jen plucked at her blouse, which she wore tucked into a pair of belted black jeans.

Paz focused on the road, too easily distracted by the woman at his side. "Yaron is our medic. He plays the larp, a stringed instrument, and likes to sing. Being a Drift Lord wouldn't be his first choice of an occupation."

"Is it anyone's?"

He winced at her perception. "No, but we do our job. We cannot deny our destiny."

She compressed her lips. "You're communications officer, right?"

He nodded. "Kaj is our engineer, and Dal is demolitions. Then there's Lord Magnor, a swordsman of the Tsuran. He was assigned as bodyguard to Prince Zohar by Primer Pedar, Zohar's regent. Magnor is working on our team, but he's not an official member."

Jen counted on her fingers. "You, Zohar, Kaj, Dal, Yaron, and Magnor. Six of you."

"Normally the Drift Lords work in teams of seven. We had two more members when we first arrived here. They were killed." He counted the traitor as good as dead in his mind.

"I'm so sorry." She tilted her head. "Tell me the prophecy again."

"The six daughters of Odin must join with the six sons of Thor to utter the ancient words and defeat the coming darkness."

"So there are six of you now, counting Magnor."

He tightened his grip on the wheel. "Actually, Kaj is still missing. Dal has made it back with a woman in tow."

"Made it back? From where?"

"He'd been ill, poisoned. He checked himself out of the hospital and disappeared. Zohar said Dal would tell me his story later. Our mission takes precedence. Shutting down the rifts is our number one priority."

Chapter Twenty-Three

Jen approached the safe house with trepidation. At last, she would meet Paz's team. They should be on their way to Palm Beach, but she couldn't begrudge him this opportunity. It's why he had come to Florida.

She was familiar with the Dr. Phillips area off West Sand Lake Road in Orlando. Restaurant Row was one place she always visited when in town, not that she got here that often. Her parents hadn't been fond of the local attractions. They considered themselves above the masses that waited in line.

The suburban street where Paz had parked their loaner car held single-story ranch houses with attractive landscaping. One home with a sand-colored exterior and white tile roof had decorative garden poles out front. Were those the perimeter defense rods Paz had mentioned?

As they neared, the door flung wide and a tall, handsome man strode outside. He wore his dark brown hair slicked back from a striking face. His confident posture and regal carriage told Jen this must be Zohar. His turquoise eyes shone with warmth as he gave Paz a quick embrace and slap on the back.

"I am glad you are safe," the man said in a deep tone. He turned to Jen, his gaze friendly as he appraised her. "And you must be Miss Dyhr."

"Please call me Jen… your highness."

His eyes twinkled. "And I prefer Zohar. Formalities are a waste on a mission."

She liked his forthright attitude and followed him inside.

She didn't miss how his glance scanned the road before he closed the door behind them.

"Come, we're having our strategy session in the dining room," Zohar said, leading the way. They'd entered through a foyer facing the living room. Around the corner, several people were seated around a long cherry wood table.

Jen's eyes popped. Who was that arresting man with the cape and sword? Good God, he looked as though he'd stepped from the pages of a comic book. That must be the alien Paz had mentioned, Lord somebody or other.

"Jen, this is Nira Larsen. Nira, meet Jennifer Dyhr."

Jen spun at the sound of her mythical sister's name and faced a cute redhead with a warm smile and wide brown eyes.

"I'm so happy to meet you." Nira gave Jen a hug as though they were long-lost siblings.

Nira wore her chin-length layered hair in tousled waves that flattered her face. A chunky turquoise and silver necklace adorned her neck above a cotton blouse. The woman would be fun to dress in her daywear designs, Jen thought, gauging her size.

Nira gestured to a guy with a trim beard and kind eyes. "This is Yaron, our resident medic and musician."

Yaron shook her hand. "A pleasure to greet you, mistress."

A wiry fellow sidled up to her. He appeared to be all sinew and brawn. His stern visage didn't once crack a smile.

"I'm Dal." He gestured at a woman who hovered shyly in a corner. "That's Lianne."

The woman looked like an earth goddess with wavy auburn hair, a smattering of freckles across her nose, and intelligent blue eyes. Her patterned maxi dress swayed at her ankles as she approached. Coral beads dangled from her dancer's neck.

Dal was the explosives expert who'd been poisoned, Jen remembered. He'd vanished from the hospital and reappeared later with this woman. Their story should be interesting.

"And you must be…?" Jen asked the swordsman.

"Lord Magnor, mistress." Sweeping his forest green cloak

aside, he bowed. He, too, had a beard. His dark hair brushed his shoulders, and his eyes held a sad, regretful look. His brooding presence cast a pall over the company.

Nira tapped her arm. "We'll be eating lunch soon, unless you're hungry now. Would you like something to drink?"

"No thanks, I can wait."

"Then let's be seated and continue our briefing." Zohar claimed a chair at the head of the table.

Jen sat between Paz on her left and Nira on her right. The other women's presence brought her a measure of comfort. Paz cracked a few jokes about how everyone had thought he was dead, and that eased the tension in the air.

At Zohar's nod, he launched into an explanation of how he'd ended up on Jen's film set, his concern when no one from the team answered his calls, and his efforts to get to Florida.

"We changed frequencies after our ship got destroyed." Zohar's brow creased. "It's enough that we have to fight the Trolleks without my political opponents entering the mix."

"What happened to the traitor who betrayed us?" Paz, his jaw taut, clasped his hands together on the table.

"He died in battle after saving Yaron from suffering the same fate as you. I listed it as an honorable death."

Paz nodded his acceptance. "We have located the rifts now that the jamming device was destroyed?"

"That is correct." Zohar drilled Paz with his laser gaze. "We have the targets but not the means to destroy them." He paused, while the other men shifted restlessly. "Do you remember how we determined the Trolleks were shipping solar calculators to a storage room in Drift World and mirrors to a Windermere address?"

"Yes, and I have a theory about their purpose, but go on."

Zohar scowled. "We tracked the address to an estate owned by a wealthy businessman from Hong Kong. His name is Ra Mat Shlom."

"Shlom!" Paz half-rose from his seat. "That liver-bellied son of a snipeling. I didn't realize he had a connection to the Trolleks."

"You've met the man?" Zohar glanced between him and Jen.

Jen cleared her throat. "Paz neglected to mention he got shot during his last visit to Togura Island. Shlom's family is involved in the manufacture of a popular healing balm. That's how we got onto him. He must be working with the Trolleks under his own will, because he didn't turn us over to them. Or maybe he wasn't aware we were on their wanted list."

Paz had been applying the balm and his wound had nearly healed. She filled his team in on their encounter with Dikibie and the dragon as well as Agent Monroe and their excursion to Manga World. "The Feds think the Trolleks are aliens who are invading Earth."

"I wonder if they're clued into the sleeper agents." Everyone perked up at Nira's words. "The Trolleks have been confounding people and sending them home for some time now. We don't know how far their network reaches, but government officials must have caught on to people acting like puppets."

"They've noticed individuals have gone missing," Jen added.

Zohar hunched forward. "I'm concerned that King Jorg may be pushing ahead his agenda."

"What about Algie's role?" Jen shivered as she recalled the dank room in Shirajo Manor where she'd been held.

"Oh, you've met the witch?" Nira raised her eyebrows. At Jen's affirmative nod, Nira said, "My sympathies. I suppose you had a delightful conversation with her in Tent Ten."

"Yes, I did. Algie explained her goals. She hopes to repair the damage to their males' defective genes. She calls it the SARB project. SARB stands for Stabilize and Reboot."

"We know about her project. Algie has been inserting Trollek DNA into humans with the intent of finding a stable recombinant strand to fix their faulty genome."

Yaron gazed at Jen with narrowed eyes. "Did the female scientist say how close she is to attaining her objective?"

Jen regarded him from across the table. "Her subjects still die, so I'd say she's not there yet."

Yaron scowled. "She's a monster. We have to stop her."

"For more reasons than one," Nira inserted. "Algie is ambitious. Females in Trollek society don't hold positions of authority. She's an exception because her father is a clan chieftain, but being top scientist isn't enough for her. She wants more power, and she's using the Videns to support her goals."

"I'm more worried about her husband." Paz told them how Jen's apartment had been violated and her assistant compromised. "General Morar wants to recapture us. We made him lose face with our escape."

Zohar jabbed his finger in the air. "Maybe we can use that to our advantage. If we draw him out, Algie might follow."

"Let's not lose sight of our prime target." Paz withdrew a crystal from his pocket. "I was able to get a scan of the dimensional rift at Shirajo Manor with a makeshift PIP and transfer it to this storage unit. The data I recorded is on here, along with information on the power source."

Zohar gestured. "We salvaged your things from our previous safe house. We'll use your reader to access the contents. Dal, get his pack."

Paz's face brightened. "Supernova! I've missed having my equipment."

"We'll replace your lost items," Zohar assured him. "Give me a list later on."

Dal left the room and returned a moment later to shove a backpack into Paz's arms.

"Thanks, bro." Paz unzipped it and rummaged inside.

"Bro, what does that mean?" Zohar asked, scratching his head.

Nira smiled and patted his hand. "It's shorthand for brother, my love." She winked at Jen. "He's constantly confused by our idioms."

Jen smiled back. "I know the feeling."

Paz nudged her. "Hey, I do pretty good with your language." He addressed his comrades. "Any news of Kaj? The Trolleks who held us spoke of him. He's still alive."

Lord Magnor growled. "We have been searching but no trace of Kaj has surfaced. We will increase our efforts." Magnor handled his sword hilt as though preparing for battle.

Zohar cut in, his voice somber, "Let's concentrate on our primary objective. Paz, show us what you brought home."

Paz placed the crystal in a square device and put it in the middle of the table. A 3-D holographic display sprang up. Data scrolled down, pages and pages of it in a foreign language.

Jen rubbed her throbbing temples while the men leaned forward to study the information.

"This is incredible," Zohar remarked. "How did you acquire these scans?"

"I jumped the rift and took a reading."

"You did what?" Zohar slapped the table. "Are you insane? You could have been killed."

"It was the only way. The main generative thrust is coming from the other side, and I think I know how to neutralize it."

"We're lucky Paz has an engineering background," Nira said to Jen.

Jen frowned at her, bewildered. "What do you mean? I thought he repairs space relays for his real job."

"He does, but he's a communications system design engineer. Paz didn't tell you?"

"Hell, no."

Paz's expression froze as he overheard them. "I am employed as a field technician."

Zohar chuckled. "You may fool SattCom Networks, but not us. We know your true capabilities. When are you going to finish fiddling with your—"

"By the Creator, this confirms my theory." Dal pointed to the scrolling holograph, his face ablaze with excitement. "Wait here." He leapt up and hurried from the room.

"You're a full-fledged engineer, are you?" Jen glared at Paz. "You let me believe you were just a repairman. Why didn't you correct me?" *And why aren't you working at a job more appropriate to your experience and education?*

"I have my reasons."

"Oh, and you don't care to share them with me?" Jen pressed her lips together. She'd been right about him not being ready for emotional intimacy. After all they'd been through, he still refused to confide in her.

"I'll explain later. Now isn't the time."

Feeling shut out by his terse tone, she fell silent.

Dal returned a few minutes later holding a metal box. "It wasn't easy to obtain this, but I figured we might need it."

"I'll say." Lianne glanced shyly at the people around the table. "That thing almost got us killed."

"Paz, your scan shows traces of malnatium." Dal's eyes gleamed with fervor. "I was thinking along the same lines."

Paz nodded slowly. "Those mirror and calculator parts are being used to focus solar energy at the rift on the Trollek side. That's what fuels their generators and heats the malnatium contained within the arched canopy at their transfer stations. If we can force the cors particles at the event horizon back into the portal, it'll blow the mechanism. But we'll need malnatium ourselves to counteract the pressure."

Dal lifted his box. "And we have some here. I intercepted a shipment. Guess who sold it to the Trolleks?"

Zohar grunted. "Why does the name Timerus Halston keep popping up? My former High Exchequer may have paid the price for his treachery, but his rebel legion still has far-reaching tentacles." The prince hunched forward. "They destroyed the *Protector*. They'll do anything to keep us from going home."

Paz tilted his head. "You're saying they supplied the Trolleks with this rare element? The fools. Don't they realize their actions will lead to disaster if we can't close the rifts? The dimensional drift will expand and tear apart the multiverse."

Nira stood and paced, her feet weaving a pattern on the tile floor. "They expect to be saved, like the Trolleks. Loki is feeding them all a bunch of lies. He's another problem we have to address down the road."

Dal flexed his muscles. "I have what I need to rig an explosive device. What's the target?"

"Sire," Paz inserted, "I have reason to believe the main portal is on Togura Island. If we blow that one, it might trigger a shutdown around the globe. Let me show you why I think that would work." He pulled a stylus from his sack.

Nira gestured to Jen and Lianne. "I'm getting hungry. Let's go fix lunch while they're talking."

In the kitchen, Nira selected ingredients from the refrigerator while they shared stories. They agreed their powers were related to an ability to alter atoms at the molecular level.

"Odin had shapeshifting ability," Nira reminded them, slapping together a dozen chicken salad sandwiches. "It makes sense. We're not that different from each other in terms of our powers."

"But how are we sisters?" Jen opened cupboards until she found some plates. "I'm an only child."

"Are you? I was adopted as an infant. So, it turns out, was Lianne."

Lianne, filling plastic cups with lemonade, nodded. She was so quiet that Jen wondered what trauma she had suffered at the hands of the Trolleks.

Jen backed away from the counter. "We can't be blood related. My parents wouldn't lie to me."

"Let me see your watch." Nira put her knife down and stepped closer. "It says you're Two of Six."

"That's what Edith told me."

Nira's jaw dropped. "You met Edith? Where?"

"In Hong Kong. That's where we saw Dikibie, too."

"Askr said he was the last of the Gatekeepers. I guess he lied." Nira put a hand on her hip. "He gave Zohar a medallion to wear, saying it would protect him. So far it hasn't done anything."

"Interesting. Smitty the dwarf made a gold armband for Paz and advised him to wear it for protection."

"Read our runes, Nira." Lianne held out her wrist. She wore a watch similar to Jen's.

Nira grabbed a pad of paper and a pen and wrote down the symbols engraved on their watch faces. "It's a bunch of random words that don't make sense."

Lianne swept her arm in a broad gesture. "That's because we need our other three sisters to complete the circle."

I am not adopted, Jen thought. *I don't have any real sisters.* And yet a niggle of doubt plagued her.

What exactly was the personal issue Cousin Clifford was using in his claim against her?

Chapter Twenty-Four

Paz slouched in the passenger seat of their borrowed Acura as Jen drove along North Ocean Avenue in Palm Beach. Luxury condominiums gave way to individual mansions as they cruised up the road. There wasn't much traffic. According to Jen, most of the residents had escaped up north to their summer homes.

They'd decided to stay a couple of nights in Orlando and drive down on Friday morning. That gave Paz more time to consult with his team and Jen the opportunity to learn more from Nira and Lianne. She already felt close to the two women.

She turned down a private lane that took them past lushly manicured grounds toward a white columned two-story structure. Resembling the home where he'd grown up, albeit not as massive, it reminded him of all the reasons why he shouldn't have come. Nonetheless, he'd promised to see Jen safely home.

Besides, Dal had yet to figure out how they'd destroy the rift generators, and Magnor was following up on a new lead. An informant had indicated the Trolleks were reestablishing a recruitment center in Florida.

His team may have demolished Drift World, but the Trolleks wouldn't yield their presence in the state so readily. The confluence of sea currents and solar energy suited their purpose. Zohar wouldn't allow the beasts to gain another foothold there.

As soon as Paz dropped Jen off and fulfilled his obligations, he'd rejoin his friends.

Meanwhile, thanks to a comm link Paz had set up, Zohar was attempting to reach Primer Pedar on Karrell to request a new ship. He also meant to order Imperial Space Command to patrol Earth's orbit to repel any further attacks from outside.

Paz swiped a finger inside his collar. Jen had requested he wear a dress shirt rather than his usual T-shirt and jeans. She wore a sexy sheath dress that made him glance repeatedly in her direction.

The soft, vulnerable woman he'd come to know had gone. In her place was a sleek, sophisticated ice queen. Jen had tied her hair into a twist and carefully made up her face. The only finishing touch she lacked was a jeweled necklace to complement her graceful neck.

She parked at a circular drive in front of the stately house. A short staircase led to a set of double wooden doors with inset glass panels.

An older fellow emerged. He wore a slate gray suit that matched his color hair. His face split into a wide grin as he approached them.

"Miss Jennifer, it's good to see you home." His eyes crinkled with genuine warmth.

Jen gave him a hug. "Thanks, Eduardo. I am so glad to be here. This is my friend, Paz Hadar. Paz, Eduardo has been on our staff for years. He's like family to us."

The men shook hands, then Jen handed Eduardo the car keys.

"We borrowed this baby from a colleague. I'll need to find a driver to return her to New Jersey."

"I can make inquiries, miss. If you don't mind, your parents are in the dining room. They'd like you to join them for lunch."

"Of course, they would." Jen strode inside with a stubborn tilt to her chin.

Paz's booted footfalls echoed on the marble floor as he followed Jen past a wide curving staircase and a living room with ivory upholstered furniture, decorative art, and enormous vases of fresh flowers. Tall French doors revealed a pool deck beyond with extensive amenities.

His neck itched and sweat popped out on his brow. An urge to bolt grabbed hold of him. He focused on Jen's swaying derriere, telling himself he was doing this for her.

Nonetheless, he'd rather face a roomful of armed Trolleks than her parents.

Eduardo led them past a kitchen with gleaming stainless-steel appliances and maple cabinets and into a formal dining room. A wide glass table held a gleaming silver bowl of fresh fruit, crystal stemware, and porcelain china plates. An aroma of baked goods made his mouth water.

"Mom and Dad, it's good to see you. This is my friend, Paz Hadar," Jen said with a wave.

A blond lady with an upswept hairdo, pearl jewelry, and a tanned face rose at their entrance, as did the burly man to her right. The woman extended both hands to Paz in a warm greeting. He wasn't sure what to do so he took her palms and bowed.

"I'm Lydia, and this is Jen's dad, Robert."

"Call me Bob," the big man said with a broad grin. He shook Paz's hand, pumping it with vigor while scrutinizing him. Then he gestured toward the table. "Let's eat or the food will get cold. Eduardo, you can serve us now."

Paz claimed a seat beside Jen and across the table from her parents. He sat back, waiting for the butler to drop the cloth napkin into his lap. When Jen took hers, shook it, and opened it herself, he copied her motions.

Their customs may be different. Observe and learn.

They began desultory small talk as Eduardo served a starter course of a sweet green melon dribbled with red juice. Its succulent flavor dissolved in his mouth.

"So how did you two meet?" Robert asked between bites, while Paz wondered at the formality between Jen and her folks.

They'd been anxious for her return, and yet neither one of them had embraced her. She sat stiffly at his side.

He cleared his throat. "I don't know what your daughter has told you, but I got a gig on her film set in Tokyo when their lead character fell ill." He hoped he'd gotten the slang correct.

He and Jen had agreed on their story during the drive south. It had been an awkward trip. She was still miffed he hadn't revealed his background, and although he longed to tell her the truth, part of him hesitated to expose his secrets.

He sipped his white wine, swirling the cool liquid in his mouth and appreciating the tang on his tongue.

"So, you just hitched a ride to Florida with Jen on her jet?" Her father gave him a skeptical glance over his water glass.

Paz waited until Eduardo had served their next course, a fish dish from the smell of it. "My travel documents had been stolen, and Jen took pity on me as a fellow American. I had to get home."

Robert lifted his fork. "And what is it you do when you're not working as an actor, Mr. Hadar?"

"I repair communications equipment."

"I see." His mouth puckered like he'd eaten a lemon pit.

"He's being modest. Paz is actually an engineer." Jen clapped a hand on his shoulder and dug in her fingernails. "It's a good thing he came along. When our plane developed engine trouble, he took over the controls and landed us safely."

Paz, playing his role, grinned and nodded.

"What happened to the pilots?" Robert's gaze skewered him.

"We got hit by lightning," Paz lied. "They were incapacitated."

"Well, I guess we owe you a debt of gratitude. Tell me, how did you acquire piloting skills? Are you a flight engineer?"

"Not exactly, but my job can involve aeronautical systems. And I've taken some flying lessons along the way."

"You should have come right home after you reached safety, Jen. We were worried about you."

Jen swallowed a morsel of food. "I know, and I'm sorry, but that storm hit Hong Kong and flights were cancelled. We did the best we could."

"Does it matter, Bob?" Lydia's voice wavered. Jen's mother hadn't eaten much, mostly pushed the food around on her plate. "She's here now."

"Right, and we need to discuss strategy before this afternoon's meeting."

Paz studied Lydia from under his drawn brows. She was nervous about something, but what? When Eduardo delivered their roasted fowl, she barely touched her portion. Whatever was in the wind, he had a feeling Jen wouldn't like it.

"Mr. Hadar, I'd be happy to show you our gardens," Lydia said after the butler took away the remains of his dessert.

He'd thought *ice cream* a peculiar name for the cold gooey mound but liked to taste different flavors since he'd encountered the sweet on a previous sojourn to Earth. He could easily gain weight if he lived on this planet.

"Sure, that would be great." He rose, dropping his napkin on the table.

Robert stole Jen away for a private conference. She didn't even give him a backward glance.

He followed Lydia outside, around the pool area and down a flight of steps to a gravel path shaded by tropical shrubbery. A yellow and black butterfly took flight as they strolled along. Lydia identified the plants in a rote voice as though her mind were elsewhere.

Paz plunged his hands into his pockets, making inane remarks about the greenery as he'd learned to do growing up. He felt as out of place here as he did at his parents' formal estate. Jen's father had evaluated him as a possible suitor and found him lacking. He could read it in the man's eyes and in the way he lifted his nose.

Clearly, Jen agreed with Robert's opinion. She'd dismissed him without even a word of gratitude. In her view, he'd fulfilled his duty in taking her home. He should set up some perimeter rods so she'd be safe here and then leave. Yaron would pick him up in the shuttle a short distance away.

After all, what reason did he have to stick around?

****

Jen had been surprised by Paz's smooth manners and how easily he'd fit into the moneyed setting. It didn't jive with his background, what little she knew of him.

His contradictions intrigued her. She wanted to puncture his emotional armor and learn his secrets, but how could they have a relationship when he wouldn't bare his soul?

As she followed her father down the hall, she thought long and hard about what Paz meant to her. Did she want to continue their association? Was she prepared to let him go? Was her offer of a modeling job merely an excuse to keep him close? Did he even want to be with her anymore?

The overwhelming scent of lilies hit her nose as she entered her father's study. Her mother loved fresh flowers, and Jen had grown up with the heavy fragrance throughout the house. It reminded her of funerals and dead people.

"Jen, have a seat." Robert gestured to a chair opposite his favorite La-Z-Boy.

She sank down, her mind already segueing into the distant past. The smell of flowers changed into a cloying perfume. A woman's familiar face materialized from the haze that enveloped her. They stood inside a thatched roof hut.

"Jorunn, what shall we do? The berserkers are gathering their forces to invade. Their soldiers will march on the village by nightfall." The woman twisted her hands, her blue eyes wide and fearful. Long blond braids hung past her ears.

Jen's, or Jorunn's, stomach roiled. "We have no defense, sister. Our people aren't any match for those ugly beasts. Mayhap we should save our jewelry. We could use it to bargain for our lives."

"How? Oh, if only the warriors were here."

"They will arrive too late." Her husband and his friends would be away at least another fortnight. "Come, we can sew our jewelry into our clothing. We must hide our valuables before the berserkers get here."

Freydis laughed with little mirth. "Do you really think that will help? They will drag our people from their homes and ravage the women. Men with any strength left in their limbs will be forced into labor. As for the old, infirm, and very young... well, they'll likely feel the axe."

Jorunn grabbed a shift dress and looked for a tool to rip the hem. She felt compelled to save her jewelry, even knowing the gesture was futile. The invaders would strip them bare and give the garments to their own women.

She and the others would become thralls. Life as she knew it was about to end. She'd be forced to leave her home, her family, and her friends. They'd be separated and sold off as prizes of war.

Panic blossomed in her chest, making it hard for her to breathe. Never to be free again, to make her own choices, to feel her husband's loving touch. Only beatings and worse awaited them. Moisture tipped her lashes as her gaze swung to the dagger in her boot. One last choice remained.

"No, Jorunn. There is another way," Aunt Alba said from behind her.

"What other way?" She whirled but her aunt wasn't there. Jorunn rushed to the door, glanced outside, but only the wind blew sea air into her face.

"You'll find it," her aunt's voice said in her ear. "It's your destiny. Pray to Odin, child. With his guidance, you can save your people."

"How? Tell me what to do!"

"Jen, hon, are you okay?" Her father's voice snapped her back to reality as the cobwebs of the past dissolved.

"I'm sorry. What were you saying?"

Robert shrugged his powerful shoulders, his characteristic gesture denoting anxiety. Jen straightened her spine, retaining a sense of dread from her vision.

"You need to hear this before we face Clifford at the Board meeting." Robert's compassionate gaze held hers. "There's no way to put it gently. We'd hoped to keep it from you, at least until you got married, but Jen, your mother and I adopted you when you were a baby."

"What?" Her blood ran hot and cold. Icy tendrils pierced her skin. She shot to her feet. "You're joking."

"No, I am not." He leveraged himself upward, stepped forward, and placed his hands on her shoulders. "We were desperate to have a child, but Lydia couldn't conceive. Then one day, her sister Alba said she'd heard of a pregnant teen who wanted a home for her infant. Would we be interested?"

Jen's mouth dropped open. Aunt Alba had been involved?

"We jumped at the chance and took you as a babe. I didn't want to tell you like this, but Clifford is challenging your right to inherit his family shares. You need to know what you'll be up against. Of course, our attorney has been advising us. Alba definitely left her portion to you in her will. But Clifford's smear campaign can have harmful repercussions."

She pursed her lips. She'd never liked her cousin and while she could understand his motives, he'd still gained his mother's other assets, including her two homes.

Never mind Clifford. What about the repercussions of the bomb her father had just dropped?

She'd been adopted—like Nira and Lianne.

Her throat constricted. Was that why her mother had constantly criticized her as a youth, because she blamed Jen's heritage for their differences? If only Lydia knew how astute she'd been. Jen shared far more with her so-called sisters than with the parents who'd raised her.

She swallowed her shock, planning to revisit it later.

"What happened with Yeager Capital Investments? Did they come around with an offer?" She hoped her dad had acquired the extra financing needed to dodge Clifford's bullet. Her cousin's proposed merger was merely a ploy to push them out the door.

A grin split Robert's face. "Yeager signed the deal. The company will be okay once the Board votes in our favor." He paused. "I hope you'll forgive your mother and me for not telling you the truth sooner. We just didn't want to hurt you. We'll always love you as our daughter."

"I know." She hugged him, savoring his comforting embrace even as anger swept her. Would he have revealed this news if Clifford hadn't posed a threat? And if not now, when?

She could understand his motives. He and Lydia had probably been afraid of her reaction. She might turn away from them. But while an adjustment to their relationship would be necessary, they were still the folks who'd raised her.

Behind his back, she squeezed her eyes shut. This revelation had only plunged her deeper into the morass opened by the Trolleks.

****

When Jen returned home after the exhausting Board meeting, Lydia intercepted her in the foyer. Robert had gone to the company office following their appointment.

"How did it go?" Lydia asked, wringing her hands.

"We won. I'm just glad it's over. Clifford wasn't happy, but he had no choice with a unanimous vote."

"Thank heavens." Lydia's face sagged with relief. "Um, did your father talk to you about…?"

"Yes, and don't worry, you'll always be my mom." Swallowing her mixed feelings, Jen gave her adoptive mother a quick embrace. Then she stepped back and peered into the hallway. "Is Paz still here?"

"He's exploring the wine cellar."

A rush of pleasure pricked her skin. She'd expected him to leave shortly after her departure.

Lydia lowered her voice. "He's a nice, polite fellow, but how serious are you about him?"

Jen grimaced at the worried frown on Lydia's face.

"We work together, Mom."

"Come on, I see the way you look at each other. And while he's presentable enough, you can't exactly expect us to introduce him to people as your boyfriend. He's a part-time actor and a repairman, for heaven's sake." She said it as though he had a disease. "Imagine what our friends would say."

"Oh, like they don't have their own boy toys?"

"That's different. They don't marry them."

Jen's eyebrows lifted. "Who said anything about marriage?"

"Then why bring him home?"

"He wanted to make sure I got here safely."

"That's very sweet of him, darling. I suggest you send him on his way before he gets other ideas."

Jen clamped her lips tight. "I'll do what I damn well please." Brushing past, she descended into the brick-lined chamber where her father kept his collection of vintage wines.

Paz lounged on a couch, a glass of red wine on the cocktail table in front of him. A frown of concentration creased his face as he tapped on his PIP. He glanced up at her arrival.

"I'm surprised you're still here." She kept her tone light and casual.

He regarded her with a steady gaze. "Dal hasn't finished his calculations, so we don't have to regroup yet. By the way, your mother liked the new garden decorations I put up at the corners of your house."

"Those wrought iron rods suit the landscaping. Good idea."

His comm unit buzzed. He studied a text message that popped up. "*Smark*, I should have known."

"What?"

"Lord Magnor confirms our friend the general is establishing another recruitment center in Florida. We should take Morar out while he's accessible."

"Is Algie there?" Excitement laced her tone. If General Morar plus Algie were eliminated as a threat, she'd sleep easier at night.

"We can deal with Algie later. Besides, she's only part of the equation. We'd have to destroy her research, too."

"You heard what Nira said. Algie's ambition is what makes her truly dangerous. She doesn't care who gets hurt along the way. Plus, if we put her out of action, it might discourage her supporters."

He compressed his mouth. "General Morar is in charge of the Togura Island facility. With him out of the way, we'd have one less worry when we go in there to blow the rift generator. He's a more important target."

This debate was useless. "Then why are you still here?"

He stretched to his feet. "I wanted to know how your meeting turned out."

His idle tone made her ponder his true reasons for remaining. "Oh. We won. The merger was defeated."

"Congratulations. Now you can relax on that score. Tell me, you're good with corporate types, aren't you? I mean, you know how to market your company and attract new clients?"

"Yes. What are you getting at? Do you want me to introduce you to people for a modeling career? I thought you had only pretended to be interested, although you'd make a lot more money as a male model than you do repairing space relays."

He stiffened. "Money isn't everything."

"Maybe not, but don't you want to advance your career? If you're really an engineer, why not use your talents to their full potential and start your own company?"

"It doesn't work that way." His expression shuttered.

"Why not? Are you afraid to rock the boat? Upset the apple cart?"

His forehead scrunched. "What do you mean?"

She waved a hand. "Are you stuck in a rut because you're afraid of change?"

"There are certain issues to consider."

"Such as?"

He stuck his hands in his pockets. "Why do you care? Is what I do not good enough for you?"

She tried to make him understand. "It's fine, Paz, but you're so intelligent and skilled, you shouldn't be working in such an inferior role. You're capable of more."

"Where are you going with this?"

Jen tilted her head, taking the plunge. "I'm just wondering where we're going with us."

"Are you embarrassed because of my job, is that it?"

"I brought you home to meet my parents, didn't I?"

"That's not a proper answer."

She folded her arms across her chest. "All right, I really like you. I want to be with you. But what happens when your mission is over?"

His eyes hardened. "I go back to my job."

"Exactly. You leave me. You leave Earth."

"Why, would you come with me?" For a moment, something flickered behind his expression.

"Not if you're a space jockey hopping from one port to another. I want to settle down and have a family."

"Well, then I guess you'll have to look for someone more stable and suitable to your goals."

Hurt and disappointment slashed through her. "I guess so. Someone like you can never understand drive and ambition. You just know how to kiss women or kill people."

She regretted the angry words as soon as she flung them at him, but his refusal to consider her feelings wounded her.

He grinned, but his eyes were two cold ice chips. "I'm very good at killing, Jen. It's my best trait. Too bad you don't count that among your requirements for a mate."

"Paz, please, you're—"

He cut her off. "Thanks for your hospitality." He stuffed his PIP into a pocket, his movement jerky.

Without another word, he stomped up the stairs, banged open the front door, and left.

Chapter Twenty-Five

Paz pressed his foot to the accelerator and raced down the road. He'd taken the borrowed car, planning to return the vehicle to its rightful owner eventually.

How dare Jen imply he was afraid to take risks? She'd seen him put his life on the line for his job as a Drift Lord. But no, that wasn't good enough for her. *He* wasn't good enough to meet her ideals.

That's why she wanted to remake him into a supermodel. Being a comm tech was beneath her class. Her parents had made that clear, and obviously she shared their opinions. Jen couldn't accept him for who he was. His character didn't matter. She thought he should push beyond his boundaries to become someone better.

Good thing he hadn't told her about his experiments. She'd jump on him to complete his prototype and to maximize his potential. He'd trained as an engineer, so why was he working as a technician?

If he stuck with her, she would hound him until he went insane.

Smark, he should never have gotten involved with her. As he sped past the mansions with glimpses of the ocean on his left, he gripped the steering wheel with white knuckles.

Someone like you can never understand drive and ambition. Her words cut worse than a knife. If only she knew. Once he brought his plans to fruition, he'd make billions in credits and would become a name recognized throughout the galaxy. His revolutionary design would bring real time communications to the interstellar networks.

And yet he held back. Why? Because he lacked business acumen and marketing skills. Because the enemies he'd face in the corporate boardroom and from opposing military factions would be worse than the Trolleks.

Dammit, he needed her professional skills. Together, they'd be formidable. But even if she accepted him without reservations, he couldn't ask her to leave her home and family. She'd hate living on an isolated estate in the desert.

Meanwhile, she regarded him as—what was the slang term—a slacker who liked following the pack and who would never strike out on his own.

His eyes narrowed, and he focused on the road as he drove over a bridge across the Intracoastal. Zohar was busy planning their attack on the dimensional portal at Togura Island. Dal was constructing the explosive device they'd deploy to blow the generator and seal the rifts shut. Yaron monitored communications in Paz's absence. His team had things under control. Meanwhile, Lord Magnor had pinpointed where General Morar was establishing his new recruitment center.

Paz had unfinished business with the general. He'd prove to Jen he could take risks, but he would do it on his terms, in the way he knew best.

****

"Jen, what's bothering you?" Lydia sat beside her on their family room sofa where they had a wide view of the rear lawn.

"I miss Paz," she told her mother, already dressed to the hilt even though it was just nine o'clock the next morning.

Her mother had a charity lunch to attend that day and wore a canary yellow dress with pearl jewelry. She'd pinned her hair in a twist.

Good God, she was more like her adoptive mother than

she'd realized. Had she received parental approval only because she constantly imitated her? After all she'd been through, that seemed like such a shallow life. Paz had shown her what really mattered.

His absence caused a hole in her heart. She should be happy to resume her normal routine, but the prospect didn't thrill her.

The Trolleks invaded her mind and shattered her peace. Possibly more of her friends would be compromised like Sandi. Were they being targeted because of her involvement? If so, what made her think she could walk away?

One truism made itself clear: her role wasn't over. If she wanted to protect the ones she loved, she needed to accept her destiny. It did no good to deny her part in things to come.

Paz had tried to tell her, but she'd closed her ears. If his claims about destiny rang true, that made him Mr. Right.

She'd been wrong to denigrate him. He was the most courageous and selfless man she knew, putting himself in jeopardy to save her countless times. Without his skill and prowess, she and Smitty wouldn't have made it out of Morar's prison, off the island, and safely to Hong Kong. They owed their lives to him.

And she'd just cast him away like a defective cut of fabric.

She met her mother's concerned gaze. "I realize you think Paz isn't good enough for me, Mom, but he's the bravest man you could know. He's intelligent, honest, and devoted to his ideals. Aren't those qualities more important than money or status?"

"You can't live on character traits alone, darling. Money makes your life a whole lot easier."

"Sometimes it makes things more difficult. People expect you to behave a certain way, and if you don't, they scorn you."

Her mother smiled and patted her hand. "Maybe it's best if Paz left. His departure was rather abrupt, don't you think?"

Jen's lips pressed together. The woman she called mother would never understand.

She stood and smoothed down her cropped tan pants. "I'm glad Dad has things under control now with the company back on track. The capital from Yeager Investments will put us on solid ground. Cousin Clifford no longer poses a threat."

"Thank God we dodged that bullet." Her mother rose and tucked a tendril of hair behind her ear. "I hope you forgive Dad and me for not telling you about the adoption sooner. You know we love you as our own child."

"I do." Jen hugged her. Despite her prejudices, Lydia tried to be a good mother. She just deluded herself into thinking her advice was for Jen's benefit. "I have an appointment in town later this morning for our upcoming trunk show and then I'm leaving to head north. I'll take my Lexus."

She didn't need a car in New York and kept it parked at home. To her annoyance, Paz had taken their loaner. What would she say to Ted?

"Won't you be flying back to Manhattan?"

"I have to go somewhere else first. Tell Dad goodbye for me." He'd gone to work early that morning to get things rolling with their new opportunities.

Jen packed a suitcase and then headed out to see her client. Hours later, she turned onto the highway toward Orlando.

She couldn't believe she hadn't told Paz about her adoption. It showed what little regard she'd had for him to focus only on his personal attributes. She'd become as much a snob as her parents. Guilt weighed her down and gnawed at her stomach as she drove north.

By the time she arrived in Central Florida, Saturday traffic on I-4 crawled in both directions. Exhaustion claimed her as she reached the safe house and knocked on the front door. She wasn't tired from the three-hour drive but from anxiety over Paz's reception when he saw her on the doorstep.

Nira greeted her. "Why, hello, Jen. We didn't expect to see you back so soon."

"Is Paz here?" she asked in a hoarse voice.

"I'm sorry, but he hasn't checked in. We thought he was still with you."

"No, he left yesterday. Where could he have gone? Did Zohar give him a new assignment?"

"I don't think so, but let's ask the prince. Come on in."

Zohar denied contact with Paz and gathered his team. When they were seated, he paced the living room, riffling his fingers through his hair.

"He's not answering his comm unit, and his locator beacon has ceased functioning or else he's deactivated it."

Nira, Yaron, Jen, and Lord Magnor sat around with worried frowns. Dal was busy assembling his energy weapon in a bedroom converted into a laboratory. His muttered curses sounded from down the hall.

"Paz mentioned that General Morar was establishing a new recruitment center in Florida." Jen clasped her hands in her lap. "What if he's gone there to confront the Trollek commander on his own?"

"Fires of Agathorn, he'll be killed." Zohar stared at her in consternation.

"We must go after him." Magnor, standing, grabbed for his cloak draped over a chair.

"Our priority is to destroy the rift generator." Zohar's authoritative tone resounded through the room.

"Holy Guacamole, you can't be serious." Nira shot to her feet and prodded his chest. "You wouldn't abandon a member of your team. Leave no one behind, remember?"

He gazed at her in exasperation. "As soon as Dal completes his device, we will deploy it. That is our prime objective."

"Fine, but until then, we can help Paz." Nira's keen gaze swung to Jen. "Did you two have an argument?"

Jen gaped at her. "How did you know?"

"He'd only be so dumb if he was trying to prove something. Paz can be impulsive, but he wouldn't knowingly walk into the lion's den unprepared, unless—"

"I never meant for him to put his life in danger." Jen's voice cracked. "Please, help me find him."

It was her fault for driving him away. She prided herself on her self-reliance, but this was one time when she couldn't manage alone. Maybe it wasn't so bad to be a team player. Maybe she should learn how to be one herself.

****

Paz cut a hole in the wire fence surrounding the Trolleks' proposed new theme park at Tampa Bay. It was just past dawn on Sunday morning. Hopefully, any construction workers would be off for the day.

The invaders had purchased this acreage for an attraction to rival Busch Gardens. According to the advance publicity by their front company, they planned to include thrill rides, live performances by popular bands, shops and restaurants, plus animal exhibits and other zoological wonders.

After he'd left Jen's house and driven to Florida's west coast, Paz had cashed one of the kewa stones Zohar had given him and used the money to buy supplies. From a hotel room, he'd hacked into city government files to access the park's proposed site plan. He figured whatever the Trolleks built here would in reality be more extensive. Likely any documents they'd filed were just smokescreen.

As commander of the Earth-bound Trollek army, General Morar would be present to supervise the center's initial construction. This gave Paz the perfect opportunity to take him out. Despite his differences with Jen, he still intended to protect her. This was the only way she'd be safe.

Paz knew he was an idiot for coming here alone and not summoning his team for backup. But they were busy building the destructive device to take out the rifts. That was their prime objective, and rightfully so. Besides, he didn't want to involve anyone else. This mission was personal.

Wishing to remain under the radar, so to speak, he'd deactivated his locator beacon and turned off his wrist comm. If he survived, he'd accept the consequences for insubordination at that time.

After shoving his backpack through the gap in the perimeter fence, he fitted himself between the cut edges, careful not to snag his assault vest. No high-tech security systems here. The Trolleks must have other priorities or else they didn't expect the locals to pose a threat.

He'd entered the construction site through the northeast quadrant, the main entrance and visitor parking lot being further south. A forest of pine trees blocked his view forward.

Slinging his sack over his shoulders, he advanced slowly through the woods, well aware that cameras could be hidden among the trees. His boots crunched on dead pine needles. The debris could hide trip wires, so he placed his feet carefully. The fresh pine scent cleared his nose. He didn't detect any cors particles. So far, so good.

He emerged from the copse of trees and scooted down a hill. A high wall faced him with barbed wire on top. He'd need his grappling gear and work gloves.

Fifteen minutes later, he stood on the other side gaping at the recreation of a Viking village. The thatched roof structures appeared deserted, but he checked the empty buildings and narrow lanes with his spare Monix T-6 laser pistol in hand. Its heavy weight reassured him.

Sweat poured down his back. In ninety-plus degree heat, his vest felt like a personal sauna.

At the opposite end of the quiet village, he faced another high concrete wall. He paused in the shadows to take out a bottle of water and pour the liquid down his throat. Was he missing the mark here? Were the Trolleks working underground to build a series of utility tunnels beneath the theme park?

He put away the bottle and scratched at a bug bite on his arm. *Maug* mosquitoes. He could live without those pesky insects.

He adjusted the bulky pack on his back. Besides neutralizing Morar, he intended to set charges and take out the entire site, or at least the portal. Trolleks would have to vector in from somewhere else to staff this place.

Once over the wall, he surveyed the area beyond. His heart lurched at the sight that met him. A vast sandy field stretched ahead with row upon row of solar panels aligned toward the west. These panels rose on silver pedestals looking like elongated sheet music stands. Not a single weed or bush sprouted in the aisles between them.

To the right of this array stood an outdoor amphitheater. Its arched white dome gleamed in the sunlight. Presumably the dirt expanse in front was destined for seats. On his left, a cylindrical stone tower rose several stories high. It was shaped like a ridged goblet with a flat top.

In the far western corner, behind the solar panels, stood a three-story rectangular building. A hive of activity circulated around this structure. He took out his long-range scope for a better view.

A scruffy group of humans labored under the direction of uniformed Trollek troops. They dug some sort of trench. Other slaves unloaded supplies from parked trucks and carted them into the building.

He scowled in puzzlement. Other than the recreated village, there didn't appear to be anything comparable to the site plan. If not a theme park consistent with other Trollek recruitment centers, what was the purpose of this facility?

The jamming device his team had destroyed at Drift World had been powered by a confluence of ocean currents and solar energy. Could they be attempting to construct something similar here? But that wouldn't make sense. His team had already pinpointed the rifts. So why wasn't General Morar busy bolstering defenses at Shirajo Manor instead of appearing here? What was so important about this site?

Paz contemplated notifying Zohar, but he needed evidence

of this place's true function. He had to get inside that rectangular building, and only one way presented itself.

He shed his backpack and assault vest, reluctant to leave his gear behind, but he had no choice. His gaze zeroed in on a dead tree stump. He'd leave his equipment beside it as a marker.

His burden lightened, he zigzagged across the sandy ground, veered around the tower, and approached the workers by the bunker's loading bay. When an opening occurred, he slipped into their line and copied their actions.

Each man grabbed a carton from an open truck and then headed inside the structure. The work crew wore street clothes so he blended in with his black jeans and matching T-shirt.

Focusing his gaze straight ahead and slouching his shoulders, he shuffled by a couple of armed Trollek sentries. His group entered a cavernous space with crisscrossing pipes, metal grating, conduits, and steel. Two other levels rose above the ground floor via interior stairs. Some of the space around the inside perimeter was delegated to offices.

Clanking and grinding noises nearly drowned out the orders barked by the Trollek overseers. Paz dumped his box in a separate storeroom with the others as directed. When his fellow humans turned to leave, he dodged behind a tall stack of cartons. He wouldn't have much time to see what was going on before the next group arrived. He planned to exit the same way he'd come in.

A guard had the bad luck to stride into the room at that moment. Paz made quick work of flooring him. He wriggled his fingers, tingling from the impact of flesh to flesh. Thank the stars he'd remembered to polarize himself that morning so he didn't have to worry about being confounded.

Having a sentry lying at his feet changed his plans. Paz grabbed the beefy fellow by the ankles, dragged him into a corner, and then stripped off his outer clothes. Now he needed a place to hide the guy. His gaze alighted on a nearby box with the proper dimensions. He pulled out the dagger strapped inside his boot and cut it open. After shoving the Trollek inside, he donned the beast's uniform and hat, pulling the brim low.

Outside in the hall, he climbed a set of metal stairs. At the top landing, he peered over the rail at the vast interior illuminated by warehouse-type lighting. He noticed a huge white bifurcated pipe. His gaze followed where it joined into one piece and thrust toward the opposite side of the room. There it disappeared into the wall.

With a purposeful stride, he advanced along the third level catwalk until he came to an office. It had a glass wall so the occupant could inspect the big hall. The other side held a view of the solar panel field. When no one appeared to be near, he slipped inside. A black leather seating arrangement filled one corner in the office. Files, cabinets, and a wide desk completed the furnishings.

Paz aimed for a row of lit displays on a wall. His heart quickened as he studied them. One was a plant schematic. His pulse throbbing in his neck, he traced the blue, white, and red demarcations. As he had guessed, tunnels ran between the structures, but he still couldn't fathom the facility's purpose.

Wait, some of those designs looked familiar. A frown creased his brow and dread pitted his gut. Oh, no. Suddenly, he knew what the enemy planned to do.

Further inspection revealed the big pipe led to a room with a circulating mechanism, the source of the clanging noise. At the far end, this room narrowed to a tunnel where steam hissed from overhead conduits and metal barrels rode on a conveyor belt toward an unknown destination.

Paz's blood ran cold as he put the pieces together.

The pistons and steam-driven devices, the solar panels, the sun, and the nearby Gulf waters. The amphitheater shaped like a giant arch and the parade field in front of it. The presence of General Morar and his elite troops. He bet if he'd opened one of those cartons in the storeroom, it would contain calculator components and broken mirror parts.

Hounds of Hel, the Trolleks were constructing a supergate, a portal much bigger than previous ones and at a more strategic location. Once activated, this gate would permit the Trollek army to invade the country on a massive scale.

Chapter Twenty-Six

Paz considered how to prevent the Trolleks from activating their supergate. His best bet would be to divert the plant's stored energy so when they turned on their rift generator, an explosion would result. He'd brought along some dythium charges. Those should do the job.

The rectangular building served as a storage tank for the voltage produced by the solar panels. He wasn't sure what purpose that outside tower served, but it was tied into the network. He'd take a look over there later.

Inside the room with the metal barrels, he strode down a catwalk along one wall. The barrels sat on a conveyor belt that led to a closed circular door at the far end. All was quiet for now. He selected a barrel in a central location, pasted on his charges, and wired them together.

He set them to blow either when the beasts turned on the system or if he pressed a remote detonator. According to the schematics he'd studied in the main office, blowing this critical juncture would start a ripple effect, igniting the rest of the stored energy. Cracks caused in the understructure should tear the complex apart. Or so he hoped.

Pipes ran overhead, hissing steam that heated his skin. Sweat dripped down his face. He needed to get out of there before their security monitors registered his presence.

Uh-oh. Too late. A line of red lights on the wall began to blink in a steady sequence.

After verifying his work one final time, Paz leapt onto the

catwalk and charged toward the exit. He dodged metal gratings and skirted cables along the way. But as he neared the door, a squad of armed Trolleks surged inside.

He spun and ran in the opposite direction amid their shouts and laser fire.

A metal ladder beckoned. He scrambled up the rungs to the upper level, meaning to find another way out, but he ran smack into General Morar himself. Straightening, Paz pressed his lips together.

The Trollek commander glowered at him, his bristled jaw clenched, and his cauliflower ears flapped forward. "You!" He slugged Paz across the mouth. "What are you doing here?"

"What do you think?" Paz sneered as a couple of muscular troopers grabbed his arms. "I'm here to stop you."

Morar whipped out a shock stick. "You're wasting your time, human."

He jabbed Paz repeatedly until his knees sagged and agony pierced his ribcage. His lungs burned for a clear breath. If not for the beefy soldiers holding him up, he'd have been on the floor by now.

"Tell me, what have you done? Where is the rest of your team?" Morar's face mottled with rage.

"I came alone." A jolt to his kidneys made him swear aloud.

"Liar. What have you learned about this place?"

"Enough to know it has to be destroyed, *donik*."

Morar punched him in the face. He tasted blood on his tongue.

"You'll tell me what you know. Maybe another episode with the boratus worms will loosen your tongue."

His gut clenched. "It didn't work on me before. It won't work now."

Morar bared his teeth. "We'll see. We have other means we can use." He gestured to his soldiers. "Lock him up for now. I'll question him after the test run." The troopers tightened their grip on his arms.

"Wait." Morar held up a hand. "I have a better idea. We'll let the Drift Lord experience our operational status firsthand. That might be more amusing. Tie him to a barrel."

Panic flared in Paz's chest as they dragged him toward the conveyor belt. If they discovered his set charges, his death would be pointless.

Luckily the soldiers didn't take him far. One of them kicked him behind his knees at the second barrel. His legs folded, and he sank onto the rubbery surface of the conveyor belt.

The guard yanked his arms upward and handcuffed him to a protrusion on the barrel. At least he was on the opposite side of the room from that enormous round door.

They kicked him a few more times before leaving him alone. General Morar chuckled on his way out.

"Goodbye, Drift Lord. May we never meet again."

His body ached from their blows, but he steeled himself against the pain. The outer door clanged shut. He heard the hissing steam, the distant grind of machinery, and his own labored breathing in the sudden emptiness.

A vibration shook the room.

Oh, no. They were starting their test, whatever that meant.

His throat clogged when the round doors at the far end slid open and the machinery noise ratcheted up in decibels. Peering past the row of barrels obstructing his view, he gulped. The room beyond held a wide maw that swallowed each barrel.

A thump sounded. With a jerk, the conveyor belt started moving. He yanked on his wrists, but the handcuffs held him secure. Steam blew into his face and sweat oozed from his pores. Wedged between barrels, he could barely twist his body.

Up ahead, the first barrel entered the next room, swirled around a turntable, and then shot into the gaping machinery. Paz rattled his handcuffs, his heart thumping wildly in his chest. The cuffs bit into his skin but they wouldn't budge.

The next barrel met its fate as the conveyor lurched forward. As soon as the barrel with the dythium charge got there, it would all be over.

Do something!

His breath coming in short, hard bursts, he bent one knee and raised his foot. He'd use his teeth to grab the lock picks inside his boot. He hunched forward, straining his arm sockets.

Before he could achieve his objective, something whacked him on the head, and all went black.

****

Paz woke up outside on the ground. His head throbbing, he forced himself to a sitting position.

Whoever had knocked him out had also unlocked his handcuffs and dragged him here. He'd like to thank his ally but didn't have a clue who it might be.

The tower loomed at his side, and he remembered his intent to determine its purpose. Morar must have halted the test when he realized Paz had escaped. Whoever had helped him would have had to disable the security monitors. They'd be searching the grounds for him. He had to hurry.

He staggered to his feet and rounded the concrete base. It appeared solid with no door or other apparent entrance. The only way to reach the summit was to climb the ridges.

He was halfway up the tower when the solar collectors in the field below changed position to follow the sun. At the same time, flaps unfolded and extended from the sides of the tower, leaving him clinging to a ledge.

He scrambled upward, hauling himself from one shelf to another, gripping metal bars along the way. Finally, he heaved himself over the roof's edge. Only then did he realize the tower's function.

Standing upright, he surveyed the property from his high vantage point. The tower panels were mirrored. They intensified the radiant energy collected by the solar units. This energy then transferred to the storage facility. Considering the body of water off the west coast, he figured the Trolleks might have a hydroelectric plant in the vicinity that fed into this place as well.

When they opened the dimensional rift from the Trollek world, the combined forces on both sides of the gate would ensure its integrity. An entire army could march through that archway below.

He had to stop them before that happened.

From his pocket, he pulled out his remote detonator. But before he could press the button, someone kicked the small device from his hand. He raised his head to view General Morar's snarling face.

****

Jen gazed out the window of the shuttle transporting her to the Tampa location where Lord Magnor had pinpointed the new recruitment center. Zohar piloted the ship with Nira beside him. Yaron, Jen, and Magnor sat in the back. Dal and Lianne had stayed behind to work on his weapon.

Jen would never forgive herself if Paz had gotten himself killed. Clamping her lips tight, she gripped the seat cushion as they veered into a steep descent. A cloaking device ensured their arrival would go unnoticed.

She got a quick view of the terrain as they approached. A squat multi-story building sat at one end of the property, while solar panel collectors, a simulated Viking village, an amphitheater, and a big tower made up the rest.

"I'll put us down by the village." Zohar maneuvered the craft, his face grim. "Most of the activity is at the other end. We need to acquire Paz's exact location for an extraction."

"This doesn't look like a theme park." Nira peered out the transparent viewscreen in front.

Zohar pulled back on the throttle. "No, it doesn't, but we're not here to investigate. Our prime objective is to retrieve Paz and get out of here."

He put them down then killed the engine. Like Yaron, he wore his uniform tunic and trousers. The fabric served as lightweight body armor. Lord Magnor wore his sword and cloak like a modern-day Robin Hood.

They entered the village and split up. Jen and Nira stuck together. Jen took only two steps down the main street and froze. The scene was eerily realistic. She could almost smell the aroma of fish cooking and the scent of peat smoke trailing from the thatched roofs.

Her mind segued into a vision that made her heart flutter: *Armed Trollek soldiers amassing on the border. An invasion force poised to attack while their menfolk were away. Her humble abode, where she scrambled to save her jewels in a last, desperate attempt to save herself and her sister.*

Comprehension made goose bumps rise on her skin. That hadn't been a vision from the past. It had been a harbinger of the future.

This place, right here, was the spearhead for a massive invasion.

"Nira! Jen! Over here," Zohar hollered. "I found Paz's gear."

Jen's spirits soared. He must be nearby. That meant they'd guessed correctly as to his intent.

As she raced toward the prince, the solar collectors arrayed on the sandy field swiveled toward the sun. The tall tower unfolded like layers of a flower, its petals opening. Except those petals were actually mirrored panels.

"Look!" Nira pointed to the tower's flat top as they got close enough for a better view.

Two figures stood by the edge battling each other.

Jen's blood iced as she recognized them.

"It's Paz and General Morar. We have to hurry and reach them before they kill each other."

****

General Morar's tall, powerful figure blocked Paz's view of the sky. He must have gained access to the tower roof through a trapdoor. Perhaps the opening to the structure was underground, with an interior staircase or lift to the top.

With a snarl, the Trollek commander swung a fist at him. Paz dodged the blow and lunged for his detonator. The general intercepted him with a kick to his kidneys. Paz dove to the side and rolled on the roof, then leapt to his feet again.

Morar aimed a beefy paw at his nose next, but Paz ducked and came up swinging. His blow missed. He launched at the beast with a flying kick. Morar dodged him with accelerated speed. Every time Paz kicked or jabbed out at him, the *riff* shifted places in a blur. He snickered, enjoying the game, while Paz's breaths came more rapidly.

"You have caused enough trouble, Drift Lord." Morar's eyes blazed with hatred. "Let us end this." He yanked a disruptor from under his uniform jacket and shot Paz straight in the chest.

Paz glanced down in stunned disbelief. *No, that hadn't just happened.*

That instant was all it took for Morar to shove him over the edge.

As he toppled backward, he flung out his arms. His fingers caught on the rim. He hung there, his feet dangling over empty space. His vision dimmed, and yet he didn't feel any pain.

Morar sauntered over, no doubt to stomp on Paz's hands with his heavy boots. Paz saw the whites of his eyes, the spittle on the side of his ugly mouth.

He'd failed. All he had to do was push that button, and he had dropped the detonator. Now the Trolleks would succeed in their invasion. He couldn't guarantee the charges he'd set on the barrel would explode on impact. Morar might find them first and deactivate the bomb.

Or not. As long as breath remained in his body, he had a fighting chance. He would destroy this facility if it was the last thing he did. His body trembled, and his grip loosened. He just had to hold on long enough to finish the job.

A hooded figure emerged from the trapdoor on the roof just

as Morar raised his foot. In the next instant, a blade whizzed through the air and landed with a sickening *thunk* in General Morar's spine.

The general's eyes widened. Then he began a slow fall off the roof. With a bloodcurdling scream, he bounced from one flap to the next and finally landed on the ground amidst the sound of shattering glass.

Paz's unknown ally reached down to grasp his arms and haul him onto the roof where he collapsed on the deck. Too short of breath to move, he watched the hooded figure turn away and scoop up the detonator. Surprise crossed his features when the ally brought it over and placed it in his palm.

"Why?" he croaked as blackness encroached on him.

Algie flung back her hood. "It's fortuitous that you escaped from the operations facility and killed my husband, Drift Lord. Now there will be a vacuum in command—a vacuum I intend to fill."

"Not if I can help it." One final job remained before he passed out.

He pressed the button at the same time that Algie pushed up a sleeve and touched the armband all Trolleks wore. In the next instant, she vanished in a shimmer of air.

A huge boom sounded followed by a concussive blast that tossed him into oblivion.

****

Horror blossomed in Jen's chest when General Morar pulled out a disruptor and shot Paz point-blank in the chest.

"No!" She charged forward, but her beloved warrior had already tumbled over the roof's edge.

Vaguely aware of the others on his team following at her heels, she raced ahead. But when she reached the tower's base, Paz wasn't there. She scurried all the way around. Had she imagined him being shot?

Nira and the Drift Lords caught up to her just as a massive explosion cracked the air. A hot blast knocked her over. Tremors shook the ground. She covered her head with her arms as debris rained down.

When silence returned, she glanced up at a field of smoking rubble. All was gone: the rectangular building, the tower, the amphitheater, and the array of solar panels. Only the village remained standing.

Omigod, she spotted Paz lying motionless on the ground.

She scooted over, soot floating in the air. He had a scorch mark on his chest and blood on his face. She felt for a pulse and got a faint beat in his neck. He was still alive!

Morar lay a few feet away, a knife in his back. One glance at his vacant eyes told her their nemesis would bother them no more.

Yaron rushed to Paz's side, knelt, and panned his PIP up and down the fallen warrior's body. A grim expression washed over his bearded face.

"It's not good. His injuries go deep. I do not know if I can heal him."

"Paz." Zohar sank to his knees and gripped his comrade's limp hand. "You fool. Why did you do this on your own?"

Jen bit her lower lip. "It's my fault. I think he meant to prove himself to me." A tear leaked down her cheek. She gazed at Nira's sympathetic face. "I criticized his lack of ambition. If he's so skilled, why didn't he get a better job than fixing space relays?"

Zohar raised a dark eyebrow. "He didn't tell you about his research project?"

Too choked up to speak, she shook her head. *What project? Was that the secret he'd been keeping from her?*

"We need to get him to the shuttle," Zohar stated.

Yaron glanced at his commander. "He may not survive the trip. I need to stabilize him first."

Nira's eyes scrunched. "He's still critically injured. Even if he makes it to the safe house, that might not be enough. You should take him to the Norns."

"What's that?" Jen asked, despair dampening her spirits.

"They're the three goddesses of Fate. They guard the Urd Well, which we know as the Fountain of Youth. It's in St. Augustine."

Jen snorted. "That's just a fable."

Yaron glanced between them. "You're mad. His wound is severe. Myths and magic won't help him."

"If there is any truth to the legends, a drink from the fountain might heal him." Nira shoved a wisp of hair from her forehead. "Do you really think your treatment will work?"

Yaron's lips firmed as he studied Paz's pallid complexion. "There's only so much I can do. His pulse is weak and erratic. He may have internal bleeding." His voice deepened with sorrow. "I can't repair him without a full surgical suite, and we've lost our ship."

Jen gripped Nira's arm. "If you think there's any chance—"

"I wouldn't have mentioned the Norns otherwise. They can read the past, present, and future. Ask for their help."

"Then tell me how to get him there. I could use my watch. The vector device will take us to their location."

"That won't work. You'll need a car. I don't know exactly where the Norns are located in St. Augustine."

"Listen, here's the plan." Zohar jabbed his finger in the air. "While Yaron stabilizes Paz's vitals, we'll search for the car he drove here. Once we find it, the two of you will get inside. We'll use our towing beam from the shuttle to transport you. Upon arrival in St. Augustine, you'll be on your own. We must return to help Dal complete our primary mission."

****

An hour later, Jen drove through the streets of Florida's oldest city while Paz lay unconscious on the rear seat of Ted's Acura.

292

Tears clogged her throat and nearly obstructed her vision, but she followed the signs down King Street into the center of town.

Flagler College stretched on her left while the Lightner Museum stood on her right. At the corner of King and Menendez, she turned left onto A1A. A bridge stretched over the water to the east, boats at anchor on the Bay. She followed the signs, passing the Old Jail until she reached the parking lot for the Fountain of Youth tourist attraction. That seemed the likeliest place to start her search.

Instead of turning into the main entrance, she drove around the perimeter searching for another means of entry. Between a pair of cedar trees, she found her spot. She parked, hoping the property didn't have security cameras in this remote corner.

It was too hot to leave Paz in the vehicle. Using a beach towel she'd discovered in the trunk, she spread it on the ground and tugged Paz onto it. She used the towel to drag him into the shade.

Aware that every minute ticking away was another minute he couldn't afford to lose, she propped him against a leafy oak, kissed him on the mouth, and then bounded across the grass.

Pines, magnolia trees, and sabal palms dotted the grounds. A sea-scented breeze plied the air, reminding Jen of her first visit here as a tourist.

This time, she avoided the stone buildings, statues, and Indian exhibits that drew visitors and aimed for something else she remembered from the past.

Wary of observers, she approached a stone ring on the ground in the middle of an open field. Concrete filled the interior of the circle, out of which stuck an open pipe. She'd seen the thing on her last visit and wondered if it might be an air vent.

Her stomach churned with acid. The heat and the stress were taking their toll. She sucked in a breath of warm, humid air. Her own discomforts didn't matter. Saving Paz was all that counted.

She pressed along the stones, considering what she would do if this turned out to be a dead end. She'd have no option except to drive Paz back to Orlando, and by then, she would be driving to his funeral.

Nira had to be right. Down below lay the Urd Well, the true Fountain of Youth. A drink from this magic fountain would restore Paz's vitality.

She heard a latching sound and something moved beneath her fingertips. Her pulse accelerated.

The concrete disk swung aside, revealing a gaping hole. A flight of stone steps led downward into the depths.

Chapter Twenty-Seven

Jen reached the bottom of the stairs and peered around. A tunnel led away in a westerly direction. She'd had the foresight to bring a flashlight but didn't need one. Rocks imbedded in the walls glowed with enough light to illuminate the way.

Moisture beaded on the stones and water dripped in the background as she proceeded along the dirt path. A few feet ahead, the trail aimed downward. Descending deeper into the earth, she sniffed a damp, musty aroma. The passage narrowed and she squeezed herself between two protrusions.

Did the Norns really live here? Was this the site of the legendary Fountain of Youth, aka the Urd Well of Norse fame?

Or was it merely a forgotten limestone cave system? North Florida was riddled with them.

As though to confirm the latter theory, gnarled calcite columns, stalactites, and stalagmites came into view as the tunnel widened into a cavern. Jen watched her footing as she climbed over a ridge, scrambled across a pile of rocks, and curved around a boulder. At the far end, another narrow passage with a low ceiling made her crouch to proceed. The dripping noise turned into a steady flow the deeper she went until it drowned the echo of her footsteps.

Her knees quaked, and she breathed in rapid, short bursts. She didn't want to be trapped here.

She couldn't think of that now. Paz's life hung in the balance. He could be dead by the time she returned.

Her hair hung in damp clumps as she skittered over a

flowstone floor and scooted into a knobby passage. Her limbs trembled from fatigue. What would she find at the end?

More importantly, how would she find her way back?

She could swear she'd been in this cavern before. Like Hansel and Gretel, she should have left a trail of string or pebbles to follow back to the surface.

Her heart thumping, she prayed her faith would be justified. She kept on, her love for Paz propelling her forward.

Love? Oh God, yes! She hadn't realized it until now.

The thought of losing him brought tears to her eyes. Regardless of what he did in real life, the man was her hero. He appreciated her for who she was, not for who he wanted her to be. She was guilty of that sin. If he revived, she'd tell him how she felt. She had to save him, no matter the cost.

Her head jerked up. Was that a voice she'd heard?

Creeping ahead, she listened acutely. Her pulse thrummed in her temples. Someone laughed, and a low murmur followed. Sucking in a breath of rust-scented air, she squeezed through a tight gap toward the sound.

A bright light shone ahead where the cave widened. The rush of water thundered in her ears. Was this where the three Norns lived? She pictured a trio of hags stirring a spoon in a giant cauldron. Did they peer inside at the swirling brew to read the future?

She emerged into a massive cavern with a ceiling so high, she couldn't see its top. A waterfall gushed from way up on a wall, dropping several stories into a pool below. From there the water tumbled onward as a river, disappearing into a crevice at the opposite end.

Three people glanced up at her arrival, their faces showing rapt interest but no surprise. She stared at them, taken aback by their unexpected appearances. Then her astonished gaze swung toward the furnishings: an upholstered seating arrangement and a fully functional entertainment system. Was this for real, or could she be hallucinating?

A young girl with blond braids bounced up from the couch where she'd been playing a video game.

"Jennifer Dyhr, come and play with me. I'm tired of these two. They're no fun."

The oldest woman had scraggly gray hair that reached her shoulders, a lined face, and the translucent skin of the very old. Her companion looked to be fortyish. She had brown hair cut in a short bob and pleasant features. The pair had been engaged in a discussion, interrupted by Jen's arrival.

"Sylvia, don't bother the young lady," the brunette admonished. "She needs our help."

Sylvia sighed and threw down her controller. "Don't they all. I suppose your sister Nira sent you."

"Um…" Jen didn't know what to say.

The middle-aged one waved. "We should introduce ourselves. I'm Verdandi. I control the Present. This is Urd who rules over the Past." She indicated the older lady. "And Skuld is the Future, although she prefers for you to call her Sylvia."

While they dressed in normal street clothes, their eyes glowed with an ethereal light.

"I'm honored to meet you, although I don't understand all this." Jan gestured at the array of furniture.

"Well, what else are we supposed to do? We're stuck down here. We deserve our comforts." Verdandi advanced toward Jen. "It's been so long since we've had anyone visit us. Please, sit down, dear. Can I get you some tea?" With a wriggle of her hand, she conjured a tea set on the coffee table.

"Don't be so formal. She's in a rush, aren't you?" Sylvia said with a smirk.

"Yes, I am. Can you predict what will happen in the future?" Jen couldn't keep the anxiety from her tone. "Is Paz going to live? Will the Trolleks be defeated?"

Gray-haired Urd cackled. "That depends on you, missy."

"My friend is injured. Nira said you'd be able to help. Does the river water have healing properties?"

Urd shook her head. "So impatient, you modern women. You never want to sit down and have a chat." She sat in an armchair and picked up her knitting. Her project must have been in the making for a long time, because a huge clump of it cluttered the floor.

Sylvia bounced over to the coffee table and grabbed a cookie from a platter that hadn't been there a moment before. "Everything comes with a price. Ask Nira about the shoes I gave her. She had to fetch some yellow flowers for me first. Too bad she forgot about those blossoms since their sap can heal wounds."

"What would you have me do?" Jen asked, wishing things could be simpler.

"This water nourishes the root of the great world tree that supports all of the realms. You've heard of Asgard?"

Jen nodded. "Asgard is the home of the gods in Norse mythology."

Sylvia lifted her chin. "It is where the mighty Odin once resided. Some of his handmaidens, the Valkyries, still exist. They're keeping the hall ready for his return."

Verdandi strode to a bureau and examined herself in the attached mirror. She patted the fine lines beside her eyes. "We may decide man's fate, but the Valkyries determine which soldiers die in battle and which ones shall live. If you want to save your fallen warrior, you must steal one of their feathers. Then you can command the Valkyrie to give your mortal his life. Bring this plumage to us, and we'll supply you with a ladle of water from the Urd Well to restore his vigor."

Jen had no choice but to accept their terms. "Tell me where to find these creatures."

Sylvia regarded Jen with a sly grin. "You have the power. Use your watch and go there."

"But I don't—" Even as she spoke, her vision receded and she dropped into endless space.

Jen blinked as her sight returned. She stood in a forest with tall leafy trees and a lake sparkling through the branches. Birds twittered and leaves rustled in a warm breeze scented with honeysuckle. A yellow butterfly took flight while a lizard scampered under a rock.

Now what? Laughter rang out amid the splash of water. Jen followed the sounds. She came upon a small clearing overlooking the lake. A group of swans floated on the surface, their regal necks extended. A young woman swam laps beyond them. She dove under and resurfaced with water streaming down her face. Her straight hair was such a pale gold as to be almost white.

Jen envied her skin, creamy without a single blemish, and her perfect form. Embarrassed by the woman's nudity, she swung her gaze away. By the shore, she spied the feathery plumage of a swan.

She crept closer and had almost closed her fist around a cluster of plumes when the young woman shrieked at her.

"How dare you steal from a virgin maiden of the Lord, Odin." She emerged from the water, her eyes flashing with rage.

Jen held up the fistful of feathers. "I command you, Valkyrie. Do as I say."

The woman sank to her knees. "State your wish, mistress," she said in a sullen tone.

"You will allow Paz Hadar, Drift Lord, to survive this battle and all others yet to come."

The Valkyrie bared her teeth. "He shall live, but I cannot promise you that he will thrive. That is beyond my power."

"I'll take what I can get." Their business concluded, Jen turned away.

"Wait, you cannot steal my entire coat!"

"You're right." Jen plucked a few feathers from the bunch and tossed the rest back. The Norns had instructed her to bring them only one plume, after all. "Remember my command. I still hold sway over you with these in my possession." Then she touched her watch, and in a shimmer of lights, she transported back to the cave with the Norns.

Jen didn't understand how the device operated despite

Nira's instructions, but it seemed to work with focused determination rather than emotion.

She held out the cluster of feathers. "Here, I have done as you ordered. Paz will live but he is weak. I need your magical water to restore his strength."

Verdandi snatched a ladle, procured some water from the flowing river, and funneled it into a vial. "This will improve his health," the goddess said, offering Jen the sealed container. "But if you drink it instead, you will forever maintain your youth and beauty."

Jen sucked in a sharp intake of air. "What do you mean?" She tucked the vial inside her pocket.

Verdandi's eyes twinkled, the first sign of a sense of humor Jen had seen thus far. "Contrary to legend, the Fountain of Youth does not provide immortality. But as it nourishes the great tree, it will feed you with vigor and allow you to bloom with your full potential. You will journey thus to the afterlife when your time comes, maintaining your youthful beauty."

Jen touched her face. She could look like a model forever? Never get wrinkles like Urd and never get old and feeble?

She shook her head. "It's not for me. I must get back to Paz. How do I get out of here? Should I go back the same way I came?"

The trio ignored her. Sylvia plopped on the couch and picked up her video game controller. Verdandi poured herself a cup of tea, and Urd returned to her knitting. Jen couldn't see what they'd done with the plumage.

She glanced at the walls of the cavern and the multiple passages leading into the gloom. Having lost all sense of direction, she had no idea which one led to the surface.

She'd have to use her watch for transport again.

Before she touched her wrist, her gaze caught on a cluster of stalagmites jutting from the cave floor. The pattern looked familiar. She spun around.

"I've seen something similar in my dreams, except the spires are gravestones." Her voice shook with excitement. "In the dream, I'm with Aunt Alba in a graveyard. She always indicates one of the stones. There's lettering on it that I can't make out."

Urd glanced up, a small smile on her mouth. "Ah, Alba. I remember her well."

"Is she sending me a message?"

Verdandi knitted, her fingers going faster. "You must find your own path, daughter of Odin."

Jen's teeth clenched. "I didn't come all this way for riddles." She spied the feathers laying on the coffee table and lunged forward, grabbing them in her fist. "You want these back? Give me answers."

"Find the stone." Sylvia spoke in a calm voice as though she'd anticipated Jen's actions.

"In a graveyard? Where?" Jen strode to a ledge that overlooked the gushing river and poised her hand threateningly in the air. Spray wet her face. "Talk, or I'll let these go." She spoke loudly to be heard over the waterfall.

"There's no need for dramatics, young lady," Urd said with a disapproving frown.

"The gravestone represents a rune stone." Verdandi, still seated and holding a teacup, fixed her gaze on Jen. "Loki is trying to reach you through your dreams, and Alba is warning you. The demon wants you to find the spell that will unlock him from his eternal prison."

"Loki?" Wasn't he the evil spirit manipulating King Jorg, the Trollek ruler? According to Nira, Loki meant for the beasts to keep the rifts open until the widening drift caused a catastrophic blast, tearing apart the multiverse. Then he would rule over the ensuing chaos.

"Find the wrong rune," Verdandi added, "and the Dark Lord will be free. Find the right one, and it will seal him away forever."

"You'd better hurry." Sylvia spoke in an idle tone. "Ragnarok nears and then he will have no more need of spells."

"If I recall my mythology correctly, the gods were defeated

in the last great battle. Do you want to risk the same thing happening again? What do you see in *your* future?" Jen asked.

Sylvia narrowed her eyes. "You must unite with your five sisters," she said without answering Jen's question. "Your timepieces hold the key to reading the rune stone."

"The prophecy says we have to join forces with the six sons of Thor." Jen stepped closer so she could hear more clearly.

"Sylvia, tell her about the other weapon. You don't have to let her know the outcome." Urd conjured a plate of sandwiches on the coffee table. The aroma of bacon entered Jen's nose, making her mouth water. Her stomach rumbled. How long had it been since she'd eaten? She suddenly felt ravenous.

The child pushed a braid over her shoulder. "There is a way to dispel the beasts who follow the demon's bidding. So it is written in the Book."

"What book? You're not the first person who has mentioned one to me." That tempting fragrance pulled her closer. She was *so* hungry.

Sylvia bounded to her feet. "Want a bite?" She picked up the tray and held it out.

Urd smacked her lips. "It's sliced turkey on a croissant with Swiss cheese, bacon and avocado. Your favorite." She rose, her skirt swaying at her ankles. Hadn't she been wearing pants before? The older woman looked spruced up, like a lady at a luncheon.

Verdandi stretched and stood. "Take a few sandwiches along with you. You can give some to your young man. He'll be starving when he awakens."

That's true. She couldn't stand smelling the tantalizing scent without grabbing a bite.

Jen moved forward but her steps took her toward the precipice instead. The three Norns faced her in a semicircle, standing between her and the exit from the cavern. She teetered on the riverbank, the rush of water loud in her ears.

Verdandi approached, her eyes glowing, her thin mouth spread in a deceptive grin.

While Jen stood stupefied, Verdandi nabbed the feathers from her grasp. And then the goddess of Present shoved Jen in the chest, pushing her over the edge.

Jen screamed as she toppled into space. Images swirled around her, a mixture of past memories and faces of loved ones. Dust spun in a vortex, gathering her into its embrace, while lights sparkled in the gloom. The light grew brighter until it blinded her in a white flash.

She landed with a jarring thump onto a soft surface. Her vision returned. She'd come to rest outside next to Paz under the oak tree. Birds twittered and leaves drifted down from an overhanging branch.

After taking a moment to calm her racing pulse and regain her equilibrium, she leaned over Paz's still form. His chest rose and fell in a steady rhythm, but the scorch mark remained on his chest and his skin was pale as a cream camisole.

The Valkyrie had promised he would live but didn't say if he'd regain consciousness.

She scrubbed her face then stared at her hand. Her skin wouldn't always stay so firm. One day, she'd be like Urd, her flesh wrinkled, her veins prominent, her skin texture like tissue paper.

Unless she drank the water from the Fountain of Youth.

Jen withdrew the vial from her pocket and stared at the clear liquid below the stopper. To be youthful and retain her beauty for the rest of her days… it was tempting. Paz might never recover. He wouldn't know the difference, and neither would his teammates. She could say he had succumbed to his wounds.

She would look the way her mother had always wanted her to be—slim, lovely, and blemish-free forever.

But then Paz would never wake up. He'd never gaze at her with his intense blue eyes or make love to her with passionate fervor. She would never again feel his warmth next to hers, his hard body against her pliant form.

She let out a shuddering breath. This sacred water was

meant for him. She hadn't come here to sacrifice her Drift Lord to a selfish whim. They could grow old together. He wouldn't care if she looked like Urd in her later years.

That is, if he'd have her. She wouldn't blame him if he walked away after the way she'd treated him. But she wouldn't let him go without telling him how she felt.

She stroked his cheek, admiring the angles of his jaw, the peacefulness of his face in repose, the tilt of his lips.

He was *her* warrior, and by all that was holy, she'd go to the stars with him if that's what it took.

Jen uncorked the vial and dribbled some of the liquid on his chest wound. Then she pried open his mouth and poured in the rest. She squeezed his jaw shut. He coughed and swallowed.

And she waited.

She rocked back and forth with her arms around her knees, praying this effort would make a difference. If only she could prove to him that he was her hero, no matter what challenges he faced or what job he held. It was the man who mattered, and she accepted now that they were meant to be together.

"Jen?"

Paz's raspy voice made her head turn. He'd opened his eyes and gazed straight at her.

"I'm here, my love." Her spirits lifted with joy. Moisture flooded her eyes as the bluish tinge to his lips receded and healthy color filled his face. "How do you feel?"

"Not bad, considering I'm still alive. My skin tingles all over." When he noticed the charred mark on his shirt, he grunted with dismay. But as he lifted the fabric, his skin showed clear, unbroken flesh. His brow furrowed. "I don't understand. How am I healed?"

She leaned over and kissed him. "I'll explain later. It's time to go home."

Chapter Twenty-Eight

"Are you sure I'm not hurting you?" Jen tickled Paz's arm as they sat on the couch in the safe house. A crime show played on TV but their attention focused on each other.

Paz wore jeans and no shirt. The air-conditioning ran incessantly in the August heat.

"*Leera*, your touch will always electrify me." He put his arms around her and kissed her with the hunger of a depraved man.

She tangled her fingers in his hair. She had on shorts and a tank top, and he slid his hands underneath to fondle her breasts. The circular motions of his thumbs made coils of warmth shoot straight to her groin. Her lips answered his quest, and their tongues danced a duet until she came up for air.

"Did I express my gratitude to you yet?" He nibbled on her ear. "You saved my life."

"You can show me *again*." She couldn't get enough of him and splayed her fingers on his powerful chest.

A week had passed since their return, and despite Paz's claims to be well enough for duty, Zohar had ordered him to remain in the house and monitor communications.

He'd established an uplink to Primer Pedar on Karrell and confirmed that the regent had sent a new ship their way, this time an armed cruiser with a full crew complement.

Meanwhile, Zohar and Nira had left with Dal and Lianne to deploy their weapon at Shirajo Manor. The resultant collapse of the main rift had a domino effect as Paz had theorized and shut down the entire sequence of inter-dimensional gates.

While on Togura Island, Zohar had received a tip about where Kaj was being held. He'd left on a rescue mission immediately following their success at the fortress. Nothing remained of Morar's headquarters except a huge crater. Reports of hot ash and rocks spewing from the island's volcano had authorities alarmed, and they'd warned residents to evacuate. An eruption appeared imminent.

Zohar figured he'd angered Loki by disrupting the demon's well-laid plans. Earthquakes and other natural disasters were rising in frequency. If the rifts wouldn't cause Ragnarok, Loki must be looking for another means to bring about worldwide disaster.

Paz had mentioned a heavy presence he felt each time he passed through a rift. Zohar shared the experience. They figured it must be Loki, attempting to drag them down into the depths. The demon's power would only get stronger as the end of days approached.

In the meantime, a sizable force of Trolleks remained stranded on Earth. True to her word, Algie had stepped into the void and declared herself queen. With King Jorg on the other side of the dimensional barrier, no one refuted her claim.

Zohar had assigned Yaron the task of tracking the Trollek scientist with the goal of sabotaging her experiments and destroying her research.

There was also the army of mind slaves to consider, sleeper agents who may have already been called to active duty by their new liege. When the team's ship arrived, Zohar wanted Yaron to continue his lab work on board. He'd been analyzing Nira's blood in the hopes of devising an antidote to the confounding spell.

Kaj's assignment, when he recovered from captivity, would be to contact Agent Monroe to evaluate the government's position.

Meanwhile, Magnor had set off to look for the Book of Odin that Jen had heard mentioned several times. She'd told the team it might hold information on a weapon to defeat the Trolleks.

They had plenty to do. The women still had to locate their three other sisters and then find the rune spell that would banish Loki forever. Zohar had promised to help them. Meanwhile, they needed allies against the demon's power.

After their ship arrived and Paz established a comm uplink, the prince wanted him to contact the Videns. Did this Trollek faction of disgruntled scientists support Algie or oppose her? What other allies could they gather?

For now, Paz and Jen had to hold down the fort. Holding down their need for each other was another matter entirely. Jen could barely control her response to Paz's rising passion. The evidence bulged between his thighs, giving her a thrill knowing she'd been the cause. She wanted to feel him against her, flesh to flesh.

She snatched at his belt, fumbling with the buckle. He helped her relieve him of his pants and then she followed suit. Jen tackled him on the sofa, pinning him down, and then showed him how much she cared by sheathing him in her heat.

His head fell back and a look of bliss enveloped him. "Ah, Jen, I can't live without you."

He filled her in more ways than one. As she rode him, her hair hanging down and sweat beading her forehead, she absorbed his words.

"You don't have to," she said when it was over and they lay naked with their limbs twisted together.

"What?" He disengaged himself, leaned up on an elbow, and regarded her with a tender expression.

"Live without me. If… if you want, I'll come with you."

"You would do that for me, give up your work here, and travel the stars?" He spoke in a husky tone, his gaze sweeping her face.

She traced her finger along his biceps. "I don't want to live without you either. You make me whole. When I'm with you, I can be myself and not worry about what people think. You were right when you said we're meant to be together. I love you."

His eyes sparked. "You are mine, *leera*. I love you, too. But there is something you should know. I haven't told you the truth about my work."

"No kidding. Nira said you're a communications system design engineer. So why do you have a job as a field tech?" Was he about to finally open up to her? She hoped so. That would bring down the last remaining barrier between them.

He frowned. "I've lain low for two reasons. One, it pleased me to annoy my father by being a lowly technician."

"Why is that?"

"The old man didn't approve of me, ever since my genetic ability to sniff cors particles manifested itself. He called me a freak for my differences from other kids."

"That's horrible."

"He'd had such high hopes for me, you see, and then I had to go for Drift Lords training."

"I gather this was mandatory?"

"The trait is rare. Those who possess it have a duty to defend our worlds."

"Your father should have been proud."

Paz snorted. "My father had a great deal of pride in his bloodlines, and he regarded mine as tainted. Plus, he ruled our household with an iron hand, if that's the proper expression. He expected us to live up to his standards. My goals weren't the same."

"What did he do for a living?"

Paz's lips curled in a cynical smile. "He owns a merchant space fleet. It's been in our family for generations."

Whoa, they owned a shipping fleet? No wonder Paz acted at home in her family's moneyed presence.

"Oh, so that's what you meant about having experience on various ships. I suppose your dad put you to work to learn the business?"

Paz nodded. "He had posts ready for me and my elder brother, Renslow. Renslow was always the perfect son, conservative and yet ambitious. My brother had a good head for leadership, while I wanted to travel and see the stars. Father meant for me to take a financial position in the company, but I didn't want any part of his plans.

"During the Great Purge, he paid big credits to stay off the Royal radar. Father should have utilized me in the company then in a way that benefited us both, but he couldn't get past his disappointment in me."

"I'm so sorry."

Paz rolled on his back and folded his arms under his head. "I had a gift for different languages. Whenever we had guests for dinner at home, I'd listen to their dialects and practice them in private. I wanted to learn how to better communicate with people from other worlds."

"I'd think that would be useful even in the merchant fleet."

"Yes, but it wasn't the role Father wanted for me. When he wouldn't agree to pay for my advanced education, I left home and never looked back." He stared at the ceiling. "After I completed Drift Lord training at the Academy, I joined SattCom Networks. The job allowed me to travel and paid well. I saved my money and used it to study engineering."

"Didn't you keep in touch with your mother or brother?" A surge of sympathy washed over her. It must have hurt to have been rejected by his father that way.

"Mother was afraid to defy my father, so she never answered my messages. As for Renslow, he considers me nothing more than a construction worker. He thinks I go off with my buddies on mysterious trips just to risk my life for no reason. There is little affection between us."

She gave him a misty smile. "I'm glad you're telling me these things, Paz. You know, my hang-up has always been that I've wanted to be accepted for who I am, and not remade into the image my mother wanted for me. And yet, I internalized her values and then tried to change you the same way."

His lips pressed together. "That's why I didn't want to reveal my background. I wanted you to like me for myself, especially because you represent the very wealth I'd turned my back on. And inside, I doubted you'd care once you got to know the real me."

"I'm not your father." She leaned over and kissed him. "You have my heart and my love, no matter who or what you are."

"You, too."

They spent the next several minutes cuddling and kissing, then she broke away, unanswered questions still hovering on her tongue.

"So you trained as an engineer with the money you saved as a technician, but you didn't let your employer know about your step up in qualifications?"

Leaning on an elbow, he shook his head. "We build comm platforms throughout the Star Empire. But the relays are slow, especially between star systems when there's a delay between transmissions. I've been working on a new system. It will create artificial wormholes to allow for real-time communication. There wouldn't be any lags like we have now."

"That sounds like a revolutionary design."

"It is, but I've never built the prototype because it's too dangerous. If people learn about my research, they'll try to steal it. If put into use, this invention would give our military an advantage, so our political opponents might attempt to stop me. So would SattCom, because my architecture isn't propriety like theirs. They'd lose their monopoly. But the real thing holding me back is that I don't have the necessary skills to bring the prototype to market." His eyes glittered. "However, you do."

"Is that right?" Evidently the man needed her talents to complete his work. A warm glow filled her. Together, they could accomplish anything they set out to do.

"Your actions with the Norns taught me that some risks are worth taking." Paz stroked her arm, making sensual circles on her skin. "If you join me, I'll quit my job at SattCom and move my laboratory here. There's no need for you to uproot yourself."

What? He only wanted her as a business partner? Her heart sank. Had she misinterpreted his intent?

"Y-you want me to work for you?"

He tapped her nose. "No, *leera*, I want you as my mate. I've made a good income at my job, enough so that we won't have to worry about money. And if I sell my Morata estate, it'll bring in more. We can have a grand wedding that will make your parents proud."

Jen's eyes widened as hope swelled within her. "You space rogue. Are you asking me to marry you? You'd really settle on Earth?"

His mouth curved in a sexy, dimpled grin. "If you're willing to take a chance on me, Jennifer Dyhr, the answer is yes. Together, we can bring progress to the stars."

She arched her eyebrows. "You already make me see stars when I'm with you. I'll go anywhere you want to take me. I accept your offer, Paz Hadar, my Drift Lord and warrior of my heart."

THE END

Author's Note

Some of the scenes in *Warrior Rogue* are set in places I've visited, albeit with a bit of creative license, such as Tokyo, Hong Kong and the South Pacific. I had fun mixing myth and magic with modern times. It's always interesting to learn new things along the way. For example, did you know gold is insoluble in nitric acid? That's where the term *acid test* originates. I hope you enjoyed Paz and Jen's adventures and will look for *Warrior Lord* to see what happens next in the Drift Lords saga.

****

For updates on my new releases, giveaways, special offers and events, join my reader list at https://nancyjcohen.com/newsletter. Free Book Sampler for new subscribers.

Thank you for taking the time to read my book. If you enjoyed the story, please consider writing a review at your favorite online bookstore. Your recommendations are critically important in helping new readers find my work.

Warrior Lord Excerpt

Here's a peek at book #3 in the Drift Lords Series

Where else but Las Vegas could a bearded man wearing a cape and sword swagger inside a casino without drawing attention?

Erika Sherwood stared at the man who peered around, a bewildered look on his face until his gaze slammed into hers.

Her heart slowed, as though the world had frozen in that moment. Despite the bells ringing and people chattering and roulette wheels spinning, her awareness narrowed. She couldn't drag her eyes away from his searing glance.

Her pulse jumped when the man strode purposefully in her direction, his cape flapping behind him. With his powerful physique and resolute jawline, he looked like a superhero come to life. She supposed he'd bought that fabulous costume at a store along the Strip.

He claimed the empty seat beside her, exchanged a few words with the blackjack dealer, and set out a pile of chips. Tension charged the air around him. Her sideways glance absorbed his longish black hair and trim beard and the wide breadth of his shoulders. She pulled her skirt down, aware it had hiked up indecently, but his gaze didn't go there. Instead, his dark eyes fixated on her wristwatch.

"Miss?" The dealer's questioning glance fell on her.

"Oh. Hit me, please." She grimaced at the eight of spades she'd drawn. Drat, now she was over the limit.

"Not having any luck?" The newcomer nodded at her diminishing pile of chips. "Maybe this isn't your game."

"Excuse me, mister…?"

"My name is Magnor." He quirked an eyebrow when the waitress came by with another round of free drinks.

Erika lifted her third Viking Volcano from the tray. Who could resist? The fruity drinks were on the house, a popular ploy to keep gamblers in their casino.

She raised her glass in a friendly gesture before taking a sip. "Is Magnor your first name or your last name?"

"It's my only name." His mouth curved as he watched her reaction.

"O-kay." She wasn't in the mood to challenge him. Those drinks had already gone to her head, making her happy to accept his remark along with his blatant stare. Probably half the people in Vegas used false names anyway.

"Do you work here?" she asked, realizing his outfit matched the resort's Nordic theme.

He stiffened. "I should say not. I am a guest, like you."

"Sorry to have asked, but you fit the part."

"It is my customary attire as a warrior of the Tsuran."

"I see," she said in a noncommittal tone. Maybe he was an actor deep into his role. He could be taking a break from a movie set. Were they filming a sequel to Thor in the area?

"Nice timepiece you're wearing." He nodded at the object of his scrutiny.

Erika slid her hand under the table. "It was a gift."

Her parents had given her the watch for her sixteenth birthday with the caveat that she ask no questions about its unusual properties. It ran with no visible mechanism and no battery and had a peculiar symbol engraved on its face.

Her forehead wrinkled. Why had Magnor chosen to comment on her watch when most men would offer a line about her flaming red hair or her flashy clothes?

Come on, Erika, why do you care what he thinks? You came here for the art show, remember, and not to meet men?

It must be the alcohol causing that low buzzing sound in her ears and not his imposing presence.

"This announcement is for all of our engaged couples out there," blared a loudspeaker voice. "It's the last call if you want to enter our exciting contest. The lucky winners will be married on live television, after which they'll receive a complimentary stay in our honeymoon suite, fifty thousand dollars, and a new car. Entries are being accepted in the Green Room all day Friday until four o'clock."

"Fifty thousand dollars," Erika muttered. "Man, could I use that money!"

Magnor nudged her, a grin on his face. "Why don't we enter the contest together?"

The smile transformed his features, making her want to study the craggy lines and furrows that made his visage so interesting.

"What?" she said when his words finally registered.

"I need a room, and the hotel is full. If we win, that will solve my problem. You can keep the car and the cash."

"B-But the winners have to get married. On live television."

He waved a hand. "Oh, that. Las Vegas is all about fantasy, is it not?"

Her eyes widened. "You mean, the wedding will be filmed like a reality show, but it isn't real?"

He winked at her. "All of the contestants get bonus credits on their club cards. What have we got to lose?"

Erika stared at her diminished pile of chips. She'd lost two hundred dollars in less than an hour.

She scooped the remaining credits into her purse while considering the man's outrageous suggestion.

In her earlier days, she'd have accepted his proposal without a second thought. Back then nothing had mattered except her plants, her pottery, and her own pleasure.

Eventually, she'd erected an armor of self-discipline around herself so she could accomplish her goals. However, this resolve had evaporated under the influence of the drinks and the man's piercing gaze. Who wouldn't want a hunk like him as her fake fiancé?

Her head spinning, she wondered how a few cocktails could affect her so strongly. She'd been better able to hold her liquor in the past. Was there something else in those fruity drinks that made her so amenable?

Ignoring the warning bells in her mind, she scraped back her chair. Her knees wobbled when she stood. Magnor rose and steadied her with a firm grasp on her elbow.

"I accept your offer," she told him with bravado. "If we lose, at least we'll be ahead by several credits. And it might be fun."

"We should seal the deal if we are to play an engaged couple," Magnor said, closing the distance between them.

His head descended before she could protest, and his lips met hers. The pressure of his mouth electrified her and left her breathless. When he stepped away, she staggered.

He gripped her arm and guided her along. "This way, my lady. I believe the Green Room is just past that shiny black Jaguar on the rotating platform."

She let him steer her, berating herself for not heading toward the exhibit hall instead.

Then again, she'd already set up her booth for the art show on Saturday, so there wasn't much else for her to do the rest of today. She deserved a break, especially since this was the only getaway she could afford for the year.

When she'd wandered into the casino earlier, she'd quickly forgotten her purpose. The free drinks and enticing games had tempted her to relax and enjoy the resort amenities. Tomorrow would be time enough to get back to business.

People jostled them as they hurried along. Allowing the caped man to hustle her past the flashing lights and dinging sounds of the slot machines, she breathed in a deep breath of cooled air. Thankfully, this was a non-smoking casino. She hated the places where clouds of smoke pervaded the atmosphere.

Viking-garbed attendants stood at attention at various entrances, most of the men having deformed features like they all went to the same makeup artist. Mythological lore being the theme of the resort, she didn't find it odd. Instead, tipsy from the cocktails, she gauged their appearance to be appropriately troll-like. Their beady eyes watched her as she moved through the throng.

In the Green Room, an elevated dais held an arched canopy decorated with white tulle and tiny white lights. A pair of contestants sat in chairs on stage while their interview was filmed for broadcast. Wearing a portable microphone, an official questioned them. He had on an emerald robe more suitable to the Wizard of Oz. Why not? In Vegas, all was flash and little was substance. People expected weirdness.

Grabbing her hand, Magnor rushed forward as a clerk behind a corner desk called for final entries.

"Picture IDs and sixty dollars cash, please," the clerk said as their turn came in line. He had them fill out and sign several forms each. "There, you're all set if you win. Take this number and wait over there." His gesture indicated a queue of other hopefuls.

Erika's stomach turned cartwheels as they advanced. How would she answer those questions the official was asking? How long have you known your fiancé? Where did you two meet? What made you know you were right for each other?

Her frightened glance met Magnor's laser-beam gaze. He touched her lips with a gentle forefinger.

"Do not worry. Say whatever comes to mind. It'll be the right thing."

As she gazed into his mesmerizing eyes, she felt an irresistible compulsion to learn more about him. His slate gray irises glinted under her observation. She glanced away, discomfited by the reaction he aroused in her. They were strangers, and yet something sizzled between them.

Whoever this man was and for whatever reason he showed interest in her, she acted like putty in his hands. Since clay was her medium for sculpting, that said a lot.

It said more than she wanted, truth be told.

She approached the steps to the dais with trepidation after

the official, Dennis Slate, called their names. Was it her imagination, or was the crowd of observers thickening around them? More of the hefty attendants moved to strategic locations at the perimeter of the room, their abnormally large ears and long noses making her wonder if they were related.

Her pulse leapt when a pretty blonde grasped her forearm. The buzzing sound in her ears increased to painful decibels.

"Be sure to stop by the Longhouse Restaurant for a complimentary breakfast buffet in the morning," the lady said in a sugary tone. Her cold blue eyes sent a chill skittering along Erika's spine.

She withdrew her arm, her skin tingling where the woman had touched her. "Sure, I'll do that."

The blonde turned to Magnor at her side and made him the same offer. He snatched his arm away as though he'd been burned. His face flushed, and his mouth tightened. With a slight shove at Erika's back, he hastened her along, but not before she'd caught the flash of alarm in his eyes.

****

Sweat popped out on Magnor's brow. Great Cosmos, that had been close. If he hadn't kissed the fiery-haired Earth woman, he might have been confounded by now. Once spellbound to the Trolleks, he'd have been forced to join their sleeper army of mind slaves.

Hopefully, they didn't recognize him as one of the Drift Lords. He considered himself a team member even though his status was provisional. And while he lacked the unique genetic trait that his fellow warriors possessed, this difference might be what kept him off the enemy's radar. At least, Magnor hoped the Trolleks regarded him as another weak human.

Unfortunately, he'd run out of the elixir from his home world that had protected him from the Trollek mind spell, and since he'd been banished from his land, the chances of getting any more were nil. Either he had to resort to the painful means used by the other Drift Lords for immunity, or he'd have to taste his lady's lips on a regular basis. Erika Sherwood had no idea of the power she held or of her role in the ancient prophecy.

Magnor didn't realize she'd be in the casino when he had stepped inside. His mission was to obtain the sacred Book of Odin. Supposedly, the ancient text mentioned a weapon that could defeat the Trolleks. He'd received a tip that a clue to the text's location was hidden at the resort.

The beasts roamed everywhere in the casino. Their alluring females passed around free drinks while their disguised troops made sure none of the humans strayed to forbidden areas.

He wondered where their recruitment center was situated. Doubtless this resort had one, like other tourist attractions commandeered by the invaders. He could explore later, once he and Erika had won this game and settled into the newlywed suite.

Her wristwatch had identified her as one of the six Earth women in the prophecy. Instinct must have drawn him to her. Now she'd become a target for the enemy, since his arrival may have activated her dormant power. Once they went upstairs, he could set up a protective perimeter in their room.

It was imperative she marry him for her own safety. Magnor regretted the trick he was playing on her, but she'd understand the necessity for it later. If not, he'd risk her ire.

She could divorce him after the threat to their worlds had been resolved. In the meantime, she'd have to rely on him to keep her safe, at least until she learned her role. Her participation was crucial to the success of his team's mission.

With an insistent pressure on her spine, he urged her onto the dais where their fate together would be sealed.

****

"Tell me, Miss Sherwood, how did you meet your fiancé? Oh, and where's your ring, dear one?"

Dennis Slate, the justice of the peace, peered at her with a kindly expression. He sported a white goatee that matched his sparse hair. The years had etched fine lines onto his tanned visage and around his firm mouth. He had a mole on one upper cheek and wispy eyebrows.

"I-I left my ring in our room safe," she said in a hesitant tone. "I didn't know we'd be entering the contest."

"I see." His eyes twinkled while the cameraman aimed his portable lens at them. "And your first meet?"

She cast a frantic glance at Magnor, seated reassuringly at her side. He grasped her hand in his large palm and gave her an encouraging smile. For an instant, it looked as though his eyes glowed, but it must have been a reflection of light from the overhead chandelier.

Now where would she meet a hunk like him in real life? A logical answer popped into her mind.

"We met at an art gallery. I have an exhibit in the show starting here tomorrow. I run a pottery studio in my hometown."

Dennis's brows twitched upward. "How did you get his attention? Was he interested in your work?"

Magnor leaned over to address the man. "Actually, I was there on behalf of my sister. I'm not into art myself, you see. But Sis couldn't go, so she asked me to, er—"

Erika caught his fumble. "To pick up a brochure on my classes for children," she finished, offering the camera a beaming smile. "I love working with kids. If we win today, I'll use my portion of the money to get an education degree so I can teach arts and crafts to special needs children."

"That's an admirable goal." Dennis tilted his head. "But tell us more about you and your fiancé."

Her pulse raced under his keen glance. "We liked each other on first sight. He asked me out, and we went to dinner at a Mexican place."

"Very good." Dennis signaled to an assistant, who handed Magnor a placard and a black marker. "Sir, please write your answers to those questions on the other side of the card. We'll see how well your fiancé knows your tastes."

Erika's gut twisted. Now surely, they'd be unmasked as frauds.

When Magnor was done, he handed the card over to the emcee.

"Miss, give us your responses, please. We'll start with the easy ones. Your fiancé's favorite ice cream flavor?"

Oh, gosh. Her preference was chocolate, but what would he like? Squinting at his costume, she compared him to Robin Hood, a nobleman turned woodsman out of necessity. Was Magnor's background similar in any way?

"Strawberry," she blurted on a whim.

The emerald-robed official beamed at her. "Score one! Next, briefs or boxers?"

Her gaze widened. "Uh, briefs." She didn't dare look Magnor in the eye. Heat suffused her cheeks as the erotic image of him in the aforementioned undergarment came to mind.

"Right, again. Where was he born?"

How would she answer that question without any clue as to his origins? Wait, another place where a costumed character might go unnoticed popped into her head.

"Orlando, Florida."

Dennis's startled gaze met hers. Clearly, he hadn't expected her to get that right.

"Location of a birthmark?"

Color warmed her skin. "His butt."

How did she know that? Was he beaming the answers directly into her brain? A tantalizing fantasy distracted her from that thought. Without his voluminous cape, linen shirt, and dark trousers, what would he look like? All rippled muscles and lean, hard body? Man, she'd bet he looked good in the buff.

Dennis didn't reveal her score. "Thing he most hates about his job?"

She squirmed in her chair, conscious of the hot stage lights aimed at them and the surrounding throng. A cacophony of background noise from the nearby casino competed with the low buzzing in her head. Her upper lip beaded with sweat. She shouldn't have consumed all those drinks.

"Can you repeat the question?" she asked.

Agreeing to this farce had been a bad idea. They'd never win. And—oh, God—what if someone from home saw her on television? This would totally confirm her family's opinion that she was too flighty to ever settle down.

Her mind absorbed what Dennis had said. "He dislikes having to depend on others," she replied with an assertion she didn't feel. She supposed a man like Magnor would take pride in his accomplishments, although she didn't have the slightest idea what he did for a living.

A depressing thought crossed her mind. The man could be a boring accountant from New Jersey or a farmer from Nebraska, for all she knew. She'd never suit him in either case. But then, he'd have to be a bodybuilder as well. No one could fake the way his chest stretched the fabric of his clothes, or the way his hand hovered over his sword as though he knew how to use it.

"Let me in!" a portly fellow shouted from the doorway. He barged his way inside past the attendants. "Listen to me! This is all a ruse. You're in grave danger. Don't let these monsters take you downstairs!"

As the bouncers approached him, he dodged them and sped toward the dais. A blond woman carrying a tray of drinks stuck out her foot and tripped him. As he toppled over, costumed male employees grabbed him and hauled him away. The gaping crowd parted to allow them passage.

What had that been about? Erika's thoughts scattered as Dennis grinned into the camera.

"Don't mind him, folks. He's merely another zealous fan. Let's finish this contest. Erika, here's the next question."

She stumbled through the rest of her responses, then stood aside with Magnor and the other contestants until the last couples had their turn. The robed official rambled on about the resort into the camera until another woman brought him an envelope with the tally from online viewers.

Erika frowned. She hadn't noticed before, but all of the female servers were blonde and beautiful. Why was that? To counter the ugly faces of their male co-workers?

Dennis flourished the opened envelope, diverting her attention. "And the winners are, Erika Sherwood and her partner, Mr. Magnor!"

Erika spun around as wild applause sounded in her ears. What? They had won?

Magnor pounded her on the back. "I knew we would do it. Congratulations!" He turned her toward him and planted a triumphant kiss on her lips. The crowd cheered louder.

"Miss, we have to get you ready for the wedding," Dennis said with an indulgent smile. "Please follow Sylvia to the alcove where we have a stylist ready to dress you."

A young teen showed up at her elbow. "This way, lady." When Magnor stepped forward to accompany her, Sylvia held up a hand to stop him. "You're not allowed to see the bride again until the ceremony. Wait here."

"What about the rest of our prizes?" Magnor said to Dennis as she strode away.

Erika's temples throbbed, and her gut churned. She needed food to settle her stomach, although she suspected it was upset more from nerves than from hunger. The nuptials might be a show for the broadcast audience, but the idea made her quake. Or maybe it was the after-effect of those cocktails she'd consumed.

She tottered after the girl, who wore a long blond braid down her back. They went behind a partition, and Erika gasped. A rack of wedding dresses stood by the wall, along with a dressing table stocked with hair implements and cosmetics.

The stylist introduced herself before instructing Erika to select a gown in her size.

"Have a seat," the woman said after she'd made her selection. "I'll fix your hair and makeup."

Once she was prepped, Erika donned the strapless white satiny gown she'd chosen. Her eyes misted as she regarded herself in the mirror. The sleek design complemented her figure, but it wasn't her appearance that made her teary-eyed.

She'd been a bridesmaid so many times that it seemed as though her own chances of wearing a wedding dress someday were nil. Adam, her latest boyfriend, had validated that belief when he'd left her in the dust. Her ambitions seemed to chase men away, but she wasn't about to give up her dreams in exchange for a wedding ring.

At least, not until now, but this marriage wasn't real.

"You look beautiful," Sylvia said after the stylist settled a short gauzy veil on her head. The teenaged girl drew Erika aside. "Here, take this." She held out a shiny gold-colored ring. "Put it on your man. Make sure he wears it all the time."

"Thank you." Erika took the ring, puzzled to feel its weight in her palm. Was it real gold?

Sylvia gripped her arm. "Tell him this talisman will protect him against the coming darkness."

The stylist approached, and Sylvia vanished around a corner before Erika could ask her what she'd meant.

"Miss, here's your bouquet. It's time to go." The woman thrust a flower arrangement into Erika's hands.

As Erika followed the woman, she noted a red carpet had been rolled down the aisle toward the dais. Cameras aimed at her, and a wedding march blasted from the speaker system. She resisted the urge to press a hand to her aching temples. Man, those drinks must have been strong.

Magnor waited for her under the canopy where myriads of tiny lights twinkled. He looked proud and tall, an unreadable expression on his face as he watched her step forward. His cape swung behind him, making him look like an avenging god with his impressive height and sword.

She took her place at his side and together they faced Dennis. The official had exchanged his emerald robe for a somber black garment. He held an open book in his hands. Dennis began the brief ceremony, his words bypassing her brain as she stood rooted in place, immobilized by the rapid pace of events.

"With the power invested in me by the State of Nevada and the city of Las Vegas, I now pronounce you man and wife. You may kiss the bride."

Erika's head whirled. Not even fifteen minutes must have gone by. Was this what passed for a Las Vegas wedding?

What a sham. She supposed that every minute they were on the air, it cost money.

Magnor's head descended, and he pressed his mouth to hers. As far as the TV viewers were concerned, they'd been married. The exchange of rings had felt real. She wondered who'd given him the one he'd slid onto her finger. Dennis, most likely.

The ruddy-faced official shook their hands, gave Magnor the key to the honeymoon suite, and said their car would be available for pickup from the valet. As for the cash, it was theirs for the taking. He handed them a large-sized signed check made out to Mr. and Mrs. Magnor.

"Oh, and one more thing," Dennis said. "I'll need your signatures on these documents, please. It's simply a formality, but we do need permission for the resort to use your likenesses for publicity. These papers also include transfer of title to the car, tax forms and such."

Erika signed with a shaky hand. In her frazzled state, she couldn't be bothered to read the details.

Magnor followed suit, then grasped her hand in his and raised it in the air. The watching throng cheered loudly.

"That's it then, wife." His low, rumbly voice broke through the haze in her head. "You're mine now."

Order Now at https://nancyjcohen.com/warrior-lord/

Norse Creation Myth

Author's Note: This is my interpretation that served as the basis for my story.

These tales derive from the Edda, an epic of Germanic origin. As the story starts, a great void stretched between the land of ice and darkness in the north (Niflheim) and the land of fire and light in the south (Muspell). When warm air met the ice, water formed, and the droplets produced the first Giant, Ymir, along with a cow who fed him.

While the Giant slept, a male and a female grew from his armpit. They were Frost Giants who had human form and supernatural powers.

The cow licked the ice and brought forth a man named Buri. Buri's son married a descendent of Ymir, and they in turn produced three sons. These offspring became the Gods, including Odin.

Odin and his brothers killed Ymir and used his body to create Midgard, the middle land, from the void. Then they made the oceans and the earth, the heavens and the stars, and the cycles of night and day. After Ymir died, dwarfs formed from the maggots in his flesh.

Meanwhile, the Gods split into two families, the Aesir and the Vanir. Odin and his son Thor belonged to the Aesir. They were warriors, while the Vanir became farmers and merchants. Odin ruled over them all as King of the Gods. Thor was a great warrior who carried a magic hammer called Mjollnir, which returned like a boomerang when he threw it.

The Aesir Gods lived in Asgard, a celestial palace. A rainbow bridge named Bifrost connected Asgard to Midgard. Odin created humans to occupy Midgard, surrounded by an ocean inhabited by Jormungand the serpent. The God Heimdall guarded the Bifrost bridge, prophesied to collapse at Ragnarok, the end of the world.

The Frost Giants inhabited Jotunheim. The Goddess Hel ruled over Niflheim, the Land of the Dead. She lived in a palace like the Gods. It wasn't considered a punishment to end up there.

Yggdrasil, an ash tree, connected all the realms. The World Tree was fed by three sources of water under its roots. One of these was the Fountain of Wisdom, guarded by the god Mimir. According to legend, Odin sacrificed an eye to drink from this fountain. That's how he gained his powers of prophecy.

The Urd well, or Fountain of Youth, was protected by the Norns, Goddesses of Fate. Their root supported the tree at Midgard, so they ruled the destinies of men. A dragon named Nidhog guarded the third spring and gnawed on its root.

As the first living creatures, the Giants were angry when the Gods dispelled them from their rightful home. They gathered their allies in preparation for an attack on the Gods. This great battle was called Ragnarok.

Loki, a companion to the Gods, caused much mischief. As a shapeshifter and descendant of the Frost Giants, he delighted in causing trouble. Eventually, the Gods banished him. The Giants released Loki so he could lead them in battle against the Gods.

At Ragnarok, the Gods battled monsters and Giants. Thor fought the sea monster of Midgard. He killed the serpent with his hammer but not before the monster fatally slashed him with poison. Odin was defeated by the wolf Fenrir. Loki fought Heimdall and they killed each other.

The rainbow bridge collapsed, and the great World Tree burned down. Each of the realms fell. Fires, earthquakes, and tidal waves swept the earth and wiped away the human race. Consumed by fire, Midgard sank into the sea.

But all was not lost. Earth reemerged from the ocean, and the sons of the dead Aesir returned to Asgard to rule again.

Members of the Aesir who had no part in the combat survived the cataclysm. Balder, a son of Odin who'd been killed through Loki's trickery, came back to life after his sojourn in Hel's realm. Accompanied by his brother, Hoder, he took his seat on the divine council. Two of Odin's other sons also returned. These were Vidar and Vali. Odin's brothers, Vili and Ve, were also among the survivors. And so the world was renewed.

The Völuspá holds the words of the prophetess who predicted that after the catastrophe, the world would arise again, and peace and happiness would prevail.

Glossary

ACTUATORS: Engine parts.

AESIR: The warrior gods in Norse mythology.

ALAMIR: A battle during the border dispute with the Morano Confederation.

ANRIAT: A planet with an unsavory underworld of criminals and desperadoes.

ASGARD: The celestial abode of the Aesir gods.

BERMUDA TRIANGLE: Also called the Devil's Triangle, this area in the Atlantic Ocean ranges from Bermuda to Puerto Rico to Miami. It is the site of anomalies where ships and planes disappear, and radios and compasses stop working.

BOGGER: Derogatory Trollek term for a female.

BORATUS WORMS: Creatures that bore into nerve ganglia.

CARONA: Karrellian term of endearment.

CAVENDII TWO: A military base of the Star Empire under command of Colonel Yaloom.

CORS PARTICLES: Matter produced at the event horizon of a dimensional rift.

DAZLITE: A thumb-sized pocket light.

DISRUPTOR: A hand weapon with two settings—stun and kill. Disrupts neural pathways. Used by planetary patrols and local military units for crowd control. May be assigned as a secondary weapon to ground troops, more often to officers. Class One military use restricted armament. Blue beam.

DOKTER: Trollek word for doctor.

DONIK: Curse word equivalent to bastard.

DONJON: Tower.

DRAGON'S TRIANGLE: Also called the Devil's Sea, this is an area in the Pacific basin southeast of Japan between Iwo Jima and Marcus Island that is the site of anomalies where ships and planes disappear, and radios and compasses stop working.

DRIFT LORD: A warrior who has the special ability to sniff cors particles and who is trained to fight Trollek incursions.

DRIFT WORLD: An adult role-playing theme park in Orlando, FL. "A place where your fantasy job becomes reality. Whatever part you want to play, it's yours for a day."

DROTT: Trollek military form of address for superior officer.

DWARFS: Short-statured men who live underground. They have pale faces and long beards. Skilled metalworkers and goldsmiths who craft magical items for the gods. Greedy fellows, they can make themselves invisible. Weakness: Their power is woven into their hair.

DYTHIUM CHARGES: Explosive compound.

EDDA: An epic of Germanic origin.

ELVES: Nocturnal beings that live in wooded areas. They enjoy dancing and gambling, but people who dance with them must be wary.

EMP GRENADE: A grenade that emits an electromagnetic pulse of a high intensity, short duration burst of electromagnetic energy.

EVENT HORIZON: Rift caused when dimensional plates grind against each other.

FAFNIR: A giant disguised as a dragon to guard his treasure.

FARARRA: A pleasure planet with resorts, emporiums, eateries, and entertainment complexes.

FENRIR: A son of Loki and a fire giant disguised as a wolf. He killed Odin at Ragnarok.

FOUNTAIN OF WISDOM: A source of water under the roots of the giant World Tree. Guarded by the god, Mimir.

GATEKEEPERS: Allies of the Drift Lords, these shapeshifters help protect humanity during Trollek incursions on Earth.

GIANT: According to Norse mythology, giants were the first living creatures. They have the gift of disguise. Two types: Fire Giants and Frost Giants.

GJOLL: A river in the underworld that souls must cross to reach Helheim.

GLITTER BUG: A lightning bug type insect on Paz's home world.

GRAND MARSHAL: Governor of Trollek towns. Addressed as "Your Eminence".

GRIMSHAW: Lord Magnor's name for his sword.

HAGRET: A bird with outstretched wings.

HAS'PUTE: A Karrellian curse word.

HEL: Goddess ruler of Helheim and Loki's daughter.

HELHEIM: The realm of the dead ruled by the goddess, Hel.

HERIS: Form of address for a Trollek landowner, second in rank to a Grand Marshal.

HYPERSPACE: Faster than speed of light travel via a distortion of the space-time continuum.

IMMOBILIZER: Stun weapon used by Star Empire military units in covert ops. Class Two restricted armament.

JADLOK: Elven liege of the lake's region.

JAK'TAR: The Trollek home world.

JAWANI: A standard universal language.

JORG: King of the Trolleks.

JORGONAUTS: Followers of the Trollek ruler, King Jorg.

KABAK: Trollek who commands a confounded human.

KAG: Man who likes boys.

KARRELL: Home world of Zohar Thorald and training ground for the Drift Lords.

KASH: A Trollek dice game.

KEWA STONES: Diamonds.

KIMMLEBUSH: A curse word in Dwarf language.

KLICK: A kilometer or approximately .6213 miles.

KNESTA: "Beloved" in Lord Magnor's tongue; a term of endearment.

LASER CARBINE: RAD-4 Rifle with enhanced infrared scanner; used by military troops.

LAVA BOMB: Explosive device, similar to a grenade.

LEERA: A term of endearment in Paz's native language.

LIEMA: A long-necked animal that moves with grace, native to Paz's home world.

LEY LINES: An energy grid intersects Earth at twelve distinct geographic points called Vile Vortices. Ley lines are the lines connecting these points of the electromagnetic field.

LEYTNANT: Officer in Trollek military force.

LOKI: Loki is a mischievous trickster and shapeshifter who was banished to an underground prison by the Norse gods. He is a malevolent being bent on revenge and galactic domination.

LOXOTAN: A painkiller.

LYTHIX SERUM: Truth serum used by the Trolleks.

MALNATIUM: A volatile but powerful energy producing compound.

MAUG: A curse word used as an adjective; a derogatory term.

MENIG: Lowest enlisted rank in Trollek military force.

MIDGARD: The middle land occupied by mankind in Norse mythology.

MIMIR: God who guards the Fountain of Wisdom.

MIMIR'S WELL: The Fountain of Wisdom guarded by the god, Mimir. This water supplies one of the roots of the great World Tree.

MIN DROTT: Trollek form of address for superior officer.

MINGLING: Sexual intimacy.

MJOLLNIR: Thor's magic hammer, forged by the dwarves. When thrown, it returns like a boomerang.

MODGUD: Giantess guardian of the bridge over the river Gjoll leading to Helheim.

MORABI NERVE JAB: A hand chop to a sensitive bundle of nerves.

MORANO CONFEDERATION: An alliance bordering the Star Empire.

MORATA: Paz's home world, a desert planet in the Zood System.

NEUTRINO: A small elementary particle that carries no electric charge.

NIDHOG: Dragon who gnaws on a root of the World Tree and guards the spring Hvergelmir.

NID RUNE: A curse.

NIFLHEL: A lower level of Helheim where the evil dead suffer endless torment.

NORNS: Three Goddesses of Fate who guard the Urd Well.

ODIN: Ruler of the Norse gods.

ORIGINALS: Early sentient beings who inhabited Earth.

PAMADORE: A type of poultry consumed on Karrell.

PFRELL: Flying creatures with sharp talons and spear-like beaks; a hunter species native to the Trollek world.

PHASE GUN: Type of energy weapon. The Drift Lords carry Monix T-6 laser pistols. Three settings—stun, kill, vaporize. Spare power packs (miniature energy cells) are carried in utility belt pouches. Older model: T-4, has to be reloaded more often.

PHASE RIFLE: Long-range version of above. Powered by portable energy converter.

PIP: Portable Intel Platform; handheld data unit with sensors and scanning capability. This device also has a levitator beam to move heavy objects.

POLARIZE: The means by which Drift Lords protect themselves from the Trollek spell.

PURPURA BLOSSOMS: A sweet-scented flower on Karrell.

RAGEESH: Honorary form of address for the Crown Prince of the Star Empire.

RAGNAROK: End of the world and destruction of the multiverse.

RIFF: Karrellian term for lowlife or thug.

SCREEN (verb): To hide from sight.

SHAPESHIFTER: Beings who can alter their form.

SHELL SHEDDER: Old-fashioned projectile weapons favored by the Trolleks. Drift Lords' lightweight clothing armor protects against these projectiles.

SHIRAJO MANOR: Trollek stronghold on Togura Island.

SHOCK STICK: Rod-like punishment device used by the Trolleks for slave control. It delivers a painful electric shock.

SIRE: Honorary form of address for royalty on Karrell.
SIRA: Honorary form of address for noble ladies on Karrell.
SKAP: Slang term for a Viden.
SLOGG: Trollek word for slave.
SMARK: A curse word in Paz's native tongue.
SNIPELING: A reptilian creature that lives in rock crevices. Poisonous venom.
SONIC GRENADE: Weapon used by Star Empire troops. It causes a blast of sonic waves.
SPATIAL SHIFT: Instantaneous transport from one place to another.
STAR EMPIRE: An alliance of sentient planets ruled by a hereditary Emperor.
TEECAHT: A derogatory name for a Trollek woman who steps out of bounds.
TENT TEN: Site of Trollek medical experiments on humans.
THOR: Warrior god of Norse legend who carries Mjollnir, a magic hammer.
THOR'S HAMMER: Thor's magical weapon, Mjollnir, returns to its thrower.
TROLLEK: Intelligent creatures derived from the Originals, the Trolleks revere nature, despise humans for chasing them from their land, and believe in taking by force what suits their needs.
UGRON: A grizzly bear-like creature.
URD WELL: Fountain of Youth protected by the Norns, its spring feeds the root on the World Tree that supports Midgard.
VALHALLA: Odin's Hall where dead warriors reside and prepare for Ragnarok.
VALKYRIES: Warrior maidens of the god Odin, these women carry warriors who die in battle to Valhalla. Also called Shield Maidens.
VANIR: Norse gods who were farmers and merchants.
VECTOR: An invisible line on the time-space continuum.
VECTOR SHIFT: See spatial shift.
VEILED: Shielded from view.
VIDENS: Faction of Trolleks who support science instead of conquest as a solution to their problems.

VILE VORTICES: An energy grid beneath the earth's crust intersects the globe at twelve distinct geographic points called Vile Vortices. These are often sites of anomalous activity. Five each of these vortices are at an equal distance above and below the equator. Two are located at the north and south poles.

WAGMIRE: A type of rodent.

WIGONK: A domesticated canine on Karrell.

WONK: Trollek slang term for male appendage.

WORLD TREE: The great ash tree that connects all nine realms of the universe. Also called Yggdrasil.

YMIR: The first Giant in Norse mythology.

About the Author

Nancy J. Cohen writes the Bad Hair Day Mysteries featuring South Florida hairstylist Marla Vail. Titles in this series have been named Best Cozy Mystery by *Suspense Magazine*, won Readers' Favorite gold medals and the RONE Award, placed first in the Chanticleer International Book Awards and third in the Arizona Literary Awards.

Her nonfiction titles, *Writing the Cozy Mystery* and *A Bad Hair Day Cookbook,* have also garnered numerous awards. These include gold medals in the FAPA President's Book Awards and the Royal Palm Literary Awards, First Place in the IAN Book of the Year Awards and the *Topshelf Magazine* Book Awards. *Writing the Cozy Mystery* was also an Agatha Award Finalist.

Nancy's imaginative romances have proven popular with fans as well. These books have won the HOLT Medallion and Best Book in Romantic SciFi/Fantasy at *The Romance Reviews*.

A featured speaker at libraries, conferences, and community events, Nancy is listed in *Contemporary Authors, Poets & Writers*, and *Who's Who in U.S. Writers, Editors, & Poets*. She is a past president of Florida Romance Writers and the Florida Chapter of Mystery Writers of America. When not busy writing, she enjoys reading, fine dining, cruising, and visiting Disney World.

Follow Nancy Online

Website – https://nancyjcohen.com
Blog – https://nancyjcohen.com/blog
Twitter – https://www.twitter.com/nancyjcohen
Facebook – https://www.facebook.com/NancyJCohenAuthor
LinkedIn – https://www.linkedin.com/in/nancyjcohen
Goodreads – https://www.goodreads.com/nancyjcohen
Pinterest – https://pinterest.com/njcohen/
Instagram – https://instagram.com/nancyjcohen
BookBub – https://www.bookbub.com/authors/nancy-j-cohen

Books by Nancy J. Cohen

The Bad Hair Day Mysteries
Permed to Death
Hair Raiser
Murder by Manicure
Body Wave
Highlights to Heaven
Died Blonde
Dead Roots
Perish by Pedicure
Killer Knots
Shear Murder
Hanging by a Hair
Peril by Ponytail
Haunted Hair Nights (Novella)
Facials Can Be Fatal
Hair Brained
Hairball Hijinks (Short Story)
Trimmed to Death
Easter Hair Hunt
Styled for Murder
Star Tangled Murder

The Drift Lords Series
Warrior Prince
Warrior Rogue
Warrior Lord

Nancy J. Cohen

Science Fiction Romances
Keeper of the Rings
Silver Serenade

The Light-Years Series
Circle of Light
Moonlight Rhapsody
Starlight Child

Nonfiction
Writing the Cozy Mystery
A Bad Hair Day Cookbook

Order Now at https://nancyjcohen.com/books/